SHADOWS ON THE SUN

Kathryn Haig was born in Scotland. She has
been an officer in the Women's Royal Army
Corps, a civil servant and a computer program-
mer. She lives in the New Forest with her husband, daughter and an assortment of animals.
Shadows on the Sun is her first novel.

SHADOWS ON THE SUN

Kathryn Haig

This edition published 1994 by
Diamond Books
77–85 Fulham Palace Road
Hammersmith, London W6 8JB

A Fontana Original 1992

Permission has been requested to reprint the following:

Extracts from *Broken Doll*, by J Tate & F Clifford Harris,
pub. Francis, Day & Hunter, 1916

Extract from *Oh, Johnny*, by A Olman & E Rose,
pub. Francis, Day & Hunter, *c.* 1914

Set in Bembo by Input Typesetting Ltd, London

Printed in Great Britain

CONTENTS

HISTORICAL NOTE

I have appropriated a portion of the Devizes Division to form the fictitious Wiltshire parliamentary constituency of Upper Avon. I fear the successful candidate for Devizes, Lt Col. W.C.G. Bell, would not have forgiven me the theft.

For Hugh

Why should I blame her that she filled my days
With misery, or that she would of late
Have taught to ignorant men most violent ways,
Or hurled the little streets upon the great,
Had they but courage equal to desire?
What could have made her peaceful with a mind
That nobleness made simple as a fire,
With beauty like a tightened bow, a kind
That is not natural in an age like this,
Being high and solitary and most stern?
Why, what could she have done, being what she is?
Was there another Troy for her to burn?

No Second Troy, W. B. Yeats

PROLOGUE

My daughter is nearly a woman. Under her blue, ruched cotton bathing suit, her chest is still flat, but where the skinny ribs end, her body swoops into a proper waist and flares out again into softly rounded hips. Her legs are long and honey gold, a shade darker than the sand that dusts them.

Soon – before the summer ends – I shall have to talk to her and soon after that she'll stop being a child. My little girl, my war baby, born as the first sirens wailed, competing with them in vocal power.

What shall I tell her? Facts alone are not enough to explain the perverse wonder of a man and a woman together.

But for now, she is still a child munching gritty sandwiches and wiggling her toes in the damp sand. Her head is close to her brother's, as they pore over the booty of shells they collected together. Their hair mingles in the silver gilt haze that skipped a generation and passed me by. It may darken in time – although my mother's never did. I hope for his sake it does. It could be a terrible trial for a boy at school to have hair like a Filippo Lippi angel.

They're not friends – not really – they couldn't be, with such a gap in age, but they get on in their own, very different, ways. They may not always. There's nothing I can do about that but hope. I can love them for the rest of their lives, but I can't make them into

11

what I want them to be. I can't make them love each other.

The two births were separated by the years their father spent in a German prisoner of war camp. The Germans kept him safe for me from Dunkirk until VE Day. He wasn't the boy who went away when he came back. But he came back. I ought to be grateful to them for that.

If I squint under the brim of my sun hat, I can watch him. He's stretched on the sand, on his back. His eyes are closed and his limbs are loose and comfortable. His hair is tousled by the breeze. From this angle, I can't see the scars of the skin grafts done in a German hospital.

He doesn't know I'm watching. Oh yes, he does. He reaches out and smooths his hand down my thigh and under the hollow of my knee, in promise.

Tonight, I'll tell him. And we'll make love in that slow, easy, tender way that's so different from the storms of our pre-war young love. And he'll cup my swelling breasts and put his lips to them and lay his cheek on my belly, listening, too early, for the new heartbeat. And we won't sleep until we're drugged and sated with each other.

The children have finished their picnic. They rush down to the water's edge, jumping back from the icy bite of the sea, daring a little further each time, wild as gulls. Their father gets up and, limping only a little now, goes to join them, to skim ducks and drakes across the breaking waves. Their shouts blow across to me, tiny and distant.

Maybe I'll walk down there, too. I love the feel of the sea sucking the sand from beneath my toes. But behind the sheltering rock it's still and warm. The stone is baking in the afternoon glare. I'm heavy with the sudden drowsiness of early pregnancy. I watch them

– my husband and our children – through half-closed eyes.

Supposing he hadn't come back . . .

But that wouldn't mean that there never was such a person. He still would have existed. There still would have been this man in the world for twenty-four years. He still would have been a son, a brother, a lover, a husband, a father. There would have been memories, photographs, talk. His place in the world would have been empty, but there still would have been a place.

Our daughter would have had a father. He would have been as real to her as I could make him. I would never have let her experience that sense of loss, of not belonging anywhere . . .

Strange . . . so far behind me now, but after all these years I can still recapture the feeling . . .

I never had a mother. Or that's what I thought, until I was nearly eight years old.

That's silly. Everyone has a mother. I knew that, really. Or to be more accurate, everyone must have had a mother at some time. Whether now dead, missing, or estranged, at least for as long as it took to let out that first, outraged yell, everyone has had a mother.

The sun's so bright. I close my eyes to shut out the stumpy little figure, freckle-faced and plain, who trots busily across the sand. Alone.

I knew a lot of things. I had watched the frogs of the forest ponds spew out their babies, like spilled helpings of black-eyed milk pudding. I knew that in May the roaming, sway-bellied mares would be followed by dear little foals on string-puppet legs. I had seen the stable cat lying on a sunbeam washing her face, while her belly was pummelled and paddled from the inside by tiny paws. I knew where her secret place was, in the darkest corner of the old harness room, and I saw her

13

lick the blood from her blind, mewling family. I'm going to have one of the kittens for my own.

I knew – I *know* – though no one would dream of letting me into the secret – that the only way I could have come into the world was if my mother, somehow, had put me there.

Then where did she go?

If I try very hard – if I rock to and fro, until I can't hear Nanny shouting at me to stop, until all the colours of the nursery are whirled into a bright, white light – I can see a woman and I know she's my mother. She has sunshine in her hair and her chest is soft – not like Nanny's – soft enough to go to sleep on and she sings and kisses my nose and blows on my neck like a pony and I want her.

When I stop rocking, she's not there any more and I feel cold and sick and Nanny gives me a good, big dose of Gregory's Mixture.

'That'll stop your nonsense, young lady,' she says.

There are photographs in the drawing room and in the library and on the desk in the study, but I know all the faces in them. They are not the person I'm looking for. And the picture in my mind is getting fainter and fainter. It's fading away.

Daddy must know, but they say, 'You mustn't worry Daddy – he hasn't been well – run along and play.'

Everyone has a mother – except me.

Then where did I come from?

MICHAEL

The Cuckold

Twenty-one million, six hundred and forty thousand people died of influenza that year. I, who had nothing left to live for, did not die. Men who had survived four years of trench warfare died. Women who had kept their families together through four years of loneliness and grief died. Children who had never known their fathers died. I lived.

Some people said it was all his fault. They said that Philip Malyon was well-known as an accomplished libertine. They said he had taken disgraceful advantage of my illness, seduced my wife right under my feverish gaze and made off with her.

Some people blamed Helen. They said she was a heartless hussy. They said she was no better than she ought to be, that a woman had no business looking as beautiful as she – that skin couldn't be natural – that she had cuckolded me as I lay helpless in bed and run away without a backward look.

My brother Anthony, with his usual unwelcome frankness, said it was nothing but lust. He ought to know. And what else could I expect, marrying a woman more than twenty years younger than I?

I knew better. It was love. It was passion, adoration, ecstasy, sorcery. It was madness; it was idolatry. It was a *coup de foudre*. They could no more help themselves than the birds could help mating each spring.

And I knew exactly how they felt. Because that was

how I had felt on the day I first set eyes on Helen Leckford.

Of course, some of the lesser newspapers adopted their usual hypocritical stance over the sordid business. Not that I ever read them, but I knew that they were circulated below stairs. The *Daily Mail* panted over it. I shudder to think what the *News of the World* wrote – probably my chauffeur could have enlightened me. The papers would probably never have been interested had Helen not been one of *the* debutantes of the last season before the war. The face of the year, she had been called, that long-ago summer before Europe slid into slime and decay.

So the hacks dipped their nibs in vitriol and gave their readers what they clamoured for – prurience disguised as a social conscience. And I lay in bed and ached and sweated and longed to die.

And I thanked God in his mercy that at least Hermione was too young to understand what people were saying about her mother. I did not realize until too late just how a sensitive child might be affected.

Anthony came running over to Ebury Street as soon as the news reached him. Of course. He would. He strode into my bedroom and the door banged back off the wall at his entry. I tried to slide under the bedcovers and pretend I hadn't heard him.

'Good Lord! It's like a hothouse in here! You'll never get better if you mollycoddle yourself like this, man. Get out and get some fresh air. Get some colour in your cheeks. Work up an appetite.'

I started to explain that the doctor had forbidden me on pain of death – literally – to catch a chill, but a fit of coughing seized me. By the time I had caught my breath again, Anthony had closed the dampers on the fire and thrown open a window.

'Well, perhaps not,' said Anthony, looking at the sulphurous vapour that writhed into the room, and he shut the window again. 'Best thing you can do is get home to Buckholt and get some clean sea air into your lungs. Leave me to sort out this godawful mess.'

My heart sank. At all costs, I had to prevent that. 'This isn't a mess that you or anyone else can sort out,' I wheezed.

'Nonsense! A few home truths will bring Helen to heel quickly enough. Pity about the papers. It's an awful stink. Still, all we have to do is get her home, then keep our noses clean for a month or so. The fuss'll die down soon enough. Someone else'll make some juicy headlines and we'll be forgotten.'

'Helen won't come,' I said.

'Won't come? What do you mean, won't come?'

'They are in love.'

Helen had never loved me, of course. Respected me, liked me, even. We were friends. But she had never loved me. I knew that and I was prepared to put up with it. I was grateful for every careless little scrap of affection she tossed in my direction. Because how could I expect a woman like that to love a dry old stick like me?

I was the 'extra' bachelor, the steady older man that hostesses liked to invite to their dinner parties and dances to make up numbers, safe in the knowledge that I could be relied on to get a conversation out of a sticky spot and was unlikely to seduce a virgin in the conservatory.

Not that I hadn't thought about it. I was not as immune to their tender charms as my hostesses would have liked to think. Night after night, I danced with one fresh young body after another in my arms. And I would be lying if I pretended to be unaffected by the tender slope of shoulders and plump, satin-skinned bosoms. Once a week I would call at a discreet house on my way home and finally reach my own bed long after the sun had risen.

But my heart remained as untouched as these young girls' bodies. If the thought of marriage occasionally strayed into my mind, it never stayed there long. Over the years, now one debutante, now another, might catch my fancy and I would think, 'I'm not getting any younger. It's about time I settled down and made some fond mother happy.'

But closer acquaintance always revealed some petty little imperfection that I knew I could never live with. One girl, the possessor of a stunning figure, had a laugh like a braying donkey. Another, whose hair would have made Titian gasp to paint her, bit her nails to the quick. A third had bad breath, as I discovered to my cost one evening behind a potted palm.

Call it fussy, if you like, but marriage is for a long time. If some little something sets one's teeth on edge right at the start, how do you suppose one might feel after ten or twenty years of it?

If I had been less of a perfectionist, I might be a happier man now. But that is hindsight.

And so I reached the age of thirty-eight content to leave my older brother to carry on the line. He seemed to be making a good job of it. More and more frequently I was deserting the ballroom for the smoking room, there to drink B and S with other middle-aged men. I was beginning myself to believe in 'dear Michael, so kind and sensible, but just a tiny bit – you know – dull'. I was bored with the season before the first fortnight in May was up.

And then I met Helen Leckford.

How can I describe Helen as she was in May 1914? I lie in bed now, with every limb aching and my lungs feeling like a pair of sodden bath sponges, and that far-off, impossibly golden summer seems like another world. The mud and pain and grief of the intervening years have separated us from it as cruelly as the angel with the fiery sword barred the return to Eden.

'I don't like rock gardens,' she said. They were such ordinary words, but her voice was a cello played by Casals.

I had been escorting Lady Haxton and her faded daughter around Chelsea Flower Show – a deplorably tedious task, but the sort of thing an ageing bachelor is frequently asked to do. Those stupendous banks of colour and perfume seemed less impressive every year. That snowdrops and chrysanthemums could be induced to flower in the same week no longer amazed me. It seemed the height of folly to transport tons of Lakeland slate three hundred miles in order to build a tiny Lakeland replica.

Left to myself, I could quite happily have spent the afternoon on a folding chair beneath the flowering chestnuts listening to the Guards band, leaving my charges to ooh and aah their way round the dismally suburban displays. But good old Michael would never have dreamed of pleasing himself.

'I don't like rock gardens,' she said. 'All those tortured rocks dragged out of the ground and displayed on the surface. Like a body with its skeleton on the outside.'

That voice stopped me as we passed the competition rock gardens that were such a feature of Chelsea that May. And when I looked back to pinpoint the owner of the voice, I could not pass on further.

Of course the birds still sang. Of course the band still played. I know that. And all the rest is just fancy. A silence more intense than sweetest music. A stillness so absolute that all London seemed to be waiting. A light as dazzling as the light that hurled Saul to his knees. Of course it wasn't like that.

The point is – I thought it was.

I dare say a woman could describe to the last scallop and button what Helen wore that day. My dazzled eyes only took in the silver-gilt halo of hair that feathered around her cheeks in the light breeze. She was tall – as tall as I was – and with a lush figure that was beginning to be unfashionable, even vain, but which promised untold delights to a masculine connoisseur.

I know now that her eyes are violet, with long, arched lids and sweep of lashes. Then I was conscious only of the way she seemed to look straight at me – at *me* – across those ridiculous little squares of garden, across time itself. I returned her glance – and was lost.

I would laugh now, if it didn't hurt so much.

I was quite well aware of all my deficiencies. I was thirty-eight years old, not quite plain but certainly not the answer to a maiden's prayer. My barber and I both knew about the thinnning circle at the back of my head. Polo and hunting in their seasons had kept my body hard, but I was not above middle height and was inclined to stockiness. My mind and manners had been left far behind by the mad, ragtime world I was living in.

I looked what I was – a staid bachelor, verging on early middle age. And I was in love. Madly. Fiercely. Joyously. Pathetically.

The next morning I sent my man out for as many back copies of *Tatler* and *Vanity Fair* as he could find. He looked at me a little oddly, but went anyway. Humouring me.

It didn't take me long to find her. Helen Leckford. Her picture looked back at me, but the photographer

22

had not done her justice. How could he portray skin that was ivory brushed with rose? How could he capture the mellow sensuality of her husky voice? The picture was a travesty. Yet I cut it out and folded it in my pocket book. Then I burned the magazine, in case anyone should discover the mutilated page. I may have been mad, but I was not eager for the whole of my staff to discover it.

Once I knew who she was, I could plan my campaign. Helen was one of those well-bred, well brought-up young women, coming from a family of high hopes and little means. She lived in Thurloe Square with her widowed mother and was doing the season sponsored (and paid for, I guessed) by the generosity of an aunt and uncle.

There were numbers of these girls every season – poor, pretty, with pale pink dresses from Debenham & Freebody and hopeful pale blue eyes. *Tatler* would never normally have bothered with a girl like Helen Leckford. But a face like that could not be ignored.

Best of all – I knew her generous aunt and uncle. Well, as good as. They were friends of friends of friends of mine. The rest was easy.

I laid my plans with military precision: an introduction at a dance to establish my bona fides; a dinner party or two; tea with her mother. That should do it. We could be married in August. A prolonged honeymoon on the Continent – Deauville perhaps, Biarritz, Baden-Baden, Menton, Firenze – and then back to Hampshire. I would give up London. I had no intention of risking my treasure in that trashy social circuit. I would become a model husband, a loving father.

My fantasies took on a life and colour all of their own. They seemed more real than the dusty streets outside, more credible than *The Times* editorial. Yet I was sufficiently realistic to appreciate that miracles don't

23

happen all by themselves. Not nowadays, anyway. They need a bit of assistance. I would have to *make* them come true.

I picked up the telephone and began a series of calls that ensured Helen and I would be invited to all the same thrashes.

I proposed to Helen at our first meeting.

That was a grave tactical error. It very nearly frightened her off completely. And I thought I was in such control, with every move in the campaign planned down to the last horseshoe nail. That night's dance at Molly and Denzil Clifden's was meant to be only a preliminary skirmish. It turned out to be nearly my last stand. It just goes to prove that men – poor fools – are completely at the mercy of their bodily impulses.

Blame the fashions of that year, if you like, those frail and fragmentary Greek tunics designed by Poiret that were all the rage among the young and quite shocking to the more sedate, amongst whom I had numbered myself until I held Helen in my arms.

Casano's Band was everywhere that year. I heard it night after night. But that night was the first time for years I had twitched to get onto the floor. I had sat out the bunny hugs and turkey trots and cakewalks – I had no intention of making a complete ass of myself at my age. But I was in a fever of impatience for a waltz. My name was on Helen's programme for the supper dance, but as soon as she was in my arms, I knew I wasn't going to make it to supper.

Being strangled must feel a lot like that, only the choking sensation was not inside my collar, but inside my trousers. Sweat prickled in horror under my arms and between my shoulder blades. The more I tried to ignore it, the more urgent the demand became. I tried to distance myself from her – God forbid that she should touch me, even brush against me, there – stiffening my arms and jerking round the floor like some ridiculous marionette.

But there was no escape for me. Her slender gloved hand was in mine. My arm was around her waist and through the wisps of chiffon that covered her nakedness, I could feel the perfumed warmth of her skin. All the blood in my body seemed to be surging to one only too obvious spot. The pressure was agony. I could barely take another step.

I began to panic. Everyone in the room must notice. They would think me a monster, a pervert, not fit to be in the same room as their virgin daughters. My control was slipping away. At any moment, the unthinkable was going to happen.

She knew. Oh yes, she certainly knew. Her eyes flicked open, startled and wide, the eyes of Danaë as the golden shower fell. Then they were veiled again. God knows what she thought – that I was going to ravish her in the middle of the dance floor. I cursed these modern diaphanous gowns. Only a few years ago a girl decently corseted and covered would never have noticed my predicament. But then there probably wouldn't have been a predicament to notice. I stifled a groan as the music quickened.

'It's awfully hot, don't you think?' Helen said and I croaked something in reply. 'Do you think we could sit down somewhere?'

We retired behind a six-foot bank of rhododendrons in full flower and perched on some ridiculous little gilt chairs. Her legs were bare – oh God! – and the flimsy tunic moulded itself over firm, rounded thighs.

She ought to have looked like a whore. In the same style of gown, Diana Manners looked as good as naked and Nancy Cunard looked as though she had had a stand-up fight with her mother before being allowed out in a gown that was half daring, half demure. But Helen looked untouched and untouchable. She drooped in the little chair, looking as spotless as the Parianware nymph that had stood on my father's desk until a careless housemaid had knocked off the head.

That made it worse. I had revealed the basest and most animal passions. I had sullied her purity in unforgivable fashion. An electric fan whirred over a gigantic block of ice buried somewhere in the rhododendrons. The cooling breeze dried my brow, but was too late to do anything to save the wreck of my shirt front. The throbbing in my parts receded, but my brain was still on fire.

Sounds were muffled behind the floral display, but I guessed people were going in to supper and decided that I couldn't face the crush. Yet we couldn't sit here in silence. Perhaps I could offer to fetch her some champagne or lemonade. Perhaps I could make her laugh. I racked my brains for something suitable and witty, something that would make her forget my crassness in a tinkle of laughter.

'Helen – you must marry me – soon – you must,' I blurted and cringed inside at the sound of my voice. I wasn't supposed to be saying that – not yet.

'Isn't that rather an extreme reaction,' she answered coolly, dropping a slow glance below my belt and back again, 'to what was, after all, just a passing discomfiture?'

'No, no – you don't understand,' I blundered on, 'I've wanted to marry you forever.'

'For about four days at the very most. Isn't this the proper moment for me to say "But Mr Frampton – we hardly know each other"?'

'I don't need any longer. I adore you, worship you. I must have you for my own.'

'You don't know anything about me.'

26

'I know enough. You're beautiful, pure, an angel and I must have you.'

'You know *nothing*. You talk as though I were a collector's item, a desirable acquisition.'

'You *are* desirable – the most desirable creature I've ever seen. I would keep you, treasure you . . .'

'I'm not an artefact! I want to be loved as a woman,' she said and her voice husked over the last word in a way that made my nerves tingle. 'I don't want to be a plaster goddess in a museum.'

She rose and I made what was nearly a fatal error. I grabbed her by the elbow as she started to leave the shelter of the rhododendrons. The look she turned on me withered my manhood. She was taller than I had thought, taller than I, and I felt as though I had indeed offended a goddess.

I slipped away from the dance without thanking my hostess. Behind that familiar discreet door in Caroline Terrace I sweated and groaned, but that monstrous priapism could not be recaptured.

At home in Ebury Street, much later, I unfolded Helen's picture from my pocket book and found lonely solace.

I like to think that my obsession was a well-kept secret – except from its object, unfortunately. No one else could have guessed that dear, dull old Michael Frampton was seething with passion. After my frightful faux pas at the Clifdens', I decided to allow Helen a little time to forget. So I restrained myself from pursuing her for almost a week and few acts in my life have ever been so difficult.

Her likeness appeared several times in society papers during that period of abstention. London had its 'Three Graces' that year – Diana Manners, Nancy Cunard and Viola Keppel – but, to my mind, not one of them could hold a candle to Helen Leckford. And Nancy had that little, squeaky, toneless voice that made me think of an ant in a hurry. Whereas Helen's low, mellow tones could send shivers down my spine. The memory still does.

Yes, I was a little mad that last gay summer of a dying age. Only two people knew it – but I wish the secret could have been confined to only one.

Towards the end of May, I decided it was time to make my next move. I don't have much of an ear for music – opera always seems like much ado about nothing to me – but I had made it my business to know that Helen's aunt, Mrs Hayler, would be accompanied by her niece to the Russian Opera Company's opening night at Drury Lane.

Against my better judgement, I was dazzled. *Boris Godunov* flared like a comet across a dark sky. There was a blast to waken the dead, a blaze of blinding gold, the Kremlin bells clanged and clashed. Chaliapin's towering figure dominated the whole theatre. And, by swivelling around and annoying my neighbour, I could watch the face of my love a dozen seats further along the row.

Helen's pure, perfect profile was lifted to the stage. All the glamour and excitement of the story was reflected in it. Would she ever look at me with that breathless wonder? Her lips were just parted in rapture. Would they ever part like that beneath mine?

Helen's aunt was a remarkable woman in a close-fitting turban with towering aigrette and a peacock-blue brocade kaftan. Not the sort of person I would willingly seek to introduce myself to. She was the first woman I had ever met who painted her face – or rather, who painted it with the intention of being noticeable. The effect of those thin arched brows and that carmine gash of a mouth was unnerving. She held out a hand whose nails matched the lips.

'So you know the Nisbets,' she drawled. 'How splendid. Isn't Isobel looking a perfect *fright* these days? But what can you expect after all those children? Douglas just can't seem to leave her alone! Now, you must meet my niece . . .' She swivelled to right and left as though looking for a mislaid book. '. . . now *where* is she?'

A lady should always be allowed to claim acquaintance first and should be given the opportunity to acknowledge or repudiate a past meeting. So I waited to hear if Helen would say that we had already met at the Clifdens' disastrous dance. But she said nothing and let her aunt introduce me.

'Helen darling – this is Mr Michael Frampson . . .'

'Frampton . . .' I corrected.

'. . . and he's a friend of the Nisbets, so isn't that *nice*?'

It was so sweet of Helen. So typical of her. By not reminding me of our past meeting, she was saying that it was forgotten, that we could start again afresh.

Either that, or she really didn't remember me.

No, not that. She couldn't possibly have forgotten my grossness. But she wasn't going to recall it, either. That awful, awful evening had been put behind us. I felt a surge of optimism. This time – this time, I was not going to make a mess of things.

We shook hands and I was aware of a strong smell of petroleum. The dear child couldn't afford a new pair of gloves and was forced to clean the grease off an old pair. Perhaps the very pair she had been wearing . . . no, that evening was behind us and I would never think of its horrors again.

Her eyes were smoky in the dim light, as dark as the violets in the flower seller's basket outside the theatre – I wished I'd thought to buy some for her, or would that have been too obvious – and shaded by those perfectly arched lids. She could have enslaved me for life with one glance that night, if I had not already been hers to tread upon if she wished.

'I'm having a little party for Helen on Wednesday next,' said Mrs Hayler as the warning bell rang to mark the end of the interval. 'You *will* come, won't you? Now, don't forget . . .'

As if I would.

'Don't know what you want to go there for,' grumbled Anthony as he stood in the window with a whisky in his hand, watching the world go by. 'All tomtits' toes on toast and long-haired pretty boys.' Anthony's visits to town are fortunately infrequent.

'I thought it might be amusing,' I answered, making myself very busy with the decanter.

'Didn't know your taste ran in that direction.' He gave a coarse chuckle and drained the glass. 'Though Clemmie was saying just the other day . . .'

'What? What was Clemmie saying . . . ?'

As I lifted my head abruptly from the decanter I caught a glimpse of my face in the looking glass above the fire. Shock had drained the colour from my face, leaving me completely grey – grey hair, grey eyes, grey face. Anthony must have seen the reflection too.

'Oh nothing, nothing . . .' he mumbled.

'What was Clemmie saying?' I demanded.

'Nothing really . . . you know Clemmie.'

'Yes, I know Clemmie. What has she been saying about me?'

'It was just her little joke . . . just a bit of night-time fun . . .' Anthony looked acutely embarrassed. He must have wished he'd never opened his mouth.

I drained my glass. 'That woman thinks the whole world revolves around sex.'

'You do remember you're talking about my wife.'

'Yes – and I'm sorry for you. Just because I didn't marry as soon as I could get it up – unlike you – she thinks . . . she suggests . . .' It was too horrible. I couldn't go on.

'Oh come on now, that's going it a bit strong.'

'Well, it may give you – and your wife – some relief to know that I expect to be married some time in August.'

'Good God!' said Anthony.

I had plenty of time to repent of that stupid scene with Anthony before the night of the Haylers' party. He had taken it very badly, had stormed out of the house promising never to enter it again unless I apologized for my remarks about his wife. In turn, I had said he would not be welcome unless he apologized for Clemmie's insinuations. It was all very stupid and unnecessary.

It had all happened before, of course. Anthony and I were continually at each other's throats about some silly thing or another. That didn't mean we didn't care for each other, in an undemonstrative, brotherly sort of way. But somehow, things seemed to have gone too far this time and things were said that should never have been said. Only a timely telephone call for me stopped us from laying bare the hidden resentments of our lives, that had been decently hidden since boyhood.

But brothers are brothers. You can always go to your big brother for help.

Even when you wake up in the dark, in pain, afraid and alone.

'Nanny,' I'd called, 'Nanny, where are you?'

If I'd ever called out before – ever – she just seemed to be there. I'd never hear her come in, but she'd be there. A smell of soap and flowery talcum powder. A rustle of nightgown. Her long plait of hair the colour of ripe

31

wheat slipping with a whisper from back to front as she bent over my bed.

'There,' she'd say, 'there, Michael love, I'm here. It's all right.'

And it was all right. She'd put her rough little hand on my forehead and stroke away the bear from behind the curtains or the witch who lived in the cupboard.

'Nanny, I've got a pain. Where are you? I need you.'

She'd always come before.

If there had been a bear behind the curtains, I'd have pulled the bedclothes over my head. If he couldn't see even a tiny bit of me, perhaps he'd go somewhere else for his supper. Perhaps he'd go and try to eat Anthony, but Anthony'd take his gun and shoot him dead. Just like the rabbit he'd brought in that evening, dangling by tied back paws from a hazel stick, blood dripping from its soft, twitchy nose.

But there wasn't a bear, so I could get out of bed without being eaten and look for Nanny. And the pain in my tummy was like a knife.

Nanny's bed was there, turned down and looking inviting in the firelight. Her clothes were there too. Her brown dress and starched apron, clean for tomorrow, hung from the hook on the back of the door. Some more clothes lay across a basket chair. I picked them up, one by one, trying to work out what they were all for. So many things. Floppy, frilly things, they were, with pink ribbon threaded through, much prettier than her day dresses. Wouldn't it be nice if she could wear clothes like that all the time and not cover them up with dull brown holland? And she could wear her hair in the plait every day, not tucked up into an ugly cap. Or loose and fluffy, like when she dried it in front of the fire after it was washed.

I thought about trying on the pretty, frilly things, but

the knife in my tummy was slicing it up now, like carving the roast meat I only saw on Sundays.

Anthony would know what to do.

Anthony was nearly a man now, or so he said. At any rate, he didn't sleep on the nursery floor any more. He had a room on the floor where the grown-ups slept. He had his fishing rod there and his gun used to be there too, until Father found out and made him lock it in the gun cupboard. He had a ratting terrier called Meg who slept on his bed and an ants' nest in a glass case, so you could look at all the ants scurrying around. He said I might look at it any time I chose. It was capital fun to scatter crumbs on the surface and watch the ants drag them all below.

But Anthony wasn't in his room either. Meg was there, curled up on the pillow. She growled when I went in, but when she saw it was me, she wagged her stumpy little tail and rolled over with her paws in the air. I tickled her tummy and felt those funny little pink bumps of skin – four on each side of her chest, but I had only one each side. I wondered what they were for.

I wandered over to the window to see if ants sleep at night, but it was too dark to see. They were so busy during the day, they must need a lot of sleep. Nanny said, 'Early to bed and early to rise' and ants certainly rose early.

Now I didn't know what to do. Nobody was where they should be. Nothing was in its proper place and the world was turning upside down and my feet were cold and the pain in my tummy was getting worse and I thought I might be sick.

When I slipped back out into the corridor, Meg followed me. I felt better with her trotting on little scuttering paws alongside me. Her toenails clicked along the polished floorboards. The corridor was so long and only the glass dome above the stairwell gave it any light.

There was no one left who could help me except Mother. I'd never been in Mother's bedroom, ever. I knew where it was, of course. It was next to the little morning room where she saw Cook every day and where she wrote all her letters – she wrote a great many letters. I was allowed in the morning room, but I'd never, ever, been invited into her bedroom. But my tummy was so bad.

I stopped outside the door. There were voices. Mother's of course – and Father's as well. And that was odd, too, because he had his own bedroom on the other side of the corridor, with a dark dressing room that smelled of pomade and cigars. But now he was in Mother's bedroom.

What a funny night. No one was where they should be. Nanny wasn't in her room. Anthony wasn't in his room. Father wasn't in his room. I wasn't in my room either. Perhaps it was always like this, only I'd never been awake before to find out.

I opened the door very, very softly, so as not to wake up anyone who just might be where they ought to be. A shaft of light sliced through the darkness in the corridor. Just like in the transformation scene in the Christmas pantomime, the corridor was transformed from cold and ugliness into a place of warmth and perfume and light.

There were scented hangings, lace and bows. A dressing table by the window was covered with silver-topped jars of delicious potions. Here was the source of the perfume that always floated with Mother wherever she went. There were silver-backed brushes, too, and a square, leather-covered box that spilled strings of pearls and topazes and the amethysts that Mother always wore because they were the colour of her eyes.

To my enchanted gaze, it was like discovering the cave that opened before Ali Baba when he cried "Open Sesame".

Mother was in bed, sitting up straight against big, soft pillows. She was wearing a nightgown the colour of the cream I was sometimes – not often – allowed on my stewed plums. The gown was all floaty and silky and covered in lace. Not at all like Nanny's. The lamp by the bed made her hair glitter as though it had been sprinkled with diamond dust.

She ought to have looked happy, sitting there in that big, soft bed and wearing a beautiful, floaty gown, but she didn't. She looked as though she felt sick, as sick as I did.

'You disgust me,' she said. 'You make me sick.'

So she did feel sick too, I thought. Perhaps we both had a germ, she was always terrified of germs.

Father was wearing his silk dressing gown, the purple one with the embroidered dragon on the back.

'Eleanor, please,' he said. 'Please.' And his voice was all funny and muffled and not at all like his usual big, gruff voice.

'You are beastly,' she said. 'Beastly.'

And then Father turned round and he *was* beastly. He didn't have his evening trousers and his hard shirt on without the collar, like he usually had under his dressing gown. On this funny night, he had nothing on – and his thing had gone beastly.

My thing didn't look like that. Anthony's didn't either, even though it was bigger than mine. Father's was all swollen and out of shape and purple, like a broken leg I saw once. It had grown too big ever to be tucked into his trousers again. He would have to go around like that forever. It was sticking straight out from a bunch of curly hair and it had a big red knob on the end. Mother covered her face in her hands.

Then I saw Father's thing go small again. It shrivelled right away, like a slug when the gardener puts salt on its tail, but it still wasn't the right colour. Father got down on his knees and put his face on Mother's tummy and cried.

I turned my face neatly away from the bedroom carpet and was sick on the polished floor.

My parents got the best man in, of course – Sir Frederick Treves, no less, although I didn't know it at the time. Nanny had come to see me when I woke up after my appendix had been cut out. She said she was very sorry she hadn't been there to make me better, but she didn't tell me where she'd been.

Just to make her feel bad, I repeated the words I'd heard floating above me before I was completely awake. 'I was very ill,' I said. 'They despaired of me, you know.'

Anthony had come to see me too. He'd said, 'What on earth were you doing wandering around in the dark?'

'I was sick and you weren't there. No one was there.' But I didn't tell him about Father crying because his thing had gone beastly.

Anthony didn't tell me where he'd been either. He'd just said, 'Sorry, old chap.'

Anthony was always very good about saying he was sorry, but this time no apologies were forthcoming on either side. And that nymphomaniac bitch of a wife of his was at the bottom of it.

Not the least of my anger had been caused by the fact that I had given away what had been until then my own treasured hope. And to have told Anthony – of all people – that I expected to marry soon. He was consti- tutionally incapable of keeping his mouth shut. And

Clemmie could wheedle his secrets out of a father confessor.

I had seen her sometimes with Anthony. She was quite shameless. She would come up behind him, draping herself sinuously against his back, her arms like twin snakes over his shoulders, breathing her poison into his ear. And what her fingers were doing under his coat, I blush to think. The besotted grin on his face told me quite enough.

Yes, there was no doubt that Clemmie would know all before nightfall. Thank God our quarrel had been too explosively sudden for me to tell Anthony just who it was I had such unexpected hopes of marrying. I wasn't ready for that – not yet.

I behaved impeccably at the Haylers'. No embarrassing occurrences, no impassioned outbursts. Perhaps I may have paid rather too obvious attention to Helen, in the most gentlemanly fashion, of course. But then, who would think badly of that? That was what the season was all about, wasn't it? A marriage mart. A glorified slave market, where the highest bidder had the first choice of goods. Untouched by human hand.

What other future was there for the daughter of a well-connected but impoverished army officer (recently deceased) and a fluffy, plump widow? I offered Helen escape from the trap that fate had closed around her. And what is more – and very unusual these troubled days, if my married friends are anything to judge by – I offered her lifelong devotion. What more could she ask?

Given Mrs Hayler's choice of costume for the opera, I didn't expect a conventional evening. And I was not disappointed. Their house in Grosvenor Street was furnished – I think the word is – eclectically. That means it was an appalling jumble of styles and dates that looked as though it had been furnished from a Cairo bazaar.

In a hall of peacock-blue de Morgan tiles, a marble Renaissance fountain splashed. My hat and stick were taken by a little Negro, no more than nine years old, dressed in a top-heavy pink turban.

Everyone knows that a garden is no place to hold a formal party, but there, it appeared, my hostess was waiting to greet me, in a tiny paved courtyard sickly with the perfume of white flowers – lilies, mock orange, lilac.

If Eglantine Hayler could just about get away with her eccentric appearance in the exotic atmosphere that had surrounded the performance of *Boris Godunov*, here under a perfect June evening sky she looked utterly raddled. She wore yet another preposterous turban, this time in the shade of ochre that adds years to the complexion of an older woman. Her shapeless, floating garment was a sort of shimmering kingfisher. Beads, bangles and brooches – some real, some not – glittered like a huckster's stall. The clear light showed just exactly how much her skin owed to artifice and, as a final catastrophe, she waved about a black Turkish cigarette in a long amber holder. She looked like Scheherazade after every single one of the thousand and one nights. Thank God she was only Helen's aunt and not her mother.

'*Wonderful* of you to have come, Mr Frampson,' she whispered. 'As you can see, we're having a little musical evening. Do sit down.'

I looked about for a chair, but everyone seemed to be sprawled on gigantic tapestry cushions. Anthony had been right about the guest list! One beautiful young man lay full length, trailing his fingers idly in a pool of water lilies. I thought about hitching up the knees of my trousers and joining everyone on the ground, but decided against it.

'Thank you, I'd rather stand,' I whispered back.

The finest musicians of the day often played at private

parties then. I had heard Casals, Rubinstein, even on one occasion Debussy himself give an impromptu recital. But no one seriously expected one to *listen*. And there was always a bolt-hole somewhere for those who wished to escape. Tonight, however, it was obvious that one's whole attention was meant to be devoted to the music. And such music! Stravinsky, Prokofiev, Ravel, Strauss (Richard, not the Viennese waltz man). The combinations of notes frequently set my teeth on edge! And the rhythms – they were totally degenerate.

No one talked. I suppose they must have breathed, but not so that one would notice. They probably thought it was all very avant-garde, those extraordinary people sprawled out on the cushions, but it was something very close to hell to me.

Standing under a drooping lilac, as far back from the source of music as I could get, I was at leisure to watch Helen as long as I liked and no one need notice. She was so lovely, so pure, in something floating and silvery that matched the spun silver-gilt of her hair. She made all the other women in that garden look garish and sullied. As long as she was there, I could have stood and looked and looked and never minded the cacophony that was crashing around my ears.

I was not alone in my tastes. After a chord that sounded like a cat being skinned alive, there came a chorus of jeers from the other side of the garden wall. The jeers were quickly followed by a more tangible expression of distaste. A perfect bombardment of fish heads and rotten eggs came sailing over the wall onto the heads of the languishing listeners. The first casualty was Clive Grayson. A rotten egg impaled itself and exploded on one of the large pearl studs which closed his exquisitely laundered shirt front.

Some wild party of subalterns, I suppose. It was all quite *glorious*. I cheered as the bombardment continued and those effete pansies ran like rabbits. But Helen was standing quite still, in the middle of the chaos, and her shoulders seemed to be heaving. I ran to her, gathering her in my arms and shielding her from the missiles. We joined the stampede for the house and she was buffeted by the press of bodies further into my arms. It was like holding a moonbeam.

In the blue-tiled hall, servants were adding to the confusion by trying to wipe down splattered guests. The little Negro boy, his pink turban knocked askew, was crying, but no one paid him any attention.

I looked anxiously at Helen, fearing to find that she might be doing the same, and was amazed to discover that her shoulders were heaving with laughter, real laughter. She flung back her head and laughed. The superb column of her throat was like living alabaster. I put out my hand to run it down the pure lines, but just managed to stop myself in time.

'Wonderful! What fun!' she cried, clear and loud. 'This party will be remembered long after all the other insipid ones have been forgotten!'

To be honest, I was just a little bit shocked. I hadn't expected such a forthright reaction. Perhaps she was overwrought. The attack had been a shock to all of us.

'Are you hurt at all?'

'Not at all, though I expect my aunt's pride has received a mortal blow.'

'You have some yellow powder – I think it's lily pollen. Would you permit me . . . ?'

With tender fingers I brushed the bridge of her narrow nose, her brow, her cheeks. Her skin was cool and firm, yet it seemed to scald my fingertips. I could feel the beginning of another unwanted sweat break out beneath my arms. Just like a schoolboy with his first housemaid in his embrace. I hated myself for my lack of control.

There was still some pollen on her lower lip, a tawny powdering as though a bee with heavy pollen sacs had wandered across a flower. Her lip was full – in another woman it might have been called sensual – and the colour of a petal. I wanted to put my head down and lick the dusting of colour from her mouth. I wanted to suck further still, to probe like that wandering bee, and taste the honey deep in her throat.

I might even have done it.

No, of course I wouldn't. Not there, in the hall, surrounded by a milling of guests and servants.

But I wanted to.

That disastrous evening had a happy result for me. By the time the dishevelled guests had left, I was still there, in the hall, with Helen in my arms, delaying my departure as long as I decently could. Eglantine Hayler fluttered towards us and, like her niece, she was laughing.

'*Such* a pantomime,' she giggled. I have always thought that giggles should be forbidden by law to women over twenty. 'But I am determined to educate my philistine neighbours and I shall, if it costs them whole crates of eggs!'

'I'm relieved to see you're not too distressed, Mrs Hayler.'

'Distressed? Not at all. I enjoyed every minute of it. *Did* you see Clive with that egg impaled on his shirt stud? And Athene Palmer swept out the door with a fish head peeping out of her tocque. I could have *died*!'

I had a sudden impulse. 'Let me make up for your spoiled evening by inviting you both to have dinner with me.'

A couple of telephone calls and we were all in a taxi on our way to the Berkeley. Its heliotrope and white grill room was very fashionable that year. It was crowded, of course, and I knew that being seen with

41

Helen in such a public place, with what amounted to a family party, was a statement of intent. Her mother would not need to be told after this that I was interested in her daughter.

Eglantine Hayler did most of the talking, I seem to remember, but what she said I had forgotten by the next sentence. She used the amber cigarette holder much as a conductor uses his baton and scattered ash not only over her own plate, but over mine as well.

Helen was very quiet. It could have been shyness, but somehow I didn't think it was. She was watching me, not warily, but as though she really wanted to get beyond the starched shirt front and social chit-chat. I felt a moment of panic. Supposing she didn't like what she found there? Supposing she was silent because she thought me just too dull for words? I couldn't bear it.

'Let's have some fun. Let's go on to a night club,' urged Eglantine as we left the Berkeley. 'It's still much too early to go home. Do say yes, dear Mr Frampson. I feel as though I could dance all night.'

Dear God!

'Yes, of course, if you'd like to. But I'm afraid I can't suggest anywhere. Bit too much of the old bachelor, you know.'

'I know a simply *divine* place, with a wonderful Negro band. Don't you think Negro music is *too* exciting – all that primeval energy!'

So we spent the rest of the evening at the Lotus and I must confess that the music was no more to my taste than Stravinsky. I completely failed to see what was 'divine' about the place. It was dark, hot, overcrowded with fast young women and with young men who ought to have known better. Eglantine drank cherry flips at an alarming rate. The band hooted itself hoarse with whip-poor-will cackles.

It seemed a very overrated, overpriced way of spending a summer's night. Not that I'm mean, of course, but I do like to see some value for my money.

As escort to two ladies, I could scarcely sit out all evening. Dancing the bunny hug with Eglantine, I felt very much like a spider's next meal. She seemed to have more than the usual complement of hands and she used every one of them in a most unusual way.

By the time I took the floor with Helen, the tiny room had become so crowded that there was no point in trying to dance. The air was thick with smoke. Most of the lights had been extinguished.

She was folded in my arms in her slip of silver lamé. Her silver sandals had little heels on them which made her still taller than I, but I didn't care. We were so close we seemed to be breathing in counterpoint, in and out, out and in, sharing the breath of life. She must have been able to feel the way my heart was battering my ribs. We were quite still, the eye in the frenzied hurricane of motion around us. The gossamer thread of her hair tickled my cheek. My lips were on the sweet, scented skin of her neck.

'Helen,' I whispered. 'Helen, do you think you could love me? Just a little bit?'

She didn't answer. Perhaps, with all the noise around us, she didn't hear me.

I wish I had taken her silence for rejection. I wish that I had just walked away, there and then. I wish – God help me, I must be going mad – I even wish I had been able to find that sort of unthinkable solace that Clemmie suspected me of. I wish . . .

I suspect that Eglantine Hayler took charge of my court-ship of Helen from that time on. After all, she was spending a good deal of money in bringing her niece out. She wanted it all to be worthwhile. Things moved with a speed that was very satisfying to me. It was suggested that I might like to take Helen to the theatre – chaperoned by Eglantine, of course. Finding something suitable for a well brought-up young woman was not easy that summer. So many of the box office successes were what might be described as rather louche.

Eglantine suggested *The Dangerous Age* showing at the Vaudeville, but I could not approve of a play enacting the love of a forty-year-old woman for a boy young enough to be her son (yet Helen could have been my daughter – why did not that seem as absurd?). *Uncle Vanya* at the Aldwych was a very strange play. And even the playbills for *Pygmalion* were offensive. I could not conceive why the Lord Chamberlain's office allowed the word *bloody* to appear in public view like that.

In the end, we settled for *The Passing Show*, like most of London that year, and I was thoroughly bored all evening. Only the consolation of sitting thigh to thigh with Helen made the endless hours worthwhile.

An invitation to tea with Helen's mother followed shortly and I knew that I was coming to the final furlong. Thurloe Square is in an area of utmost, if slightly fallen, gentility in the maze of South Kensington streets. The fine family houses had been split, since the turn of the century, into smaller apartments frequently rented by genteel windows in reduced circumstances. I scarcely knew where my cabby was taking me. I knew Helen's father had not left his widow well-provided for, but as we drew up before the cream stucco-faced building, I approved the well-whitened steps and the polished knocker. She seemed to be managing to keep up appearances as well as she could. As I walked up the steps, I was conscious of curtains twitching at the windows of other apartments.

There are so many women like Mrs Leckford. Their courage is not the courage of men. No blaring trumpets

44

or waving flags accompany their acts of heroism. And yet they are brave – daily, weekly, monthly, yearly brave. Keeping up appearances on a minute pension. Never letting down the side. Never giving way to despair. Bringing up a family that will one day take up a rightful place in society.

I expected a faded, nervous, gentle widow. I found a ruined Helen – tall, handsome, ravaged, dauntless. And the greatest shock of all was that Mrs Leckford was younger than I.

The shock made me nervous. I fluffed our introduction fearfully. Suddenly it seemed so absurd, so indecent, that I should be pursuing the daughter of this woman who herself was the right age to be my wife. I looked into her violet eyes – Helen's eyes, sharpened by worldly knowledge – and read the same thought there. Helen's mother thought I was too old, too plain and too dull for her glorious daughter. No doubt Helen *could* do far better for herself, if I were to stop monopolizing her and allow her to meet other eligible men. Yet for reasons of her own, Mrs Leckford was prepared to admit my courtship.

I know I did not show myself to best advantage. I seemed to myself to be even duller than usual. I perched awkwardly on the edge of an atrociously ugly chair, making less than scintillating small talk about the weather and the various parties I had been to. We sat in a room shaded with green holland blinds against the glare of the pavements beyond the window. And not once did I tell Helen's mother that her daughter was my lodestar, that I must have her for my own or live a twilight life.

I was stifled. My collar seemed to have become half a size too small. My hat was balanced awkwardly on my knee with the grey kid gloves inside. My stick was propped against the arm of the chair and I knocked it over twice. I felt like a shop assistant being interviewed for a new post.

The atmosphere was heavy and dusty and there was a curiously sweet smell that I couldn't quite place. Helen slipped away and it was only when I heard the rattle of teacups approaching that I realized she had been preparing tea herself.

Not even a daily woman! I promised myself there and then that Helen would never have to do another hand's turn when we were married. I would give her anything – everything – if I could make her happy.

I could not have been more relieved when tea was finished. The air in that stuffy, shaded room was unbearable. Surely they could have lifted the blinds a fraction, let in a little daylight? Helen rose to pick up the tray and I bounced up to help her. My ebony stick fell again to the floor with a clatter.

'No. Stay,' commanded Mrs Leckford and when Helen had left the room, 'Open the blinds please.'

When the blinds were opened, I had my second shock. Mrs Leckford was dying. The splendid bones on her face looked sharp enough to pierce her parchment skin. The hair that once had been gilded as Helen's now was a dusty ash, as though she had been cleaning out a grate without wearing a cap. Her fine, long-fingered hands were folded in her lap. They looked at rest, but as I watched, I saw that she was clenching and unclenching her fingers every few seconds.

'I see by your face that I don't have to tell you, Mr Frampton.'

I made a sort of noncommital mumble.

'Let me be frank. I don't expect to survive this summer.'

'Surely something . . .'

'Nothing. And, now that I have no false hopes, I am

46

longing for the end. But I must live long enough to see Helen provided for.'

'I would give my life to make her happy.' Not the most felicitous remark in the circumstances and one that made me cringe in the silent hours of that night.

'I know. Mr Frampton, people who are dying don't have time or energy to waste on polite conversation. If circumstances were otherwise, you are not the husband I would have chosen for Helen . . .'

'I'm not worthy of her.'

'. . . but you are a generous and kind man. Kindness is the only thing worth having when passion has died. I think you will take care of her.'

I bowed my head. She was giving me a trust. She was passing on her daughter to my charge. And I was deeply grateful.

'But a word of warning, Mr Frampton. Never forget that she is only – a woman. Helen, dear . . .' She swivelled in her chair with a tight smile as the door opened. I was close enough to hear the brief, indrawn gasp of pain. '. . . why don't you take Mr Frampton for a walk? I don't suppose for one moment that he has ever been for a walk around here before.' The laugh she gave was like listening to Helen's ghost.

The heat in the streets was punishing that day. It bounced off the paving stones and sneaked underneath hat brims. It seared through the soles of shoes. It dried the horse dung in the road to a powder which was scattered by a scorching wind. The narrow streets around Thurloe Square trapped the stifling air and released it in eddying whirlwinds of dust that might have blown off the Sahara. We walked slowly, breathing in air that seemed to have had all the oxygen sucked out of it. Helen's arm rested lightly on mine.

She had been given to me. She had been bequeathed to me as a sacred trust. It was almost as though I had been left her in a will. She was mine. A legacy of love. Absolutely. For ever.

And now her mother's narrow stucco house was in view again and nothing had been said. Not one word had been spoken between us. I felt I could not return Helen to her mother without a commitment having been made. I tried a gate in the railings that surrounded Thurloe Square gardens and walked her twice around the cinder path beneath dusty plane trees.

'Helen,' I said as we began our third circuit, 'will you marry me?'

'If you like,' she answered softly.

Not the most ardent reply to a proposal of marriage. An omen. If I liked. Not if she liked. Or if we liked. If I liked.

And I did like. I felt giddy, sick with relief and excitement. I lifted her hand and pressed it to my cheek in thanks and homage. The long bones were so slight, so fine. Everything about her was so beautifully made – God's perfect handiwork. And this glorious creature was mine.

Helen turned to look at me, her head slightly at an angle to compensate for the fact that mine was a little lower than hers. Her smile was a heady compound of shyness and invitation.

It was appalling really. So careless of her reputation. Even now I am embarrassed by the memory. But my excuse is that I was carried away by joy and relief.

There in the public park, within sight of her mother's windows, I kissed her with a lover's kisses. Deeply. Hungrily. And she answered me.

Our bodies seemed to fit together, moulding – breast to breast, thigh to thigh we fitted in a jigsaw of love. Her arms twined round my neck and I felt the softness of her fingers interlocking against my skin. Her full lips parted beneath my own and I tasted the warm places of her mouth – sweet and sharp, unforgettable flavour. She nipped my tongue with teasing teeth and the brief tang of blood heightened my passion. She was fire and ice, temptation and dark, dark excitement.

I shall never forget it.

And then my hat fell off. And with that came the shocking realization of what we were doing. I was treating my future wife as a whore. Worse. At least a whore is dealt with in decent darkness.

'I'm sorry. I'm so sorry . . .' I picked up my hat and dusted it with a cuff, turning my face from her to allow her time to recover her composure. 'That was beastly of me. Beastly.'

She was looking at me with those wide eyes that seemed to be accusing me of all sorts of horrors. They were very bright, suspiciously bright. Her lips looked swollen and there was a red abrasion on her chin where my late afternoon beard had rubbed. I couldn't bear to think that I had caused her that hurt.

'I'm so sorry,' I repeated. 'That will never happen again. I promise. Please forgive me.'

'If you really think you need forgiveness,' she said gently, 'you may have it.'

And she turned to walk towards home. I suppose she must have been disgusted with me.

Helen's mother died on the day war was declared. It seems incredible now that I had not noticed the shadows grow long. My own private obsession had obscured my vision. My horizon began and ended with Helen. The sun rose on thoughts of her and often rose again before I managed to sleep.

But I was not the only one wearing blinkers. It is fashionable today for people to beat their breasts and say that they had an uneasy feeling of coming wrath, that the decadence of society had to be purged, that the heart of the rose was cankered. But I heard no one say that in August 1914.

Schools broke up for the summer and senior boys expected to be back at their desks in September. The schools' cricket match was held at Lords. The Subalterns' Cup was played for at Hurlingham.

His Majesty did not go to Goodwood, however, and perhaps that was a pointer to growing anxiety. At the end of Goodwood week, the bank rate doubled to eight per cent.

But Anthony said, 'There won't be any war. The City would never allow it.'

Eglantine Hayler set herself to plan our wedding with gusto. I managed to veto every extravagant idea she came up with.

'But it's Helen's day,' she protested. 'Don't you want it to be a memorable one?'

'It will be quite memorable enough without eight attendants in Louis Seize dresses. I want this to be a simple, dignified ceremony, not a peepshow.'

Helen said nothing. I scarcely saw her these days. I saw less of her now that we were betrothed than I had in the days of our courtship. Her mother was failing fast and Helen was spending every possible hour at her bedside. She spent the long, weary hours of that stifling July in the stale atmosphere of the sickroom. Now that her daughter's future was secure, Mrs Leckford had loosened her grip on life, but life would not loosen its grip on her. Her last days were hard ones.

On the morning of 5th August, I was still at breakfast and staring in incredulity at newspaper headlines which informed me that our ultimatum to Germany, stating that we would 'uphold the neutrality of Belgium and the observance of the treaty to which Germany is as much a party as ourselves', had not been accorded a 'satisfactory answer'. Our ambassador had asked for his passports. We had been at war with Germany since 11 p.m.

All night cars decorated with the Tricolore and the Union Flag had driven around, hooting. Crowds had sung the *Marseillaise* in Bedford Square. His Majesty and Queen Mary had appeared on the balcony at Buckingham Palace to an excited, optimistic crowd. But until I saw it in unarguable black type in *The Times*, I could not believe that the impossible had happened.

I heard my door bell ring, but, as I had no doubt Anthony would be on the doorstep at the first sniff of gunpowder, I paid it no attention other than an inward groan. Then Helen was shown into my breakfast room.

'It is over,' she said simply.

I had risen in haste at her entry and knocked over my chair. I turned to set it right before answering. 'Come now, my dear, I know the situation seems grave this morning, but there is no need for despondency.'

'I had nowhere else to go. I couldn't stay in that house.'

I looked again at her drawn face. The fragile skin under her eyes was smudged with plum-coloured shadows. Her glorious hair was slipping from its combs and had not been tidied that morning. Her mouth was tight, drawn like a tremulous line. She was standing very erect with shoulders as taut as a soldier, as though the least hint of weakness would cause her to collapse totally.

'Your mother? Oh, Helen. My poor, dear girl.'

I helped her to a chair and sent my still hovering man for brandy. She gulped it down, with none of the girlish grimacing and coughing I had expected.

'I don't want to disturb you. I just didn't know where else to go.'

'But my dear, we are about to share the rest of our lives. To whom else would you go?'

51

'It was so . . . so awful . . .' A shudder passed along the whole slender length of her, like the first warning tremor of a coming earthquake.

'It was a happy release,' I said, sententiously.

'Could I have some more of that brandy, please?' She held out the glass with an arm that was extended to its limit to still the shudder.

'I'm not sure . . . Is that wise?'

'Please, Michael? Please?'

I poured another tot and she downed it in one. Her skin grew less waxen.

'Have you had time to tell your aunt yet? Would you like me to telephone her?'

'Yes, please. No . . . not yet . . .' She grabbed the edge of my dressing gown as I turned for the door. 'Don't leave me. Not yet.'

I drew up another chair and sat by her, chafing her icy hand and wondering if I ought to call a doctor for a soothing draught.

'It was cruel . . .' Her voice was a hoarse whisper. '. . . cruel. People don't die like that in books. They have time to make speeches and give deathbed blessings. My mother died screaming. She didn't know I was there. I was just something solid to hang onto.'

She held out her other hand and I saw with horror scarlet crescent-shaped weals on the white skin.

'Couldn't the doctor do anything?'

'He said . . .' She gave a short barking laugh. '. . . he said any more painkiller would kill her. I begged and begged . . . but he wouldn't do it.'

'The man should be shot!'

The spasm began at her head. I didn't know people's teeth chattered in real life. They do. The sound is like bones being rattled in a hellish game of dice. The spasm spread until her whole body was in its grip, jerking and twitching as the horror of the night took hold.

I picked her up and staggered at the statuesque weight of her. One-handed, I eased open the door and started upstairs to the guest bedroom, calling as I did so for my man to ring the doctor. He can't have heard me.

I laid her on the bed and pulled the covers over her. The artificial colour the brandy had left in her cheeks had faded, leaving her the colour of putty. Her knees were drawn up to her chest and she gripped them with her arms.

'You're so cold, my darling, you must have a hot water bottle and a doctor.'

'Don't leave me.'

She grabbed again at my robe as I turned to organize help. I knelt by the bed and stroked her dishevelled hair back from her brow.

'Only for a moment, darling. Just to get help for you. I'll come back, I promise.'

'Don't leave me.'

I tried to find her pulse, but wasn't quite sure where to look. The beat in her wrist seemed too threadlike to be accurate. I must have done it wrong. Her skin was clammy and icy at the same time.

'So cold . . .' she moaned.

Supposing she died? Dear God . . . supposing she died of shock? Was that possible? No time to call for servants. No time to wait for kettles to boil.

I pulled back the covers and slipped into bed beside her. I opened my dressing gown and pulled her body close against mine, willing the heat to pass from me to her. Still she shivered. I opened my shirt. I unbuttoned her blouse with fumbling fingers. Perhaps with our skin together, the heat would pass more effectively.

I swear I didn't mean it to happen.

She opened her eyes, huge and bruised in her chalky face. 'Don't leave me,' she pleaded. 'I'm so alone. Don't leave me.' And she laid her icy lips on mine.

Helen. My goddess. My queen. My wife.

★
53

I never meant it to happen. I took advantage of her grief and horror. I shamed myself before her. And when I rose, shaking with self-disgust, there were white stains on the front of my robe and on her skirt.

I couldn't speak, couldn't explain that all I had meant was to give her comfort. Thank God, at least I had withheld from the final, bestial defloration. She was still intact and the shame was mine alone.

When she looked at me, the pain in her eyes was almost more than I could bear. And it was mixed with something else too, something too complicated for me to understand. I was prepared for shock, for accusation, but not for the pity in her gaze. I didn't expect that. I must have misread it.

'I'll have a doctor brought to you at once,' I said, making ineffectual attempts to straighten the bed covers.

'I don't need a doctor. I must go home.'

'But you are in a state of shock.'

'Not now. My mother is out of her pain now. So I should stop being selfish and be glad. Would you be kind enough to send up a housemaid to help me with my hair before I go?'

'Your aunt should be notified. Would you like me to contact her?'

'If you would.' She swung her legs out of bed. Her skirt was crumpled and stained. 'And I would be glad of some hot water and soap, please.'

'Of course. Of course.'

'Michael . . .' Her voice recalled me at the door. 'You mustn't be ashamed. I wanted . . . I *needed* more than you . . . well, never mind. It doesn't matter.'

I didn't believe her, of course. She was only trying, in her sweet way, to make me feel better.

'You're a good man, Michael. I shall be glad to be your wife.'

We were married quietly two or three days after the declaration of war. There seemed no point in waiting. Her mother's death and the uncertainty of the nation would have made any ostentatious display quite distasteful. Even Eglantine saw the propriety of that, although she abandoned the Louis Seize dresses and the flower-decked arbours with great reluctance.

'Not even two attendants? That's not overdoing it, surely?'

But we held firm, Helen and I. And I was deeply relieved, despite the awful circumstances, to have been spared the vulgar performance we could otherwise have endured.

The service was dignified, restrained and beautiful. Exactly as I would have wished it. I sat in my lonely pew in the front, with Anthony at my side, and I dared not turn round. The church was nearly empty. There were so few people we really wanted to invite.

Clemmie was there, with her narrow, clever face, her Irene Castle-style short bob, her little mocking smile that I hated so. Her two awful boys were there too. The afterthoughts, as Clemmie called them, with distressing frankness. A daughter was already married and in India. Their eldest son had joined his regiment on 5th August. I could hear the boys tussling together and was deeply grateful that we had a good excuse for not choosing them as attendants.

At the other side of the church Eglantine Hayler sat by herself. Her appearance could only be described as devastating. She looked as though she had escaped from one of Diaghilev's more fanciful productions. And that was all. Not exactly the society wedding of the year.

The rustle in the church told me Helen had arrived at the door. Even those dreadful boys were still for a moment. But I couldn't turn round. The tension was too fierce. I was too close to tears. The sight of Helen drifting up the nave in a foam of white, the sun-bright glass staining her gown with a kaleidoscope of crimson and azure, would have unmanned me completely.

Anthony had to give me a nudge in the ribs to make me move. I stepped forward to the altar, to wait for the moment when meek little Mr Hayler would put Helen's hand in mine, finally and forever.

Even at that sublime moment, when I put the ring on Helen's finger, I had not the courage to look at her face. There – it was done! She was mine!

Brides are usually described, by newspaper hacks, as radiant. The report of our wedding too, describes Helen as thus (and myself as distinguished, which made me laugh!). But if the camera does not lie, Helen was not radiant. Our wedding pictures show her as beautiful (of course), calm, but thoughtful looking, even pensive. I managed only to look foolishly doting and proud.

There was a whirl of congratulations at the church door. Eglantine gave each of us a kiss that left the imprint of her (that day) deep purple lips. Anthony shook my hand with a grip that crushed my bones. He had a wide, foolish grin on his face. Clemmie cocked her neat, bird-like head on one side and said, 'Well, well.'

I knew exactly what she meant. And for a moment I hated her with an intensity that clouded the bright day.

The war, too, curtailed our wedding tour. I was more sorry about that than about the abandoned festivities. I had had such plans. I wanted to show Helen all the places I had loved in the past. I wanted to show her off in all the fashionable watering places. She had never been to the Continent and I wanted to be the first to show her the Alps, Venice, Menton. I wanted to lay the world at her feet.

Instead, we were forced to content ourselves with a few days in Cornwall. We stayed in Penzance, in an hotel with sea views. The sea breeze was so welcome after London's stifling streets and the scenery was idyllic.

And it was there, if I am honest, that things started to go wrong.

Lying in bed, with a temperature of one hundred and something, one hovers between reality and unreality. But sometimes that unreality leads to a clarity of thought that one could never achieve in the healthy state. Perhaps one's inhibitions are down, even the internal ones that put barriers around the dark places of the mind. One's secret fears are brought out and examined, before delirium clouds the issue again.

I remember Helen sitting up in the wide hotel bed, propped up on big, soft pillows. I came out of the bathroom, my dressing gown still girded around me, and she was there, waiting. Her nightgown was of creamy silk, clotted cream, as rich as the cream I used to be allowed on my stewed plums, sometimes. It was nearly a match to her skin, so fine, and her nipples were darker shadows peeping through lace. Her hair was brushed into a gossamer web and spread across the pillows. The lamplight shimmered on a strand that curled around her left breast. It glittered as though it had been sprinkled with diamond dust.

I felt sick.

It had been a long day. I had been too nervous to eat anything and Anthony had made sure we had not stinted on the champagne. It was quite natural to feel a little queasy. Anyone would have done.

I turned away to unfasten my dressing robe. I slipped quickly beneath the covers. The sheets on my side of the bed were icy, slippery with starch.

I stretched out to switch off the light, but before the

room was dark, I looked at Helen's face. She was smiling. She was welcoming me.

Of course, I had been around a bit. I was not like Ruskin, who is said to have fainted when he discovered that women had pubic hair, and Helen's was such a sweet, golden puff on top of a perfect, ivory-skinned mound. Nevertheless, my goddess was gone, replaced by a woman.

The vivisection of a failed marriage is very dull to outsiders and the most exquisite torment to those involved. My illness has brought down some of the barriers, but I will *not* allow it to shift these ones. It would be too cruel.

Last night cars drove up and down hooting, people sang in the street, the church bells rang. The flickering of bonfires lit the sky, challenging the Zeppelins and Gothas to come and get us if they could. There was dancing on the tables in restaurants and those women who still had hair to let down, let it down. The munition workers from Woolwich roamed the streets, like yellow maenads, demanding kisses. Men and women, total strangers, copulated in the parks, Anthony told me.

My marriage lasted almost exactly as long as the war. Does that mean that without the impetus of hostilities, without the subconscious urge to marry and procreate while there was still time, it might never have happened? I don't know. I don't think so. But I am still too close to the glass to see a clear reflection.

Neither of us did anything wrong. There was nothing I could point to and say, 'This is a problem between us'. We both led blameless lives of domestic harmony. She bore me a healthy daughter (though it would have been better for Hermione's sake if she had looked less like me).

Perhaps if I had not left Helen at Buckholt. Perhaps if I had put up a stronger fight for what was mine by law and custom. Perhaps . . .

I cannot blame Philip Malyon for causing the rift between us. I can and do blame him for exploiting it. But I was not seriously worried at first. Philip was an attractive young man with an impressive war record. Helen was a beautiful woman married to a very dull dog. A walk in the garden, a laugh, a smile, the fleeting touch of fingers. These things meant nothing. She was my loved and loving wife.

Then I looked into her eyes and I recognized what I saw there. I saw the same expression that I remembered from my own mirror in those lost, perfect days when I had first met Helen.

'They are in love,' I said and before Anthony's horrified gaze, I turned my face into the pillow and wept and waited for death to take away the pain.

CLEMENTINE

The Organizer

Helen was a virgin when she married. That goes without saying. She was pregnant when she returned to Buckholt from the honeymoon. And she still had virgin written all over her. Michael had wasted no time in doing his duty by the family, but he had left his beautiful wife untouched in all the ways that matter.

There was still a purity about her, that brief innocence that women lose so soon. And when she looked at Michael, it was with curiosity – as if to say, 'Well, is that all there is to it?'

I recognized the look, but that's not to say I had ever shared Helen's problem. Ant has his faults – the old sweetie – but he keeps me well satisfied in that respect.

I don't suppose anyone else but me noticed it. Any more than anyone else guessed she was pregnant – least of all Helen herself. But it stood out a mile. There's something about the eyes. She just had to be.

Some people have accused me of resenting Helen from the start. They said I made her life so difficult that when she went off with Philip Malyon, it was me she was running from – not Michael. What nonsense! That's just not true. When Ant told me the astonishing news that Michael was getting married – now *that* was a surprise – I was delighted. Really.

It might have been such fun having another woman around. Buckholt is lovely, but it is rather out in the sticks. Just too dreary sometimes. Especially when the mist floats in from the Channel, shutting off the view, swaddling the fields in cotton wool, muffling every sound except the moan of the lighthouse.

With the boys away at school and Ant ferreting around the estate in his usual bumbling way, the house can be utterly deadly. At times like that I just ache to leap into the train at Brockenhurst and disappear up to town. And never come back, I sometimes threaten. But I don't mean it. Really.

And then Ant comes in, with the mist beading his eyebrows, rubbing his big, mottled hands and heading for the whisky decanter.

'Parky today,' he'll grunt. 'Real brass monkey weather.'

And if he's in the right mood and I wheedle nicely, sometimes we might spend the rest of the afternoon upstairs. Well, it helps to pass the time. And Ant is good at it. Very good. Not very subtle maybe, but with bags of energy. He's got staying power and that's very important to a woman like me. I need a man with stamina. We shout a lot and roll about a lot. We have been known to start off in the bath, progress to the bed and fall onto the floor for the finale. I'm very lucky. Really.

I saw Helen's arrival as a life saver. We could get up to such japes together, she and I. I was missing Viola dreadfully at that stage.

It seemed an age since she had married and India was so very far away. Now, why couldn't she have found someone sensible and gone to live somewhere nearby? There'd been masses of nice local boys she might have been very happy with. Why on earth did she have to choose a career soldier? I had nothing against Harry Firth, of course. He was a nice enough boy, if a bit gauche. Viola was mad about him – though what she saw in his callow fumblings, I'll never know. But India?

From all I heard it was just like Salisbury Plain with beggars.

Helen just might have been a substitute for Viola. And though I didn't like to think of it, she was more of an age to be my daughter than my sister. Perish the thought!

There'd be someone to have a good moan about Ant to and enjoy her moans about Michael back again. Someone to go shopping with. Someone to share a pre-dinner cocktail with when Ant had gone to sleep in the library. Someone to swap girl talk with.

So when we heard the car bringing them back from the station after their journey up from Cornwall, I absolutely ran down the front steps to greet them. Michael handed Helen out of the car as though he were unpacking a piece of particularly precious china.

She was shy. Of course she was. I remember clearly what an ordeal it was when I first arrived at Buckholt – even *I* was nervous, believe it or not. Although Ant's mother was alive then, so that made it a million times worse. Five feet two inches of steel and whalebone. Mrs Frampton could have raised the siege of Ladysmith all by herself! Pity poor little me!

Anyway, I reached up to give Helen a welcoming, sisterly kiss on her cheek. She must have been a good six inches taller than I.

'Goodness! What a beanpole you are! I shall need a stepladder!' I laughed, but it was meant as a good-humoured, friendly tease. You know.

Helen bent her stately neck and received my kisses, but managed to manoeuvre at the last moment, so that my lips just grazed her jawbone. There was no answering warmth. Her skin was chill as marble. I might have been kissing a statue.

Right, I thought, if that's the way you want it, that's the way you'll get it. But then I saw the telltale puffiness

65

around the eyes – you can always tell – and I felt sorry for her. A honeymoon with Michael would have left anyone feeling a bit limp! So I decided to give her another chance.

Ant gave her a kiss then. With more than necessary gusto, I thought. He always was such a goose over a pretty face. I thought about kissing Michael. Tit for tat. But really – enough was enough!

'I'll bet Helen doesn't do this for Michael!'

Ant arched his back. He has such sensitive nipples. Not everyone knows that men's nipples have feelings. I do and I make the most of it.

He didn't open his eyes as he answered, 'You're not supposed to think of other people at times like this!'

'I can't help it. I just can't imagine Michael looking like you're looking now.'

'And just what do I look like?'

'Mmm. Ecstatic!' I circled his nipples with a hard, pointed tongue. He grunted and his hips jerked forward. A snail's trail of silver decorated my thighs. 'But seriously, can you?'

'Can I what?' Ant moaned.

'Imagine them like this?'

'No and that's their loss.'

'I'll bet Michael is very brisk and businesslike . . .'

'Sssh. Stop talking, won't you?'

'. . . and then he thanks her politely afterwards like a well brought-up child after a party. Do you suppose Helen gives him an orange to take home?'

'You are a wicked little cat!' Ant bit my ear – hard.

'You beast!' I squealed and slapped him. 'And she's so young, too – what, seventeen, eighteen at the most? Michael must be a good twenty years older than she is. It's barely this side of decent. Still, perhaps that's what he needs to get him going these days – a virgin sacrifice.

After all, he's hardly been noted for his enthusiasm in the past.'

'Clemmie, *do* stop talking.'

'But I don't suppose he'll be doing very much of anything now. Not for the next nine months anyway.'

Ant sat up then. 'For the next nine . . . You're joking! Has Helen told you?'

'Of course not. She doesn't know herself yet. But I know . . . you can always tell.'

'Well, well, the old devil . . .'

'He's younger than you.'

'He hasn't wasted much time, has he?'

'He hasn't got much time to waste. I hope he hasn't developed too much of a taste for it on honeymoon. It might seem a long nine months.'

'What difference does that make?' Ant was still talking, but his hands were working enthusiastically to end the conversation. It was becoming difficult to concentrate.

'Michael's much too much of a gentleman to have a go at Helen when she's pregnant.' I adjusted Ant's fingers slightly. 'Not like you, you beast! We were at it so late last time, you almost met the twins coming the other way!'

'I didn't notice you complaining!'

I laughed, but breathily now. Ant took my hand and into the open palm laid his deliciously heavy balls. I stopped talking.

So you see, I really did mean to be friends with Helen. It wasn't my fault things didn't work out that way. We were two different women with two different natures who just happened to be living in the same house. Under any other circumstances, we would never even have dreamed of trying to be friends. It wouldn't have worked.

But because we had married brothers, the world expected us immediately to dote on each other. Why should we? That's the tragedy of families. Too often, they consist of groups of totally incompatible people who have nothing in common but their names. It's all very sad and silly.

I tried with Helen. I made all the right sisterly noises. And it didn't work.

We had a good war, down at Buckholt. As good as anyone else's, that is, and a whole lot better than most. As soon as it became clear that it wasn't going to be all rushing around on white chargers and waving flags, as soon as we realized that men were actually going to be hurt, I persuaded Ant to offer Buckholt as a convalescent home for officers. He wasn't very keen at first.

'Why on earth should we do a thing like that?'

'For the simple reason, my darling, that if we don't offer, then Buckholt will certainly be requisitioned.'

'Then what's the rush? Why not wait until then? It might never happen.'

'Oh, it will, it will. And if it's requisitioned, then we won't have any say in what it's used for. Would you like to see the house turned into a rest home for common soldiers, taken over by some do-gooding, stuffy charity? Or even have colonials billeted here – or Indians?'

Ant stuttered. 'Surely not? That couldn't happen?'

'Oh yes, it could certainly happen. Make no mistake. This way, we take the initiative and choose how the house will be used.'

Ant saw my point. He usually does. So we offered Buckholt to the War Office, making much of its healthy sea air, and the offer was accepted with thanks. As well as making sure that we had only desirable occupants, we got the credit for being selflessly patriotic as well.

Charley got a spot of leave from his training camp

and turned up when the conversion was at its messiest. He stood in the middle of the landing, like a militant angel in his spanking new uniform, and gaped.

'Good Lord! Have you got the bailiffs in?'

'Now come and give your mother a kiss and don't let's have any of your usual boring stuffiness, Charley dear,' I answered. 'This is war work.'

'What on earth are you trying to do, Mother? Turn the place into a munitions factory overnight?'

'Stop exaggerating, darling.' I pulled the protective scarf from my hair and linked an arm through one of Charley's. 'Come and see what I'm doing. Buckholt's going to be an officers' convalescent home, that's all. Some of the bedrooms are being divided into private cubicles. I've sent a special order to the Army & Navy for lockers and folding beds. A little improvement on the plumbing. And that's about it.'

I threw open a door and Charley looked around the bare cubicle, his expression like a new boy surveying the dormitory. 'I wish you hadn't been in such a hurry about it. When I go to France, I want to remember Buckholt as it used to be, not looking as bare as a monastery.'

'You're being very silly,' I answered brightly, but the thought of Charley in France lanced through my busy preoccupation. 'Downstairs will hardly change at all. I want it to be a home from home.'

'I'd put away your favourite pictures and bits and bobs, though, if you want to see them again after all this is over.'

'But it will all look so bare. And after all, they will all be *officers*.'

'That's what I mean. You should see the ante-room after a mess night!' He leaned forward and wiped a smut from the end of my nose. 'Do you know, Mother, I believe you're actually enjoying all this.'

'Well, it's certainly more fun than knitting sleeping helmets!'

Charley met Helen for the first time at dinner that night. Her pregnancy had been officially announced by then – with much blushing on Michael's part at the coarse ribbing he got from Ant – but she was still at the pale and interesting stage.

Charley was sitting across the table from her and his worshipping gaze was beginning to irritate me. Fortunately, Michael was on the same side as Charley and couldn't see the way the boy was looking at his wife.

I don't know why I said fortunately. I just did.

Out of uniform, Charley looked more like the boy he was. His carefully tended moustache somehow made him look younger rather than older, as he had hoped. His mousy brown hair still had that cow's lick that Nanny had spent years trying to plaster down. One day he might be as weighty as his father, but at the moment he was just chunky.

He was my son, my first born who came into the world nine months to the day after I married Ant. And now he was a man – or thought he was – and talking excitedly about killing some other mother's son.

Don't go, my son, oh don't go. Your country says it needs you, but your mother needs you more.

'It had to come, of course,' Ant pontificated from the end of the table. 'The build-up of the German fleet ought to have told us long ago what the Kaiser had in mind.'

'Only we weren't looking,' added Michael.

'Well, we're looking now,' laughed Charley, 'so the Hun had better watch out.'

'Why?' asked Helen in that affected voice of hers that always seemed to make Michael go weak at the knees.

And I saw the same besotted expression cross the face of my son.

'Why?' His voice broke on the question as though he had still been only thirteen.

'Why should the Germans watch out?'

'Well because, because . . .'

'If you don't know by now, Helen,' Ant growled, 'then all your commonsense must have drained down into your womb.'

'Anthony, please . . .' came Michael's scandalized protest. Even I thought that remark was a trifle coarse and Charley positively crimsoned.

But Helen didn't even seem to notice. She leaned forward, elbows on the table, and fixed Charley with her twilight gaze as though he were the only poor fool in the room.

'I read in the newspaper,' she said, 'that German-owned shops – like Appenrod in the Strand – are being smashed and looted. Veterinary surgeons cannot cope with the demand from doting owners to have their dachshunds put down. Does that sort of thing make you proud of your uniform? Is that what you mean by saying that the Germans should watch out?'

'They're vile, snappy little dogs anyway,' I interrupted – anything to break the web that Helen used to ensnare my son's attention.

'That's nothing,' Charley defended himself. 'The Huns are savages. Do you know, in Antwerp priests who wouldn't ring the bells for their German conquerors, were hung upside down . . .'

'Barbaric!' exclaimed Michael.

'. . . inside the bells and used as living clappers! That's the sort of enemy we're fighting.'

'We're fighting for civilization as we know it,' added Michael.

'Poor little Belgium,' I quoted with malicious glee.

'A country raped by its invader. I hear that even pregnant women have been . . .'

'Clemmie!' Michael cried in disgust. 'This conversation is becoming quite degrading. I hoped that you at least – another woman – might shield Helen from knowledge of these atrocities.'

'Helen's a big girl now, Michael,' I teased, 'or hadn't you noticed?'

'I'm sorry, Helen, I didn't mean to upset you,' said Charley with his best play-up-play-up-and-play-the-game expression. He was still just a boy, after all. 'But I hope we've said enough to make you understand that we're fighting for honour.'

'I know you believe that, Charley,' Helen said softly and something in her voice made me feel like a cat with its fur being stroked the wrong way. 'I hope nothing ever happens to make you change your mind.'

'It's not going to be easy,' said Charley modestly. 'I'm not fool enough to believe we'll walk over them. It'll take a month or so to roll them up. But we'll do it, all right.'

Charley left next morning. He was going to Winchester to rejoin his battalion and then on to 'somewhere in France'. He said goodbye to his father and uncle at breakfast. I was glad the twins were away with friends. Their exuberance would have tested my temper that morning. Helen was still in bed, prostrated by sickness – these willowy, fade-away types always seem to get it badly. I was glad. I wanted to save Charley's last few minutes for myself. I wasn't going to share him with another woman.

I didn't cling to him. He'd have hated that. I handed him his stick and hat at the door and resisted the urge to straighten his tie.

'You will . . . take care, won't you, Charley?'

'No need for you to worry, Mother. After all those

72

OTC camps on Salisbury Plain, I ought to know what I'm doing.'

'Yes . . . yes, of course.'

'I'll write as soon as I can. But don't worry if it's not straight away. Might be a bit busy at first.'

'Of course.'

'Well . . .'

'Well . . .'

'Goodbye for now, Mother.'

He gave me a quick kiss on the cheek. Then he stood for a moment looking round the hall, before turning and running down the steps to the waiting car.

'That's it, then, Liddell,' I heard him call. 'Off to war!'

After he'd gone, I looked around the silent drawing room and thought about his advice to put my treasures safely away from rampaging young men. And I suddenly realized what a convalescent home actually was. It was somewhere where young men – young men like Charley – could come to recuperate from their wounds before being sent back for more. The idea didn't seem such a good one any more.

Once French's little army had crossed the Channel, the newspapers went very quiet. It was hard to believe there was a war on. Charley sent us a card to say that he had arrived safely, but wasn't allowed to tell us where he was. And since the card was a picture of some simpering French girl in very scanty draperies, we couldn't work it out for ourselves.

The silence in the newspapers was eerie. It was as though our boys had just vanished in mid-Channel. After several days without news, the first lists of casualties at Mons began to come through. It was ghastly. There were friends of Charley on it, boys I remembered coming to stay in the long hols, boys with spots and blushes and too long wrists grown out of coats. And now they were men and dead. But Charley's name was not there.

I didn't want to know. But one had to look, just in case. I made a rule, after that, that newspapers were not to be opened until after breakfast. Ant grumbled but he saw my point. We owed it to the boys at the front to keep up morale at home.

We expected a flow of convalescents when the lists were published, but day after day went by. The British Expeditionary Force fell back before the Hun and names like Le Cateau and Néry appeared in the newspapers. We got used to the sight of people in black.

That long, golden, breathless summer was passing. Swathes of heather purpled the forest heathland. And our brand new beds remained empty. I couldn't understand it.

Our first 'clients' arrived in early October. By then I thought the War Office must have forgotten about us. It made all that bustle in August look unnecessarily keen and I was beginning to regret having ruined the proportions of the guest bedrooms. So when the telegram finally came, I scanned it with relieved enthusiasm.

'Six – that's a good number.'

'Six what?' Ant wiped marmalade off his moustache. He looked so naked without a newspaper at breakfast, but I stuck firmly to my rule.

'Six convalescent officers. They arrive this afternoon.'

'Thank goodness for that. Give you something to do. Your own little bit of war work.'

'Well, I absolutely refuse to tear up perfectly decent sheets for bandages and I wouldn't even know how to start knitting socks. I leave all that to bank clerks' wives. My gesture is a grander one.' I gulped down my tea. 'Six. So we'll be ten for dinner. How nice. It'll be just like a house party.'

I thought Helen hadn't been listening. She never seemed to listen to what anyone said to her these days. She went around with the dreamy, inward look of the breeding woman that painters used to give their Madonnas. Michael, I know, found her detachment very beautiful. He used to look at her as though she were a holy vessel for his seed. I'll bet he never ever thought of touching her.

I found her expression intensely irritating. It made her look like a broody hen. But if she didn't often join in the conversation, she obviously kept an ear open for what was going on.

'They're sick men, Clemmie. It won't be like a house party at all. They'll need rest and quiet.'

'Nonsense. They must be better or they wouldn't be coming here. The least we can do is give them a little fun before packing them back to France. Liddell can meet the train with the brake.' And I skipped off to make arrangements.

All right. Helen was right and I was wrong. As soon as the brake drew up at the door, it was clear why our beds had remained empty for so long. The men who had been only slightly wounded never came back to England at all, but were patched up in field hospitals. The ones who needed convalescence had spent a long time in hospital before they arrived at Buckholt.

The six were only the first in a long procession of damaged men who arrived at our door – men on stretchers, men in wheelchairs, the blind, the halt, the maimed. A long line of them shuffles through my nighttime memory even now – coughing, crying, laughing, trembling, shouting – nameless, faceless men in a line that stretches to nowhere.

Ant complains that I sweat and shake in the night. His dreams must be sweeter than mine.

But because these six were the first, they still have names and faces in my dreams. I remember the shock of seeing them slowly help each other out of the brake. I was standing at the top of the steps in a very clever afternoon frock of black and white striped taffeta piped with emerald. It was a favourite gown – smart, modern, with a peg-top skirt that emphasized my minute waist. I knew I made a striking picture at the top of the long flight, just touched by the shadows of the portico – a hostess waiting to greet her guests.

They emerged from the brake one by one, with Liddell's help, each one caring for the other, brothers in pain. I couldn't move at first. I remembered being kicked by my pony Flossie when I was about eight years old. I remembered gasping with shock, remembered the way the breath had exploded from my body, remembered that I thought I would never be able to breathe again. I felt like that when I saw them.

But one does breathe again, of course. And just as I had known instinctively that I must not betray my shock to Flossie, so I knew that I must shield these men from my automatic reaction. So I pinned a bright smile on my face and went down the steps to greet them.

Later that afternoon, when the six officers were resting after their journey, I went over some points with the housekeeper.

'Captain Ridley has suffered a stomach wound. So something light, I think – custards, rice. Cook will know what. Have the sofa table in the drawing room removed. In fact, have all the small tables removed. They'll only get in the way of Mr Christie's crutches. Arrange a clear path through the drawing room and into the dining room. I'm told Mr Pemberton is determined to find his way around without any help, but there's no need to make his job even more difficult.'

I looked around the drawing room and said goodbye to it. I looked at the delicate *bergère* chairs that I had rescued from the attic when Ant's mother had died, replacing them up there with her own cumbersome Victorian mahogany. I looked at the satinwood Pembroke table with the pictures of the children on it, at the Carlton House writing table with its harewood inlay and ebony stringing. I looked at the pair of Chelsea lovebirds that old Mrs Frampton had relegated to doorstops.

I had promised Charley that Buckholt would never change downstairs. Already that promise was impossible to keep. Buckholt would have to change. Everything would have to change. Nothing would be the same again.

The six came and went and others took their place. Christopher Ridley's stomach wound healed, but how he would manage in the trenches on Fray Bentos and plum and apple jam I couldn't imagine. Anything heavier than sieved chicken still made him vomit, even when he was declared fit enough to leave us.

The various legs and arms of the others healed – more or less – and back they went. Johnny Pemberton stayed longer than the others, but even he eventually went home.

I remember one afternoon in January – I was on my way out for a much needed breath of air and I passed Johnny's room. The door stood open and I could hear Helen's voice. She was reading a letter to him. Johnny's face was turned to where he thought her voice was coming from. His glance reached somewhere over Helen's left shoulder. She came to the end of the letter, folded it up and put it back in his hand.

He gripped her fingers hard, crumpling the letter, and his blank eyes poured tears, bitter tears that must have seared the wrinkled, hairless, papery new skin of his face. His mouth opened in a soundless wail.

I shouldn't have stayed. I shouldn't have watched. I couldn't help it. Helen put her arms around him and let him lay his tortured head on her bosom. She was rounding out nicely by this time, her belly ripening like a seed pod when the petals fade. Her breasts were already changing shape, losing their upward thrust, softening at the outer curve, indecently swollen. They probably ached every time she turned over in bed.

Poor Johnny Pemberton buried his raw face in Helen's fertile softness. Slowly, she rocked him back and forth, her face turned down into the tufts of his hair that were beginning to cover his scalp again. He slid lower, his sobs muffled by the mound of her belly. Gently, gently, she rocked him. I felt like a voyeur.

Behind me, I heard steps coming along the landing. Turning, I saw Michael coming towards me. I didn't want to be caught watching what no one else had a right to watch. So I hurried away. As I slipped downstairs, I heard the sound of Michael's feet pause by Johnny's open door. I ought to have shut that door. I meant to shut it. Really.

Of course, Helen had no idea how to behave towards these wounded boys. Sympathy was absolutely the worst thing to offer them. They wanted to take bright memories back to the trenches with them, memories of fun and gaiety. So many young girls at that time were beginning to look very drab and serious. Their talk was of nothing but war work. An awful mistake, I thought. That wasn't what the boys wanted. They wanted pretty girls and bright lights. They wanted to remember how life used to be and how it would be again.

So I pinned that smile to my face and kept it there, no

matter what. I filled Buckholt with music and dancing and laughter. Ant used to complain now and then. But I soon put a stop to that.

'They want to have fun,' I said. 'When they go over the top, they need to know that they're fighting for the girls at home.'

Round about this time, Michael started to withdraw inside himself. He had a huge map table set up in the library and followed the campaigns intently. Well, we all did, of course. All the newspapers carried maps and people made little flags on pins to move back and forth across the Franco–Belgian border.

There was a grotesque fascination in watching the little flags creep forward or flutter back in panic. Often, one would find they were retreating back into the identical pinholes they had advanced from weeks before.

But there was something distasteful about Michael's fascination. He would shut himself in the library for hours. Ant said that he was punishing himself for being too old to fight. For a man with Ant's limited imagination, that was quite a penetrating remark. Though why a man of thirty-nine, with a young wife and first child imminent, should want to slog along French roads beside men half his age, I couldn't think. Thank God Ant was even older.

Helen's baby was born early in May 1915. About as soon as it could decently be born, in fact. It only needed to be just a little premature and tongues really would have wagged.

But no. Probably not. No one looking at Michael or Helen could have imagined them anticipating their marriage vows. Helen still looked as though she were the surprised victim of an immaculate conception. And Michael – to quote Ant's memorably vulgar phrase – had about as much poke as a capon.

Throughout that long, hot day Michael managed to get on everybody's nerves. After an hour or so of tension, Ant disappeared with his rods and I knew we wouldn't be seeing him again until well after dusk.

Michael just sat, right where he was most in the way. Buckholt was full at that stage – the maimed remnants of the Aisne, Neuve Chapelle, first and second Ypres cluttered every corner. And Michael just sat.

Every new father is nervous. When Charley was on the way, Ant kept popping his head round the door, just to 'check the score'. I was screaming the house down, but I still managed to laugh at the colour of his face, which got steadily greener as the hours went by. He was a perfect nuisance. Eventually his mother frog-marched him downstairs and force-fed him brandy. When Charley finally arrived, Ant was dead drunk and snoring!

But Michael just sat. Every new father ought to be nervous. Michael really annoyed me, sitting as calmly as though he were waiting for a train, as though the drama upstairs were nothing to do with him. Someone had to bring it all home to him.

'For goodness sake, why don't you take yourself off for a walk?' I said brightly. 'Nothing's going to happen for hours yet.'

'I didn't know these things took so long.'

'Oh ages, sometimes. But you've waited nine months – a few hours won't matter.'

'I suppose not.'

'Helen's being awfully brave. Ant's mother said you could hear me screaming out at sea!'

'Have you seen her? How is she?'

'I wouldn't dream of going in. Having been the principal actor in that particular drama three times already – and once it was a double feature – nothing would induce me to play a supporting role!'

80

'I wish I knew what was happening. Why doesn't that doctor come and talk to me?'

'Oh, he's much too busy to bother about a mere father. Never mind, Helen's such a strapping, healthy girl – not like tiny little me – it'll pop out like a piglet when it does come.'

He was beginning to look more normal now – more normal, that is, for an expectant father – pale and sweaty.

'Does it hurt very much, Clemmie?'

'Hurt?' I shrieked. 'My dear Michael – it's absolute bally agony! Like being sawn apart with a rusty knife!'

That got him going, all right. 'Dear God! I must go to her.'

He started up out of the chair, but I put a hand on his shoulder and pushed him down again. 'I wouldn't if I were you. You might faint at the mess. And Helen certainly wouldn't want you to see her with her nightgown under her armpits and her legs apart!'

Michael gave me a look of utter loathing. 'You're so crude, Clemmie.'

'Childbirth *is* crude, Michael. You can't just shut your mind to that. It's messy and painful. Helen won't look like your plaster goddess now, you know, she'll look like any other suffering woman.'

'You are *disgusting!* I don't know how Anthony can stand your vulgarities.'

'Ant can stand my *vulgarities*,' I spat, 'because he's a real man – not a poor, spineless replica. It amazes me that you've managed to father anything at all!'

If I'd slapped him round the face, it would have been less cruel. He positively staggered. I felt sorry for him then. After all, I'd only meant to ginger him up a bit.

'Well, not long now,' I said, comfortingly, as I turned to go, 'and then we'll discover who it looks like.'

'Like Helen, I hope,' he answered wistfully. 'It would be a shame if it looked like me.'

'That's honest, at any rate, but sometimes babies look like someone else entirely,' I said mischievously, just to give him a final jolt. It gave him a jolt all right.

'What do you mean?' he demanded. His face had gone quite grey. 'Who else could it look like?'

'Just a joke, you old silly. I'm sure it'll be beautiful, whoever it looks like.'

She wasn't beautiful, of course, newborn babies never are. But I just can't resist them. I just happened to be passing along the corridor when I heard the first sound from Helen's room. She gave a great yell of triumph and then there was the sound of a tiny, echoing yell. I slipped in, hardly noticed in the bustle.

A girl child, slippery, indignant, her tiny fists balled in helpless fury. Dark-haired, grey-eyed, sturdy. A real Frampton.

I was still there when Michael came in. The room had been tidied up by then, of course, and Helen made decent, but there was still a smell of blood in the air and of dark, unmentionable, female rites. I saw his nostrils quiver as he stood uncertainly in the doorway.

He did all he was supposed to do, but like a man sleepwalking. He walked over to the bed and gave Helen a kiss. Not the kind of kiss Ant had given me, of triumph and relief and adoration, but a kiss all the same – a chaste one on the brow. Her hair was damp and I watched him push it fastidiously aside before his lips touched her skin. Then he picked the child up from the crook of her mother's arm and walked over with her to the window.

He didn't know what to do with the poor mite, that much was obvious. He held the bundle of shawls and napkins, with a crumpled, angry face in the middle of it, and he just didn't know what to do. There was nothing to see. No starfish hands with seashell nails to marvel over, no minute toes to tickle, no vigorous limbs to be tested for presence and function. Nurse had wrapped the infant firmly and she wasn't going to have any nonsense about 'just having a peek'.

I don't know what Michael was expecting. What he was given was just an armful of draperies and a gaping mouth fringed with wrinkled gums.

'She looks like you,' said Helen and I could have wept at the anxious, longing-to-please weakness in her voice.

'Yes,' said Michael. 'Somehow I didn't think she would.'

'You know,' I said to Ant as we snuggled together in bed that night, 'just for a moment today, I envied Helen.'

'You what?'

'I envied her. We had four lovely babies and now they've grown up and gone away.'

'Well, we can soon solve that!' He hauled up my nightgown and rolled onto me like a beaching whale.

'Only for a moment,' I giggled, 'and the moment has passed. So you can just get back down again – right now!'

Ant reared up on stiffened arms. His weight pressed my thighs down into the mattress. 'Do you really mean that?' he demanded.

'What do you think?'

They called her Hermione, such a pretty name, but not the name one would have chosen for that plain little girl. She looked like a Jane or a Mary. Pure Frampton. Thank goodness Viola looked like me. I was only grateful they hadn't named her after Helen's dotty aunt, Eglantine Hayler. But given the way Michael felt about Eglantine, the odds were fairly long.

She – Eglantine – arrived for the christening in a spanking new 'Prince Henry' Vauxhall, driving herself with her meek little husband at her side. She drew up with a lurch outside the front door, spattering the gravel from the huge white-walled tyres, before reaching outside to pull on the handbrake.

She wore a leather helmet with a spangled veil wrapped around and streaming back in the wind of their passage, goggles and a dusty paletot of khaki. What a guy she made of herself! We hadn't seen each other since the wedding. Our opinions of each other hadn't changed.

'And where is the little darling?' she cooed, sweeping past me and leaving her husband to be polite to Ant and me.

The momentum of her entrance kept her going on up the stairs to the nursery at the top of the house. Ignoring scandalized Nanny, she leaned over the baby's cradle, still wearing that absurd costume, the sun glinting off the goggles. I fully expected Hermione to scream blue murder at the sight. I wanted her to, then I would be justified in picking her up and giving her a comforting cuddle.

But she didn't. Her wandering baby eyes seemed to steady and fix on Eglantine's face. I'd swear she smiled if I didn't know it was only a windy grin.

'There – see – she knows her great aunt!' Eglantine gurgled. 'Who's a clever girl then?' And she swept the baby out of the cradle without supporting her head and pressed her to the dusty, oily paletot.

'Mrs Hayler, if you please . . .' protested Nanny. Hermione's soft cheek was smeared with engine oil. '. . . You're disturbing baby's nap.'

'Nonsense, Nanny, I thought *you'd* know better than that. Don't you know it's bad for children to sleep too much? Their little brains need constant stimulus – I read that only the other day, I forget where – if they are to reach their full potential. You're horribly old fashioned.'

'Well, really . . .'

'Now,' Eglantine said, turning imperiously, 'show me to my niece.'

A troublemaker, if ever there was one.

Helen burst out laughing when she saw her. 'Good heavens, Aunt Eglantine, you look as though you're about to go down a coal mine!'

Underneath the coverall, Eglantine wore something that could only be described as a bundle of odds and ends. She looked as though she had dressed in the dark from some labourer's cupboard. I believe the garment is now known as a 'boiler suit', but then it had no name. It gave her the figure of a bifurcated cottage loaf!

'What,' I asked scornfully, 'is that?'

Eglantine looked at my lavender self-striped zephyr frock, up and down, up and down, as though she were about to hire a parlour maid.

'There *is* a war on, you know. This is my contribution to the war effort. Strictly practical. Minimum dressing time. Easy to launder. Think of all the seamstresses and laundry hands and ladies' maids who could be released for essential war work if everyone followed my example.'

Dotty. Quite, quite dotty.

'Perhaps,' I suggested, whisking away a chair before she could settle her filthy costume on it, 'it might be pleasant to have tea outside. Now do tell me – I'm dying to know – has your maid gone into a munitions factory yet?'

'Well, not exactly – not yet. But she could if she wanted to.'

'So all this . . . this . . .' I gestured, '. . . is so much window dressing?'

'Nonsense!' When Eglantine bridled, she was quite six inches taller than I. 'It's a patriotic gesture and I fully expect this will be universal dress before the end of the war.'

'God forbid,' I shuddered. 'And do you really think that, with the German blockade biting, it's patriotic to drive a private motor car at all?'

'Of course. I couldn't carry on my committee work without it. And just what, may I ask, are *you* doing for your country?' asked Eglantine in tones that recalled Mrs Pat at her soupiest.

We were all in the garden by this time. Before us, in groups dotted about the lawn, were men on sticks, on crutches, in wheelchairs. I held out my hands in a simple, unaffected gesture.

'I have given my home.'

That silenced her for a moment or two, but not for long enough.

'Helen, darling,' she said, 'you look quite, quite dreadful. I should scarcely have known you. You look positively wan. Doesn't she, Clementine?'

'A little pale, perhaps, but that's only to be expected.'

'Are you sleeping well . . . eating well . . . ?'

'I'm perfectly well, thank you,' Helen answered, a little tersely I thought. 'Just a bit tired, that's all. Hermione . . .'

'You're not feeding her yourself?'

'Of course.'

Eglantine gave a fastidious shudder that scarcely mixed with her extraordinary garb. 'I don't know how you . . . I could never bear . . . I was reading only the other day – modern mothers insist on Cow & Gate. That way Nanny can deal with the night feed.'

'Wincarnis and raw liver,' I put in. 'That's what she should be eating – Helen, I mean, not Hermione – lots

86

of raw liver. Minced, if it helps, with lots of parsley. But she won't touch it.'

'Oh don't.' It was Helen's turn to shudder now. 'The very idea makes me ill.'

'No wonder you're anaemic.'

'I'm *not*!' There was a brittleness about her, like the spun sugar cages Cook sometimes makes to sit over a selection of sorbets. A touch of the spoon and they shatter into a million razor-sharp shards. 'There's nothing wrong with me. I don't need raw liver. I don't need a tonic. I'm just tired. I . . .'

Slow, painful drops beaded each lash and when each one grew too heavy it rolled down her cheek. It was like watching the tears of a miraculous statue.

'Helen, darling.' Eglantine drew Helen's head onto her own scrawny, khaki bosom. 'We only want to help you.'

'I don't need help, thank you.' Helen struggled out of her aunt's embrace and wiped her cheeks with the heel of her hand. 'I'll feel better soon. Michael . . .'

Ah hah, I thought, so that's the problem.

'You'll have to speak to Michael,' I told Ant firmly that night.

'That sounds ominous. What about?'

'About Helen. She's exhausted. She will insist on feeding that child herself and it's taking too much out of her.'

'And what do you expect Michael to do about that?'

'Silly!' I punched his ribs. Playfully. 'He ought to leave her alone until she's feeling stronger.'

'And you expect me to tell him *that*?'

'Of course. He ought to have more consideration for her. She hasn't recovered her strength yet – though I'd have thought a big, strong girl like her would be bouncing around by now. Still, it is very hot. Michael should lay off until she's stronger.'

'Good God! I can't tell him that!'

'Why not? You're his brother.'

'That doesn't make me his keeper.'

'Helen really isn't well. In fact, I don't think she's far from a nervous collapse. If you don't tell Michael – I will. I warn you!'

'You can't do that!'

'Try me.'

'Anyway – I'd be very surprised if that's the problem.'

'Oh?'

'Some men – ' Ant said slowly (the old dear, he was embarrassed) ' – some men can't wait to know their wives again after a baby . . .'

'I know!'

'Don't interrupt. This is serious. And some men don't . . . they won't . . . can't bear to . . .'

'Oh!'

Yes, we had a good war at Buckholt. When other people complained about the servant problem, I could say that it didn't really affect us. Working at Buckholt was classed as war work and so we were able to have girls (not men, of course) drafted in to help. And there were VADs – such self-sacrificing girls – to take care of the more intimate needs of convalescing officers. I didn't enquire too closely what those needs might be. After all, the nurses were all over twenty-one (or were they?). On reflection, I might perhaps have been just a little too open-minded. Still, if a girl is old enough to leave home, she's old enough to look after herself. Or should be.

So all I really had to do was organize everything – although that was no kid-stakes. (I learned that wonderful phrase from a one-legged Anzac who came to us from the New Zealand Hospital in the Tile Barn Fields. He taught me all sorts of things!)

Even the blockade didn't affect us all that badly in the early days. Of course, the little luxuries were hard to find – you had to be prepared to pay through the nose – but almost anything was obtainable somehow or other. And since we qualified for military rations and Cook was very clever, we didn't suffer in any real sense.

As I said to Ant many a time, 'Whose idea was it to hand over Buckholt to the War Office?'

And he would pinch my cheek until I squeaked and ask, 'Who's a clever little girl, then?'

It wasn't all roses, of course. Viola's husband Harry was sent to France with his regiment of native cavalry. God knows what the Indians thought of Flanders. There were camps and convalescent homes at Brockenhurst, Milford and Barton. Sometimes one would see them wandering around, looking as miserable as it's possible for human beings to look. Some had arrived from India in their usual uniforms and, due to cloth shortages, hadn't been kitted out properly. It was January and snowing.

Khaki cloth completely ran out at one point and newly-joined soldiers were kitted out in navy blue serge, looking like a monstrous army of postmen. When it rained, the blue seeped out and stained their skin.

Having Viola back was a comfort, of course. But she wasn't the sweet, jolly girl who had boarded the boat to India. Silly of me to expect it, really. Nothing stands still, no matter how much we want it to.

She would mope around having long, morbid conversations with our 'guests' about the horrors of Flanders. It was a bad time for everyone. Viola would go into a blue funk and have nightmares about rats. She might wake up screaming any night. Since some of our officers suffered from neurasthenia (shell shock was for other ranks) and were quite likely to do the same, our nights were not peaceful. The recovery of some of our visitors was quite definitely put back by Viola and her 'little chats'.

Viola struck up a friendship with Helen. A funny sort of friendship, but I can't think of another word to describe their relationship – unless it was that of faithful hound and master. Viola would trail after Helen, especially after a bad night, looking for comfort and, perhaps, finding it in Helen's calm.

Well, they were both much of an age – Viola a little the older, if truth be told. I didn't much like to think of that. In fact, with Viola back, I was very obviously relegated to the older generation. It was very difficult to act as though I were Helen's sister, when my own daughter was around.

And then there was Charley. He'd managed to wangle a few '72s' but that was never enough time to come home, so I used to dash up to town to meet him. We'd eat at the Savoy Grill, perhaps go to a nightclub or two – Murray's was Charley's favourite. Army officers weren't supposed to enter nightclubs in uniform – it was lovely to go out with a man who wasn't in khaki – and the 'beauty sleep order' meant that the clubs were supposed to close at the same time as restaurants, but no one paid any attention to that. Young men were old enough to get themselves killed for their country, but not old enough to decide at what time they would go to bed? Absurd!

We'd shop during the day, buy him boots at the Army & Navy, bags of socks, order a hamper from Fortnum's – the greedy boy loved Abernethies and Elva plums. We'd drop exhausted into the Ritz for tea.

It was so stimulating to get up to town. The sight of

all those poor convalescing men used to get me down a bit. And Viola's moping around made me want to scream.

When I got home, there was always something to talk about – something to make Ant laugh or make him growl into his pre-dinner whisky. Once we got caught in a Zeppelin raid. Such fun!

We were just coming out of the Cabaret Club in Beak Street – so naughty, Ant would have been furious with me. Those violent black and primary colours – like a child let loose with a palette – were a bit overpowering, even for me. (What is a Vorticist, anyway?)

We were wondering where to go for a little late supper. Champagne, a spot of caviar, an oyster or two. You know. And to think we could all have as much fish as we wanted with a clear conscience! I suggested the Carlton and Charley was just about to call a cab, when we heard the police whistles blowing. At first I thought it was a robbery, but then realized, of course, it was a Zeppelin raid warning.

The buildings in Beak Street blocked our view, so we bolted across to Regent Street to have a look. The pavement was packed with people staring and the traffic had stopped in the road. The atmosphere was just like a street party. There was even a little man in a greasy cap selling hot pies from a tray.

Charley bought two and said, 'No need to go and look for supper now. Supper's come to us!'

I bit into it and the thick, hot gravy dribbled down my chin. I scooped it up and licked my finger. It tasted wonderful. Or was it just the freedom, the fun, the escape from humdrum Buckholt?

The airship scarcely seemed to move. It hung over some luckless part of London, silent and silvery, while the searchlights of the anti-aircraft batteries quartered the sky.

Someone said the Zeppelin was looking for the docks; someone else said the railway lines; someone else again said Buckingham Palace. If that was so, the captain was well out in his navigation. To judge by the noise, every gun in London, whether in range or not, seemed to take up the challenge thrown by the silver ghost. We all cheered the gunners on wildly. Then came the heavier crump of falling bombs. Someone, somewhere, was getting it. We stopped cheering then.

Then, unharmed, the silent killer just floated away. I found it impossible to believe that there were actually any real men aboard. It was as though we had been attacked by one of Mr Wells's more fanciful creations. It had drifted in, killed – I heard next day – seven or so poor people down in the East End and then simply drifted away again. And that despite every searchlight and gun in London being trained on it. Eerie.

Charley put it down to plain bad shooting. He said that, with half the practice our gunners got in Flanders, it would have been brought down.

'But Charley, dear,' I argued, 'the only way to get more practice would be if more of these horrid things were to turn up. We can't have that, you know. Not if innocent people are going to be killed.'

'And who is innocent, Mother?'

And although we did go on to the Carlton for what was left of the evening, Charley didn't say much more.

So you see, every moment of his leave would be accounted for. And if Charley was a bit quiet, I put it down to tiredness. Time was so short, it felt like a crime to waste a second. London was full of young men bent on having a good time – and of girls who would give it to them.

And I would keep up my animated conversation and bright smile until his train pulled away from the platform. Even then, I didn't dare relax, in case he just might be able to see my mask crumble. It always did crumble – but in private.

And then the telegram came. Viola fainted as she saw the postboy cycle up the drive. Damn the War Office for those little yellow envelopes. One died just trying to open them with stiffened fingers. There should have been one colour to announce death and one colour to announce wounds. That way, one would have known the worst or the best of it before the flap was ripped apart.

Charley was wounded. A Blighty one. He was in hospital at Étaples, but would be sent home as soon as he was fit to move. I was all for catching the first available boat to France, but sensible old Ant held me back.

'Don't be ridiculous,' he snapped. 'What sort of chaos d'you think there'd be if every mother dashed over there to mollycoddle her son?'

'Isabella St John did. She got all the way to Hazebrouck to see her son.'

'And probably thoroughly embarrassed him. The front line could be swamped with anxious mamas!'

'And a good thing too! It's men that started this wholesale murder. How many mothers willingly sent their sons over there? If women really banded together – we could stop it tomorrow!'

'But you won't, will you?' Ant queried with a twisted smile – quite unlike himself, 'because if there's one thing women won't do, it's stick together. No one can be crueller to a woman, than another woman. You're your own worst enemies.'

I flounced out of the room, slamming the door. I was being too hard on him. Ant was every bit as worried about Charley as I was. I had no right to act as though I were Charley's only parent. But I couldn't help it.

The Charley who came back wasn't the Charley who had left. Just like Viola, the war had left a permanent mark on him. He came home without his right arm and without the joyous sparkle that had once turned a rather plain young man into an attractive one.

He'd lost weight, but that was probably not a bad thing. Pain had left a tension around his eyes and mouth – eventually there would be harsh lines there, when his skin stiffened into permanence, but at the moment, the expression sat oddly on his young face. He never looked me in the eye, but always seemed to be looking just over my shoulder, seeing something that the rest of the family couldn't see.

He was still taking morphine for the pain in his stump. Often I would hear him rise in the night, blundering around his room in the dark, and I wanted to go to him, but Ant wouldn't let me.

Charley wasn't content just to be with his family again. He didn't want to pick up with his old friends – those few who were not already in Flanders. He most definitely didn't want to meet any nice girls. When I suggested holding a little dinner party – only a little one, nothing too ostentatious – he just walked out of the room without saying anything. And that night I heard him walking again.

Dear Sir,

Just a line to let you know that your parcel arrived safely here and the Woodbines and Dundee cake were much appreciated by all. We are all as well as can be expected. We took a bit of a pasting near St Eloi the worst shelling I think we have ever had and we were lucky not to lose more but Cpl Brightman was buried and we couldn't get him out in time. I am sorry to have to tell you that Mr Withers and Mr Stuart got it that day. I know they were particular chums of yours. However it could be worse keep smiling and now we are in the rear for a few days and hope to catch up on a bit of sleep and have a bath. I was sorry to hear that you lost your arm but it could be worse. Well Mr Frampton sir I must close now as it is time for church parade. Hoping this finds you as it leaves us in the pink.

Yours respectfully
3287 Fielding A W Pte

Reading other people's letters is just about as low as you can get, Ant says, but after all I am his mother. And Charley obviously had no more use for his batman's scrawl on lined paper with blue indelible pencil, or he wouldn't have thrown it away like that.

'He's not trying,' I would complain. 'Other men try to get over their disabilities. Charley could learn to eat with one hand. He could easily teach himself to write with his left hand. He's just not trying.'

'Leave him alone,' said Ant. 'He'll come back to us, but in his own time.'

The only people he wanted to be with were the other wounded officers we had staying with us at Buckholt. They would sit in huddles, smoking far too much, and talk. Mostly they would talk, on and on, late into the night. Sometimes they just sat in silence, but it was the sort of silence that formed a protective barrier around them.

They didn't want us – none of them. We were from a different world. We were still in a state of innocence; they had tasted of the tree of knowledge of good and evil – and the tasting of it cut us off from our sons for ever.

But watching Charley – watching them all – I suffered too. Like a loaf of bread being sliced, our family was being separated into its constituent parts.

'Soldier on,' said Ant. He never did have much imagination.

★

To the astonishment of all of us, Michael announced one morning at breakfast that he had volunteered to be an ambulance driver.

'I'm too old to fight,' he said, 'but when I look at the brave young lads around us, who have given their all, it shames my manhood.'

I'm sorry to say that I snorted into my tea in a most inelegant fashion. Ant just roared.

'You're off your chump,' he exclaimed. 'I suppose you've forgotten you're over forty years old – must be having a young wife that makes you feel so spunky! This is a young man's war!'

'Conscription extends up to forty-one.'

'But only single men – by the time they get round to old married men like you, the war'll be long over. We're not that desperate yet!'

Charley pushed back his chair so abruptly that it toppled backwards. 'If Uncle Michael wants to go and pick up arms and legs and clean up puke and stuff guts back into bellies, then let him go. We're all mad out there. One more won't make any difference.'

'Charley – not at the breakfast table,' I gasped, but he was gone and the door bounced back on its hinges after him.

'Charley – come back here at once!' Ant roared. 'At once – do you hear?'

He was all for going after the boy and dragging him back to apologize, but I managed to calm him down.

'Helen – can't you talk some sense into your husband?' I begged.

'Michael must do whatever he feels he must,' she said with an eerie calm.

'You can't leave Helen, Michael,' I urged. 'And what about Hermione? She's still so little.'

'There are hundreds of thousands of wives and children left alone at this moment. Helen and Hermione will be better off than most. They at least will not want for food and warmth while I'm away.'

'There's more to marriage than having enough money to live on,' I retorted, 'but I don't suppose you would realize that!'

'Clemmie,' said Helen and there was a dreadful weariness in her voice, 'Michael and I have discussed this at length – at great length. If this is what he wants to do, then I've no right to stand in his way.'

'He seems to have pulled the wool over your eyes as successfully as over his own. If you ask me, he's just looking for an escape . . .'

'Clemmie,' said Ant in a warning tone, but I was well away by this time.

'. . . because he can't cope with married life. He's not volunteering – he's running away.'

'Clemmie – this is between Michael and me,' Helen warned.

'You mustn't come between man and wife,' Ant growled, glaring at me along the length of the table.

'Why not? It's about time someone spoke the truth about this sham of a marriage. Michael can't cope. He should never have been a husband – he should have been a monk. He wanted a virgin to worship and he got a real, live woman.'

Michael went so pale, he looked like an over-developed photograph. Helen pressed her napkin to her lips, as though she was trying to keep from vomiting.

'It's Helen I feel sorry for,' I finished with cruel accuracy. 'Just look at her. Look at that face and figure. If ever a woman was made for loving, Helen is. You took her, Michael, before she even knew what life was all about. What will you do when she finds out what she's missed?'

It all looked a bit like a scene in a play – and I must admit I'd really enjoyed my dramatic monologue. I'd really made the most of it. Viola was struck dumb. Helen had bowed her lovely head in shame. Ant was grinning – yes, damn him, actually grinning.

When Michael rose to his feet, I must say I admired his restraint. He must have felt like throttling me.

'You foul-mouthed slut!' he hissed. 'Anything you don't understand, you sully.'

'Yes, the truth hurts, doesn't it? You're not half man enough for Helen!'

'Stop talking about me as if I were a statue,' Helen screamed and threw her napkin across the table, 'and stop meddling in something you'll never understand – never!'

Well, I must say, that took me by surprise – the ice maiden had feelings.

'What chance does my marriage stand – ' Michael flung open his arms melodramatically, but the anguish in his voice was real enough. I felt sorry then, for having started this, but I wasn't going to say so. ' – when I have to live it in public, day in and day out?'

'Don't be surprised,' I called after his retreating back, 'if she isn't here when you come home again.'

Afterwards, Ant was very cross with me. He said I'd been very wicked.

'Well,' I justified myself, 'Michael's so pompous and blown up. I can't resist giving his bladder a little prick now and again. It does him good.'

But I had been rather naughty.

Hermione didn't seem to miss her father. But then she had been so young when Michael left, she probably never knew who he was. She wasn't a pretty child – too much of a Frampton for that – but she had charm. And as her Great Aunt Eglantine frequently said, if she had to choose between beauty and character, she'd choose character every time. Funny how you never hear a woman under forty making statements like that!

I have no criticism to make about Helen as a mother. If anything, she was too devoted to that stodgy little girl. Nanny threatened more than once to give in her notice.

'Mummy must learn that children need regular habits. It doesn't do to overstimulate them,' she complained. 'It took me hours to settle Baby last night because Mummy insisted on walking her round the garden to look at the bats. Bats! The very idea!'

'I'll speak to Mrs Michael about it, Nanny,' I promised. 'It won't happen again.'

Heaven forbid that we should lose Nanny. A dragon she may have been, but what should we have done without her?

Perhaps Helen was lonely. Looking back, I do feel a little twinge of conscience about that. But if she was, it was her own fault. She never tried to come halfway to meet me. After all, as they say, it takes two . . .

It was wonderful to have a child around the house again. A big house like Buckholt was meant to be full of children. It was once, but children grow up and leave an empty place behind them. And now we had another excuse for Christmas stockings and birthday parties and a pony in the stables. We'd have such fun.

As Hermione became mobile and learned to prattle, she gathered up all the scarred inmates of Buckholt into one huge family with herself at its centre. It didn't matter to her whether a man was horribly burned, or had no legs, or was coughing his lungs into bloody rags. Hermione just accepted them all. She was the only outsider who managed to penetrate the barbed wire defences that Charley had wrapped around himself.

I wish Viola had had a child. She'd been married two

years before Harry went to France and not even the hope of one in all that time. It might have helped her.

This time the yellow envelope was for her.

'Deeply regret to inform you . . . Captain Henry James Firth . . . Army Council express their sympathy . . .'

Harry was missing, presumed dead. Viola was astonishingly calm, now that the moment had arrived. She just handed the telegram to me and walked out of the room. I dropped it and started to run after her, but Ant said no. When Viola came back, she didn't look as though she had been crying. She had lived with the fear since leaving India, grown accustomed to it, it was almost a part of her by this time. The actual moment was no worse than the anticipation.

A letter followed from his company commander, telling Viola that they thought Harry had been sheltering from sniper fire in a shell hole with two others. Another shell had landed in the hole – a direct hit. If Harry had been in it, he wouldn't have known a thing about it, the letter said, he wouldn't have suffered. Viola believed that. It was a kind letter to send. It was a comfort to her.

'But maybe he wasn't in there,' I said hopefully to Charley, 'maybe he's been captured. After all, they've no proof that Harry was in that shell hole. Perhaps we'll find it's all been a ghastly mistake.'

'Oh, he was there all right,' said Charley bitterly. It was the first voluntary remark he'd made to me all that week.

'But he's only been declared officially missing.'

'Don't you know what that means? Don't you really know, Mother?' Charley was very close, so close that I could smell the brandy on his breath. It was ten in the morning. 'Missing just means they couldn't actually find him. It means that of those three men hiding in the shell hole, there was nothing left to identify. Nothing at all. Vanished. Napoo. Kaput.'

'Oh God,' I whispered, 'poor Harry.'

'Poor Harry nothing. He was one of the lucky ones. He wasn't crucified on barbed wire for three days and nights. He wasn't drowned in mud. He didn't have his face eaten by rats because he was too weak to fight them off.'

'Charley!'

'Charley! Charley!' he mocked. 'You know nothing! Harry was one of the lucky ones. I wish I'd had his luck!'

I slapped his face then – hard – and watched shock unfocus then focus his eyes. They began to water and I thought he was going to cry. Charley, oh Charley. My fingers were livid on his unshaven cheek.

'How dare you! Yes – you've lost your arm and it's going to be hard for you and I'm sorry for you. But you've still got your strength. You're not broken like some of the men we see here. And you're not dead like Harry. I'm sick to death of you moping around the house!'

Oh God, it broke my heart to see him, my beautiful boy. I wanted to put my arms around him, to kiss away the pain. I wanted to make it all better.

'You don't know . . . you can't know . . . you haven't seen . . .' he snivelled.

'Nobody forced you to go to war,' I reminded him coldly. 'Nobody forced you to sign up on the first day. It was your choice – remember? It just hasn't turned out the way you thought it would. And if you ever – ever – tell Viola what you've told me this morning, I'll throw you out of this house with my own hands. I swear it.'

In the autumn that followed the push on the Somme, it was full house again at Buckholt. We ran out of space and had to subdivide the cubicles to make extra bed-rooms. You couldn't have swung a cat in one, even if you'd wanted to. Another change at Buckholt, but by then Charley didn't seem to care. It seemed so long since that bright-eyed boy had gone to war making me promise not to change a thing.

Michael wrote frequently to Helen and she always read his letters to us – or those parts of them that were fit to read. Although, knowing Michael, they were probably all fit to read. I couldn't imagine him making love to his wife on paper. The letters were models of propriety – bright, sensible, so patriotic that the censor rarely had to put his pen through a word.

But now and again, Michael wrote privately to Ant. Ant never read those letters aloud at the breakfast table. He would skulk off to his study and lock the door so that I couldn't interrupt. I must say, I resented that. Michael was miles away and he could still manage to come between us.

I suspected that Michael's letters to Helen told us what he wanted us to know and that his letters to Ant told him what it was really like out there. Michael wasn't a young man – although quite robust – and it can't have been easy for him. Ambulance drivers were almost in the front line. Their casualty rate was surprisingly high. Whatever I said about Michael – and I said plenty – one had to respect his courage. Thank God, Ant was too old.

If I had been Helen, I would have been worried out of my mind. But if Helen worried, she kept it very much to herself. We never knew what she thought.

God, I was bored! I was bored with the streets a mass of dull khaki and blue, bored with having to justify every little necessity. I never seemed to get up to town any more. I was bored with winter in England – Keep

Warm, You Will Need Less Food, but if it hadn't been for our allocation of wood from the forest, we certainly wouldn't have kept warm at all.

I was bored with the sight of women in lumpy uniforms and big boots. I was bored with Viola's meek acceptance, bored with Charley's sulkiness, bored with Helen's good manners. I was bored with the sight of the maimed and the blind and ugly disabilities everywhere. I was bored with pages and pages of close-packed printed casualty lists – the *Daily Telegraph* and the *Morning Post* gave up printing the names of other ranks after the Somme, but *The Times* kept it up until the end of 1917. I made Ant change our newspaper.

I was bored with meat and sugar and fat rationing. We had narrowly escaped prosecution for hoarding. It could have been *so* embarrassing and with Ant on the bench too, but I pleaded that Buckholt was equivalent to a hospital and we provided little luxuries for our guests that they wouldn't get on army rations. I was bored with the way the forest was gradually encroaching on the lawns and engulfing the flower beds. I was bored with talk of mining strikes and engineering strikes and shipbuilding strikes. I was bored with fears of Bolshevism.

I was bored with Ant's plain, jolly face, that seemed to get redder as the years went by – he hadn't followed the King's example and given up his brandy and port for the duration.

I was bored, bored, bored!

The two young men who came to visit Charley were different. They were whole. I can't tell you what a pleasure it was to see them. Buckholt had been full almost without pause since the Somme push and the coughing of gas victims kept me awake at night.

And now here were two hale and hearty young men.

You could see Charley brighten up at the sight of them. They sat under the cedar tree in the long, slow, Daylight Saving twilight. In the dusk, you couldn't see the way the garden was slowly reverting to heathland. It was almost – almost – like the old days, the days when Buckholt was filled with laughing, noisy friends of our children, when Viola was a flirting child making eyes at poor Harry and any other young man within range, when Charley was famous for his lob shot.

And yet – and yet. It's hindsight, of course. There was nothing about the pair that made me wonder. It's only now that I look back and tell myself that there was always *something* I didn't quite like. They were an unlikely pair, really. Not boys who would automatically have been friends before the war. But the trenches threw up some strange bedfellows.

Archie Byatt had known Charley at Charterhouse. He was not only older than Charley but a good deal cleverer (that wouldn't have been difficult), so they had not been friends exactly, but they knew of each other, and then they had found themselves in the same company in 1914. Archie was a stocky powerhouse of a young man, built like an inverted bullet, with a smile that showed two rows of perfect teeth and stopped just above his upper lip.

Patrick Snape was what Ant called, with a contemptuous snort, a 'T.G.', a temporary gentleman, commissioned as the ranks of nature's officers thinned. He didn't look like a fighting man, but then who did, in these days when the most unlikely were being forced to the front line? He looked more like a master from a minor prep school. He would be kind to the little boys newly away from home, a hopeless disciplinarian, fall tragically in love with some child's older sister glimpsed across the field on sports day and end his days a bachelor. If he didn't drown in an evil broth of mud and dead horses' entrails and chlorine gas first.

They were beautiful because they were untouched. No scars, no missing pieces, no tremors. And on Archie's left breast, below RFC pilot's wings, was the white-violet-white ribbon of the Military Cross. Patrick, too, wore a ribbon. Not one I recognized, but I dare say Ant knew what it was. No rear echelon staff officers, these.

The only flaw was Patrick's vowels – perhaps not a prep school master after all, perhaps a scholarship boy, son of some shop owner or manufacturer aiming for acceptance in the next generation. The sort of people who say 'Pardon?' if they haven't heard something. You know what I mean.

Ant joined me at the window, where I stood watching the three young men. Archie lounged in a basket chair with his legs hanging over one armrest. His brightly-polished boots were in Patrick's lap. All three of them were laughing. If they had been girls, I would have called it giggling.

'It's so good of them to come and see Charley,' I said, leaning my head back against Ant's chest. 'It's done him so much good. He's quite excited.'

'Mmm,' Ant answered.

'I'm afraid he's getting so bored at home. It's good for him to see old friends.'

'Mmm.'

'It's a terrible thing, darling – I'm ashamed to admit it – but I'm glad Charley was wounded so soon. It's got him away from all those horrors. It means he'll live. Is that very wrong of me?'

'Mmm.'

'Ant? ANT? You're not listening to me!'

'Sorry – no – sorry.'

'What're you thinking that's so much more important than what I'm saying to you?'

'Nothing. Nothing really. Just wondering . . . nothing really.'

Eglantine Hayler found any excuse to dash down to Buckholt. Somehow she was still managing to run her very masculine motor car.

'War work, darling,' she would say every time Ant queried where she found the petrol for that greedy brute, 'war work.'

She was more extraordinary-looking than ever. The last few years had not improved her. Some time in 1917 she had lost all her teeth. The first time she opened her mouth and smiled at Hermione with two rows of bright white china, I expected the child to scream herself into a fit. Instead, she just gaped in wonder, then put out a square little hand and, quick as a magpie, whipped out the top set! Eglantine's top lip fell in like the rim of a shell hole. What fun! Though to be fair to Eglantine, once she had got over the shock she laughed louder than any of us.

Eglantine had become very thin, so that the khaki dungarees she still affected had to be belted in tightly with a Sam Browne belt. She wore this with flying officers' sheepskin-lined high boots and heavily car-mined lips. Her eyes were outlined in kohl, making her look rather like a raddled Pola Negri. Horrible!

But not boring – never that. And in that dreary, khaki-coloured time, I was actually beginning to look forward to the volcanic eruption of Eglantine's visits. But I wouldn't dream of telling her so!

Eglantine was in the grip of yet another of her enthusiasms. She tore up the front steps and tossed her leather helmet and gauntlet gloves on a hall chair.

'You know Cassandra Malyon, don't you?' she

asked, indicating the slender, fashionable woman who followed her out of the car. 'You must – everyone knows Cassandra. Where's Viola? Not moping, I hope?' She burst through the drawing room in a haze of Mitsouko and engine oil and the two women finally tracked Viola down in the garden. 'Viola, my dear, I've met the most amazing person and I thought immediately of you!'

Cassandra Malyon was a younger Eglantine, right down to the tips of her scarlet nails. But whereas the kindest word one could use about Eglantine's appearance was 'eccentric', Cassandra had an *outré* kind of chic that was very individual. Her hair was very short, emphasizing the whiteness of a drooping neck. The handkerchief points of her sea-green georgette frock floated somewhere around mid-calf. Black pearl teardrops swung from her ears, matching the black pearl rope that dangled over the barest swell of bosom. She drifted across the lawn after Eglantine on narrow, narrow feet, looking like a mermaid uncertain of the advantage of her new legs.

And flesh-coloured silk stockings, sheer and shimmering – delicious! Right there and then I resolved never to wear anything but on my legs again.

It was not quite the thing these days to wear mourning. Most people made do with a black armband. When every family in the land had been bereaved, sometimes many times over, to flaunt one's own losses seemed tasteless. Yet Viola still clung obstinately to unrelieved black. She had grown so thin that the low-waisted crepe tunic hung on her as shapeless as a nun's habit. To my censorious eyes, it was as though she were play-acting the part of the young widow – pale, brave, with a gravely sweet smile for everyone. And her audience was not her family, but the poor, besotted fools who went back to the trenches knowing that they were fighting for young English widows like Viola. That might have been believable in 1914, but in 1918? They should all have known better.

Look at her now – reading to one young man with a shaved head. Another lay on the grass at her feet. A third had propelled his chair as close to Viola as he could. It was a picture straight out of the pages of a minor Victorian novel.

Had she really loved Harry so much, or was she just in love with the image of the dead war hero? Terrible thoughts for a mother to harbour.

Eglantine's loud hail broke up the pretty picture. 'The *most* amazing woman, my dear. Quite remarkable. A natural.'

'Whatever are you talking about, Eglantine?' I hissed as I scurried across the lawn keeping up with Eglantine's giant strides. 'I won't have you upsetting Viola.'

By the time she and Cassandra Malyon had reached the little group, they had outdistanced me by quite a few paces. 'She has *contacts*,' Eglantine explained, clouding the issue still further. She sat heavily on a chair vacated for her by the subaltern with the shaved head.

'I'm afraid you've quite baffled me, Mrs Hayler,' Viola said. 'Who has contacts – and where?'

'Her name is Mrs Olive Graham and her contacts,' Cassandra Malyon's voice was a hoarse whisper, 'are not of this world.'

'Oh no,' I interrupted, coming up in time to hear this. 'I won't allow Viola to dabble in any of that nonsense.'

'What nonsense?' asked Viola. 'And what has this Mrs Graham to do with me?'

'She has uncanny powers,' said Cassandra.

'She is a medium,' said Eglantine.

'She is a charlatan,' I said.

Eglantine bridled. 'On what grounds do you say that?'

'As far as I'm concerned, the two words are synonymous!'

'Typical! Dismissing something you know nothing about!'

'Please – stop bickering,' begged Viola. 'I'm old enough to make up my own mind, Mother.'

The young men who had surrounded her had quietly faded away and we four were left together to argue things out.

'Olive Graham has a most impressive client list. The greatest in the land have consulted her and declared themselves astonished by her powers,' Eglantine persuaded. 'She has testimonials from members of the aristocracy, from professional people, even from members of the War Cabinet.'

'I don't find it at all reassuring that the politics of this war are being handled by Mrs Olive Graham,' I scoffed, 'and if they are, she's not making a very good job of it. Can't her Red Indian guide, or whatever he is, do a better job? We'd all be very grateful!'

'You may mock, Mrs Frampton,' Cassandra said in that startlingly deep, hoarse voice, 'but what do you know – really *know*? We are all like children locked in a dark cupboard, crying for the light. Why turn your back on it when it comes?'

'Viola dear,' Eglantine picked up Viola's little hand with its bitten nails, 'wouldn't you like to know if Harry is happy?'

What impressionable young widow would have been able to resist finding out the answer? I raved, Ant put his foot down firmly, even Helen came out of her isolation to say that she thought it unwise to meddle in the unknown. Viola refused to listen to any of us. She set her stubborn little mouth in the expression I remembered so well from her childhood and told us all that she had made up her mind.

Surprisingly, Charley supported her decision. 'If she needs consolation, what harm can it do?'

'A great deal,' I answered. 'She's much too impressionable. She could be frightened into fits.'

'We all need comfort. I get mine from a brandy bottle. Viola gets hers from table-rapping. What's the difference? Both methods are bad for us, but what else have we got?'

'The difference is that you're ruining your body and Viola risks ruining her mind.'

'So what? Anyway, who knows? It just might be true. And there's no need for her to be frightened of poor old Harry. Unless they couldn't find all the bits and pieces when they put him together on the other side – like doing a jigsaw with all the best bits missing!'

He laughed and reached for the decanter again. There was no point in trying to reason with him.

I certainly wasn't going to let Viola go off to meet Mrs Olive Graham accompanied only by women as dotty as Eglantine and her languid friend, Cassandra. Besides, I hadn't been up to town since Charley's last leave from the front. Perhaps I might be able to whisk Viola quickly in and out of the medium's lair, leaving us enough time for a decent lunch and a spot of shopping.

It was all very disappointing. London was *so* dreary. Buckingham Palace looked like a poultry run, draped with anti-Zeppelin steel nets. The lake in St James's Park was drained and its surface covered in nasty little huts. There were naval guns in Regent's Park and gaps in bombed facades left by the Gotha raids. The recruiting banners strung around the Carlton sagged in the rain. The messages ran into each other in a stream of unpunctuated, patriotic gibberish: 'WE MUST HAVE

110

MORE MEN MEN OF BRITAIN UPHOLD YOUR COUNTRY'S HONOUR WE ARE FIGHTING FOR A WORTHY PURPOSE BRITONS ENLIST AT ONCE.'

London wasn't fun any more. I was beginning to regret our journey.

Mrs Graham lived in irreproachable respectability in Maida Vale. Her double-fronted villa sheltered behind a dusty laurel hedge and there was nothing eerie about it to mark it from its neighbours. Mrs Graham herself was a perfectly ordinary woman – neither old nor young, neither fat nor thin, dressed in perfectly ordinary clothes.

I don't know why, I had expected flowing draperies and a vulgar profusion of necklaces and rings. In other words, I had expected yet another woman rather like Eglantine – as though there was a particular type that could be associated with this new craze for spiritual dabbling. What I had not expected was a woman who might have been a headmistress or a bank manager's wife, with greying hair and a well-corseted figure. The only feature worth remarking on was her voice. She had a fine voice, clear, resonant – an actress's voice.

She welcomed us with dignity and even offered us refreshments, which were brought by a neatly dressed maid (and that was a rarity these days – how did she manage to keep hold of one – I longed to ask), and we talked about the weather.

'Now,' said Mrs Graham, 'if you are ready . . . ?'

I saw Viola turn pale. 'You don't have to do this, darling,' I whispered.

'I beg your pardon, Mrs Frampton,' interrupted the medium. 'Your daughter does have to do this. There is a great turbulence in the air around her. There is an unquiet spirit near her.'

This was said in such a matter of fact manner it

111

almost took the breath from me. Almost. 'If there *is* an unquiet spirit, then it's her own,' I snapped, 'and no wonder!'

'Mrs Frampton, I must ask you to be quiet or to leave. You are standing between your daughter and her husband. Let no man put asunder . . .' she quoted and, despite my scepticism, I felt fear at that moment.

The blinds were not drawn – I had expected they would be – but only a greenish twilight filtered through the high laurel hedge. Mrs Graham sat with her back to the window and in a breath of air the hedge fluttered and rustled behind her. I felt my breathing slow to match the medium's, but on my right I could hear Viola panting like a terrified rabbit.

The atmosphere changed. I sat there willing nothing to happen, but it grew steadily colder and colder. The rustling in the hedge grew louder, until the noise seemed to be coming from somewhere in the room. I don't know how she did it. I watched her intently every moment we were there and I saw nothing – yet the atmosphere *did* change. It was very clever.

'Captain Firth is here now,' the medium said quietly. Viola gave a little gasp and looked wildly around the room as if searching for Harry. It was cruel.

'He wants to tell you he is quite happy,' Mrs Graham went on. 'He says that he was very confused for a while, but now he understands where he is and is happy. He is glad you've come to talk to him. Is there anything you want to ask him?'

'Is he . . . is he lonely?' Viola faltered.

'Not at all. So many of his friends are with him. Frank Pryor is there and Dick Royden – so many of his friends. They're not lonely. The spirits were alerted, you know, to the needs of all these young men flung hastily into the next world.'

'I see,' I interrupted, 'a sort of spiritual officers' mess!

Do they still play billiards and drink brandy and soda up there?' Eglantine gripped my arm with bruising force.

The medium smoothly rode over my interruption. 'Is there anything else you'd like to ask your husband?'

'I . . . I want to see him.'

Believe it or not – and I still don't believe it myself – the intensity of light behind Mrs Graham's head strengthened. The greenish pallor increased until it was like the halo one sometimes sees around the moon on frosty nights. That phenomenon has a scientific explanation and, although there were no ice crystals in Mrs Graham's room, I am convinced that her halo could be equally well explained. A look at Viola's face told me that no scientific facts were going to get through to her.

The light faded and was gone. 'He has tried but he cannot come any closer,' said Mrs Graham. 'He is not yet strong enough.' She paused. 'He has gone.'

'Now just a minute – you bring him back here – if you can,' I demanded. 'He's told us nothing yet. How can you prove to us that Harry Firth was really there?'

'His last words – they were very faint – but I think he said, "*I miss her little icy paws*".'

'Harry . . . oh, Harry. He always used to complain that my feet were cold at night. He called them my icy little paws. Oh, Harry . . .'

Viola looked on the verge of hysterics. 'Now look what you've done,' I snarled at Eglantine, 'you and your spook-hunting friend! For heaven's sake, Viola, don't be fooled by all this mumbo jumbo. It was just a stab in the dark. Millions of women have cold feet. Millions of husbands must complain about it. The odds were all in her favour when she said that.'

'Then what about quoting the names of Harry's friends? What about that?' Eglantine defended herself.

'And to think I used to believe you were an intelligent woman! Frank Pryor and Dick Royden were in Harry's company. They died on the same day. Their names were in the same casualty list, on the same page of *The Times*. Is that supernatural knowledge or a bit of basic detective work?'

When Viola turned to me, the hostility in her eyes was like a slap across the face. 'No wonder Harry wouldn't stay. He knew you didn't believe. He knew you were trying to send him back. You kept him away from me!'

Dear God! What could I say?

'Next time,' the medium said soothingly, 'next time Captain Firth will be feeling stronger. It is so difficult for the spirits to come. It takes so much energy. Next time will be better.'

'Next time?' I demanded. 'Who says there'll be a next time?'

Mrs Graham looked at me with her respectable, bank manager's wife's face. 'There's always a next time.'

'Like a drug?' I queried. She didn't answer, but I didn't need her answer.

I *wish* Viola had had a child to occupy her mind. I *wish* Eglantine had never dragged her mermaid friend Cassandra into our lives. I *wish* . . . oh, what's the point?

Viola had had a taste and, like an addict, she craved more. Ant agreed with me that it was undesirable, but he didn't seem to see how unhealthy all this longing for the impossible was.

'Leave her alone,' he said, 'she'll grow out of it. Or Eglantine will grow out of it – which is quite likely any day now – and stop encouraging her. In the meantime, it may comfort her and can't do any harm.'

Oh, but it could, I thought. And it wasn't Eglantine's influence I was worried about, but the languid Cassandra. One afternoon I went up to Viola's room to ask her about some small thing – I forget what. I knocked briefly and went straight in. The room was darkened, with curtains shutting out the bright August sunlight. Viola and Cassandra sat around a small table with pieces of paper laid out in a large circle. Each had a forefinger on an upturned tumbler in the centre of the circle.

Should I have crept out and shut the door quietly? Should I have breezed in and swept back the curtains with a bright remark about the weather? Whatever I did would have been wrong.

That night after dinner, Viola came to me with an open book in her hand. 'Listen,' she said, 'this is what Conan Doyle says in *The New Revelation*. "What is done must be done with every precaution in a reverent and prayerful mood. But if you are earnest you will win through somehow, for someone else is probably trying on the other side." If Harry is trying to reach me, how can I turn my back on him?'

She looked so young, so lost.

'Listen darling,' I said as gently as I could, 'Harry is gone, along with thousands of other brave young men. He wouldn't want to think of you wasting the rest of your youth pining. You've still got a life to live and I'm sure Harry would be happier to see you live it to the full.'

'You don't understand . . . you'll never understand,' she moaned and somehow evading my comforting arms, she ran out of the room.

The twins were particularly trying that summer holiday. They thought Viola's preoccupation with the spirit world was hilarious. Their idea of a huge joke was to hide in the wardrobe in her room, then leap out gibbering and groaning. Once they found an old chain trace in the coach house and clanked it along the corridor in the middle of the night, wailing.

Somehow or other they got hold of a copy of Sir Oliver Lodge's notorious book *Raymond, or Life and*

Death. One has to be sorry for a man who has lost a beloved son, but to hear the twins quoting great chunks of that drivel at meal times was more than I could stand.

'Do you know,' Rupert might giggle, 'that chaps can have cigars and whisky and soda up there? Just like a London club!'

'Do you know,' Rudolf would continue, 'they're having terrible trouble with premature cremations up there? People are so careless!'

Like some awful music hall turn, they would carry on about playing ragtime in heaven and singing comic songs and missing arms or legs and spiritual love between the sexes and mansions made of bricks manufactured from earthly emanations. In the end, Ant exploded and banned them both from the dining room for a week.

But if anything was likely to shake Viola out of her preoccupation with matters spiritual, it was the twins and their heavy-handed mockery. Certainly, she became very much less secretive afterwards and I had hopes that the craze might be over.

Michael came home early in September 1918. He was no longer fit for ambulance service after suffering repeated attacks of dysentery. Helen went to meet him in London and travelled back to Hampshire with him on the train, so none of us saw their first meeting. By the time they arrived at Buckholt, Helen had had time to adjust herself to the shock, so we only saw the familiar, calm Helen. But her beautiful eyes were red and swollen. Of course, that might have been from tears of joy. Or maybe she wept because of the change in poor old Michael. Or perhaps for some other reason. Who knows?

Michael looked like an old man. He had lost so much weight that his suit hung straight down from his square shoulders. His face was like well-proved bread dough. One had the feeling that if one poked his cheek with a fingertip, the indentation would remain. He was forty-two and looked like Helen's father.

I sympathized with her later that afternoon, when Michael had been ordered to bed by Dr Hawley.

'He's been very ill,' she said, 'but there's nothing actually wrong with him now. Nothing that rest and careful diet won't cure.'

'Well, we've certainly had plenty of practice with convalescents here – he's come to the right place!'

I spoke cheerfully, but was far from feeling it. Why did they have to live with us? Why couldn't they open up the London house again? Why couldn't they buy something small and convenient, preferably a long way from Buckholt? Michael fit was a brooding presence in the house. The thought of Michael ill was really depressing – it would be all meals on a tray and hot water bottles and night nursing. Of course, one had to feel sorry for him, but really . . . !

Yet he made surprisingly little complaint. Perhaps he had seen so much suffering in the past two years, that his troublesome bowels did not seem all that important. He would sit in the garden in the mellow autumn sunlight. He sat apart from our convalescent guests, not talking, not reading, just sitting. I suppose he was thinking, but about what?

Often Helen would draw up a chair to join him, but she never seemed to stay for long. And when she came back to the house she frequently seemed close to tears, but, being Helen, she confided in no one – least of all in me. One would think that after four years together in the same house, we might have become closer. It wasn't for lack of trying on my part. Really.

Michael didn't want company – anyone's company – except perhaps Hermione's and that only within his own strict limits. As long as the child would sit and look at a picture book, or draw, or play with building blocks, he would allow her to stay. But she was a chatty little soul and soon she would be on his knee, demanding a story or a game of I-Spy. She was used to a constant turnover of strangers in the house and this man was just one more stranger. I don't think she really knew what a father was. I certainly don't think it ever occurred to her that she ought to have one of her very own.

Then Michael would try to oblige and would open the story book, but soon his voice would fade and he would just let the child drift out of his arms. Then she would run and look for another man – for Captain Boxall, perhaps, or Major McCarthy, who were never too tired for the latest exploits of Peg and Weg and Golliwogg – any man would do. Or Nanny would come out to move Hermione on to walk, or tea, or bath, or whatever the next event in her strictly time-tabled day might be.

Michael began to look better. The autumn sun gilded that awful hospital pallor. A diet of bland, sieved food relieved his belly cramps. Slowly he seemed to realize that he was not the only person in the world who had seen the pit of hell. All these men around him had been there and back and yet they were not too tired to let Hermione win at noughts and crosses. Michael was coming back to the world and Helen learned to smile again.

Eglantine was responsible for introducing Cassandra Malyon, whom she had met at a seance, into the family. So I suppose Eglantine was responsible for what happened next, although she would certainly deny it. But someone must have been to blame. These things just don't happen by malevolent coincidence – not unless there really is a higher power directing our lives. And in that case, I fail to see what amusement that power derives from some of its more bizarre decisions.

If I had a criticism of Philip Malyon on that wet October day when his sister introduced him to us, it was that he was just too good to be true. He had the high gloss and sleekly-muscled power of a very well bred racehorse. He had its fidgety manners too. If he *had* been a horse, he would definitely have been a crib-biter. As it was, he prowled the drawing room, picking up ornaments, adjusting pictures, flicking purely imaginary dust from his glittering boots.

Goodness knows what incentive Cassandra had offered her brother to make him drive her to Buckholt without protest. Whatever it was, it did not seem to be forthcoming. Cassandra and Viola disappeared upstairs, bound on who knows what unsavoury project. Philip was left to make polite conversation to a middle-aged couple and stare out at the sodden lawns.

Somehow or other, all our residents seemed to have found something vital to claim their attention. No one was winding the gramophone or flicking through *Horse and Hound* or playing unwinnable games of patience. There was no interest in the giant jigsaw of the late Queen's Diamond Jubilee that always lay partially completed on a table by the window. Apart from the sound of Rex Crawshaw's appalling cough reverberating from the library, the house was silent.

It was the red tabs that did it – the red tabs of the gilded staff – that and the blank space above the left breast pocket and the beautiful, unlined face and the supple athlete's body. Philip Malyon was all that those poor maimed boys might have been and never would be now. His very presence in the house was an affront.

And then Helen came into the room. I looked at Philip's face and I realized just exactly what diversion his sister had promised to induce him to make the boring drive down from Wiltshire.

Now don't misunderstand me. Philip Malyon wasn't my type at all. I like my men to *be* men, if you know what I mean. A man needs something more than a pretty face to attract me. And if that means that the route from stable to bedroom isn't always via the bathroom, then I don't mind too much. Strike while the iron's hot ought to be Ant's motto! And if it means that the hand that caresses my softest places is sometimes calloused and rough, then that's all right too.

But it seemed a long, long time since Ant – or any man – had looked at me the way Philip looked at Helen that wet afternoon. She drifted into the room with Hermione in her arms. The child was much too large to carry by that time. She had tangled her fist in her mother's hair and soft, silken cobwebs escaped from their combs and curled around Helen's ears and the nape of her neck.

I was in the middle of describing to Philip how boring London had become. He leaped to his feet, ogling Helen in the most obvious way, as though I didn't exist at all. Stupid boy – captivated by a vapid, pretty face. It's a wonder he didn't roll over there and then and beg for his tummy to be tickled!

And suddenly I could see what was going to happen as clearly as though it had all been played out on a stage in front of me.

Could I have stopped it? I don't know. I don't know now if I even wanted to try. Life was *so* dull. What harm could a little amusement do? Then the rain stopped and Philip suggested that he and Helen might take a stroll in the dripping wet garden. And after that it was too late to do anything but watch.

'You must spend Saturday to Monday with us,' An

invited Philip before he left for Wiltshire. 'Charley has asked some chums and I'm sure they'd be glad to meet you – swap war stories and all that.'

And of course Philip came – frequently. Barely a month later, Helen had gone.

A nervous breakdown is quite respectable now. Before the war, it was something to be talked about in whispers, if at all – and then only to near relatives. It didn't surprise any of us. Michael had really suffered in France, then, coming when he was barely convalescent, Spanish flu had all but killed him. Ant went up to town because he was sure he wouldn't see Michael again.

The shock of Helen's deceit finally pushed him over the brink. One had to feel sorry for him. He really didn't deserve to be punished like that. Pompous, dull, well-meaning Michael. His idol lay shattered at his feet and he didn't have the courage to pick up the pieces and put them together again.

But I'll never forgive him for what he did to Hermione. Never.

The war was over and we all had pieces to pick up. To read the newspapers, one would have thought that we might all suddenly be transported back to August 1914, that everything was going to be just the same again, that we could all start living exactly where we had left off. I looked around at our family and wondered how. Our daughter was a widow and caught up in the unhealthy circle of Cassandra Malyon's friends. Our son was maimed and dependent on the brandy bottle for his solace. The last, precious few years of my youth had been squandered in the war and it looked as though Helen's life was just about to begin. I felt drab and middle-aged and very, very bitter.

Michael came back to Buckholt in December, after

the doctor had finally allowed him to travel. He didn't look fit to be out of bed. A constant high temperature had dried out his skin. It was flaky across his cheeks and his lips were cracked. He walked stiffly, as though the pains in his joints had become permanent.

'Early bed for you, old man,' decreed Ant cheerfully. 'Let me pull this chair closer to the fire and you might go upstairs after tea.'

'Your room's quite ready,' I said. 'I've put you in the guest wing. I thought you might not want . . . might prefer . . .' I began to flounder.

'If you mean that I might not want to sleep in the bed I shared with that whore, you're wrong.' His voice sounded like a cracked record. 'She means nothing to me. I've made a fool of myself and now it's over. I don't want to talk about her again.'

Ant gave me an expressive look across the tea table. 'Whatever you say, old chap. I dare say you'll feel better after a good night's rest.'

'Don't try to humour me, Anthony.' Michael took a cup from me and, although he steadied the wrist with his other hand, the saucer was full before he managed to put it on the little table beside his chair. 'I'm not an idiot and I'm not a child. Just because I've been ill, it doesn't mean that I'm not perfectly aware of the implications of what I'm saying.'

'Of course, of course, but you're just a bit tired now.'

'I'm not the first man to have been deceived by a pretty face. I dare say I won't be the last,' Michael said calmly. He began to stir his tea, round and round, round and round. 'So we don't have to talk about it again. I'm not going to think about that whore laughing at me while she fornicates . . . I'm not going to talk about that filthy harlot again . . . she's not going to get into my dreams . . . that fucking bitch . . .'

On and on – words I knew existed, but had never

actually heard before. And to hear them from Michael, that scrupulously polite man, was more shocking than the words themselves. Ant wanted to telephone the doctor there and then, but I said no. I thought that once Michael had spilled out all the shame and degradation he would feel better. I always think that I know better than Ant.

Michael stopped swearing at last. There is a limit to how many such words a man knows – even a man whose education has been broadened in the trenches. After a while, the repetition merely becomes monotonous. He held out his cup and saucer to me.

'Do you think I could possibly have some more? I seem to have allowed this to become cold. I'm so sorry.'

And we talked about the peace plans and the future of the Kaiser and about returning Buckholt to normal. I wanted to strip out all the cubicles upstairs and redecorate the whole house. Ant thought we ought to close off both wings and all but the family rooms because of potential staff problems.

'In fact, we could be worse off,' he said. 'The extra staff we had for our residents will leave and you won't get girls wanting to go back into service. Think of all the men who have died or are disabled. Who'll do their jobs?'

'Nonsense,' I said. 'In a few months girls will be clamouring for jobs here. The war's over. Who'd be a bus conductress or a chimney sweep by choice?'

And we talked about votes for women – too dull. I would be the only woman in the house eligible – that is old enough – to vote and I certainly didn't intend to exercise that right. It was tantamount to admitting one's age! Of course I was well over thirty, but why should I dream of broadcasting that fact?

Much more exciting was the news of Ant's OBE. It would be made public in the New Year list, but we didn't mind Michael knowing in advance. He wouldn't gossip. We'd go to the Palace for the investiture and London would be just the same as it ever had been. Of course, Ant deserved it. He'd given up so much for the war effort.

'Other Beggars' Efforts,' he laughed. 'It should really go to you, darling, you did all the work.'

And Michael congratulated Ant and ate a second slice of Dundee cake and was really quite nice about everything. I relaxed and thought, thank goodness Ant didn't panic and telephone Doctor Hawley. All Michael needed was to get a few things off his chest.

Then when tea was finished, Nanny brought Hermione down for her usual half hour with us. The poor little mite needed to know that some things didn't change, even though her mother had disappeared – gone for a little holiday, we'd told her. Where had she gone, Hermione kept on demanding, why had she gone, on and on, until we were forced into a tissue of unsustainable lies to shield her from the truth.

'Hermione, come here,' Michael said.

Such a plain little girl, so sturdy and square, her father's image. She skipped over to his chair and tried to climb onto his knee, but he pushed her back down again. He took her by the shoulders and stood her straight in front of him, like a little soldier.

'Stand there, Hermione – yes, just like that. Now, I want you to listen to me very, very carefully.'

I looked across at Ant in alarm. I had an awful feeling about what was coming next.

'Your mother has been very, very naughty,' Michael said, slowly and carefully. 'Do you understand?'

'Steady on, old chap,' warned Ant.

'Do you understand?' Hermione looked at him in total amazement. 'Your mother has been a wicked woman – very wicked indeed.'

124

'Michael, you can't do this . . .' I gasped.

'It's not on, Michael,' said Ant.

'So we're never going to talk about her again. Are we?'

The poor little thing had stopped looking amazed. Her face was so pale that the freckles on her nose stood out like paint spots. 'Never?' she quavered.

'If Daddy hears you talking about her, he's going to be very cross with you . . .'

Ant made a move towards Hermione, but the ferocity in Michael's glare stopped him. 'Now look here, Michael,' Ant soothed. 'Aren't you going a bit over the top?'

'You mustn't, you mustn't,' I protested. 'It's too cruel.'

'We don't talk about wicked people. We shut them out of our minds and out of our lives. Hermione!' His voice cracked out suddenly and Hermione flinched in fright. 'Look at me when I'm talking to you! You never had a mother . . .'

'Michael, stop it! For God's sake, do something, Ant . . .'

'. . . there was a wicked woman who used to live here, but she's gone and you must rub her out of your mind, like a dirty mark on a page. You never had a mother . . .'

I picked Hermione up and ran with her out of the room. Ant hurried out to the hall to telephone Doctor Hawley.

ADRIENNE

The Refugee

How can a woman leave her child? How can a mother just walk away from the child of her body? Soldiers were shot for deserting their posts, weren't they? What is the difference?

I look at Helen and think of that poor deserted little girl, without a mother, with a father – by all accounts – in a mental institution, left to be cared for by an aunt and uncle. And I think, how can she do it, has she a heart at all, is she really a woman?

When I ached for a child of my own with such ferocity that I couldn't even bear to see a woman pushing a pram through the streets or to pass a washing line fluttering with tiny clothes, I used to think about Hermione and grieve for her. I would never have left her to run off with any man. I would never have abandoned my child to be cared for by some other woman. How could Helen?

It's not easy to be the only ordinary person in a household full of extraordinary people. I am not plain, I am not dull, I am not unintelligent, but compared with everyone else at Knapp Hill, I am very, very ordinary.

Price is fiercely proud of his working class roots (I don't understand this English obsession with class – at home it never mattered) and he is even more proud of capturing his clever and artistic Harriet. Cassandra is completely mad – I shall never understand her. Philip is too beautiful to be true. Hector is a knight errant, born six centuries after his time. And now there is Helen, lovely, heartless Helen.

When I first arrived, the circumstances were so extraordinary that the Malyons must have hoped that I would be as unusual as the events that brought me here. An orphan, a heroine from 'poor little Belgium', a victim of German atrocities. How simply fascinating! In time, they were disillusioned. I am merely ordinary and now they don't bother with me very much.

I don't really mind that. Or I wouldn't, if I had a child to love.

The purpose of marriage is the procreation of children. By that, we avoid bodily sin and glorify God. I abandoned my Church to marry Hector. My sins go unabsolved, I am cut off from the sacraments, my soul is in jeopardy. But it should have been worth the sacrifice. It would have been if, after four years of marriage, I had two or three little ones for comfort.

Instead, Hector subjects me to unnatural practices to prevent conception. His seed lies in a cold pool on my belly. Why should that hot fountain turn to ice on my skin? It dissolves and trickles around and under the curve of my waist. Wasted. Wasted. We curl around each other to sleep like spoons in a drawer and I lie in the dark and think of Hermione.

I can't talk to Hector about how I feel. I can't talk to him about anything now, not since he came back from Flanders. He lives his life and I live mine and they are far apart.

He goes out to the stables in the early morning, often taking a packet of sandwiches with him for lunch. He spends the day with the men he chose to employ after the war, all old soldiers like himself – paying back the debt, he calls it – men who converse in their own private shorthand. They discuss brood mares and stock improvement and blood lines. They talk about where they have been and who they have known and what they have done.

When he comes back he is dirty and tired. He wants a bath and a whisky. He doesn't want to discuss the procreative urges of his wife. He doesn't want to talk to anyone if he can help it.

It was different once. I had a child once.

Early on 4 August, the first invaders trotted into Belgium. Briskly, purposefully, they trotted across the border. People looked up from their breakfasts onto the twelve-foot lances passing the windows and whispered 'Uhlans!'. The frightened whisper overtook the riders and ran ahead.

Wherever they passed, the flag of my country was hauled down and replaced by the black eagle. A rash of proclamations appeared on town halls and church doors. We were to do nothing – nothing – to hinder the passage of the invader. And if we did? Protocol veiled the threat decently, but only just.

Column after column converging on Liège, monotonous field-grey, scarlet regimental numbers on helmets, great steel-tipped boots, harnesses creaking, hooves striking sparks from the *pavé*, rumble of iron-shod wheels, motor cyclists accelerating ahead to clear the next crossroads, hooting from staff cars, silent crowds in village squares.

And singing, always singing. *Heil, dir im Siegeskranz.* Even today, if I hear the British National Anthem, I don't hear God Save the King. I hear German voices. Hail, who wears the victor's crown. Singing and marching across Belgium.

The rumours travelled faster than the army. The French were coming. The French were not coming. The British had landed at Ostend. The British had decided to stay on their little island. King Albert had abdicated. He had ordered the defenders of Liège to hold out to the last man.

The burning and shooting began on the first day. Six hostages shot at Warsage. The village of Battice completely gutted. Visé. Andenne. Seilles. Tamines. Dogs scavenging in burned out ruins. Cows, udders bulging, bellowing in ransacked yards. The harvest, dusty white and ready for reaping, trampled. Bavarian was another word for barbarian.

In the gay holiday towns on the Meuse, where last summer children had paddled watched by mothers in shady hats, where fathers had fished from deckchairs, where little boys had thrown sticks for little dogs, where happy people picnicked and caught the excursion steamer from Namur to Dinant, we waited for the twelve forts of Liège to fall. They lasted until 16 August.

The day before that, the Germans arrived in Dinant and met the French Fifth Army, at last on Belgian soil.

Memory is such a funny thing. Why does it allow me to remember some things so clearly and yet it shuts other things up so tightly that I would need a crowbar to prise them free? And who knows what would fly out then? Pandora's box indeed. Perhaps memory is merciful.

I can remember the ticking of my father's watch as he held me to him for the last time. His beard was rough against my cheek. His skin was cold and yet slippery with sweat. I can remember my mother's hands – only her hands – as she clung to the skirt of his coat. They had to tear her from him, she clung so hard, and her nails were ripped to the quick.

I can remember the way the cobbles gleamed like a rainbow as the square filled up with the men and women of Dinant – six hundred and twelve of them. My father's friends – shopkeepers and clerks, artisans and labourers. My mother's friends – housewives, mothers, grandmothers. Children. Oh Holy Mother, there were children.

Men on one side of the square, women on the other, each in two rows, one standing, one kneeling – arranged to the convenience of their executioners. So orderly. So efficient. And the firing squad, marching to the centre of the square and splitting into two, facing in each direction.

But I can't remember the crash of rifle fire, volley after volley. It must have thundered back from the precipice of the Citadel, doubling, trebling in volume. I can't remember how the rainbow on the cobbles must have been extinguished, the way smoke later blotted out the town, by a steaming, sluggish stream of blood. Dinant was a charred, hollow shell.

I can remember the road stretching white and baked, the road that led to the safety of my aunt's house. '. . . the five inch crust of France's dirty dust . . .' the Tommies used to sing, but Belgian roads are just as dusty. '. . . that makes you feel your limbs are growing older. It's not the load on the hard, straight road, that drives away your smile . . .'

I can remember the carts laden with mattresses, bird cages, dinner services, pianos, children – everything people held most dear on the move from somewhere to somewhere. Sometimes, if you were lucky, you might be offered a lift on a cart, but mostly they were so overloaded that only the very young and very old rode. You would have thought that all those people would have made a noise, like an army on the move. But they were not at all like an army. The carts' wheels creaked, sometimes the children cried, sometimes the overburdened oxen bellowed with distress under the unaccustomed loads. But most people saved their breath for the effort of walking under a metallic August sky.

I can remember the shock of reaching my aunt's house at La Louvière and finding that the Boche were there before us. Tante Lili had four of them billeted on her. We walked into her kitchen, my mother and I, and there was a wonderful smell of coffee and hot bread. Tante Lili was at the stove, frying potatoes, and there were four young men, tunics unbuttoned, sprawled around her table. I can remember that they were as astonished to see us as we were to see them.

But I can't remember where I lost my mother. Sometimes in the night, I nearly – so very nearly – catch up with her. I see her on the road ahead of me, walking with her quick, bustling step. And that doesn't make sense, because her back was broken by the cart wheel. And I call out to her, but she doesn't turn round and she doesn't wait. Then I shout louder and Hector puts his arms around me in comfort. He comforts me in the only way he knows, that silent, gentle man. Then he curls back around me and goes to sleep.

Somewhere on the road to Calais, I lost my mother. She didn't have to come. She could have stayed with Tante Lili and helped her to look after the four young German soldiers. But by then there were only three of them.

My mother went into the coal shed and, when she saw what was happening in there, she took the little hatchet that was kept for splitting kindling and buried it up to the haft in the scrawny white neck of the fourth young soldier. The blood splashed over my bitten and naked breasts and over my torn petticoats, where it mingled with the blood of my pierced virginity. Then, as efficiently as she used to dismember the pig for salting after it had been bled and scalded, my mother removed his head.

We shifted a mountain of coal to bury him. We scrubbed and scrubbed and camouflaged the last stains with

134

coal dust. Tante Lili said she would get someone to come in the night to take the body away.

I don't suppose she got away with it. Once the German authorities started looking for their missing man, who else would they blame for his disappearance? Poor Tante Lili. It wasn't her fault.

It might have been better for all of us if my mother had just shut her eyes to what she saw and tiptoed away, closing the coal shed door gently behind her. The worst was all over by then anyway. She couldn't turn the clock back. She couldn't make me back into what I had been.

My mother and I decided to join the stream of refugees making for England. Somewhere along the road a cart overturned and broke my mother's back. She never reached England. She was the six hundred and thirteenth victim of the Germans at Dinant.

The English are such funny people. They pretend to be so unemotional. I think they actually enjoy their reputation for coldness. They look down on funny little foreigners, with their excitable ways and gestures. But when the stories of German atrocities in Belgium began to circulate, the English became as excited as any foreigner and they showed that their hearts are as tender.

Thousands of us made the short, terrible Channel crossing – 26,000 in one week alone. We crossed in Channel steamers, dredgers, colliers, yachts, anything that would float. Seasick and shivering, a few possessions bundled in blankets, we landed at Folkestone. It was all so bewildering. Few of us spoke English – I certainly didn't, not one word – and the English are not known for the accuracy of their French. It was even more difficult for the Flemings amongst us, I imagine.

But some things need no words. Even a cup of mahogany-coloured tea, thick with sugar, was welcome. They gave us great bowls of soup and damp English bread. There were gifts of blankets and scratchy woollen combinations. There were rows of camp beds laid down in Scout huts and pavilions and warehouses and race courses and skating rinks. And when they tried to segregate men and women, of course families didn't want to be split up, so there were tears.

Oh, they were good, these English, in their own way. All this kindness, in a country that was trying to mobilize itself to fight a terrible war. We were a symbol, we Belgians. England had gone to war to defend the 'scrap of paper' that should have guaranteed our integrity. Poor little Belgium. None of us would have believed then that in four years time we would have long outstayed our welcome.

One doctor asked, in atrocious French, if I had seen any *petits mutilés*.

'*Quoi?*'

'*Des petits mutilés? Quelques enfants sans mains? Les Allemands ont coupé les mains des enfants.*'

Dear God! But the rumour was very strong. Everyone in England believed that Germans cut the hands off children and the breasts off nuns. The truth was not nearly sensational enough for them. It was quite bad enough for me.

The urgency now was to get the refugees out of camps, where they had to be cared for by the War Refugee Committee, and into private accommodation and work of any kind.

At Folkestone, I had made a friend of sorts, a girl from Bastogne called Huguette. We were lucky enough to be transferred together to the camp that was being set up at Earls Court.

The Kentish countryside didn't look much like the hills of the Ardennes. Yet there was something about its timeless peace that reminded me of the way things had been. We looked out of the train windows and saw people working in the fields and even though they didn't wear blue overalls and sabots, I felt they were the same kind of people. Huguette and I both cried and clung to each other, but by the time the train steamed into the outskirts of London, we had stopped crying and started staring. It was all so big, so noisy, so dirty. So exciting.

And we stared even more when we got to the War Refugee Camp at Earls Court. The relics of past exhibitions were still there – the Doge's Palace, a German beer garden, an aerial railway. Huguette and I had narrow little beds in a Chinese pagoda, along with an old woman with two parrots and a circus performer with his wife and the cannon he used to fire her from. We giggled as we lay in bed and looked up at temple bells and many-coloured snarling dragons.

'This is a mad house,' said Huguette. 'The sooner we find a job the better.'

'Shall we stick together?' I asked hopefully.

'Of course. I was a milliner's apprentice. Even Englishwomen wear hats, so someone must want me. What can you do?'

'Nothing.'

'Nothing? Don't be silly! Can you sew?'

'Nothing you could wear afterwards!'

'Can you cook?'

'Nothing you could eat!'

'Well, for goodness sake – what have you done with your life?'

'My father owned a *maroquinerie* and I kept his books for him.'

'There you are then. You could be a bookkeeper or a bank clerk even, now that all the young men are going to war. You'll make so much money, you can keep me!'

It was quite exciting, really. It sounds terrible to say

that when my parents were so recently dead – and I *did* grieve for them, never think otherwise – but we were young and we'd never been away from home before. The scent of freedom was thrilling.

We were each issued with a little buff card headed *Carte de Sortie et d'Entrée* and underneath *Uitgangs en Ingangs Kaart* which told us very primly that we had to be back in the camp by five-thirty unless we had permission for absence. At that time, the newspapers were full of small advertisements in French offering '*une chambre comme chez soi*' or '*chambres avec legumes de notre potager*'. How we giggled over that one! We actually got round to visiting a few, but the landladies were not too keen on two young girls (what did they take us for?) and we were determined to stick together.

I hadn't been feeling too well for a few days, so Huguette went off by herself to look for work. She came back that evening and plopped down on the narrow bed next to mine.

'I had no idea,' she said, undoing the stiff row of buttons down the outside of each boot, 'that London was so big. My feet feel as though I've been walking on hot coals.'

'Any luck?' I asked.

'Yes!' She turned to me a face full of excitement. 'I've been offered a job in the milliner's workroom of Thomas & Freemantle.'

'What's that?'

'Only one of the biggest department stores in London. One of their girls has just got married and another has joined up as a nurse, so they're short-handed. I turned up just at the right time. The supervisor gave me a trial and she said I have a natural flair for colour.'

'How marvellous.' I tried to squeeze some enthusiasm into my voice.

138

'But Adrienne, there's bad news too. It's a living-in job. I'll have to live in a hostel with the other girls. They're very strict about that. And after all our plans . . .'

'It's all right. Don't worry.'

'I could say no,' she offered. 'I could keep on looking for something else.'

'Better not. It might take ages. I'm glad for you, Huguette, really I am.'

'But what'll you do?'

'Stay here.'

'Something will turn up for you too, soon, you'll see.'

'Not now,' I said slowly. 'It's too late for that. I'm going to have a baby.'

The shock on Huguette's face seemed to turn my words into an undeniable truth. And for the first time, I faced up to the fear I had been stifling for weeks.

'Are you sure . . . ? Maybe you've just made a mistake – miscounted . . .'

'I'm sure.'

'Can't you . . . can't you . . . *do* something?'

It was my turn then to be shocked. What did she think I was? A murderess?

After that I became someone else's problem. Now I was no longer just a refugee, but an Unmarried Mother – definitely with capital letters! I was a charity case and committees of worthy women had been set up just to take care of people like me.

Yes, of course I was grateful. How could I not be? How would I have managed in a strange land, with only a few necessary sentences of English at my command and with my body swelling daily with my enemy's child?

If only they had not made me feel that I ought to be grateful, these worthy women. If only they had not

139

looked me up and down with a silent question in their eyes. If only the dresses they handed out to cover my expanding figure had not been made for someone six inches shorter than I. If only the interviews had not taken so long, interviews with this social committee and that church committee, and I was growing all the time. If only their kind queries about my health had been made without shouting slowly at me – I was neither stupid nor deaf. If only they had left me my self-respect.

'We have found you a home,' they told me. 'Not a Catholic household, as you wished, but very good people – ' They must be, the silent stare told me, to take in a pregnant foreigner of unknown background. ' – if a little – unusual. The lady of the house is an artist, so you must make allowances for her funny little ways. Still, we hope you'll be happy there, until . . .'

'Until the little bastard is born,' I said and, though I spoke in French, the word is sufficiently close to the English. An expression of disgust passed over the face of each one of those English ladies.

They meant well. I should have been grateful. Of course, I was, really. How would we Belgians have behaved if we had been invaded by the whole population of Kent, destitute and frightened?

But I was not in the mood to be grateful to the Malyon family when I finally arrived at Knapp Hill after a long and terrible journey. The train from Waterloo to Salisbury seemed to have been diverted into every siding on the way. Priority on the line was being given to troop trains and they were all travelling in the other direction, away from Salisbury Plain. The temperature in the carriage must have been well below freezing. I managed to close one button on my coat, but although I strained, none of the others would meet.

It ought to have been a relatively short journey, but the train was four hours late into Salisbury. Somewhere past Andover, it began to snow. For the last hour, a grinding low in my belly had been starting to frighten me. It grated, like a pestle in a mortar, stopping long enough only to lull me into false relief, then it would begin all over again.

From Salisbury, I caught a connection to Collingbourne Ducis, but it was dark by the time the Malyons' dogcart let me down before their front door. The jolting of the cart over icy country roads had been agony. I was very afraid. It had been all I could do not to cry out. But what would have been the point of that? What could the poor driver do, in the dark and miles from anywhere, but be afraid with me?

When the tall, athletically-built man in evening dress came down the long sweep of staircase at Knapp Hall that evening, the last thing he expected to see was a scrawny waif with an obscene protruding belly standing in his hall. The pain was not a grinding any longer, but a ferocious propelling of something unwanted along a dark passage. I was no longer in control of my body.

I remember the terrible panic of not being able to halt the hot flood. I remember the urgency of Hector's voice calling for help as he leaped the last few stairs. I remember pitching forward into the sanctuary of his arms. He caught me and, before the darkness slipped down over my eyes, I looked up into his face and it was like coming home at last.

It was all for the best, they said, when the child slipped passively from my body. No woman could be expected to bear the fruit of violation. The shock had been too much for me and my womb had expelled this monstrous growth that had been foisted on me. Poor little Adrienne. She has lost so much – her parents, her home, her country. We must be kind to her.

And Hector was kind. So very kind.

All for the best, they said. And they thought they

were comforting me. But if I had known that I would be denied the love of a child in my marriage, if I had known that the child I lost that night would be my only child, I would have held onto it – no matter who the father. I would *never* have let it go.

You would have thought that Harriet Malyon would have been shocked, wouldn't you, when her son brought home another man's wife? But Harriet merely wiped her clay-stained fingers on her filthy coverall and refixed the comb in the slipping silvery mass of her hair.

'I wouldn't dream of interfering, my dear,' she said. 'Philip's a big boy now and presumably he hasn't actually abducted the woman?'

'Well, no, but . . .'

She leaned forward and with her spatulate thumb adjusted the nose on the bust she was sculpting. 'Well, then. You must forgive me, Adrienne, if I say that you are being frightfully middle-class about all this.'

The English class thing again. Of course I was *bourgeoise*. Why should I not be?

'And it bothers you not at all,' I asked, 'that the woman has deserted her child as well as her husband?'

'No doubt she had her reasons. It's not for me to enquire. Mind you, all this running away is quite unnecessarily dramatic. When I was a child, if my father wanted a bit on the side, he'd bring a woman home with him. Next morning, we'd all have breakfast together. So jolly civilized. None of this public breast-beating. Mind you, Mother could never keep any servants – they were always giving notice. Said they never knew how many cups of tea would be wanted in the morning!'

I had to laugh.

Price thought Philip was no end of a dog. 'If I were only twenty years younger – no, ten – I'd give young

142

Philip a run for his money,' he chuckled, giving that humorous quirk of his bushy brows that I had come to know well. It redeemed his large face from being simply plain. Looking at him then, I could well believe he had been quite a ladies' man in the days before he met his Harriet.

I tried to talk to Hector about it. He lifted his head from the pillow long enough to say, 'None of our business, really.'

'That's what you all say.'

'Then it must be true. Go to sleep, Adrienne. I'm too tired to lie awake worrying about Philip's little affairs.'

'Helen isn't a "little affair".' I was truly shocked – the *bourgeoise* in me again, I suppose.

'No, you're right there. This really does look as though Philip is serious at last.'

'But you can't condone adultery . . .'

'I'm not condoning it, but I'm not condemning it either.'

'That is typical English compromise.'

'No, just realism.'

'And what about the child? Does no one think of her?'

'I'm sure Helen does . . .'

'Then she has a strange way of showing it. Is this how all English upper-class women behave to their children? Is this why they allow their children to be brought up by nannies? Is this why they send their little boys away to school at seven – *seven* – years old? Because they don't care?'

Hector put his arms round me and drew me close. His breath was warm on my skin. I could feel the crispness of his chest hair beneath my cheek. Gently, gently, as though he soothed a nervous mare, his hand stroked the long curves of my waist and thigh.

'You don't understand,' I sobbed against his chest, 'you don't understand how I feel.'

143

'I do understand, darling, really I do. But you must try to understand how I feel too.'

'How can I? You talk such nonsense about rights and wrongs, as though having a child was a problem in mathematics.'

'This is a filthy world – it's foul and rotten through and through.' His voice cracked on the last words. 'And a child is so innocent . . . you do understand . . . you do see . . . ?'

'I see only that you won't give me what I want most.'

'I'd do anything for you, Adrienne – anything. But not this. Don't ask me. I can't.'

'You're cruel! Cruel!' I tried to pull away from his arms, but they tightened round me. 'If you really loved me . . .'

'It's because I love you. If you had seen the mess . . . the horror . . . people are evil, Adrienne. How could they do such things to each other? How could I have done them? I'm as evil as any of them.'

'Don't talk to me about evil,' I rasped. 'I'm not a milk-and-water Englishwoman. I've seen what men can do. I *know*.'

'I have done such things . . . I have no right to be a father . . . no right . . .'

I should have listened to his cry for help, but all I heard was my own voice weeping alone in the darkness.

'You have no right to deny me this,' I cried and with a fierce jerk, I broke free from him and sat up in the darkness.

There was a long silence. All I could hear was the rasp of my own breathing. The night air was chill across my barely covered shoulders, but I was too proud to snuggle back beneath the blankets as though nothing mattered. Then faintly beneath me, I could feel a tremor of the bed.

Hector was beginning to twitch. I groped in the dark

until my hand encountered his face and when I touched it, I felt a wave of panic. His mouth was distorted by that terrible tic. He had fought so hard to control it when he first came back from France. He had so nearly won. I remembered those terrible nights of his despair and the equally terrible days of hiding from his family the fact that Lieutenant Colonel Hector Malyon DSO, MC was shell-shocked.

I had seen some bad things in my twenty-three years. I had seen my father executed. I had seen my mother dismember a man. I had watched my mother's suffering body dragged out from under the wheels of a waggon. I had seen the bloody mess that was my child wrapped up in a newspaper like so many potato peelings. But nothing – nothing – had been so bad as watching the man I loved disintegrate.

Of all the cruelties of war, the most senseless is the shame of a brave man pushed to the limits of his endurance. A crippled body can be seen and understood and pitied. A crippled mind is a scar that can never be displayed with honour. It is a dark secret. It is not something that happens to one's husband or son or brother. It always happens to 'a chap I once knew'.

I remember Hector's last leave, ten months before the end of the war. I remember the brittle gaiety of his days. He was like one of the dried flowers in my wedding bouquet – one breath of harsh wind and he would have broken down into a puff of colourless dust. I remember the way he couldn't bear silence, the way he talked and talked, the dancing, the drinking, the way the gramophone ground out tune after tune long after everyone else had gone to bed.

I would lie upstairs and listen. And when there was silence, I would fear. What was he doing? How long could he go on like this? When would he finally decide that life wasn't worth living any more?

I remember the silence of our room, when he took me again and again, until my abused body was ready to scream out. He never spoke, he never whispered words of love to me in the darkness. The only sound was my breath hissing through my teeth and his grunt as he fell back from me.

But I was glad and proud to give my body to him. I knew, you see – I knew, the way no well brought-up young English wife could ever have known, what Hector was suffering. I knew that the scent of my skin, the silkiness of my hair, the softness of my breasts drove away the night-time demons of slime and blood and fear. For a little while at least. I was proud to love him.

A man is only given just so much courage: a lot or a little, the amount is finite. He can hoard it, eking it out like a miser, spending it only when absolutely necessary; or he can be profligate, spending it with a generous hand, giving it freely in a largesse that lightens the darkness around him. These men are like shooting stars. They flare across their sky, doing great things, often again and again, their glory trailing like sparks behind them. They are a source of wonder for a while and then they are either dead or burned out.

Such profligacy must come to an end. The source of their courage dries up. But they are not allowed to give up, or what might become of all those others who have come to rely on the cheerful word and the shining example? So they struggle on, the shooting star earthbound at last and stumbling in the mud.

Hector did not commit the ultimate sin against hope, the sin against the Holy Ghost that would have damned his soul for ever. Instead, he went back to face the German spring offensive and to win a bar to his DSO.

Sir Douglas Haig said, 'Every position must be held

to the last man . . . With our backs to the wall and believing in the justice of our cause, each one of us must fight on to the end.'

I remember reading the words and when I closed my eyes, I saw Hector, with his back against the wall. Alone. And I was afraid as I had never been afraid. But he returned and he brought his demons back with him.

If the pressure of my demands had driven him back into that waking nightmare, I would have done a terrible thing. I would never forgive myself.

'Hector, darling,' I whispered, 'I'm sorry.' I covered his face with tiny kisses. 'I didn't mean it. I'm sorry. I'm sorry.'

I could feel him fighting it. I could feel the tension in his muscles as he clenched them against the tremors. I could feel the bite of the nails curled into his palms as though on my own flesh. I could hear the whistle of his breath through clamped teeth.

I took one of his stiff hands and curled it around my breast. He was icy cold yet slippery with sweat. I slipped my own hand inside his pyjamas. Gently. Gently.

'I love you, Hector.' His mouth was rigid under mine. I ran the pointed end of my tongue along his teeth and nipped the soft inner surface of his lip. Gently. Gently.

And then his mouth opened to me. The spasm left his body and we melted against each other. I could feel the nudge, nudge of his response butting against my thighs and the butting grew to a demand. His lips travelled over my skin, teasing, tempting, scalding. His hands could draw the very soul from my body.

I had won. I had brought him back from hell once more. But for how long?

This time. Oh, please God, this time.

★

147

Strangely enough, of all the family, only one shared my concern about Helen's arrival and that was the one I would have least expected to be at all interested.

In her usual forthright way, Cassandra didn't bother with discreet hints. She came right out with it one cold November morning at breakfast, when Helen had been at Knapp Hill about a week.

'I think you should go home, Helen,' she said. 'You'll bring nothing but trouble if you stay.'

Philip was at the sideboard, heaping his plate with kedgeree. He threw the serving spoon back on the platter and spattered buttery rice everywhere.

'For God's sake, don't you start, Cass. What's up this time? Did the cards come out wrong last night, or did you read disaster in the tea leaves?' he jeered.

'Very funny,' snapped Cassandra. She pushed back her chair and tossed her crumpled napkin onto the table. Her lipstick had left scarlet smears on the white damask. With a rasp of silk, she crossed her legs and drew a long amber cigarette holder from the bag that hung over the back of her chair.

'Must you?' grumbled Price. 'I can't say I enjoy the taste of tobacco with my food. In my young day, a lady would no more have dreamed of smoking than she would have of drinking Bass straight out of the bottle.'

To listen to him, no one would have guessed that Papa Price's young days had been spent fighting his way up from grocer's delivery boy, through store manager, to the owner of the chain of grocery stores throughout the country that bore the name *Malyon's* in flowing gold script on maroon ground.

'The trouble with you, Daddy,' said Cassandra, drawing deeply and exhaling from the corner of her mouth, 'is that your young day was a very long time ago.'

'And does that automatically mean I'm wrong?'

'You're positively antediluvian! This is the young people's time now. You old men have had your chance and look at the mess you made of things. It's our turn now.'

'And *I'm* to blame for the war now, am I? It's all *my* fault?'

'Not exactly your fault . . .'

'Oh, that's very decent of you, Cass,' put in Philip, plainly relieved that the spotlight of Cassandra's critical gaze had been removed from him and Helen.

'. . . but you can't say that you didn't make a good thing out of the war. *You* did all right, Daddy.' There was a sneer in Cassandra's voice and she emphatically blew two slender columns of smoke down through her pinched nostrils.

One should not talk to one's father like that. One should have more respect. I know that if I had ever spoken to my father in that way, it would have been made very plain to me where my duty lay. But I never would have spoken like that. My mother would never have allowed it – and yet Harriet sat and listened to her daughter and never spoke a word in her husband's defence. But perhaps she was not listening. When she was working on a sculpture, she often didn't take time to eat or drink, let alone listen to her family bickering.

'An army has to have food, doesn't it?' Price justified himself, but his voice rasped dangerously. Cassandra would be wise to change the subject.

'And someone has to get the contract,' added Philip, 'so why shouldn't it be Father? I don't know what you've got to complain about.'

Hector said nothing, but I saw him push his uneaten breakfast around the plate, as though his appetite had suddenly left him. I tried to catch his eye across the table, to smile at him, to make him smile back at me.

149

He rose abruptly. 'Must go,' he said. 'Got the vet coming to look at Willowherb.'

And I knew he would not be back until dark.

'I played fair,' Price pursued, 'there was no sawdust in *my* jam, no sweepings off the warehouse floor in *my* tea. Not everyone can say as much.'

'Daddy darling,' cooed Cassandra, 'don't let's mince words. You're a profiteer . . . *such* a dirty word these days. One would have thought the money would have been reward enough. But a grateful country is giving you a "K" as well. So don't say you didn't have a good war.'

Thank God Hector wasn't here to listen to all this. I held my breath. Surely Price would turn on his daughter now. Instead he laughed – a huge, indulgent laugh.

'You silly bitch,' he roared, 'and what do you think pays your allowance? What do you think keeps you in lip rouge and French knickers . . . ?'

Accidentally I caught Helen's eye across the table. She was blushing at Price's coarseness and I knew her colour was mirrored on my own face. Such unnecessary vulgarity.

'. . . so if I'm a profiteer then you're profiting very nicely out of it. Let's not be squeamish. And while you're sitting at my table, eating food bought by me, you'll put that cigarette out. Understand?' Suddenly, his voice had the crack of authority. I had a glimpse of the fire and the tenacity that had carried Price Malyon up from a back terrace in Truro to his Blomfield-designed country house.

'Oh Daddy,' sighed Cassandra, 'sometimes you're positively neolithic.' But she screwed the cigarette butt into a nut of leftover butter on the side of her plate. Helen winced at the revolting mess.

I would have liked to have seen inside Buckingham Palace. Just vulgar curiosity, I suppose – a bit like staring through the windows one passes when on a bus at that strange time of day when lamps are lit but curtains not yet pulled. It would have been interesting to see the King and Queen of the country that had become my own. I don't suppose I'll ever have the chance now.

But of course, the number of guests at a Royal Investiture has to be limited, or the poor King would still be investing, or whatever it's called, for the next fifty years. Harriet, naturally, was to see her husband knighted and Price would have liked his eldest son to accompany him as well, but Hector refused to go. He was in one of his dark moods and said that he had a buyer for his mare, Belladonna, and wasn't going to lose money for the sake of a jaunt to London.

Philip was only too eager to take his place. 'Never one to miss a jolly,' he said.

Hector had seen the King twice before, when he had been awarded his DSO and later the Bar, but that had been at ceremonies in Flanders and not at the Palace. He described His Majesty as a sad-eyed countryman, who seemed genuinely distressed at the sufferings of his army.

In the end, Hector did have to put off the buyer for Belladonna. Price said we all ought to lunch at the Savoy to celebrate and it seemed too churlish, even for Hector, to disappoint his father. So Hector was to be *chevalier des dames* for the day and escort Cassandra, Helen and me to the Savoy.

Price looked magnificent dressed for his investiture. No one could have faulted him, from the sleek silver mane on his massive head to his glistening toe-caps. No one could ever have guessed that once he had worn a cloth cap and hand-me-down boots. His pride in his own achievements was innocent and very lovable.

'Not bad, eh?' he said, holding out his arms and twirling round like a little girl in a new party frock. 'Not bad for a ragged-arsed urchin from Truro?'

'You're very naughty, you know – just like a little boy. You use naughty words just to see what will happen next!' I was getting used to his raw tongue and what would once have made me blush now only made me laugh. It was only his funny way of reminding himself where he came from, that he hadn't been born to the luxury that surrounded him. 'You look wonderful, Papa Price. A perfect aristocrat! I'm only sorry you were already spoken for when I arrived, or Hector might have had a serious challenger!'

I aimed a kiss at his cheek and with a wicked grin, Price turned his face and met me full on the lips. His heavy moustache tickled. But over my shoulder, he saw Harriet come into the room and, as always, she had only to appear for every other woman in the room to be eclipsed, in Price's eyes.

Harriet topped her husband by a good four inches. Her ankle-length gown was of delphinium blue nun's veiling, topped by a seven-eighths length coat of the same colour, trimmed with sable and intricately frogged. Her sable cossack-style hat was perched cocquettishly over a mass of silver hair.

'Ah,' Price said softly, 'if I'm a gentleman now, it's because I had the great good fortune to marry a wonderful woman – and a lady in every sense of the word.' With a formality that would not have been out of place in the Sun King's court, he raised Harriet's gloved hand to his lips. 'Are you ready, Lady Malyon?'

Those of us who were not going to the Palace went up to town on a later train. We went straight to the Savoy and awaited Price and Harriet at our window table in the Grill, with its peerless view of the Thames.

They arrived in high good humour. Price pretended not to have been impressed by the ceremony, but his self-satisfied grin told us otherwise.

'My,' he said, 'you should see the flunkies – every one

152

of them dressed fit to be a king. I felt I ought to be bowing to them, instead of the other way round. When I finally got to His Majesty, it was quite an anti-climax. He looks just like a kind, red-faced country squire!'

'And what is it like in the Palace,' I asked eagerly. 'Is it like a real palace ought to be?'

'If you mean is it all gold cornices and red carpets and cut glass – then yes, it's just like a proper palace.'

'And did the King really say, arise Sir Price?'

'No, he didn't. I knelt down on a little gilt stool and he just tapped me on the shoulder with that sword and then I got up again. And it was a bit of a struggle from down there, I don't mind telling you!'

'And was that all?' I demanded, just like a child at the end of a fairy tale.

'No, His Majesty spoke to me very kindly for a moment or two. He was very sympathetic about my arthritis. Really, very kind . . .'

Price cleared his throat and I was amazed to see his eyes blur with tears. Harriet reached across the table and patted him gently on the hand.

'You old fraud,' she said softly. 'You try so hard not to show you care. But your family knows you too well for that. We're proud of you – all of us.'

'Hear, hear,' said Philip loudly and the rest of us nodded and smiled.

'Well, well . . .' Price mumbled and cleared his throat. 'Now then, Hector, have you ordered for us yet?'

The grill room was packed and by the look of it, we were not the only ones celebrating inclusion in the New Year's Honours List. The noise was rising as each new party came in. We toasted Price in Roederer '11 and then we toasted 1919 and peace and hope.

Then Hector rose from his seat very slowly and his mother looked at him in surprise. I caught her sudden anxiety. She knew. She knew it all. Of course she did –

how could she not? She was his mother, after all. I should have realized. I gave her a quick, reassuring smile, but it did nothing at all to reassure either of us.

Hector looked round us all and then around the room. His eyes came back to us again, those clear hazel eyes that once had seemed able to burn right through deceit and pettiness. I had loved their fearless challenge. But now they were clouded and puzzled. He was slipping away from us.

He was made of glass. Struck in the right way and he would give a fine, true ring. A careless knock and he would shatter into a million bright pieces.

Hector looked at us all as though he had expected to see entirely different faces looking back at him across the table. We were strangers. We loved him and we were not the people he wanted to see. He raised his glass and opened his mouth to speak, then suddenly sat down. A yellowish stain spread across the white damask where his glass had slopped.

'I thought . . .' he stammered. 'I wanted to . . . we ought to remember . . .'

'That's all right, old chap,' Philip interrupted and I could have choked him for his hearty dismissal of Hector's pain. 'Don't you worry about a thing.'

Cassandra took out her compact and began dabbing at her nose with fierce, pecking motions.

'*Must* you do that in public,' Hector snapped. 'It makes you look like a Bloomsbury tart.'

His rudeness was a relief. That strange, lost moment was over and Hector had come back to us again.

We lunched on fillets of sole and *velouté* of lobster and Price would not consider a meal was a meal unless he had had sirloin or some such. Now that the meatless days and breadless days and potatoless days were over, he could begin to enjoy his food again. Yet somehow the sparkle had gone out of the celebration. It had all gone very flat after Hector's sad gesture. When the congratulations were over, we didn't seem to have very much to say to each other.

We were eating *macédoine des fruits avec des sorbets variés* when I heard Helen give a little gasp. No one else seemed to notice that she shifted her chair sideways a fraction and began to give the view of the river more attention than it had had all lunchtime.

The room was less crowded now and I could see right across the floor. A family was just leaving. By their dress, they too had been to the palace investiture. There was a florid man with a thin, fashionable wife in a velvet tunic the colour of Parma violets. Its hemline was a good halfway up her calf. Her matching velvet hat was tipped well forward on a neat little head. They were followed by a young couple who might possibly have been married, but they looked so bored with each other that I guessed they could only be brother and sister. The young man had lost his right arm and wore the sleeve of his coat tucked neatly into a pocket.

To reach the door, they had to pass right by our table. The man gave a stiff little nod of the head as he went by and his wife passed on without turning. They were halfway to the door when she pulled away from her husband's arm and hurried back. She had an eager look on her sharp-featured face.

'Helen, my dear,' she exclaimed in a high voice. 'What a lovely surprise to see you. I wouldn't have thought you would dare to show your face in public – not after what you did.'

Philip rose and Helen put a soft hand on his arm. The large man also touched his wife. 'Clemmie,' he said, 'we'll miss our train.'

'Nonsense, Ant, we've plenty of time. And Helen must be just aching to know how her family is. It's so long since she's seen them. Aren't you just aching, Helen darling?'

Helen had gone completely white, right to the lips. I felt sorry for her then. No matter what she had done, she was about to suffer a terrible public humiliation. And what could we say? All Clementine Frampton had done was to offer news of Helen's family.

'Michael's in a sanitorium – for his health, you know. But of course, maybe you don't want to know. He went completely ga-ga, I'm afraid, in December. Not long after you left him.'

Clementine had the sort of cut-glass voice that carried right around the emptying restaurant. I saw waiters pause, fascinated, in their work. No one turned a head, yet I knew that everyone was straining to hear what might come next.

'Tried to do away with himself, poor old thing,' Clementine went on relentlessly. 'Cut his wrists in the bath. Awful mess. That sort of thing's so awkward to hush up. Officious doctors. Police. *You* know.'

Her husband was crimson now and dragging at her sleeve. 'For God's sake,' he muttered, 'keep your voice down. D'you want everyone to hear?'

'I expect everyone knows already,' she answered, not taking her pin-bright eyes off Helen's face. 'Quite a nine days wonder. Even made the London papers.'

Helen was so still, I thought she must already have fainted. Her breathing had slowed to a whisper. If someone had held a mirror to her lips then, I swear it wouldn't have misted.

'Satisfied now, Clemmie?' asked Mr Frampton.

'No, I am not. You haven't asked about your daughter, Helen. Don't you want to know how Hermione is?'

Philip started to bluster. 'If you have something to say, Mrs Frampton, I can give you the name of my solicitor . . .'

'Hermione doesn't talk about her mother. She's not allowed to, you see. Her father has forbidden it. So she says nothing. Not one word. Not ever. She is dumb.'

Harriet was quite magnificent. She turned what was rapidly becoming a very ugly scene into a spot of interesting family news-swapping. At one point, I thought Philip was going to overturn the table to reach Mrs Frampton, but Helen managed to hold him back. Hector had a look of utter disgust on his face. Cassandra was drooling over every word.

Harriet slipped out from behind the table and took Clementine Frampton by the elbow in what looked to be a friendly gesture, but was really a fierce clamp.

'How very kind of you,' said Harriet in that deep voice of hers that made Clementine sound like a shrew, 'to let us know how Hermione is getting on.' She began to propel Clementine firmly toward the door, with a grateful husband close behind. 'We do so enjoy all your little snippets of news. How nice it would be if you could visit us at Knapp Hill sometime. We must arrange it.'

Clementine's feet in their high Louis heels tip-tapped rapidly across the floor, but Harriet managed to make it look like a stately progress. At the door, Harriet bent her head for everyone to see, ducked neatly beneath the brim of Clementine's hat, and left a cool kiss on her cheek. It was a masterly performance.

When she came back to the table, she gathered us all up with her eyes, defying anyone – even Cassandra – to make a clever remark and said, 'Well, I think we're ready to go home now. Don't you, Price?'

It was no use, of course. Harriet may have put an end to a potentially nasty scene, but the newspaper hounds were back on the scent. There had been some ugly paragraphs when Helen had first left her husband, but the story had eventually died away and was overtaken by other, juicier scandals. Now the righteous condemnation broke out all over again. Helen was pilloried in three-decker headlines:

A MOTHER'S LOVE?
DESERTED DAUGHTER'S GRIEF
LITTLE GIRL SILENT

Of course, we all tried to keep it from Helen, but it just wasn't possible. What a gift for the newshounds: a runaway, an attempted suicide, a madhouse, a dumb child. If they had sat down and tried to invent a sensational story, I doubt if they would have come up with anything half so lurid. Helen was called every name under the sun. Philip blustered and threatened to sue, but he knew he wouldn't stand a chance. A good counsel would have made mincemeat of him and Helen would never have forgiven him.

'I think you ought to try to be friends with Helen,' said Hector one night.

'I'm not not friends,' I answered.

'You know what I mean. I think you ought to try harder. She needs a friend just now.'

'She has Philip. Isn't that enough for her?' I could hear myself – so virtuous, so sure, so *married*.

'That's not what I mean and you know it. She needs a woman friend. She's alone and very young – even younger than you . . .'

'. . . younger and more beautiful and a whole lot cleverer!'

'That's not worthy of you, Adrienne.'

Hector's voice was so mild and yet the reproof really stung.

'Oh, I can see she's managed to enslave you too – along with Philip and Price and that poor *farouche* hus-

158

band of hers. You're like a lot of wasps – you men – buzzing around a peach. Only this peach is *rotten*!'

There was a still, waiting silence. I had shocked myself. I didn't know I felt like that. I really didn't know. I didn't know those words were just waiting to spill out.

Hector didn't help. He didn't try to soothe me or soften the words. He just lay there, propped up on the pillow, his arms folded behind his head, watching me in the mirror as I sat at the dressing table. Waiting.

I picked up my hairbrush and began to brush my hair with long, fierce strokes. It crackled with static and followed the brush up at the end of each stroke. After a few minutes I looked like an angry Gorgon. I flung the brush back down on the table, scarring the polish.

'This is ridiculous. I'm going to have my hair bobbed.'

'You'll do no such thing!'

'Why not? Perhaps it'll make you take your eyes off Helen long enough to look at me again.'

'Because if you had short hair right now, you'd look like a furious kitten – all spit and fur! And I'd laugh at you and you'd get even crosser.'

And I looked over at him and saw what four years of hell had done to my husband. The bones of his cheeks and nose were so sharp, I fancied they might easily have pierced his skin. I saw the way the bedside lamp caught a generous handful of white hairs. I saw the way his mouth seemed always to be kept under determined control. I saw the plum-coloured bruises below his eyes that no amount of sleep seemed to fade.

His face had the permanently questing look of a man whose hearing has been damaged by the thunder of the guns. His body was reduced to wire and whipcord. Even now, when he was about to go to sleep, he looked as though he were afraid that if he let go – even just for a moment – the wires would snap under the tension of memory.

I loved him. Dear God, how I loved him. He had given me everything: name; respect; decency; faith; love. Everything. Except what I wanted most in all the world.

'Besides,' said Hector as I climbed into bed, 'I love the way your hair trails across my chest. So I'm not going to allow you to bob it. It's too . . . sensuous.' Then, after a little while, he murmured into the hollows of my neck, 'You silly little thing, don't you know I've never looked at another woman since you fell into my arms that winter night?'

And if I sometimes thought he buried himself in my body in order to bury the past, why should I care? As long as he did it.

If Hector wanted me to be friends with Helen, then I would be friends – whether she wanted to be or not. I found Helen alone in the morning room. As I entered, she whipped something quickly beneath a cushion, but not before I had seen it was the *Daily Graphic*. She'd managed to get a copy from below stairs, no doubt.

'Helen, may I talk to you?'

'Why not?'

'Hector has told me I ought to be better friends with you.'

Helen managed a laugh. 'Well, that's honest enough, at any rate. And are you going to do what you're told, like a good girl?'

'If I can.'

'Fine. Then where do we begin?'

She stood up and faced me, outlined against a window. Oh, she was lovely, Helen. In spite of all I had thought and said, I had to admit she was lovely. It wasn't just the perfect face. It wasn't just the firm, female flesh or the graceful way she moved or that mellow voice. There was something so untouched about her, something so pure. A husband, a child, a lover – and yet she could have modelled for one of Raphael's Madonnas. And hadn't I heard somewhere that his Madonna was a harlot as well?

Then she moved and the light, instead of being behind her, fell on her face. She had been crying. Even beautiful women cannot cry the way actresses do in films. The tears do not fall like raindrops on a window pane, leaving the face unblemished. Real women are different. The skin around Helen's eyes was disfigured by tiny raised red spots, where the salt had stung. Her lids were puffy. The tip of her nose was red.

She turned away and blew her nose vigorously, then turned back to me with a smile brief as a break in the clouds. 'You start,' she said brightly.

Helen had courage all right. Whatever she had done, she was suffering. And she was suffering alone, because Philip would never have noticed a little thing like her tears. Women are like that, he would have said, always bubbling over about some trifle or other.

I wanted to put my arms around her, to let her cry herself out on my shoulder. Just at that moment, I would have done anything to stop her tears. She had courage, you see, and I understood so well what it was like to be alone among strange people.

And then, when she felt better, I would have given her my advice – go home, I would have said, make the best of it and forget him. How ridiculous. Why should she listen to me? So I said the first thing that came into my head. That was very stupid.

I said, 'Do you ever think about your daughter?'

That could easily have been the end of my attempt at friendship. It was a thoughtless, callous thing to say.

My only excuse is that Hermione was constantly on my mind.

I remember the horror with which I had heard Clementine Frampton tell us that the child no longer spoke. She was not yet four years old. She should have been chattering non-stop. She should have been asking questions, finding out about the world, telling long, complicated stories to an audience of dolls and teddy bears. She should have been singing off-key nursery rhymes. She should have been trying to count the stones on the beach, the stars in the sky. If she had been *my* daughter . . .

And instead – silence. I couldn't stop thinking about a little girl who had chosen to be dumb.

My baby would have been the same age as Hermione.

So I said to Helen, 'Do you ever think about your daughter?'

It would have been kinder to have slapped her face.

'I never stop thinking about her,' Helen said and the music of her voice was choked, but she had the courage to look me straight in the face as she said it.

Then she turned away from me – why not? – and ran to the door. She was running from me and my thoughtless cruelty.

'Helen, wait,' I called. 'I'm sorry. I didn't mean to hurt you. Please – can we be friends?'

'Because Hector wants it?'

'Because I want it.' And I meant it.

Helen turned round then and the smile she gave me was so frail, but real. 'Thank you,' she said simply. 'I'd like that.'

At least one link from Helen's past life had not been cut off – her Aunt Eglantine. This remarkable woman took no notice of feuds. She came and went as she pleased amongst the Framptons and the Malyons.

I remember the first time she came to Knapp Hill. Helen had warned me that her aunt was a little eccentric, so I should have been prepared – but I wasn't.

It wasn't so much the way she looked. A few years ago she must have been wildly avant garde, but now the world was catching up with Eglantine's style. Her bobbed hair and primary-coloured face had become, if not commonplace, at least acceptable. One no longer expected dogs to howl in the street and horses to bolt at the sight of her wispy draperies. It was the wave of energy that issued from her that made her so remarkable. She was surrounded by a magnetic field that had us all skimming about like iron filings.

We had been playing the first tennis of the season on a hot, still afternoon when the trees looked like cutouts stuck on dusty sugar paper. Our shouts sounded as though they came from far, far away and the noise of the ball off the racquets was like a bowstring snapping.

I was not very good. A shopkeeper's daughter gets very little opportunity to play games of any kind, but I could muddle along. It ought to have been mixed doubles, but Hector had gone off to talk to some old soldier who had come to the door, attracted, no doubt, by Hector's reputation as a man who would never turn an Old Contemptible away. Sometimes I wondered if all the hard luck stories he heard could possibly be true.

So Cassandra had been persuaded to take Hector's place, with very bad grace. We were arguing a line decision – all of us sweaty and ill-tempered.

'It jolly well was out,' said Cassandra, 'so that's our point.'

'Out?' scoffed Philip. 'You need glasses, old dear, too much squinting into crystal balls. Must be bally boring for you to play, if you can foresee the result every time before you start.'

'It was *out*,' stormed Cassandra. She threw her

racquet on the ground and there was an ugly splintering sound.

'Temper, temper.' Philip picked up a towel and slung it around his neck.

'That sounds like the end of the match,' Helen said.

'It's a rotten surface anyway,' complained Philip. 'How can we be expected to have a decent set or two on a court that's been growing potatoes for four years?'

'It'll get better,' I soothed. 'After all, this is the first time we've used it since re-turfing.'

'And the last, if today's anything to go by. Sensible Hector, pushing off like that.'

And then there Eglantine was, gesticulating frantically through the wire. We had all been so absorbed in our quarrel, that none of us had seen her arrive.

'Thought I smelled brimstone,' Philip muttered as he bent down to pick up his jersey. 'Wonder where she left her broomstick.'

Helen hurried out and greeted her aunt with a kiss. It was when I saw their cheeks together, that I realized what was so odd about Eglantine. Her skin was brown – really quite like leather. Helen's complexion was like milk beside her.

'Goodness, Aunt Eglantine,' she said, 'where have you been?'

'I've had the most glorious two weeks. Tommy Cobham has his yacht at Cannes and we've just *lazed*.'

'But you're quite brown.'

'Of course – the sun is well known for that effect, you know!'

'But . . .'

'It's the coming thing, darling. The rays are so beneficial. Think of all those poor, starving little German children being helped by sunshine. I feel so *unutterably* healthy.'

'Very fetching, Mrs Hayler,' Philip said. 'Is it the

new fashion? Do you think it'll catch on? You look so Provençal – just like a native.'

Eglantine squinted at him to see if he was teasing, but Philip always managed to look so innocent when he was being naughty. There was something about his wide-set, blue eyes that always made him look like Nanny's darling just when he was at his wickedest.

Privately, I thought that the sun had done irreparable harm to Eglantine's complexion. The fine wrinkles around her eyes were like a white cobweb upon brown leather. The skin around the eyes is so delicate. If lying in the sun were to become fashionable, someone would have to invent some sort of protection for the eyes.

'And darling,' went on Eglantine with the sort of excitement that made her sound as though she were hugging herself, 'we *flew* as far as Paris. So *thrilling*.'

Cassandra went quite white. I saw her face quite distinctly as I rose from picking up a dropped ball.

'How exciting,' said Philip, 'did you enjoy it?'

'It was sublime!' Eglantine enthused, 'The Channel was exactly like grey panne velvet – I used to have a gown just like that before the war. I could have gone on and on for ever – all the way to Timbuctoo!'

'Rather you than me.' Philip gave a mock shudder. 'I need to feel solid earth beneath my feet. And anyway, isn't it a bit dangerous for a lady who's . . .'

'. . . who's old enough to be your mother, you were going to say! Cheeky young pup! I'd have thought the war would have put an end to that sort of talk. Who ran the country when all you men were away, I'd like to know?'

They all flopped down in canvas chairs set out beneath the cedar in the middle of the lawn. I trotted off to organize tea. The servant problem seemed to have got worse since the end of the war, rather than better. Harriet barely noticed, but Papa Price used to complain as though he'd been accustomed to being waited on hand and foot since babyhood.

As I went, I could hear Eglantine saying, 'I can't wait to get my pilot's licence – what bliss to swoop and soar above the boring old world. And I've found just the person to teach me – a friend of young Charley Frampton.'

By the time I rejoined the party in the garden, having gone via Harriet's studio to remind her that tea was ready – meals were just a distraction to her when she was working – the tea trays had been brought out. Philip had already been through the sandwiches and was making huge inroads into a Madeira cake.

Cassandra was crumbling a piece of caraway seed cake. She looked very odd – more odd than usual, that is. We all knew that Cassandra was subject to what were politely called her 'moods'. We normally pretended nothing was happening. It looked as though one was brewing now.

'Helen, darling,' Eglantine said, leaning forward and putting her hand on Helen's arm, 'I thought someone ought to tell you that Michael's come home again.' Her confidential whisper echoed around the whole group.

'What – back from the nuthouse?' chuckled Philip.

The word 'insensitive' was probably coined to describe Philip. I don't suppose he even noticed that Helen shuddered, but whether it was at that word, or whether it was at the idea of Michael's coming back, I couldn't say.

'He's had a little rest, that's all, Philip,' said Eglantine, with more asperity than I had ever heard in her voice before. 'He had a hard war, for a man of his age – harder than you, I shouldn't wonder – and he just over-reached his strength. That's all.'

'And now he's back,' said Helen softly, 'tell me – is he . . . is he . . . you know . . . ?'

'If you mean, does he still show signs of his breakdown, then the answer is 'no'. He looks very well. Put on a spot of weight, in fact. More like the Michael you first knew, before . . .'

'Before the world tore itself to pieces. I'm glad he's better,' said Helen quietly. 'He didn't deserve to suffer like that.'

Philip leaned forward and took the last slice of Madeira cake. 'Fine, if he's fit to bear it now, then I'll get in touch with our solicitor about the divorce.'

'Philip;' Eglantine said carefully, 'that's really why I came today. There isn't going to be a divorce. Michael won't hear of it.'

'What do you mean – won't hear of it? Helen's committing adultery, isn't she?'

'Philip . . .' I gasped in protest. Helen's breath hissed through her teeth.

'Well, isn't she? He can't want her back now. Not after she's . . .'

'That's just it,' Eglantine explained. 'He does. He wants her back very badly.'

'That's ridiculous,' Philip blustered. 'Well, he can't have her. We'll sue for divorce ourselves. He'll do the decent thing, won't he? Surely?'

'Can you really see Michael coming to an arrangement with some little chorus girl in Brighton? Your imagination must be more flexible than mine. Michael will give Helen no grounds. She is the guilty party.'

'Madness – we'll sue on grounds of madness,' said Philip triumphantly, 'that should do the trick. Everyone know's he's gone round the bend.'

'That won't do, I'm afraid.' Eglantine had obviously done her homework. 'Insanity is not considered a proper cause for the breakdown of marriage and, even if it were, don't forget that Michael's breakdown followed Helen's departure, not the other way round.

Helen,' she opened her bag and took out an envelope, 'Michael asked me to give you this and to say that he wants you to come home.'

It was an honourable solution. It was the *only* solution. What did life hold for Helen as a divorced woman – or worse, an adulterous one? Suppose Philip tired of her? She had lost her position in society, her friends, her pride. She had no income. She was a fallen woman, fair game for any man who might fancy a fling.

She had lost her child.

Why, then, did Helen shudder as she took the letter from her aunt? Why did she hold it as though it soiled her fingers?

'I really don't think,' I interrupted, 'that this is the right time or place to discuss such personal details. Mrs Hayler, would you like to come and see Lady Malyon's studio? She's working on a bust of Helen at the moment. It's terribly modern – you might be interested.'

'It's hideous – you'll love it!' promised Philip.

Eglantine could take a hint as broad as that one. We started to walk across the garden towards Harriet's little brick-built studio. We left Helen holding the envelope in both hands, just as she had received it, and staring as though she could read the contents through its protective cover.

'Don't do it!'

Eglantine and I both turned round in surprise. Cassandra was hurrying across the lawn towards us and, by the look on her face, her 'mood' had come to a peak.

'Don't do what?' I asked. 'Visit your mother? Is she too busy?'

'Don't learn to fly.'

'Why ever not?' asked Eglantine. 'It's so exciting.'

'I don't know why. Just don't – that's all.' Cassandra was very much in earnest. She was still very pale. There

168

was a thin white circle surrounding each of her irises, just within the arc of colour. I had never noticed that before. 'Don't have anything to do with Archie Byatt,' she went on.

'Nothing to do with Archie? If someone offers to teach me to fly, I certainly wouldn't dream of turning down the offer. Cassandra dearest, don't you want a nice lie down inside – away from this heat?'

Cassandra's eyes seemed to go quite out of focus, then slowly they focused again, so that she was able to look straight at us. 'That's what they always say,' she remarked bitterly and walked off towards the house.

'Well!' said Eglantine.

I don't remember anyone called Archie Byatt being mentioned before. How did Cassandra know he was going to be Eglantine's flying instructor?

Say what you like about Philip – he loved Helen. He was indolent, indiscreet, sometimes pompous, sometimes weak – but he loved Helen deeply and sincerely. I don't think I appreciated at the beginning just how much he did love her. I thought she was only a fancy of his, that he had ruined her life for a passing whim. I was wrong. I was wrong about Helen, too.

I was sitting out on the terrace after dinner. It was chilly, but the sound of Philip's gramophone grinding out everlasting jazz was more than I could bear that night.

Even out here, where it should have been cool and dark and silent, I could hear the silly, tinkling tune.

You called me baby doll a year ago.
You told me I was very nice to know.
I soon learned what love was, I thought I knew,
But all I've learnt has only taught me how to love you.

169

The machine whined down and back up again as Philip turned the handle.

> *You made me think you loved me in return.*
> *Don't tell me you were fooling after all!*
> *For if you turn away,*
> *You'll be sorry some day,*
> *You left behind a broken doll.*

Philip had been in a flamboyant mood all evening. He had mixed us all cocktails when we gathered on the terrace before dinner – virulently coloured concoctions with nasty sugar-rimmed glasses.

'Tarts' drinks,' Hector had growled, pouring his into a flower bed.

As though in direct challenge to the letter from Michael, Philip had flaunted his possession of Helen, handing her extravagantly into dinner, kissing her before his mother's very eyes. And Helen had caught fire too. She burned like a pure white flame of sexuality. They were both all lingering looks and trailing fingers across bare skin and silent promises across the table. They were devouring each other right in front of us. It was disgusting.

It was disgusting and yet, as I sat alone in the cool darkness, I felt a shameful, creeping warmth in my body. They were dancing now and they were so close one could not have passed a knife blade between them. They were one body. I had never seen Helen like this. She glittered, she was incandescent with promise. Philip was her slave.

I knew – we all knew – what they were going to do together later that night. They had all but performed in front of us. And I was jealous.

Somewhere in the garden, Hector was smoking a last cigar. Soon he would come in and we would go

170

upstairs, not holding hands in public, and we'd go through the nightly ritual of washing and undressing. Perhaps he might just lean over and kiss me goodnight with a friendly pat on the buttocks. Perhaps he might be in the mood for more than that. Then he'd slip my nightgown over my head and he'd . . .

I clenched my fists and wouldn't allow my thoughts to go any further down that path. Never had Hector looked at me the way Philip was looking at Helen tonight. Never had I felt as though my very bones were melting when Hector trailed his fingers across my skin. Never, never, never . . .

The curtains whispered softly and Helen stepped out onto the terrace. She slipped down into a chair beside me and I heard a breath of a sigh. Helen always looked her best in white or silver and tonight she shimmered under the moon in filmy gauze. There was a sheen of sweat, as though her skin had turned to satin, across her bosom and shoulders and the night was cool.

'Do you think you ought to be out without a wrapper?' I asked.

She shrugged. 'It doesn't matter.'

So we sat quietly for a moment, while the gramophone whined down for the last time.

> *It's naughty, it's true,*
> *But when I look at you,*
> *I feel so*
> *Oh Johnny*
> *Oh Johnny*
> *Oooooh.*

We could hear Philip cajoling his father into one last B and S. We could hear Cassandra saying goodnight to no one in particular and going upstairs.

My curiosity was a burning torment. I had watched

171

Helen tonight. I had seen her in the mornings, her lips puffy from Philip's kisses, her movements slow and sated. The looks, the little gestures . . . they were as open as a pair of mating cats. Just to sit opposite them at breakfast was to feel like a voyeur.

She stretched out her long legs. They were just a little apart, as though already anticipating Philip's bulk.

'Helen . . . I . . . Helen . . .' It was dark and still I had to look away. 'I read . . . is it true . . . is it possible for a woman to enjoy . . . you know, enjoy, like a man?'

'Yes, of course,' she answered directly, without shame. 'Don't you?'

'Oh, I don't mean that I don't. It's very nice. But a woman never wants . . . never actually . . . well, it's not the same, is it?'

'Why not? We all have needs, don't we?'

Do we? I know Hector – any man – has needs. One was brought up to recognize that. But that a woman might . . . that Helen . . . that I, even . . .

'Sometimes I do feel – ' I confided, in a rush to say the words before I could think too deeply of the consequences, ' – sometimes I feel that there is something that I can't quite – you know – appreciate. Something that seems to be waiting for me just around the corner, but I never quite get that far. It's odd.'

'Are you telling me that you never . . . ? Good gracious!'

She was laughing at me. She made me feel like a freak, two-headed, bearded. Just because I never knew . . .

'I'm sorry, that was very rude of me,' Helen apologized. 'Heaven knows I'm no expert, it's just that it never occurred to me . . . look, it's just a matter of timing, that's all. Hector should wait for you, until you're ready. Can't you ask him to? It's not a race, after all.

And then, when you're both ready . . . oh dear, what a conversation! I'm awfully glad it's dark.'

'Yes?' I asked eagerly, 'Yes?' I was conscious of an extraordinary, dragging sensation, as though a great, warm weight lay in my lap.

'Well, that's it.'

'That's it?'

'For heaven's sake, Adrienne. Do you want me to go into every lurid detail? This conversation ought to be censored. Use your imagination!'

I felt as though Helen had left the most important part unsaid. Just as in the act itself, something was missing, something was just out of reach.

'But you and Philip haven't had a baby, and you mustn't have one, so how can you . . . what do you feel when he . . . when he *leaves* you?'

'When he – ?' I could tell by the angle of her head, by the way she turned sharply, what the expression on her face must be. 'Adrienne, I can't see if you're blushing and you can't see if I am. So let's say things we wouldn't usually say. Are you telling me that Hector withdraws from you before you are ready?'

'Yes.'

'Every time?'

'Every time,' I whispered miserably. 'He doesn't want to have a child.'

'But there are other ways. That's cruel. No wonder you . . . Look, you don't have to have a baby if you don't want to. There are things you can do yourself to prevent it, things that won't interfere with your enjoyment. I can give you the name of a doctor, a woman doctor . . .'

'No, no, you don't understand,' I cried. 'I couldn't do that. It's Hector who doesn't want the child. I could never . . . it would be a sin.'

'I see,' she said slowly. 'Then in that case, I can't help you. I'm sorry – for both of you.'

We sat silently for a moment. I wanted to fidget in my chair. The things we had said, the words, the thoughts, had left me hot and sticky, unable to sit still. I wanted to go in and have a bath, but the thought of the heat and light inside, of the many goodnights to be said, of the long stairs, kept me outside a little longer.

'That's not true,' Helen said suddenly. 'I'm not sorry for you at all. You have everything and I have nothing. You have everything I'll never have now. If you weren't so nice I could hate you for it.' And she robbed the words of their sting with a sad little laugh.

Then Helen opened her little silver evening bag and took out a folded letter. She held it out to me without words. I raised my eyebrows and she nodded. So, reluctantly, I took it and unfolded it.

It was an admirable letter in its way – cool, sensible, without a trace of the bitterness that one might have expected from a man whose wife had run off with a younger, handsomer man. In fact, it was so sensible that I felt uneasy. One might write like this when requesting the return of a mislaid umbrella, but not an erring wife.

And was this the letter of a man who had gone crazy for love, who had forbidden his little daughter even to mention her mother's name? I thought not. I read it again and was certain. Either Michael Frampton was trying too hard to give an impression of sanity, or someone else had written it for him.

Even so, the meaning was quite clear. Under no circumstances would there be a divorce. The scandal would not be tolerated. Helen would be welcomed home if she came immediately. Otherwise . . . The 'otherwise' was not clearly spelled out. Nevertheless, it was there, just a hint of coercion, a hint of darkness behind the matter of fact exterior. Enough to make me uneasy. I refolded the letter and handed it back to Helen.

'What shall I do?' she asked simply.

'That is not for me to say.'

'I thought you were my friend . . .'

'I *am* your friend, but this is too private a matter. How can I judge between husband and wife?'

'Adrienne, please. Philip only laughs and says he'll tweak Michael's nose for him. Harriet is on another plane altogether. I'll go mad if I can't talk to someone. There's no one but you.'

'Helen, don't force me. You forget. I am Catholic. Because I married Hector, I am separated from my Church, but my beliefs are still the same.' I wish . . . I wish I didn't have to say these things to her. 'If I were really to give you my advice, I would say there can be no divorce. I would say you are committing a terrible sin and must go back to your husband. But because I am your friend, I can't say that to you. So please – don't make me.'

Helen stood up and the moonlight sparked off the spangles on her gown, turning each one momentarily to an icy rainbow. I don't know when she had started to smoke. I had never seen her do it before. But she took a cigarette from her bag and lit it, impatiently drawing on it before it was well burning. She took one or two deep breaths, inhaling the smoke deep into her lungs. Then she threw the cigarette down and ground it with her silver slipper.

'Ugh, filthy habit! I might have known,' she said with a brittle laugh, 'the sort of priggish advice I'd get from you. Little *bourgeoise!*' Fastidiously, she picked a strand of tobacco off her tongue. 'Listening to you is like listening to my conscience.'

'Then you should not have asked.'

'No, no, you're right. I'm sorry, Adrienne. Whatever you said tonight would be wrong. I see that.'

Helen took a couple of turns along the length of the terrace. Her arms were folded around her body, as though she were trying to keep herself from falling apart. I expect she was cold.

'He won't leave it at that, you know,' she said eventually.

'No, I don't imagine he will.'

'Michael doesn't like to be a loser. He can't stand it. And he has a very well-developed sense of property. When he married me – he bought me. When I left the house with Philip, it must have felt like a burglary to Michael.'

'That sounds very harsh. Didn't he love you at all?'

I tried to keep my voice very matter of fact. Helen was high that night – high on fear, on uncertainty, on sex – and I'm not at all sure on what else.

'Oh, yes, he loved me all right. And he loved his gilts and consoles, his bachelor house on Ebury Street, the Tissot on his drawing room wall.'

'You're very bitter, but are you being really just? Think how he must have suffered. Does a man have a mental breakdown because his shares go down in value?'

'You read the letter. He's going to try to force me to go back – I know it. But I'm not going back. He can't make me. I'm not going to give Philip up. And I'm not going to give up Hermione either. I'm going to fight for her. I'm going to fight for her with every weapon I've got. And if that means fighting dirty, then I'll do that too. But I'm going to get her back.'

She was glorious standing there – a supple, gleaming column with moonstruck hair. I believed every word she said. It was like listening to a sacred oath. Then Philip stuck his head round the terrace door.

'Ah, there you are – I've been looking everywhere for you. Coming?'

He held out his hand. Helen held out hers. And I swear that the air between the tips of their fingers crackled. Philip put his arm around her shoulders and they disappeared behind the curtain. There seemed to be a sort of afterglow left on the terrace where they had been. The air was vibrating. I felt it, low down in my body.

I would have given anything . . . anything . . . to have Hector look at me the way Philip looked at Helen.

But then, I was no Helen. I was no goddess. I was a little brown mouse with an ugly accent and a shop-keeper's sense of values. No wonder I couldn't drive Hector wild. If I were a real woman, he would never be able to control himself long enough to practise his abominable anti-conception ideas. If I were a real woman he would be helpless, he would drown himself in the pulsating darkness.

I saw Hector's starched shirtfront first, gleaming in the moonlight, and then he came up the terrace steps.

'Ready, old girl?' he asked.

I looked at the easy strength of him, all whipcord elegance. I looked at the long muscles of the horseman's legs, at his sensitive hands, at the hooded sweep of bright hazel eyes. He robbed me of my breath. He robbed me of my sanity. The desire that had smouldered in my body all evening flared with the suddenness of a brush fire.

If I were a real woman, we might have a child even yet . . .

PATRICK

The Scholar

It's a phrase proud parents are apt to use, an odd phrase – 'taking' a commission – as though commissions lie around discarded by their last owners, just waiting for someone to pick them up and dust them down. Or as though they could be acquired by stealth, stuffed in bags by men in striped jerseys and masks.

Given the choice, I would never have 'taken' a commission. Unfortunately, one was given to me and there didn't seem to be any way of avoiding it. Like Malvolio, I had greatness thrust upon me, but unlike him, I wasn't awfully happy about it.

I took a sort of perverse pride in my collection of white feathers. I kept them in a spill vase on the mantelpiece, next to the photographs of my brothers in uniform, the shell-decorated box from Eastbourne and the tea caddy that held the 'just in case' money. Mother would have thrown them out – or burned them more likely – but I wouldn't let her.

They were like campaign medals for my own, personal campaign. There was no question of my following Edgar, Arthur and William into the Army. Not if it meant leaving Mother all on her own. She couldn't possibly have managed with all of us in France. So, as the youngest, I stayed to look after her and collected white feathers.

I should have had a citation. I deserved one. For conspicuous gallantry in the face of public contempt. White feathers – a handful of seagull, some chicken, three dove and one lovely, downy swan's feather.

Phyllis gave me that one, that summer Sunday in 1915 we went on a boat trip to Kew. Best pennyworth around, Mother used to say, Kew Gardens. She always liked a trip there every summer.

She used to savour every moment of it. Even getting up early to pack meat paste sandwiches in waxed paper and to fill cork-stoppered bottles with cold tea was part of the adventure. It was as exciting as a day at the seaside, getting on the steamer that puffed upriver from Westminster to Kew. There was a smell of steam, of mudflats if the tide was out, of brackish, tidal water. Gulls used to follow the steamer, screaming and swooping low over our wake. I used to hurl my crusts to them, but Mother always complained that that was a sinful waste of good food.

We'd get off at the little landing place at Kew, then walk slowly under the echoing bridge and up Ferry Lane to the Green. We wouldn't go straight into the Gardens. There was no hurry. We'd stroll right round the Green admiring the grand houses with rare plants in their tiny front gardens – grace and favour houses, some of them, I'm told, royal houses. We always popped into St Anne's Church. It's so light, so cool, so elegant, so different from our own little red brick box of a church. Then, taking deep breaths of the drunken scent of lime blossom, we'd walk towards the ornate metal gates of the Gardens. I'd hand over three pennies to be slipped into the slot. Then Mother, Phyllis and I would filter through the turnstile.

We all had our favourite places. Mother liked the steamy heat of the Palm House and always used to say that, if she could live in a climate like that, her rheumaticky knees would be better in no time. Phyllis always went to look at the water lily leaf that was big enough to support a child. I loved the wild part of the gardens, the glimpses of the river through untouched woodland glades. Then we'd make sure that we always consulted the noticeboard at the entrance, to find out what was especially worth seeing that day.

It was very hot that Sunday. Mother got rather overheated, so we sat for a while by the ornamental lake, watching the mandarin ducks and the pintails and the swans – familiar, graceful white ones and the black swans with their scarlet beaks and matching, wicked eyes.

Phyllis looked nice, I suppose. She'd taken a lot of trouble over her appearance. She'd even put on a new frock, one of those shorter, full-skirted ones that appeared so suddenly that summer. It was striped pink and raspberry. As I watched her stripping leaves from a willow switch, I decided that I didn't much like her in pink. It made her look overblown, like a striped camellia whose petals were about to drop off in perfect, tattered formation.

Pink is for pigs. Pink is for seaside rock. Pink is for babies. Pink is for breasts and bellies and bottoms.

Mother stretched out her legs and wiggled her toes. Her little patent leather boots were pushed out of shape by her bunions. 'Ooh, that's better,' she said. 'I don't know why I even dreamt of wearing these boots in weather like this. I ought to know better. Patent always draws my feet. Well, best get on, I suppose.'

I stood up and gave Mother my arm to rise. Then I turned to assist Phyllis, but she avoided my hand. She stood up lightly, brushing grass and petals from her skirt. Then, bending as gracefully as a willow, she picked up a feather that had become trapped in the reeds and handed it to me without a word.

A white feather. A soft, downy swan's feather, newly-shed, barely damp. I took it from her.

Mother sucked in her breath and said, 'Well!' And I waited for a scandalized tirade, but Phyllis's gesture had silenced even Mother. Only her face was eloquent.

I tucked the feather into my buttonhole, my white cockade, my campaign medal. Then I held out my arms, ready crooked, one for each lady. 'Shall we go?' I said.

All the way home, I wore that feather in my buttonhole. I could just see it, from the corner of my eye, fluttering with every step. Once I nearly lost it. It was nearly plucked from my buttonhole by a sneaky breeze and whirled back over the high brick wall into the Gardens. But I managed to catch it and tucked it back in place more firmly.

I think by then Phyllis would have been glad to see it go. She had planned the whole gesture – the graceful bend, the sweet smile as she handed it over, Mother's horror, my own shamefaced reaction (but I disappointed her in that). What she had not planned was the aftermath.

She had not bargained for the sheer mortification of having to travel all the way home in the company of a man who, rather than stuffing her feather into his pocket in shame, wore it as a badge of pride. A knight used to wear his lady's favour on his helmet. I wore mine in my buttonhole.

A woman in black gave my feather a look of absolute contempt as she passed. Phyllis's face was scarlet. It clashed dreadfully with the pink of her frock. We had a bit of a wait for the train at Kew Gardens Station (the day was too short to make the journey both ways by river) and Phyllis pointedly walked over and read a poster fixed to a brick wall.

' "Is your Best Boy wearing khaki?" ' she read. ' "If not, DON'T YOU THINK he should be? If he does not think that you and your country are worth fighting for – do you think he is WORTHY of you?" Well, thank goodness,' she said, 'that *my* sweetheart has answered his country's call.'

She wasn't going to succeed in making me blush.

By the time we turned into Pretoria Avenue, I could sense that Mother was coming nicely up to the boil. There were some little girls skipping in the road, one at each end of a long rope, chanting to the tune of 'Jack and Jill'. The one in the middle had a long streak of jam down the front of her pinafore and the floppy blue bow that tied back her hair bobbed up and down, working loose with every skip.

> *Kaiser Bill went up the hill*
> *To see the British Army.*
> *Gen'ral French jumped out of a trench*
> *And drove the Kaiser barmy.*
>
> *Kaiser Bill went up the hill*
> *To play a game of cricket.*
> *The ball went up his trouser leg*
> *And hit his middle wicket.*

Mother looked like thunder. Phyllis usually came in with us to Number 32 after a Sunday outing and had a spot of tea – tinned salmon with maybe some cucumber, bread and butter, fruit salad and tinned cream. It was a settled thing, so much so that Mother didn't bother any longer to get the best service – the Paragon with the gold rim – out of the china cabinet in the front room. Phyllis was going to be part of the family, so she could just take us as she found us. But still Mother always used the dainty tablecloths and serviettes she'd embroidered herself. She was very particular, Mother.

This time Mother stood in front of the gate like Nemesis in black serge. She pointed to a card that was fixed proudly in the bay of our front window.

'Do you see that, Phyllis Norley?' she queried and didn't wait for an answer. 'Read it – go on – read it. Let's all hear you.'

'Mrs Snape, I . . .'

'Read it.'

'This house has . . . this house has sent . . .'

'Louder. We all want to hear you.'

'This house has sent three men – ' Phyllis cleared her throat. ' – three men to fight for King and Country.'

'Three men,' echoed Mother. 'Three sons gone to the trenches. One of them your own sweetheart. And now you want to send a widow's last support and comfort to his death. I hope you wake up in the night, Phyllis Norley, and blush to think of what you've done this day.'

I couldn't allow Phyllis to go on home by herself, that wouldn't have been proper. So I walked her round the corner to Ladysmith Avenue, just as I always did. She blew her nose twice into her handkerchief on the way, but I didn't pay any attention to that. I took her to the door and raised my boater to her mother and said good evening to her father. They both looked at Phyllis's blubbered face, then at the feather, then at me.

Then I said goodbye to Phyllis.

I know now why she did it, of course. It was pique. But I didn't understand it at the time. We'd known each other for years and years. We'd been to school together. We'd belonged to the same Sunday School. Phyllis had been walking out with Arthur for a whole year before the war. She was Arthur's girl – we all knew that – and I was just looking after her until Arthur came home again. It was understood. Or I thought it was.

On the night before – the Saturday night, that was –

we'd been to see *Judith of Bethulia* with both Gish sisters, Lilian and Dorothy, and Lionel Barrymore. Mother approved of that because it was biblical, suitable for a young lady. (Though why seducing a man, then chopping his head off – even if he was an Assyrian – should be thought suitable is completely beyond me.)

Besides, what harm could Phyllis come to with me? Who would choose thin, studious Patrick when she could have big, bold Arthur?

The film was wonderful – like Alma Tadema come to life. We chatted about it nearly all the way home. It was a lovely night, so we walked back and just before we turned into Ladysmith Avenue, Phyllis ducked into the entrance of Carlucci's little corner shop and pulled me by the elbow into the dark square of the doorway. She folded her arms round my neck.

'Phyllis,' I protested, 'what're you doing? You can't do that here!'

'I've never done it anywhere,' she complained. 'That's the trouble. Oh Patrick, please, just one little kiss.'

'But suppose someone sees?'

'Who'll see? Who'll care? There's a war on, don't you know?'

And she closed her big blue eyes and turned her face up to mine and waited. I went rigid. After a moment or two, Phyllis opened her eyes again.

'What's the matter?' she whispered. 'Don't you like me?'

'Of course I like you.'

'Don't you love me?'

'I like you a lot. You're really a ripping girl. But you're Arthur's sweetheart. What'd he think about you kissing another man – and his brother, at that?'

'Arthur doesn't care about me any more. He never writes, just sends those silly field service cards, with ticks for 'I am well' or 'I have received your letter of such and such'. What good's that to me?'

'Well, perhaps he's busy – you know – fighting and such.'

'*All* the time? Oh Patrick, he doesn't love me any more and I'm wasting all my youth waiting for him!'

I seemed to remember a line something like that in a picture we'd been to see a week or two before. 'Come on, Phyllis,' I said in a jolly tone. 'Time we went home. Your Dad'll think the white slavers have got you!'

Somehow or other she twisted in my arms, so that my back was against the door of the shop. The handle was pressing into my spine. Phyllis pressed against me. I could feel the cushion of her bosom against my chest. The flesh of her back was ridged where her corset cut in. Below the corset, her thighs were round and firm and just parted.

Her face was flushed pink. She licked her lips. They were moist and full.

Pink is for babies and breasts and bellies and bottoms.

I knew I ought to like it. I was supposed to like it. I was a *man*, for heaven's sake! Even schoolmasters at the elementary school round the corner in Durban Street and living with their mothers – so convenient – are supposed to be men. Yet I felt Phyllis's warm body curve against mine and it was as though my bones had turned to sticks of chalk and ink flowed through my veins.

It was the softness of her, the ripeness, the cloying texture, like bletted pears. She seemed to billow, like sheets on the line in March. Her breath was hot on my face and smelled of the cachous she had eaten in the picture palace. And there was the smell of something else, too. I don't know what it was, something sweet and acrid at the same time. She smelled the way all women do.

And yet Arthur liked Phyllis. Presumably he loved her. He said he was going to marry her when he came home.

'This is wrong, Phyllis,' I said and my voice was muffled by the fluffiness of her hair. 'You're not being fair to Arthur.'

'Is he being fair to me? I'm twenty, Patrick, twenty-one in August. And I'm tired of making love on paper. I want to live!'

I'd obviously taken her to the pictures far too often and not always to the ones that Mother would have approved.

Then she kissed me. She put her little hot, pointed tongue between my lips. It was salty and sweet and sour all at once. God knows where she learned a whore's trick like that! Surely Arthur couldn't have taught it to her?

I put one hand on each of her shoulders and pushed. She staggered back against the display window and I ran up the street. When I got to the corner, I stopped. Phyllis wasn't following me. Perhaps I'd hurt her. Perhaps she'd stumbled. I couldn't just leave her there. So I walked back to Carlucci's shop doorway.

She obviously didn't want me to see that she'd been crying, so I pretended not to notice. She lifted her head pertly and said, 'It was only a try-on, Patrick, to see if you really liked me. I was curious about you, that's all. But obviously, it's nothing to do with me. You just don't like girls at all.'

But the moonlight shone back at me from her brimming eyes. The next day she gave me the white feather.

It wasn't the first one and it wasn't the last – not by a long chalk. By the time conscription was brought in, I had quite a collection. Mother said that it was a disgrace – the hussies who stood on street corners handing them out would be better off at home, where God had always meant women to be. (Though who God thought was going to keep the country going if all the men were in the trenches and all the women at the kitchen sink, Mother didn't say.)

She said, 'Of course the country needs teachers. What would happen if all the teachers ran off and joined the Army? Where would we be then?' She never thought much of women teachers.

But nearly all the teachers at the school in Durban Street were women now, with the exception of the headmaster, who was nearly of retiring age, and Mr Symons, who could only see the blackboard if he put his face right up against it. I'd seen him marking children's work, with his face barely two inches above the blotted exercises.

It was a fine little school, relatively modern, bright and spacious. We didn't have to struggle with the problems that afflicted so many London schools. There were always a few children with the shaven heads that indicated treatment for lice. There were a few children (generally the same ones) wearing hand-me-down boots and no stockings. But that was only to be expected, even in a sturdily lower-middle-class area like Durban Street. Most of the children were well-clothed and well-fed.

Friends of mine that I'd trained with told horrifying tales of spending most of their salaries on boots and nourishing meals for their pupils. They had children whose development was so stunted by malnutrition that they would barely be capable of writing their name, no matter how long they stayed at school. They had girls who hardly ever attended class because there was always another baby to look after for worn-out mothers. They had children who were beaten and abused. There were epidemics of measles or diphtheria or scarlatina that carried off a quarter of the children in a

190

class. Then, of course, there were the immigrant children of Russians or Poles. They arrived knowing nothing of the English language or customs. Yet somehow, they often seemed to have an urge to get on that was missing in our own, home-grown slum children.

The school inspectors expected nothing of these schools and, because nothing was expected, nothing was achieved.

The classrooms of Durban Street Elementary smelled of carbolic and chalk and coke dust. In the winter they smelled of damp woollen gloves and scarves drying round the stoves and, faintly, of gas. They didn't smell of piss and river mud and unwashed clothes bought for pence from second-hand stalls.

I don't think I could have faced the day-to-day drudgery of teaching in Bermondsey or Limehouse or Whitechapel. Quite possibly, I needed shaking up a bit. Quite possibly I was becoming complacent, in my comfortable niche, although Miss Carey was doing her best to make it less comfortable.

Her campaign began with pointed remarks about healthy young men who shirked their duty and turned their backs on England in her hour of need. She carried it further by refusing to work in conjunction with me. Then she wouldn't even stay in the staff room if I was there. She'd put her head round the door and, if she saw me, would snort and slam the door shut. She was making life very uncomfortable for everyone and effectively disrupting the timetable. But the headmaster did nothing. I suspect he would have liked to have treated me the same way himself, but couldn't, because it would have been bad for discipline.

Finally, at assembly one morning, she presented me with a white feather in front of the whole school. Dried-up old spinster. Hell hath no fury like a noncombatant.

Mother said, 'I can't be expected to manage this

house by myself, without a man to so much as drive a nail in for me.'

Try telling that to the military tribunal.

On 2 March 1916, I was 'deemed to have enlisted under the Military Service Act' and nothing Mother could say or do was going to change that.

She tried, of course. When my call up papers arrived, she immediately applied for exemption, on the grounds that she already had three serving sons and that I was her sole support. In some places, she might have got away with it.

In Preston, I heard it said, senile decay seemed to set in at a very early age, so many owners of businesses were retiring and handing over to their sons, because one-man firms were often exempt. In Huntingdon, a tribunal member stepped down from the bench to argue for his own exemption, was granted it, and then reascended the bench to try other cases.

On the day I appeared before the tribunal, the chairman addressed us all before opening proceedings.

He looked round at us all from his chair behind a baize draped table and said, 'No matter what loopholes Parliament has left for shirkers, I am bound to ensure that none escape from their duty.'

I might as well have put on khaki there and then.

A self-employed chimney sweep was told to turn the business over to his wife and expect his papers within a fortnight. A conscientious objector was told he was fit only for the point of a German bayonet. Then there was the cinema producer.

'And what do you do?' asked a middle-aged lady member of the board.

'Everything from writing the scenario to superintending the production, ma'am,' he answered.

'Oh, I see,' she said with a smirk to the other members of the bench. 'You arrange for people to throw

192

each other into the river or to rub custard pies in each other's faces!'

'And for cars to be run over by railway engines,' added the chairman, chuckling. 'Work of the highest national importance, no doubt. You have fourteen days to arrange your business affairs. Next.'

Mother put up a good show, I'll say that for her. She wore her blackest black. Standing in that dusty town hall, with the sunlight that managed to filter through dirty windows catching every thread of silver in her hair, she fought for her last son.

'We're a family that's always done its duty. My husband died for his country, sir,' she said with simple dignity, 'and while he was alive he always encouraged our boys to know their place and do their duty.'

'And what did your late husband do, Mrs Snape?'

'He was a station master, sir, with London Midland, and he died on duty. He had an apoplexy right there on the platform, leaving me with four little boys to bring up on my own.'

'And a fine job you've done, I have no doubt. You have three sons already serving, I think?'

'Three sons have I given to my country, sir,' she pleaded. 'Three fine sons I haven't seen in two years. Patrick is the youngest and my sole support. He's always worked hard – he won a scholarship, sir – and now he's a teacher. He could have been promoted to a better school, he could be a headmaster one day if he wanted to, but he chose to stay with me, because I can't possibly do without him.'

'Very creditable, Mrs Snape.'

But Mother looked far too competent and formidable to get away with the 'poor little widow' act. She looked, with her upright stance and firm jaw, as though she were quite capable of beating the Kaiser over the head with her umbrella and chasing him all the way to Berlin. The three tribunal members put their heads together and then the chairman spoke.

'You have our sympathy, but is your case any different, Mrs Snape, from mothers whose only sons have been conscripted? What is worse – to lose the last son or the only one? No exemption.'

Well, it could have been worse. In fact, it was almost a relief to have things decided for me. Now there could be no tears or recriminations when I went. It was all taken out of our hands. My call up papers arrived two weeks later and by June I was in khaki. So that was that.

I was still in training when the big push on the Somme started. Seven days before that, the softening-up barrage began. Down in Shorncliffe, the ground seemed to pulsate day and night. We could feel it through the soles of our clumsy boots and in our diaphragms. The glass in every window shivered. Cups rattled in their saucers, slopping tea over the edge. The fire bell that stood on a ledge just inside the hut door gave a ghostly tinkle that kept us awake until we stuffed paper round the clapper.

It didn't take much imagination to realize that we were listening to the sound of men being blown to shreds. Whether their bodies were covered by khaki or field-grey, high explosives would have very much the same effect on the flesh underneath.

One of them was my brother William.

When the telegram came from Mother, I was wild with anger and hate. If I had met a German then, I would have been quite capable of tearing him limb from limb. Bayonet practice took on a new meaning. In, out, on to the next. In, out, on to the next.

My rage didn't last. I remembered the trophies William had brought home on his last leave. Little, pathetic, personal items. A badge. A regimental button.

A pipe. A wallet with photographs and a stained letter. I had parcelled them up and posted them to the address in the letter. I don't know whether they ever arrived. Post to Germany must have been non-existent. At least we tried to send those few remnants back to the thin, nervous-looking woman in the photograph. It was the least we could do. William had killed her husband.

I didn't tell anyone all that, of course. I wasn't totally naive. I just got on with the job of learning to be a soldier. And if I *was* going to be a soldier, I reasoned, then I might as well be a good one. So I decided to knuckle down, keep my ears open and my mouth shut.

The earth shook itself to pieces beneath our feet as we learned to strip down, clean and reassemble a Lee Enfield in less than no time. An army advanced in line of company, one hundred paces apart to certain death as we fumbled with our bayonets, learning to insert them without having to look.

'Don't look down,' screamed the sergeant, 'you'd soon find the hole if there was a fucking tart round it!'

We learned to charge, screaming obscenities, plunging with our unblooded bayonets, knowing that one day soon we'd be hanging like flies on a spider's web of wire long before our shiny bayonets could ever be used.

'You're slower than the second coming of Christ!' yelled the sergeant.

We weren't soldiers. We were conscripts, we were the lowest of the low, we were scum.

Then one day we were real soldiers.

And they sent us to Dublin to fill the gaps in a badly mauled regiment drawn out of the front line.

Three months later I was a sergeant and in the salient.

Two months later I was a sergeant major wearing the ribbon of the Military Medal.

Six weeks later I was a second lieutenant, the only

subaltern in the battalion who'd seen any active service at all.

I said that if I was going to be a soldier, I might as well be a good one. Didn't I?

The average life span of a subaltern in the trenches was six weeks, they said. Those fresh-faced eighteen-year-olds, who should have been in the last year at school and cramming for Oxford, arrived with their squeaky new boots and their tuck boxes and their blossoming moustaches, for all the world as though they were new boys at school again. They weren't the boys I had taught at Durban Street Elementary, but they were boys just the same.

They were so young, so keen, so beautiful. They even wore their tin hats at a rakish angle, as though defying school rules. But the penalty for breaking rules this time was worse than detention. It was permanent gating.

They stood on the fire-steps – any fire-step, any-where – watching the seconds tick by on their brand new wristwatches. The shrilling of whistles would come down the line, platoon by platoon. They would leap up, brandishing their revolvers, exhorting their men, and be blown to smithereens.

I wasn't that sort of second lieutenant. I was twenty-seven years old. The babies of the mess nicknamed me 'Teacher' or sometimes 'The Beak'. I was a ranker. Even just eight months of soldiering, eight months of surviving, gave me an edge over those cherubs.

They were even a little in awe of me. Strange how the flavour of chalk dust and powdered ink still seemed to hang around me. Away from the forward lines, I used to fill in the time by writing bad poetry (when I wasn't writing letters of sympathy to widows and mothers) and the boys left me in peace to scribble. Even the grinding of the portable Decca gramophone (it was impossible to get sufficient needles, so the records were gravelly in no time) didn't disturb me much.

I no longer think
  now, when I write.
The words are the same.
I fill in the blanks for number, rank and name.

Although I might
  have memories of the man
    I keep them to myself.

His mother does not need to know
  her son took so
    long to die,
      just yards from where we hid, that in the end
        I silenced his cries.

I will not share
  with his widow the glare
    of Very lights
      that turned her husband's livid skin pink,
        healthy again.

I no longer think
  now, when I write.
The words are the same.
I fill in the blanks for number, rank and name.

He was killed outright.
He died without pain.
I reach for another sheet and begin
  again.

Appalling, self-indulgent doggerel. But it kept me sane – as sane as anyone else, that is.

Harry Barclay said I was his lucky charm. He said that as long as he managed to keep next to me, he couldn't be hit. But when I slipped in the mud and the sniper's bullet that should have been for me took Harry's lower jaw off, the boys began to realize that you carry your own luck around with you.

Or you make your own luck. Just because I'd decided to be a good soldier didn't mean I was just waiting for whatever army life could fling at me. So I decided not to wait to step into any more dead men's shoes and I certainly wasn't going to wait for another man to step into mine. I volunteered for transfer to the Royal Flying Corps just before the Arras offensive of April 1917. Not long after that, the machine guns at Monchy-le-Preaux tore the battalion to pieces.

I had forty-eight hours at home before reporting for assessment and medical examination. Pretoria Avenue looked as it must have done since the day it was built – neat, introspective, constipated. A street of people who 'kept themselves to themselves' and were 'beholden to no one'. A cut above the working class, who were 'never off the top of the road'.

There were a few straggly daffodils blooming in pots on windowsills. A thrush sang from the top of a lilac heavily in bud by the gate to Number 32. I couldn't even remember what colour the lilac would be in a few weeks, though it had bloomed below my bedroom window every May since I was a boy.

I'd forgotten it was meant to be spring. There are no potted daffodils on the shattered windowsills of Château Thierry. There are no trees in Caterpillar Wood for thrushes to sing from in the green April twilight.

Mother was in the scullery, wearing the same old

wraparound pinafore, peeling potatoes. 'Patrick,' she said, 'Patrick.' Over and over again. 'Patrick.'

'Are you well, Mother?' I asked, stooping and giving her a kiss on her crumpled cheek.

She put down the knife and wiped her hands and took off her pinafore and patted her hair into place. It seemed much greyer than I remembered.

'Patrick,' she said again.

I'd forgotten how small the scullery was, how short the garden, no more than a drying green with the privy at the end and a little gate leading into the back lane. I didn't seem to be able to fit in. There seemed to be too much of me. My boots were too big. My hat had been tipped askew by the door lintel.

Mother took both my hands and held me at arm's length, looking carefully into my face. 'Don't they feed you in that Army, boy?' she asked. 'I always thought officers lived on the fat of the land, but you don't look like it to me. You've got quite scraggy. You sure you're all right, Patrick?'

'I'm fine. Don't worry about me. How are you?'

'You should have let me know,' she said, not answering my question. 'A mother has a right to know her son's comings and goings.'

'I barely knew myself, Mother, when I was going to get away.'

'Well, never mind, you're here now. That's all that matters. And Arthur's here too. Isn't it grand to have both of you together?' Then she hissed, 'And don't mention Phyllis to him, whatever you do.'

Arthur was in the kitchen, in Mother's usual chair by the range. He didn't realize I was there for a moment. His legs were spread and his forearms rested on his thighs, his big, red hands dangling. He was catnapping, like all soldiers learn very quickly to do, snatching any short moment of quiet, no way of knowing when the next one might be. He looked like every soldier I had ever met. I would not have known my brother, if I had passed by this sleeping man in a dugout. I would have moved on and let him sleep.

Then Mother bustled in. 'Arthur, here's Patrick. Isn't this a surprise?'

And the sleeping man with sergeant's stripes on his sleeve stood up, his eyes puffy with fatigue, his hair rumpled, and he was my big brother again.

'Patrick, this is splendid. How are you?' he asked, holding out his hand. Then he stopped, his hand frozen in its gesture of welcome and he eyed the single pip on my shoulder strap. 'Or should I salute you instead – sir?'

It hurt. Just for a moment, it hurt like hell. He was my brother, dammit. My hand faltered on the way to his, but I forced it on. I took his outstretched hand and shook it. 'You old fool,' I said and then we were in each other's arms.

'Don't do that,' Mother shrieked. 'Not when I've spent all yesterday delousing him.'

And she had me back out in the scullery, stripped naked and into a tub of scalding water and carbolic before she so much as put the kettle on for a cup of tea. My uniform went out the back door, carried at arm's length by Mother with the wash tongs.

'Officer or not, you've got nothing there I haven't seen before. Into that tub with you. And you're not having that uniform back,' she threatened, 'until the seams've all been pressed with a hot iron. Mrs Yates said her Henry swears it's the only way to deal with nits.'

I had changed so much and home had changed so little. Or had it? Mother was smaller, thinner, greyer. As well as the portraits – now four – of her sons in uniform, she had framed and put on the wall a highly-coloured memorial to William, outlined in black passe-partout. His photograph surmounted a parchment depicting Britannia at her sternest, her arm around a lumpish lion. 'Fallen on the Field of Honour' said the inscription in florid Gothic script. It made me very uncomfortable.

Mother saw me looking at it. 'I wrote to his officer, you know,' she said, 'asking if they could let me have a snap of his grave. When they had time, you know.'

'Mother, there wouldn't be any . . .'

I knew what Arthur was going to say and glared at him across the room, but he'd already thought better of it.

'. . . there wouldn't be time, not at the moment. Later perhaps, when things aren't so hot.'

'That's what he said. I had ever such a nice letter back, saying that "due to the exigencies of service" they didn't have time to photograph graves, but they'd do their best later on. Remind me to show you the letter after tea. He said such kind things about William.'

There was a nice bit of whiting, steamed between two plates over a pan of boiling water, for tea, with boiled potatoes and carrots, and a big dab of Colman's on the side – lovely.

'I'm only sorry I can't give you boys meat, not so much as a sausage,' Mother mourned, 'but this is a meatless day. Voluntary, of course, but I hope I'll always know where my duty lies.'

'Any bread, then, Mother?' asked Arthur.

'It's on the sideboard. Cut what you need and no more. I'm not putting cut slices on the table any more, whether any one wants them or not. That's wasteful.'

'Here – what's this?' Arthur paused with the bread knife in his hand. 'What colour d'you call this, then?'

'It's all that colour these days, Arthur love. There's been not a slice of white bread to be had for six months or more. You get used to it after a while.'

Arthur came back with a quarter loaf on his plate. 'Ever seen German bread, Patrick? Now that's an eye-opener. It's like eating a slice of grey blanket. And sausages like cardboard tubes stuffed with sawdust. I wonder they can fight at all, on muck like that.'

'It's those U-boats to blame, whatever they are,' remarked Mother with a sniff, 'trying to sink our ships. What kind of a way is that to fight a war, when their own Navy won't put to sea from Heligoland, or whatever you call it, at all? That's sneaky, that is.' She poured us all another cup of tea so strong that a fly could have walked across the surface and left its footprints. They were decent sized cups, kitchen cups, not the Paragonware she saved for visitors.

'But fair's fair, there's enough for all, if we abide by the rules. Not like some people I could name. There's hoarders where you least expect them. I'd send 'em to prison, the whole lot of them. D'you know, that Mr Norley from Ladysmith Avenue . . .' She stopped.

'No need to look like that, Mother, as though the cat got your tongue.' Arthur pushed back his chair and went over to the fire, groping on the mantelpiece for his pipe and tobacco. He took a spill from the spill vase where I used to keep my white feathers – none there now – and made a lot of fuss over filling and lighting and tamping down. When he came back, his eyes were very shiny. 'No need to act as though I've been bereaved. Phyllis got married, that's all.'

'Not a moment too soon,' muttered Mother darkly, 'if what I've heard is anything to go by.'

'Who . . . er . . . ?' I faltered.

'You wouldn't know him. The chemist in that row of new shops by the station. Pharmacist, he calls himself. Exempt conscription. I'd give him exempt, if I could get my hands on him,' she sneered and I remembered the woman who had fought to keep me safe at Durban

Street Elementary. 'There she is, four months married and as big as a house. I wonder she has the nerve to show her face in the street among decent people.'

'Let be, Mother, let be,' Arthur soothed.

Arthur and I walked down to the Coach and Horses that evening, but there was no one there we knew, so we soon came back again. There was no one to share it with, you see, no one who understood. There was no one who had seen the things we had seen or done the things we had done. There was only each other.

We sat for a little while, each buying his own pint. Because of the no-treating law, a husband couldn't even buy his own wife a drink, let alone brothers. There was no need to talk. It was a sort of companionship, that silence. We understood. No one else there did. Then we went home again.

'When did you last have any leave?' I asked Arthur as we went quietly upstairs.

'Six months ago.'

I went to bed in my narrow little room under the eaves and thought about Arthur's last leave six months ago. I thought about Phyllis with her camellia-striped frock and moist, pink lips. I thought about a frightened girl who only got out of date field service cards in answer to her frantic letters. I thought about the tremor in Arthur's fingers as he lit his pipe.

On the Monday I attended the medical board. I thought it was a mere formality, but I was wrong. The doctors were far more thorough than they had been when I was conscripted. Then they had only grasped my balls and told me to cough. (I never did discover what they hoped to find out from that!) They had lifted my feet as though I were a horse. They had sounded my chest. And that was that.

This time, as well as a more detailed heart examination, they made me see how long I could hold my breath. Something to do with having to fly at high altitudes without oxygen. I managed 47 seconds – that was quite good. Then I was told to sit on a typing chair and spun round – and round and round. When they'd finished, the doctors were supposed to check how long it took to stabilize my eye movements. There wasn't much point. I was so giddy, I almost fell off the chair.

I suppose every man likes to think that he is more or less perfect – not classically handsome, perhaps, or as plucky as Richard Hannay or as strong as Tarzan – but one does imagine that one is put together in the right order and functioning properly. I discovered I was not. The tests proved that I had less than perfect hand and eye coordination. Not bad enough to make a difference to writing on a blackboard. Not even bad enough to prevent my sticking a bayonet into a German's guts. But certainly bad enough to persuade the authorities that I was unlikely to make a pilot or even an air gunner. When it came to calculating deflections of shot, I'd be lucky to hit anything moving faster than a hangar!

They did their best. By this stage, they were desperate for flyers. They might even have overlooked my slight problem if I'd come from the right background, been made of the right stuff. After all, were aeroplanes very different from cavalry horses, when all's said and done? Even the Director General of Military Aeronautics said that flying was perhaps a little easier than riding because one sits in an armchair instead of a saddle!

Did I play any sport that required good reflexes? Not if I could help it. Did I shoot? Only Germans. Hunt? Not much chance of that in Pretoria Avenue. Pity. So when I joined 56 Sqn, it was as a desk pilot and not as a flyer.

'Bloody April' – that was what the RFC called the

month of the Battle of Arras. I'd seen war from the ground. From the air, it was pretty bad too. The myth of von Richthofen had something to do with that, but, brilliant pilot as he was, the man couldn't be everywhere at once, he couldn't be personally responsible for the massacre in the air that was taking place over Arras.

On 2nd April, von Richthofen scored his first double victory. The first luckless British pilot, making a low-level dash back to the safety of his own lines, went straight into the side of a house. The second was plucked right out of a British formation of nine machines, proving – if proof were needed – that the superior performance of the Albatros DIII offered virtual immunity from retaliation. It was a bad omen for the coming British air offensive.

Bad weather prevented much air activity on the first day of the battle, but on 5 April the RFC was in the air in swarms in their largely antiquated machines. It's beyond belief now that when such strides were being made in aerodynamics, we clung with such tenacity to outdated dinosaurs like the FE2b and the DH2 – the spinning incinerator – machines with 'pusher' engines rather than 'puller', machines that could take more than half an hour to get to any height worth talking about. Someone, somewhere, should answer for decisions that sent our men into the air with about as much chance of coming back again as a snowball in hell. I hope he fries, whoever he is, for all eternity.

On that morning of 5 April, six brand new Bristols of 48 Sqn went bouncing across the grass and began to gain height for their first patrol over the lines. Not one pilot or gunner had any operational experience of the Western Front, although they were led by a man who wore the deep crimson ribbon of the VC – Major Leefe Robinson, the man who shot down the first airship to fall on British soil.

They had been told that the Bristol had structural faults and was liable to break up if thrown around the sky. This was not true, but how were they to know? They were chary of sharp turns and steep dives, nervous of shearing the wings right off. The first time they were given a chance to test the plane was when five Albatros climbed up from Douai airfield to meet them. The leading Albatros was painted scarlet from spinner to tail.

Six Bristols went up. Two came back and one of those crashed on landing. Leefe Robinson spent the rest of the war in a German prison camp. The reputation of the Bristol took a further, undeserved knock and the type was held back at a critical time. By that evening, von Richthofen's *staffel* had claimed thirteen British victims.

On 6 April, a patrol of five FE2d's – the flying pianos – met a formation of slow German two-seater reconnaissance planes. Not one FE returned. The complete patrol had been destroyed by a machine not even designed as a fighter.

On 7 April, six Nieuports of 60 Sqn met von Richthofen. Two Nieuports were brought down and three were badly shot up. It was as easy – and as much fun – as pulling wings off a fly.

Altogether, between 4 and 8 April, 75 British machines were brought down and 105 airmen were killed, wounded or missing. At the same time, 56 planes were totally destroyed – mainly by inexperienced pilots, some with less than ten hours solo flying time – in flying accidents. This at a time when soldiers going over the top were being mown down by the thousand, but the ratio of casualties within such a tiny service was too high. The British public was horrified and alarmed by the air statistics.

The sky belonged to von Richthofen and his gaudy red circus. On 30 April, they attacked a patrol of seven

FE2d's guarded by three naval triplanes and brought down three. Six Bristols escorted by five triplanes were forced to abandon their flight. Then two out of eight FE2b's were downed and their photographic reconnaissance aborted.

The next day, von Richthofen went on leave. When he came back, things were very different.

I joined 56 Sqn just after the squadron arrived at Vert Galand. This time I was the new boy.

I'd forgotten that Officers' Messes like that ever existed. In fact, I probably never knew. I hadn't been an officer long enough. There was no such thing in the front line as a proper mess. We lived in dugouts, admittedly with soldier servants to bring hot water and tea in the morning, but in conditions little better than the men. When I thought about it, I realized that I'd never actually been in an Officers' Mess at all.

A lorry had picked me up in Arras, from the Hôtel de Commerce where I'd spent the night. If ever a woman goes to heaven, the proprietress of the Commerce ought to be there. That pinched, gallant little woman with the scrap of fur thrown always around her shoulders served daily miracles out of a kitchen shelled every night from the German trenches only 2500 yards away.

There were half a dozen of us, huddled in the back of the lorry with a litter of Wolseley valises. I'd been in France before. I knew what to expect. But the faces of the other five, all lads fresh from training, reflected their shock at the torn and featureless land. I don't know what they had expected, but it wasn't this sodden waste. I looked around at the five bright, young, scared faces and cynically calculated their survival time.

I knew, too, what the effect of a leather clutch soaked in castor oil, studded tyres at 60lbs pressure and cobbled roads could be on the backbone. I'd taken the precaution of bringing a cushion with me, but the others were jolted and bruised into breathless silence before we had travelled many miles.

Infinitely slowly, we ground along, routed by Military Policemen along seemingly pointless detours, our driver as taciturn and calm as the London bus driver he probably was. We dropped men off at the various airfields en route – Bellevue, Fienvillers, Beauquesne. By nightfall, when we turned off the road and through a farm, I was the only passenger left.

'Here you are, sir,' said the driver, ticking my name off his list. 'This is your squadron.'

The aerodrome, several miles behind the front line, was as rigidly regimented as a peacetime camp on Salisbury Plain. Around the airfield were canvas hangars: one a huge Bessoneau hangar, sagging and billowing in the squally rain; the others were portable hangars sheltering about three machines each. The aircraft were dispersed like this as protection against German bombing raids. The men were much more hierarchically organized.

The days of sleeping in barns and using aircraft wrecks as windbreaks were over. Vert Galand was neatly divided into the officers' compound and the other ranks' compound. In between were drab rows of Armstrong huts, neatly labelled according to the conventions of class: officers' kitchen and other ranks' cookhouse; officers' bathhouse and other ranks' ablutions hut. The airfield was totally isolated and self-contained, in the bleak, dead land between the war zone and the rest area.

There were cows grazing on the airfield. Chickens scattered as I carried my bags down the path. Whatever else, we were obviously going to eat better here than in the trenches. A smell of smoke came from the dying bonfire that had told returning pilots on which arm of the field to land. From the hangars came the glare of light and clank of tools, as fitters and riggers checked over machines that had just come in and would be needed again next day.

Somewhere in the muddle of huts I found the Officers' Mess. The ante-room was comfortably scruffy, with assorted easy chairs grouped round a pot-bellied stove and a half-sized billiard table at the opposite end. An upright piano stood in another corner. On a table with a wonky leg propped up by magazines, stood the inevitable Decca portable gramophone. A record had just finished and was still spinning with a crackling hiss, but the man asleep by the stove never stirred.

I had to knock twice before I could wake the orderly officer. It seemed a shame. I remembered well how rarely one could grab a few moments alone. Even when he did wake, he wasn't very talkative. Still half asleep, he led me along to a Nissen hut containing five beds and an empty space by the door.

'You can put your bed up there,' he said. 'I'll send an ack-emma along with your kit to put it up for you.'

And he went out. I sat down on one of the other beds and pulled out my cigarette case. Well, I had volunteered for this.

It was our joke that the only real elite of 56 Sqn were the musicians. Major Bloomfield, the squadron's dapper little ringmaster of a CO, had made a tour of London's orchestras and persuaded those men about to be conscripted that they should, in their own best interests, choose the RFC in general and 56 Sqn in particular. In a very short time, he had recruited the cream of London's theatres and concert halls. The squadron formed its own orchestra – well, why not? The army had its military bands.

Someone else in the squadron who loved music was Albert Ball, one of the flight commanders. Ball was an ace, a man who had survived since the early days of the war, but events were moving so fast, that even he was becoming a dinosaur. The old days of chivalrous combat, of pilot against pilot, of the knight errant roaming empty skies in search of adventure, had not lasted long. Now it was a simple matter of cunning and strategy, of manoeuvring the odds in one's favour, of maximum destruction for minimum loss. War wasn't fun any more. It was a bloody business that had to be wound up as soon as possible.

Albert Ball seemed to be unhappy in his role as a commander. He had always been a lone hunter, roving the skies, pouncing when and where he chose, now he was forced to be pack leader. When off duty, he spent much of his time in a little hut on the airfield, playing the violin and listening to scratchy records. Schubert's 'Unfinished' seemed to be his favourite. It's always been quite a favourite of mine too, even if it was written by a German!

I didn't seem to be able to settle into my new role. If it hadn't been such a crazy idea, I might even have thought I was missing the trenches. Ridiculous! Who could possibly miss the mud and the rats and the permanently peeling feet and the mind-dulling noise and the ghastly food and the smells and the ever-present fear of mutilation – and the comradeship? That was it, I suppose. From being someone, from being 'The Beak', from being the older man looked up to by the lads, I'd become less than nothing.

Not that anyone was actually rude to me. Far from it. They were all scrupulously polite. I'd more combat experience than most of them – I had the medal ribbons to prove it – and they respected me for that. But this was a different kind of war and I just wasn't part of it any longer.

No one actually raised his eyebrows if he saw me holding my knife in a different way from anyone else. No one actually smiled if I circulated the port the wrong way round the table – good God, we may have had an orchestra, but we hardly had a table, let alone port to circulate round it! And these irreverent lads were quite likely to put their boots on any table handy. Yet I didn't fit in.

They all had that indefinable public school grace, that long-legged, long-nosed, greyhound languor of the British upper classes. It's not arrogance – not really – because to be arrogant is deliberately to despise those more humble than oneself. This wasn't deliberate. They just . . . they just *knew* that I wasn't one of their sort.

I wasn't excluded on purpose. Perhaps if I'd been a flyer myself, I would have been less sensitive. I'd have become one of them by simply sharing their day to day danger. We'd have had a language in common. But, as a desk pilot *and* a scholarship boy from Pretoria Avenue, I was an outsider. I couldn't share their war. I couldn't share the frenetic speed of life that keyed them up to such mad pranks in off-duty hours.

Given a choice, I'd happily have built a little hut beside the runway, like Albert Ball, and spent my time listening to Schubert. Of course, looking back, I didn't help myself. I very soon became withdrawn and prickly. What had begun as a thoughtless exclusion on their part, very soon became deliberate avoidance on mine. And I'd only myself to blame.

I did my job. I did it well. But I was thinking very seriously of a transfer back to the infantry and the sort of life I understood. Only a stubborn determination not to be pushed out kept me at Vert Galand. It might have been better if I had gone.

I was in the squadron office one morning at the beginning of May, when a new pilot reported for duty. I heard the duty truck pull up outside the office with a grinding of gears. I made a note on the pad on my desk to check vehicle servicing records.

I've heard some people say that there really is such a thing as premonition. They say that there is a moment – the merest flaw in the perfection of time, the first hairline crack on the surface of an egg, no more – when one is warned. Other people say that we simply perform a kind of mental gear change, that we unconsciously shift a happening back from present to past and call it a premonition, or *déjà vu*, or something of that sort. It all sounds very suspect. I've always had a very healthy suspicion of mumbo jumbo.

All I can say is that, in the split second before the handle of the office door turned, I would gladly have been anywhere, rather than there. I couldn't try to explain it, or rationalize it, or even expect anyone else to believe a word I'm saying. It just happened. The dark corners of my mind were seared by an unexpected panic, as lightning imprints a view of the hidden landscape on the eyeballs long after the flash has passed.

Then the moment was gone and Archie Byatt opened the door and reported for duty. I looked into the clear water of his eyes and was lost.

Fear has as many faces as an actor and changes its costume as often. The dark has unnamed terrors for the child who lies rigid as a corpse with blankets clamped under his chin by stiffening fingers, just in case . . . Fear is just as terrible to that child as it is to the man whose bowels loosen as he waits to go over the top. There is mental fear and moral fear and physical fear . . . And then there is fear, not *of* something, but *for* something, or someone.

I would watch the flight of SE 5s bounce over the rutted grass pearly with mist, their engine note rising to a screaming roar as the end of the runway came up. I would watch them point their gaudy spinners to the sky and pull away, defenceless in the climb. I would watch them level out, heading for German lines, because the Germans rarely, if ever, crossed the front line. Still, at that height, I would persuade myself I could recognize the flaming grenade that Archie had painted on the fuselage of his machine.

'This time,' I would think, 'this time he won't be coming back.'

They might return to base quite quickly from an early patrol, then, mid-afternoon, the klaxon would rasp again and the pilots would jump up from their deck-chairs under the apple trees and run, dressing as they went. I would get up from my desk and watch them hurtle into the sun.

'This time,' I would think, 'this time . . .'

Perhaps, in the green, late spring twilight, they would be gone again, landing for the last time on a runway marked by a smoking flare path. Each time, one or more engines would be choking and stuttering, hacking like an old man's cough, streaming black smoke.

I would strain my eyes in the dusk to spot the flaming grenade as the machines throttled back to bump down, one after another, a gawky flight of ducks coming in to roost. The mechanics would run out, clumsy black shapes in the glare of the flares, to manhandle the machines off and clear the runway.

They didn't all come back. Too often, someone was missing. Too often, the flight commander would report that Jack had cooked, or that Frank had been spotted coaxing his plane down behind enemy lines, or that Ned had just disappeared. As recording officer, it was my job to turn their muddled and sometimes emotional reports into dry service language. Before they had washed or changed, while events were still as sharp as they could be in minds dazed by speed and danger, I'd listen to their view of events and transcribe it for officialdom.

'29 April 1917. Time 06.45,' I would write, 'Formation of Fokker triplanes observed locality 53QR5. Formation engaged with 1 in 5 tracer without success. Lt Barton observed on fire and spinning. Unable to follow down.'

And my spark of regret for Jack, Frank, or Ned would be extinguished by a fierce surge of relief – like a roaring of surf in my ears – that Archie had come back. This time.

The sense of anti-climax if the weather was bad was enormous. The Germans distinguished between *Flugwetter*, flying weather, and *Fliegerwetter*, flyer's weather. The latter meant low cloud, poor visibility and nothing to do – smoking, playing cards, writing letters, playing cricket. A strangely isolated patch of calm that somehow made the tension of the days before and after even worse.

And *Fliegerwetter* meant time, too, to think about the bone-splintering force of a powered dive into the earth, dislocating every joint in the body from its neighbour, leaving an unstrung puppet in a crushed shell. It meant thinking about fair young flesh crisping black, as the flames flared back in the slipstream. It meant remembering the suspicion of roasting meat that lurked beneath the smell of escaped fuel around a wreck.

Perhaps it was better never to have any time to remember, better to go on and on, answering the klaxon, never stopping to wonder.

On 7 May, eleven SE 5s took off for a routine patrol, climbing up and into a shimmering castle of high-piled

214

cumulus. I watched them disappear one by one into the shifting ramparts of cloud. I imagined them climbing, enfolded in the wet woolliness, eyes straining to catch a glimpse of anything at all beyond their misted goggles. I imagined them bursting out into the glittering air above, blinded by the icy brilliance, unable to tell for a vital moment whether the Huns were below or higher still.

Only five came back again. Captain Albert Ball, DSO and 2 bars, MC, soon-to-be VC, was one of the six who were never seen again.

The survivors were very subdued in the mess that night. No one seemed to want to talk about what had happened. The debriefing had been short and specific – they had come out of the cloud and spotted six enemy machines below. Our flight had dived into the attack, but the Germans had been flying in a stacked formation. As our pilots had engaged the visible enemy, a higher layer of Germans had attacked in turn. These had been the scarlet Albatros DIIIs of Richthofen's Circus. Ball had dived after one plane, into a bank of cloud. He never came out the other side. No one was in the mood that night to elaborate on the simple story.

At Durban Street Elementary, any boys I caught fighting could expect detention – not a flogging, not from me – and a poem or a string of dates or the 16 times table to learn. I never approved of fighting, but I did at least understand it, just. What I could never abide were the boys – and there were always some – who delighted in tying squibs to cats' tails or picking the wings and legs off flies. They disgusted me. I wanted to lash out, to hurt them so that they understood just what pain was all about. I had the power. I had the right to punish them. And I was disgusted with myself at the very idea that I might use my superior power and strength in that way.

When I first joined 56 Sqn, I had viewed the pilots in much the same way as the squalid little boys in the corner of the playground pulling a butterfly to pieces. There was something so inhuman in the way they would talk about downing machines, as though the thought that there might be a man at the controls never even crossed their minds. It was a game, with its own complicated sequence of steps, its own rules, and you totted up scores, just like in a playground.

I had killed men in the trenches. Of course I had, or I wouldn't have survived myself. But they had always been men to me. They had not been disguised under the label 'Jerry' or 'Boche' or 'Hun'. They had been men who would kill me if I didn't kill first. Like fighting in the playground.

But the pilots who said, 'I brought down an Albatros today,' (or a Fokker or a Halberstadt) never said, 'I killed a man today'.

I didn't understand, not at first, that if they acknowledged a man had died in the flaming wreckage spinning down, scattering charred debris into trenches on both sides of the divide, then they acknowledged their own mortality. Later, I understood.

Time changed my ideas. Time and the fact that the face of combat changed. The war had gone on long enough. Both sides were sick of it, sick to death. It had swallowed up the young and idealistic and eager and had spat out their bones. Our armies were incapable of ending the struggle. They had ground each other into the mud. If picking the wings off flies made of wood and wire and canvas was going to help finish it off, then the sooner the better.

Archie was very good at the game. Major Bloomfield described him as a born killer.

'He's more than a good flyer,' he remarked one evening as we watched the SEs bump in for the night. 'In fact, he's not even the best flyer we've got – just a bit better than adequate. But he's got what the others lack – the killer instinct. Ball was a hunter, but Archie Byatt is a predator. There's a difference, Patrick.'

He didn't look like one – not at first sight, that is – but appearances are so very deceptive. When you first looked at him, you only saw how short he was, how stocky, how thick-shouldered. Then you looked again and saw how well-tuned his body was, how honed, how obedient, how efficient. When other men in the mess were looking gaunt with the strain of months of active service, Archie seemed to glow. There was a bloom of health on him. His hands didn't shake, there were no shadows under his eyes, he didn't snap for no apparent reason. When two, three, sometimes more, operations a day took a terrible toll of his friends, Archie ripened like fruit on a south-facing wall.

'The trouble with you lot,' he said one night after dinner, 'is that you forget that Jerry must feel just as knackered as you do. You go up there expecting to meet someone who's fresher, better fed and a whole lot fitter than you. You expect to catch it – so of course you *do* catch it. But who says they're any better off than we are? They're only men, after all. Why shouldn't we be able to knock 'em down – just like tin cans on a wall?'

He imitated a small boy with a catapult. It was a chilling little gesture.

'All very well for you, Archie,' said 'Bloomer' Rose. 'You don't know what it's like to be shot up. I only just made it back last Thursday. The tank was riddled – fuel everywhere. A bit of a spark in the wrong place and I'd've been a grilled cutlet.'

'But I won't be,' said Archie and his smile sent shivers down my back, 'because I'm invulnerable.'

'Absolute bally rot!' shouted someone over the top of the piano.

'Balls!' roared Bob Hicks.

'How do you know?' Major Bloomfield challenged. 'What makes you so bloody special?'

'Sometimes one just knows things.' Archie made several attempts at striking a damp match and lit a cigarette. He dragged deeply, then looked round at his audience with that rapacious grin of his. 'I don't need to watch my back, because I know there's no one there. So I can concentrate on killing the chap in front of me. If I'm close enough when I fire, he'll fall out of the sky. It's as simple as that.'

Someone – I don't know who it was – threw a cushion then, hitting Archie square in the face. Archie threw it back and all hell broke loose. In the middle was a tight scrum of bodies, tussling, yelling and heaving like a family of inexpert young lions with their first kill. Around the edge, less violent spirits pummelled each other with more cushions, magazines, boots, anything they could lay their hands on. 'Bloomer' turned a soda siphon on the whole lot. A brace of the mess dogs yapped and snarled, nipping any ankle within range. When someone picked up a poker, I turned to Major Bloomfield for guidance.

'Leave them,' he said and pushed me out of the room, shutting the door behind us.

In his hut, the CO poured two stiff glasses of whisky and passed one to me. 'If they didn't let off steam sometimes,' he said, 'they'd all go mad. Better a few black eyes tomorrow than cracking up on patrol the day after.'

'But someone's going to get hurt,' I protested.

'Don't you believe it, Patrick. They're not trying to hurt each other. It's a sort of mass madness that comes over them all every month or so. Last time, there was a raid on the squadron over at Fienvillers. That one ended when someone dropped cigarette tins filled with petrol down the mess chimney. But no one ever gets hurt. That's not the point of it, you see.'

'I see,' I answered, but I didn't. No one in the trenches ever had time to scrag the next door regiment. We were too busy being scragged by the enemy.

'And if you don't understand now, you will soon.'

The CO had a rare gift of common sense. He knew when to look the other way. I relaxed a bit and sipped my whisky.

'Anyway, young Byatt asked for it,' Major Bloomfield went on, 'making bloody stupid remarks like that. I didn't have him down for such a buffoon. Invulnerable!' He snorted derisively. 'What d'you make of a fairy tale like that? What made him dream that one up?'

'Not sure, sir,' I muttered noncommitally.

But I had looked across the room into Archie's queer, colourless eyes – and I believed him.

'Game for a spot of Hun-sticking?' Archie asked, two or three evenings later.

'What's that?' I queried, looking up from my book.

'Just thought it's time you got a closer look at our sausage-eating brothers, that's all.'

'If it doesn't sound too much like boasting,' I said acidly, 'I've been a damn sight closer to the enemy than any man in this mess. And I don't have much of an urge to go out and look for more.'

'All right, all right, no offence meant. It just gets so bloody boring in this dump, night after night. Thought we might go up for a bit of a burn-up.'

When Archie was in this sort of mood, he plagued the life out of anyone unlucky enough to be around. No wonder the ante-room had emptied so suddenly. I ought to have seen it coming.

'Go and check your ammunition canisters for tomorrow.'

'I've done that – three standard, tracer, Pomeroy.'

'I thought you said you wanted to have the Lewis gun mounting altered?'

'Done that.'

'Can't you find someone nearer your own age to play with?'

'No one else wants to play my game,' he laughed, 'it's too dangerous. But you'll come, won't you, Patrick? I know *you* won't let me disappear over German lines all by myself. Will you?'

If it had been anyone else but Archie, I'd have said he'd been drinking. There was a wild glitter in his pale eyes. They sparkled like newly-washed pebbles, before the breeze dries them to dullness again. His lips were colourless as his cheeks, with two harsh lines boldly linking nose and mouth, lines that had not been there when he had joined the squadron.

He was taut with excitement, twanging like a bow string, pacing round the room picking up and putting down. He looked drunk, but knowing Archie, he wasn't. He never seemed to need the stimulus of alcohol. Danger was a drug to him and that made him a danger to the rest of us.

Marking the page, I put my book down. I wasn't at all sure I'd ever be back to finish it.

There was just enough light left in the sky to take off, but the ground was black beneath us as we slowly climbed and wheeled towards Douai. It was like travelling in a packing case. I began to understand why the FE2b was regarded with such scorn and called the 'flying piano'. Up there in the last light, it was as though the earth had disappeared altogether. The sun still outlined the edges of fantastic cloud formations.

The dark earth had vanished completely. At 10,000 feet, it was bitterly cold.

Archie had outlined his crazy plan as we were getting ready to take off. The dressing hut, brightly lit for the dawn patrols, had been nearly in darkness. Archie could dress like lightning. I fumbled awkwardly with silk underwear followed by loose woollen underwear. Then came a cellular vest, a silk shirt and a khaki woollen one, two woollen jerseys, all topped with a lambswool-lined Sidcot suit. I was stifling. Archie only laughed. There were thigh boots and gauntlet gloves, both lined with muskrat fur. A silk scarf round the neck. It was more than I could bear on a warm summer evening.

Archie pushed forward a buff-coloured form each and an indelible pencil. 'FS20,' he said. 'Got to keep to the rules. "Date. Time. Pilot's name. Thigh boots, fur-lined, gauntlets, fur-lined, goggles with triplex glasses, Sidcot suit and oversleeves. These are the property of the public. Losses due to the exigencies of campaign must be certified by the officer commanding."'

Archie signed both forms with a flourish: Charlie Chaplin; Douglas Fairbanks. I wonder which of us was which?

Where his waist ought to have been, Archie buckled a belt with a revolver holster.

'What's that for?' I asked naively. 'Shooting moles on the runway?'

'If we're a flamer – ' Archie paused while he flipped open the Webley and checked the ammunition, ' – I'll use it on you first. Nothing personal,' he laughed, looking at my scandalized face. 'I'll shoot myself next. If I miss, or I'm hit and can't shoot you – ' He pulled the belt a notch tighter, ' – then jump.'

I started to protest, my tongue tripping over itself in shock.

'I mean it!' Archie rapped, then switched on his blaze of a smile. 'But don't worry. I won't let it happen to us.'

As a final touch, we smeared our faces with whale oil, pulled on balaclava helmets and the Nuchwang dogskin face masks. We rolled onto the airfield like a pair of drunken sailors in our cumbersome kit.

'Aren't these men going to get into serious trouble?' I asked, indicating the fitter and rigger who stood by the FE2b.

'You're the senior officer,' Archie replied coolly.

We climbed up and slid into the seats. Behind me, Archie checked the machine with the absorbed air of a butler checking a dining table for an out of place fork.

Rudder bar? Throttle? Emergency fuel hand pump? An eye check of the rigging. Dashboard gauges – oil pressure, radiator temperature. Compass free? Height indicator zero? Lateral indicator bubble central?

It all took seconds rather than minutes.

Under his seat I knew Archie had the standard prisoner of war haversack containing pyjamas, underwear, shaving tackle, toothbrush and cigarettes. I didn't have one. The thought wasn't comforting.

'Ready, sir?'

'Ready.'

'Switch off, sir?'

Archie's hand went to the air intake. 'Switch off.'

'Suck in, sir?'

Archie switched on the fuel. 'Suck in.'

The mechanic had turned the propellor and there was a clonking noise as the rich fuel mixture flooded the cylinders. The mechanics all seemed to know by instinct when they had the precise required ratio of fuel to air.

'Contact, sir?'

'Contact.'

Archie had flicked on the air intake, tuned the fine

222

adjustment lever and opened the throttle halfway as the mechanic swung the propellor hard in a clockwise direction. There had been a roar and a gale of blue smoke. Archie had adjusted the revs – if we were to be stopped, that was the moment, the noise had splintered the night air. There had been a mechanic on each wing tip and one sprawled across the fuselage, countering the natural lift as the revs had risen.

Archie had given a side to side wave and the chocks had been withdrawn. A mechanic had checked the runway, saluted to indicate it was clear, Archie had given a fore and aft wave and we had taxied down the bumpy field.

His plan had sounded certifiable in the dressing hut. Now, we were heading for the front line and I knew we must both be utterly crazy. Alone in the front seat, with my nose streaming in the icy wind and my feet already completely numb, I could feel the thrum of the rear engine pushing us on further towards German lines. Short of jumping, there was no way of escape.

I looked backward, seeking some comfort in my loneliness. Archie wasn't looking. His eyes scanned the darkening sky. His head swivelled to port and starboard, above, behind and below, never fixing on anything, a ceaseless vigilance. I saw what he was then – a natural fighting man. If he *were* invulnerable, it was his own skill that kept him that way. Archie would never be taken by surprise. He would never relax his guard in the sky. It was his element. It was up to other men to show weakness and when they did – Archie would be waiting for them.

We were crossing the lines now. The land was black beneath a violet sky. The scarred, churned earth was invisible, but I could track the twisting of the trench-lines by the dotting of hurricane lamps at strategic corners. No barrage tonight, no savage slashes of light searing the sky like earthbound lightning. The poor buggers below were getting a chance to snatch some sleep.

Somewhere down there a wirecutting party might be belly crawling across no-man's-land, cringing at every sound, anticipating the limelight glare of the Very light, the crack of sniper fire. Somewhere down there a man might lie waist deep in a flooded shell hole, his blind eyes unable to distinguish night from day. From the cold emptiness of the sky, it looked so domesticated. So cosy.

Half an hour into the flight now and the icy numbness that had started in my feet had spread up my legs and round my kidneys. Yet there was sweat on my forehead. Beneath my facemask, my skin was sticky and unbearably tickly.

I leaned over the side and lost overboard the omelette I had eaten two hours earlier. I felt better after that.

Someone told me once, that all the unburied, rotting corpses in no-man's-land give off a luminous gleam at night like giant fireflies. He said you could map-read by them. When I told him that was a load of bollocks, he swore that pilots could navigate by the glow. It's not true.

Archie poked me in the back and pointed downwards. A prickle of lights in a familiar pattern told me we were above an airfield. There was no way I could tell if it was Douai or not. For all I knew, we could have been travelling in a circle and arrived back where we started. Archie throttled back and, as we swooped low enough to make a positive identification, he cut the engine altogether and glided in.

After the noise of the motor, the silence was a positive thing. There was only the harping of the rigging and the soughing of a bitter wind past my ears. As we plummeted to the earth, I felt my gorge rise. I was

224

paralysed, pinned to my seat by the stresses of the dive. The selection board had been right. I would never have made a pilot, not if it meant hurtling, powerless, towards the ground like this.

Just as I thought we would never pull out, when I thought we must plough into the ground, there was a clattering roar as Archie restarted the engine. The first the Germans could have known of our arrival was the growl of our throttle opening 150 feet above the runway.

We skimmed the grass, heading straight for the hangars. I hurled the first bomb over, with more enthusiasm than accuracy. It exploded with a searing blast that rocked our machine. I think it holed the runway, but couldn't be sure. Then Archie banked sharply for another bomb run.

In a funny sort of way, the searchlights that suddenly sliced through the dark actually helped us. The beams criss-crossed the airfield, pinpointing targets I had been unable to see before. The next bomb was more effective and caught a hangar, but the blast nearly blew us apart.

The smoke snatched at my throat and sent me into a spasm of coughing. Above that, above the crackle of fire, above the yelling from below and the rattle of rifle fire, I could hear Archie's crazy, joyous laugh.

His excitement caught me up in a sort of madness. I was laughing too as I lobbed the next bomb straight into the cockpit of an Albatros parked by the runway. It burst into flames. The draught of our low pass whirled the flames across the gap and the neighbouring machine caught fire.

The ground was swarming with tiny figures. They came tumbling out of the mess and the dining hall and the huts. Bullets twanged through our rigging and ripped through the fabric of our wings, but, amazingly, they seemed to miss anything vital. We were so low, it was like flying through a swarm of bees. Then they set up a Spandau and things began to look serious.

I fired off the first canister from the Lewis gun mounted on the nacelle. The thin white fingers of tracer could have shown me how hopelessly inaccurate my fire was, but I didn't have time to look. I hurled the empty drum overboard and snatched the next. Half standing in the cockpit, lurching with every turn of the machine, I wrestled with the second ammunition drum. My nails were broken and the skin torn from my hands. There were steamers of linen fluttering back from our riddled wings.

I fitted the second drum and swung the Lewis on its awkward right-angled mounting to bear on the Spandau crew. I let off a wild spray of bullets. I don't know if I hit anyone – probably not – but figures dashed off in every direction like rabbits at harvest and I was the grim reaper.

But with less than half the drum shot off, the Lewis overheated and jammed. Hanging onto the gun with one hand, while the aircraft bucked and jinked over the field, I groped in the cockpit for the 2½lb lump hammer in its mounting by my right hand. I gave the Lewis a couple of hefty thumps, but it wouldn't clear.

I slipped down into my seat and signalled to Archie to get the hell out! Archie kicked the rudder bar frantically, but the machine wouldn't answer. I could hear him swearing, yelling blind, meaningless obscenities. He put on full bank and slowly, slowly we began to crab round, gaining height with pitiful slowness. The engine was coughing in spasms and a spray of water was hissing from the radiator. Mixed with the smell of steam was the acrid taste of hot fuel.

The flare path at Vert Galand was lit for us. As Archie throttled back, the engine was surging and dying, vibrating the fabric along its full length. Gently, gently, he coaxed it down from the sky, with hands as soft as a lover. My own hands were gripping the edge of the cockpit with a dead man's grip. The sweat trapped under my clothes during the fight had frozen at high altitude and I was shivering uncontrollably.

Only three men had watched our take-off. Now it looked as though the whole squadron was out to watch us limp in. Behind the smoky glare of the flares, their figures were massed black.

The FE2 lurched across the grass and we both swung out as it halted before the hangars. Archie pushed up his goggles. Two white circles stared out of an oil-blackened face. His thin lips parted in a dazzling smile. He pulsated with life and vigour. He glittered with excitement and exhilaration. I felt sick.

'Looks as though we'll be picking up the kitty this week for the most bullet holes,' he laughed and his voice cracked on it.

Archie put his arm round my shoulders and we walked across the airfield to a bollocking from Major Bloomfield.

If you really believe something, is it possible to make it happen? Archie really believed in his invulnerability. He didn't try to explain it, just said he 'knew' it. In the sky – paying no attention to the possibility of a German catching him from behind, and on the ground – hurtling his powerful Douglas motorcycle along rutted French roads, he acted as though he had a charmed life.

And soon other men began to believe too. They said, 'Keep close to Archie, if you want to avoid a Hun on your tail.' They used to rub their hands for luck on his machine, some surreptitiously, some quite openly, before taking off.

Remembering poor little Harry Barclay and his shattered jaw, I had my doubts about lucky charms, but I kept my mouth shut. What's the point of smashing another man's confidence? What's clever about that? Where's the satisfaction in saying 'I told you so'?

And anyway, it just might have been true. Who can say? All I could do, counting the planes out and counting them back, was to hope that Archie's instincts were right. And soon the legend of Archie Byatt became part of the folklore of the squadron.

Just when it looked as though some of our boys couldn't take any more, the squadron was moved back to England. Our SE 5s were to be fitted with the new 200 hp Hispano-Suiza in place of our old 150 hp engines. And life in England made a pleasant change from the more primitive conditions of a front-line aerodrome.

I suppose I could have gone to see Mother in the few days leave we were offered. I ought to have gone to see Mother. But Archie persuaded me to go with him to visit an old schoolfriend who lived down in Hampshire.

'Used to be in my house at Charterhouse – dim little bugger, if I remember rightly, but quite jolly. Left an arm behind at Loos – awfully careless, what? Let's go and cheer him up.'

I didn't want to go. Archie's every phrase emphasized my feeling of inferiority. *In my house at Charterhouse*. I had nothing in common with Archie's past. We shared the present. We would share – God willing – a future of some sort. But his past was not mine and I wanted nothing to do with it.

But if Archie wanted me to do anything, anything at all – bomb Douai airfield single-handed – I would have a go. It wasn't asking so very much to expect me to accompany him to Hampshire to cheer up a wounded schoolfriend. So I never told Mother I'd had a spot of leave. And when it was over, I was too busy getting the squadron organized to return to France to get over to see her, so I never told her I'd been back in England at all.

Charley Frampton, Archie's schoolfriend, lived in a splendid pile just where the New Forest grows down to the Solent. He was very young, younger than Archie, who in turn was quite a bit younger than me. He had the sort of sturdy, healthy, outdoor looks that run to fat and red complexions in middle age. But at that moment, Charley Frampton didn't look healthy.

Archie introduced us and I automatically held out my right hand. Charley just looked at it.

'No use expecting Charley to do anything with that,' Archie chuckled.

It was so embarrassing. I had quite forgotten. His empty right sleeve was not folded up, but just neatly tucked into his pocket. One had to look twice to spot that the sleeve was empty at all.

I started to stammer an apology, but ran out of words. What does one say? Jolly bad luck? Or does one offer the left hand as an alternative, like a Boy Scout?

'Never you mind,' said Archie, putting an arm around my shoulders and squeezing. I would rather he had not done that in public. 'Charley doesn't mind. He's used to it. Aren't you, Charley?'

'Do I have a choice?' asked Charley bitterly.

I must say, Charley's mother was very decent. She made us both very welcome. The salmon we had for lunch was not tinned, but came straight out of the Avon. I don't suppose my mother ever realized that salmon came from English rivers rather than ready-packed from a Canadian cannery.

As Mrs Frampton neatly lifted portions from the bone, I could almost hear Mother's voice. 'Would you look at all that skin and bone! Oh, I couldn't be doing with that. What a fiddle!'

I wasn't all that keen on Mr Frampton, though. He had a way of looking across the table, first at Archie, then at me, from snapping grey eyes beneath shaggy brows. I knew what he was thinking. His very look demeaned us. I felt defiled. I wanted to stand up and shout. I despised his blind prejudice, his crassness. What did he know? How *could* he know?

If I had been Mr Frampton, I'd have stopped fussing about Archie and me and worried a bit more about my son. Anyone who needs to drink brandy after lunch, has a problem. Anyone who is still drinking brandy by teatime on a sweltering June afternoon, has a very serious problem.

I'm not saying Charley was drunk. Far from it. Given the amount he drank, he ought to have been. I'd have been under the table long before. But then, I haven't a head for alcohol. How could I have, growing up in the sort of low-church household where even too deep a gulp of communion wine was condemned over the Sunday dinner table? But Charley Frampton drank with a sort of steady determination. By the time his family joined us on the lawn for tea he was becoming truculent.

If I had ever imagined an upper-class family, it would have been just like the Framptons. We sat under an old cedar tree in a garden that smelled of newly-cut grass and roses, sharpened with a tang of salt. Long fingers of shadow touched the front edge of the terrace, but the upper windows still glittered in dying sunlight. If I turned my head the other way, I could see the whale-backed hump of the Isle of Wight and could only hear the invisible water that lay between us and it. It was all so peaceful, so perfect. I thought that Buckholt was the most beautiful house I had ever seen.

They were all so *nice* to each other – none of the

abrasiveness of my mother or the heavy-handed teasing that my brothers called wit.

No one said, 'Eat up, you're at your auntie's!' or 'Don't hold back, it's all paid for!'

On the other hand, there was none of the fussing with cake forks and tiny napkins – I'd stopped calling them serviettes – that seemed to dull all the pleasure of having visitors at Pretoria Avenue. The Framptons just got on with eating and talking and enjoying themselves. If Mrs Frampton wanted to laugh with her mouth full of sandwich cake – she did. Perhaps that's the difference – the middle classes worry about doing the right thing, the upper classes simply know that they are right.

I envied Charley, in a way. Of course, he had been horribly mutilated, but he belonged to such a close-knit, happy family. There seemed to be none of the stresses and strains of my own family, of wondering if one had done the right thing, or said the wrong thing. At Buckholt, everyone was so relaxed.

There was a sister, Viola, who, although widowed, had a sweet and gentle smile. Charley's aunt was there too, the wife of his father's brother. She – Helen was her name – was a classical goddess, a silver and white beauty with a voice that could call back souls from hell. There was a dear little infant stumbling around. She managed to climb up onto my knee and chattered away to me, unintelligibly but quite happily. Archie gave me a very sarcastic grimace, but actually, I rather liked it. She was a sweet little thing. Mrs Frampton was witty and charming and always seemed to know exactly the right thing to say to put one at one's ease. Yes, I rather envied Charley.

I wasn't too keen on Charley's father though. And he wasn't too keen on us either. He managed to wedge his chair between Archie's and mine. Archie said later that he thought the old ogre ought to have been grateful to us for coming to cheer up his son.

'What're you going to do when the war's over?' Charley asked.

The shade under the cedar was no deeper now than the shadow over the whole garden. The distant island had merged with a violet sky. The chittering, high-wheeling swallows were gone and two or three bats swooped on wings of crumpled black tissue paper. The smells of the evening were piercingly sweet. The war seemed further away than the three-quarters moon that was rising as red as a sun.

So when Charley asked, 'What're you going to do when the war's over?', the question was an intrusion. I didn't want to do anything other than what I was doing right at that moment. I didn't want to talk. I didn't want to think about the war. I didn't want to think at all. I just wanted to be.

Archie stretched lazily. 'What makes you think it's going to end at all?'

'But it must – surely.'

'I think we'll just go on getting better and better at it,' said Archie, 'and the better we all get, the more impossible it'll be to finish. Because each side will be too strong for the other to beat, don't you see. Neither side will be weak enough to lose or strong enough to win. It could just go on and on.'

'That's a terrible thought,' I said slowly, irritated at having been dragged out of my dream.

'It's happening already. You must have noticed. The weak ones are being weeded out . . .'

'Like me, you mean,' interrupted Charley.

'. . . and soon only the strong will be left.'

'Like you.'

'Like me,' Archie confirmed. 'I'm getting very good at war. It suits me. I'm not sure I'd know what to do with myself in peace. Maybe I'll go off and be a mercenary somewhere – Russia or Ireland – anywhere they'll have me. I'm not fussy where.'

It was like a betrayal. I felt as though Archie had swung one of his gleaming brown riding boots into my belly. He knew – for Christ's sake – he knew I wasn't a natural fighting man. He knew that I, like Charley, was one of the weak ones who would eventually be picked off. I'd been lucky so far, but, according to Archie's theory, my luck wouldn't last. He didn't really care.

'And what about you, Patrick old man?' Archie lounged back in the battered basket chair and deposited his legs across my lap. They were heavy, deliberately so. The backs of my thighs were pinched against my own chair. Even Charley raised his eyebrows. I saw him. 'What're you going to do in the Great Peace – if it comes? Go back to teaching snotty-nosed brats how to go forth and multiply?'

Charley giggled. Archie giggled. I made a positive effort to keep my voice neutral as I replied.

'Maybe. I don't know. I thought . . . perhaps . . . I might try a spot of writing . . . perhaps . . .'

'Oh yes, yes,' gurgled Archie. 'I can just see you as a poet in a soft shirt and a corduroy suit. A Panama hat. No – no hat and flowing locks like Tennyson. Very you.' He threw back his head and declaimed in a high, nasal, mocking voice,

> 'Green is the colour of
>   grass and
>   fern that shimmers,
>   frond and feather in a silken stream.

> *Green is the colour of*
> > *gas and*
> > > *slime that slithers,*
> > > > *froth and foam in a seething steam.*

> *Green is the . . .'*

'You bastard!' I had been silent, stricken, dumb with treachery. I hurled Archie's boots off my lap and when I stood up the chair toppled backwards. Archie just laughed. 'You've been through my papers. You . . .'

I could have hit him. He sat in the chair, laughing, laughing and Charley laughed too. I could have hit him. I wanted to split his wide, laughing mouth. I wanted to smash his perfect, grinning teeth.

But of course, I didn't. I wouldn't. That wasn't me.

But I wanted to.

'You bastard!' I spat again, but they could tell the fight had gone out of me.

I walked down the garden, into the dark. I walked to where the garden faded into the shore. The pebbles were awkward under my stiff, high boots and I stumbled, setting a fall of shingle off to the water. The weed and water smelled very clean. The scents of the garden cloyed in comparison. I lit a cigarette and dragged hard on it.

I would have liked to weep. I wanted to howl out my grief and rage. It might have eased so many things. But I didn't know how to do it. I'd never had enough practice, even as a child.

Big boys don't cry.

That's a brave little man.

So I didn't even know how to begin.

At that moment, I had a choice. I could have walked away. I could have turned my back and walked away. I could have slipped off into the darkness, alone, and no

234

one would even have noticed I had gone. The choice was mine.

There was a sliding of stones behind me. I didn't want to turn round. I didn't want to look at him. I took another long draw on the cigarette, then threw it into the water. It curved like a tiny Very light and spluttered out.

'Patrick?' he said softly.

And I turned and went back to him.

EGLANTINE

The Enthusiast

Clemmie blamed me for everything. That was unjust. No, dammit, it was totally unfair. And it was typical of her that she didn't accuse me straight off, as any normal person with a grudge might do, but waited ages before winging in to attack with all the venom of a wasp.

It was *my* fault because I introduced Cassandra into the house. What nonsense! It was *my* fault because I didn't run and warn the family that Helen intended to take off with another man. Am I my niece's keeper? And – and she really was scraping the barrel this time – it was irrefutably *my* fault because I had encouraged poor besotted Michael in his courtship of Helen. How *utterly* absurd!

On second thoughts, Clemmie wasn't so much a wasp as a gadfly. Attacking again and again, never successfully beaten off, and stinging, stinging, stinging.

'I know what you're trying to do,' I countered on one occasion, when only good manners had led her to offer me tea. 'You're trying to drive me off. You're trying to make me so uncomfortable by your petty hostility, that I'll fly off on my broomstick, swearing never to return.'

'What an extraordinary idea!' she returned pettishly.

'Yes, isn't it, because it's not going to work. Hermione is my great-niece and I insist on being allowed to see her as often as I choose.'

'No one's stopping you, but are you being sensible – or just emotional? You think you're being kind to her, but you're not, you know. You *will* talk to her about her mother and all you do is confuse her. That poor muddled little mind.'

'Muddled, my foot!' That really annoyed me. 'That child is as sharp as a razor. Did you know she can read? No, I didn't think you did. Of course, one doesn't know what she makes of the page, because she won't speak, but watch her eyes, next time you see her with a book. She's reading, all right. So let's have no more talk of "muddled".'

When Clemmie's annoyed, she fidgets. This time, she riffled through the pages of *Queen* and tossed it aside with an exclamation of disgust. She stood up and kicked the logs in the grate with the tip of a grey lizard-skin shoe. (Clemmie has always been very particular about her shoes – she's so proud of her tiny feet. I'm wickedly envious.) She crossed the room and twitched the folds of the long, plum-coloured brocade curtains.

'I must speak to Ant about decorating this room,' she murmured. 'It's too awful. No really, Eglantine, you force me to be blunt. Your visits are too upsetting for Hermione. You have no idea how difficult it is to settle her after you've been. After your last visit, Nanny complained to me that the child was as high as a kite. Apparently, you'd been playing some silly memory game. It won't do.'

'Pelmanism – such good training for the memory. You ought to try it. We have our own variation and Hermione places objects in order, rather than naming them. She's very good at it.'

'And won't go to sleep afterwards. Eglantine, I must draw the line.'

'Are you forbidding me the house?'

Clemmie flicked an invisible speck from her heathery tweed coat frock. 'My dear Eglantine, you must understand . . .'

'Do you intend to be not at home when I call?'

'It's for Hermione's sake . . .'

'Piffle! Let me make myself quite clear, unless your husband requests me to my face to leave his house, I will visit my great-niece as I choose.'

I knew I was on safe ground there. Ant was much too nice – and too idle – to be drawn into his wife's cattishness. He would no more consider shutting the door in my face than he would dream of shooting a fox.

So I remained a sort of go-between. I was the only person with *entrée* to both houses. I visited both my niece and my great-niece whenever I wished. I kept Helen informed about her daughter's progress and I made sure that Hermione never forgot she had a mother who loved her. I was made welcome by the Malyons and just about tolerated by the Framptons. It was a useful arrangement.

I was Hermione's Aunt Egg and I'm sure she loved me. She never exactly called me Aunt Egg, of course, but that was how I referred to myself, that was how she knew me. Aunt Egg. A silly name, but I adored it.

I was a constant in her life. And when she screamed, or kicked the nurserymaid's shins – or there was that terrible day when she sat for an hour banging her head on the table, slowly and rhythmically, not looking at anyone, not responding – when Nanny couldn't do a thing with her, it was silly old Aunt Egg who could bring her round.

Clementine and Anthony were kind to Hermione, of course. They loved her, I've never denied that. They gave her a home – something neither parent seemed capable of providing. Yet, because she chose not to speak, they were inclined to treat her as though she were in some way retarded. They shielded her from contact with the outside world. She was never allowed to mix with other children. It was unnatural. She needed friends of her own age and all she had was me.

241

Busybodying, perhaps. I do admit that I've always had a tendency to meddle – but with the best intentions. Hermione was so quick, so bright. It was a joy just to be with her. I knew she could read. One just had to watch her face to know that she had made the complex connection between the words she heard and the black squiggles on the pages of her story books. We started doing simple sums and she grasped the principles of numbers in no time. We went on nature rambles and discovered the delights of frog spawn.

And yet she would *not* speak.

That sturdy, plain little girl was so very dear to me. I would watch her drawing brightly-coloured, elongated people – her tongue sticking out and touching the tip of her snub nose – and see nothing of her mother in her. Then sometimes, quite unexpectedly, she would look up and something in the level, considering look she'd give me from huge dove-grey eyes would be pure Helen.

But, in a way, Clemmie was right. I had been the innocent cause of a great deal of unhappiness. Michael was not the husband for Helen. I ought never to have thrown them together so enthusiastically. It was a tragic mistake, for both of them.

Yet it all looked so right. What could possibly go wrong? Michael was a gentleman of independent means and impeccable character. Everyone I knew spoke highly of him. Helen was young, beautiful, innocent, ready to be moulded into everything Michael could possibly wish. The fact that he seemed to have fallen madly in love with her made his proposal as satisfactory as the last page of a fairy tale. Call me a romantic, if you like.

It was very hard not to like Michael. Even now, I still do. I pity him; he has had much to contend with. I despise him; I never thought he would turn out so weak. I don't understand him and I suspect no one else does either. Yet still I like him, that poor, tormented, upright man.

And then there was poor Celia, Helen's mother and my sister-in-law, to think about. It was all too horrible, that last summer of her life, watching that beautiful woman waste away. And suffer. Oh God, she suffered all the torments of the damned. If knowing that Helen's future was assured relieved at least some of her anxiety in those last, agonizing days, then surely I was justified in what I did. I did the right thing. Didn't I?

Of course, it goes without saying that Helen could have come to live with me after her mother's death. Celia and I were very close and Helen would have been doubly welcome for her own sweet self. Yet still her mother fretted. I suspect she thought my life-style was just a touch raffish for her daughter. She nearly said as much once. I think she was afraid that Helen's spotless character might become a trifle tarnished by my less than conventional friends. What an idea! Harold was and is the soul of respectability.

So there was every good reason why Michael's suit ought to have been encouraged.

The sight of Helen on Harold's arm walking to the altar to take her place by her husband's side was a very satisfying sight to me. It was the perfect culmination of all my hopes and plans. Helen didn't hurry. Not like me – I had dashed off, towing my poor father behind me, and arrived panting with eagerness. Most indelicate! Helen moved with no more flurry than a swan gliding over an evening lake, leaving a little eddy of admiration behind her. She was as graceful and – yes, now as I think back over the day – as remote.

I was close enough to hear Michael's breathing. He was blowing through his nostrils like a nervous horse.

243

Yet he never once turned to look at Helen, not even as Harold put her hand into his. I particularly noticed that.

The perfect ending to the perfect romance. I never imagined there'd be a problem at the bottom of the page – the bit that goes 'and they lived happily ever after'.

What else could I have done? How was I to know?

I must say, the war was very exciting. Yes, I know, awful things happened. Yet I have never felt so fulfilled. There was so much to *do*, you see, every day was bright and fresh, a new challenge.

I was on a committee for the rehabilitation of Belgian refugees. If you could have seen the plight of some of those poor people, fleeing before the Uhlan hordes. Infants. Old men proudly wearing the medals of past campaigns. Innocent girls ravished beneath the boot of the Hun. (Well, not literally, but you know what I mean!) I felt a thrill of satisfaction every time we managed to find a haven for one of them.

I was on a committee for the relief of servicemen's families, too. You'd be amazed at the plight of some of those stout women, left behind by men who were serving King and Country. Of course, some employers were very generous – Aquascutum, whose splendid driving mackintoshes I always purchased, and Malyon's, the grocery empire with the excellent tea, paid half wages to the families of employees who volunteered *and* promised their jobs back at the end of the war.

Not everyone was so patriotic and there were real cases of hardship amongst women prevented from going to work by a young family. I started a branch of the Tipperary Club nearby, which offered free fires, newspapers, books, a nursery (we didn't dare call it a *kindergarten* in those days) and wholesome food for those in need. The poor dears were so grateful.

244

*Hers the conflict, hers the conquest, hers the flag of life
  unfurled.
Hers the sorrow, hers the suffering, hers the love that rules
  the world.*

Splendid words and so true. I had them copied from
The Queen's Gift Book and framed on the wall in our
little club room.

There were women, too, who seemed to be smitten
with a bacchanalian frenzy. It was a sort of 'khaki fever'
that attacked the most unlikely of women and induced
them to offer themselves as a sacrifice to any man in
uniform.

I was told that women of other nationalities suffered
from the same extraordinary malady. One heard of the
Russian woman who tore her dress open and pressed
her naked breasts on the boots of a young officer,
crying, 'Take me! Right here before these people! Poor
boy . . . you will give your life . . . for God . . . for
the Tsar . . . for Russia.'

How grotesque. I can't imagine that English women
ever gave way to their emotions in quite such an abandoned manner. Still, one never knows.

There was a joke going the rounds that certain hotels
would install plaques after the war was over, saying 'To
all the women who fell here during the Great War'.

I believe it was the natural female complement to the
male frenzy of killing that was going on around us day
after day. It was an outbreak of primitive instinct, if you
like, easy to understand and perfectly natural. But the
perfectly natural outcome was too often that little
pledge of affection, the war baby. Not a good idea.

And then, of course, there was that scourge of the
soldier, the intimate plague not normally discussed in
polite circles. In his paybook a man would find a mess-

age from Kitchener exhorting him to 'Avoid all intimacy with women'.

'Not blooming likely. Who does he think he is?'

You can imagine.

One was scandalized by the number of men rendered *hors de combat*, not by the enemy, but by man's natural appetite. So unpatriotic. Such a complaint was, of course, regarded as a self-inflicted injury and suitably punished, but that was rather like shutting the stable door, wasn't it?

I joined one of the 'purity patrols' formed to combat this female aberration. In our dark blue uniforms – I dispensed with the heavy, hampering skirt after a few days and had a pair of navy blue breeches made for me – with high boots and hard felt hats, we patrolled parks, alleys and shop doorways, under bushes, in long grass.

My dear old Harold looked up from his newspaper the first time he saw me in uniform and said, mildly, 'Are you quite sure you know what you're doing, dear?'

'Of course,' I returned, ramming the frightfully uncomfortable hat down hard (I didn't want it falling off if I had to chase someone). 'If I can run a houseful of cantankerous servants, I'm quite capable of marching drunken girls home or splitting up overenthusiastic couples.'

And I gave him a peck on the cheek and marched out to first parade.

One got to know the likely spots on one's patch. One evening I met a young subaltern – he looked scarcely old enough to have shed his milk teeth – with a woman of a certain class hanging on each arm. I tapped him on the shoulder and he turned round, very indignant.

'These ladies are my cousins,' he protested.

I gave his 'cousins' a killing look. They were the usual type – pretty, fluffy, giggly. One of them pointed at my breeches and tittered.

'Oh gawd,' she gasped, 'if it isn't Vesta Tilley 'erself!'

'Very well,' I said to the young man. 'You are an officer and a gentleman. I must accept your word.'

A few minutes later, I heard the sound of feet hurrying after me. 'I'm sorry to have told you a lie,' he said. 'I thought you might like to know that I'm going back to camp now.'

He held out his hand and I was proud to shake it. Poor boy. I wonder what happened to him. He probably died a virgin. What a waste.

Is it very naughty to confess? It was all such *fun*!

And now there we were on the verge of 1920. It was all very exciting. I had the feeling that at last – at last – we could get on with living in a new century. The preceding twenty years had just been marking time. Waiting. There was something so inherently satisfying in the very sound of the numbers. Nineteen. Twenty. Rounded. Complete.

We had frittered away the first few years of the century under a frivolous king. We had thrown away the teen years in an orgy of destruction. Now, rather late, we were ready to begin. The new Georgians were eager to throw off the old, worn-out century.

I looked around our house in Grosvenor Gardens and it looked so *cluttered*.

'A clean start,' I said to Harold. 'Clean minds, clean bodies, clean walls.'

'What, dear?' asked Harold, looking up from the *Daily Telegraph*.

'I want to celebrate the new century.'

'A little late, aren't you?'

'Not at all. I'm just in time. The new century *begins* in 1920. I want to be ready for it.'

'If you say so,' Harold answered, turning back to the

paper. 'I say, those shipping shares you persuaded me to buy are doing rather nicely.'

I snipped the top off my egg and buttered a snippet of toast before answering. 'I rather thought they might.' A pause while I excavated the little, chopped-off end. I always start on that bit first. I don't know why. 'Harold, I met the *most* interesting young man the other night – at Dickie and Leila's, you know.'

'Mmm. Consolidated Gravel hasn't done much, though.'

'It will. Just think of all the new roads that are going to be needed. Lovely, clean concrete roads for all the new motors. And all needing masses of gravel. He's a designer, a designer of houses. So I thought . . . Harold?'

'Mmm?'

I leaned forward and whipped the paper out of his hands. He looked a bit cross for a moment – just for a moment. 'I thought I'd let him have a look at this place. Just – you know – a look. To see what he thinks.'

'I'm sure he'll think it's very nice, dear. You've always liked it, haven't you?'

But that wasn't what I meant at all.

'Clean,' I said. 'A new beginning.'

'Oh yes,' said Ronald, 'I do see what you mean.' He looked around the hall and then walked over to one of the walls. He put his hand on the peacock blue de Morgan tiles. 'Under all this, it does have the most wonderful *proportions*.'

'But it's so cluttered, so . . .'

'Oh yes, isn't it?'

We went on into the drawing room. All those draperies, I thought – the ottoman piled with cushions, the sub-Renaissance furniture. Like Aladdin's cave. Sweep it all away. I blame it all on Marcel Boulestin. In one of my madder moments, I seemed to have bought half the contents of his delicious Elizabeth Street shop. Looking round, I felt I never wanted to see another stick of *Jugendstil* again. So twee.

Ronald looked out into my little paved garden. 'What fun,' he said, 'to bring the garden into the house. I can see it all white, with touches of vibrant colour, and stark, stark, stark.'

'Oh, yes.'

There was a dangerous moment of weakness as we went up my wonderful staircase. I'd had to plead very hard with Harold for that. I ran my hand up the curvilinear rail of polished olive wood. No, no. Everything must go. We walked around upstairs a bit. I really felt quite embarrassed about some of my past excesses. A tented First Empire bed in gilt and ebony. Imagine!

'What do you think?' I asked eagerly. 'Can you do something for us?' How silly. I couldn't keep a tremor of excitement out of my voice.

'Oh, I think so. I could do a lot with this. You want something modern, something exciting, something . . .'

'Clean,' I supplied.

'Exactly.'

I don't think I've ever seen Harold so cross. I never thought he would be. I never thought he even noticed his surroundings. He just lived in them. I started to condition him to change by gradually removing photographs and horrid old wedding presents, all the bibelots and knick-knackery that one just accumulates somehow. He grumbled a bit at first.

'There'll be nothing left in here soon but two hard chairs and a coal scuttle.'

Then the real work started. Harold was *so* unreasonable! So unlike himself. Although, I must admit, Ronald's plans did seem designed to make us exceedingly uncomfortable. Chipping the blue tiles off the wall in the hall made an extraordinary amount of dust. Then the whole garden wall in the drawing room was to be knocked out and replaced by glass, with concrete piers, just like children's building blocks.

'In November?' raged Harold.

'But I want it all to be ready for spring, so we can't possibly wait for warmer weather.'

'Meanwhile that vandal of a decorator of yours goes back to his cosy digs every night. No doubt his landlady banks up the fire and feeds him steak and kidney pudding.' His voice rose to a shout. 'And warms his *slippers*!'

'Ronald is a vegetarian.'

'What's that got to do with the price of fish?' Harold walked slowly round the room, running his hand along bare plaster, where the wallpaper had been stripped off. 'French, that was. Handblocked. I've still got the bill in my cabinet.'

Goodness. I never thought he'd even noticed it. 'Look at it this way, darling. You'll never have to buy any wallpaper again.'

Harold couldn't slam the door when he went out of the room because, just at that moment, there wasn't a door. Sound seemed to echo in an extraordinary manner through the empty rooms. I could hear him slamming drawers upstairs.

'Whatever are you doing?'

'Packing.'

'Don't be silly, darling. Where are you going?'

'I'm going to live in a cardboard box under the Arches. It'll be a damn sight more comfortable.'

Harold went to live at his club for a few weeks, where he could be pampered and fed nursery food. Silly old dear. I envied him – just a bit. When the water was turned off to install my own private bathroom, I nearly mutinied. Of course, I could have gone down to the country. But then I wouldn't have been on hand to watch the fascinating process of change.

I was tempted once by some very pretty furniture in Heal's – all white, with painted swags and garlands in delicate colours, but Ronald was utterly scathing about it. I had to admit he was right. It was too chocolate-boxy by half.

There was only one item of original furniture that Ronald allowed me to keep – and, I must say, I was relieved, because it was *extortionately* expensive. That was the Bugatti chair, one of my favourite pieces. It was veneered in rare, rich woods highlighted with beaten pewter and all in wonderful, curly-wurly snail-shell patterns. I always loved it.

I felt as though I were watching a very svelte butterfly emerge from a particularly ornate cocoon. Ronald would come running two or three times a day to ask me to approve this idea, or to come and see how that idea had turned out. It was all quite *thrilling*.

I was still living in chaos, when Helen telephoned late one night to ask if she could come to stay for a while.

'Well, of course, darling,' I answered, 'but I'm not sure you'll like it. We're in rather a state at the moment.'

'It doesn't matter. Any corner will do for me. Do say yes. Please.'

I must say, she sounded a bit odd. I did hope she hadn't had a quarrel with Philip. But then lovers so often do. And it all works out for the best in the end. So they say.

Helen turned up with just a tiny bag.

'Darling, lovely to see you,' I greeted her, 'but how long are you staying?'

'Not long, just a day or two, Aunt Eglantine. If that's all right.'

'Of course, whatever you like. But I did hope you'd make a little holiday of it. We could have such fun together, get about a bit, you know.'

'I'm sorry. I just don't feel much like gadding about at the moment.'

'Oh, dear.' That did sound ominous. 'Of course, you don't have to tell me a thing, if you don't want to. But if there's something on your chest, do try to get it off again. It'll do you good. And my lips are sealed.'

Helen gave me a little peck. 'There's nothing to get off my chest, I promise. But thank you, anyway. You're a dear.'

Of course, there was. Something to get off her chest, I mean. I knew it as soon as I set eyes on her. Her nerves were drawn as fine as a wire. They positively twanged at the slightest noise. It all came out after dinner – as I knew it would. Helen had never been a secretive child.

By this time, my own little snug was more or less habitable. It looked just as I had imagined, but somehow, on a night like this, it was less than satisfying. It was a night for drawing thick velvet curtains and pulling chairs up to a roaring fire. My beautiful cream leather and chrome chairs just weren't the same. I wanted to curl up with abandon, but they were fiendishly uncomfortable. Bits seemed to stick into me in the most awkward spots. The slatted blinds rattled and made the weather sound even worse than it actually was. I suspected that the glass and chrome striplights cast a less than flattering glow on me. Still, one must suffer to be beautiful, and so must a house.

A fire would have been nice, though. Of course, we were going to have the most modern heating system – central heating, the Americans call it – but, also of course, it hadn't yet been connected. I switched on a little electric fire, but it barely took the chill off the air and fizzed in a most alarming fashion.

'Now we can be cosy. Isn't this nice – all girls together?' Helen gave me a wan smile. 'Helen, darling, I don't mean to pry, but – well, I am your aunt and I'm completely unshockable.'

'Yes, I rather think you are.'

'Well, then.'

Helen stretched out her long, graceful legs towards the silly little fire. I hadn't realized until then just how much weight she had lost. She had been a gorgeous girl before the war. Now she was a quite stunning woman. That lush figure she had had when she first married was quite gone. She had fined down to wonderful bones, narrow waist, narrow hands, narrow feet. It suited her marvellously, but I was afraid it was a sign that she wasn't happy.

'I'm going to meet Michael tomorrow.'

I racked my brains for the proper reply. There wasn't one.

'Oh?'

'He's written me a letter. Well, he's written lots of letters, actually, all of them saying the same thing. But this one's different. He says he'll bring Hermione. He says I can see her.'

'And you believe him?'

'I have to.'

'But darling . . .'

'Do I have a choice? Supposing Michael plays fair . . . supposing Hermione is with him and I don't turn up . . . what would Michael tell her about me then . . . what would she think of me?'

'She's so young,' I soothed, not really believing what I was saying, 'she'd scarcely understand what was going on.'

'Don't pretend, Aunt Eglantine. I'm not a child.

Aren't you always telling me how clever she is? I can't afford not to be there.'

'That's so unfair! Michael's using that poor child like a . . . a hostage. It's wrong.'

'You do see, don't you? I can't take the risk. She just *might* be there.'

I didn't have the heart to tell her what I really thought of her chances of seeing her daughter, the next or any other day.

'To be frank, darling, I'm surprised Philip allowed you to come up to town alone. And to see Michael . . .'

'He doesn't know.'

'I thought as much.'

'He wanted to come. We might go dancing, go to a show, have some fun, he said. I said no. He insisted. I said I didn't want him . . . it was the only way. I told him I needed some time on my own to think. You can guess what happened then.' Her voice was so low, I could barely hear her. 'We had a silly quarrel . . . oh, I'm sorry, I'm being an awful drip over this. He said horrid things and I said horrid things back . . . oh dear . . .' She drew in a great suck of shuddering breath. 'Oh dear, I didn't mean to cry all over you.'

'My poor little girl, you have got yourself in a mess, haven't you?'

Helen gave me a watery grin. 'Yes – and I don't know quite how it happened. It just did. My own silly fault, I suppose. I just seem to have been blown from one thing to another without time to stop and think about it all.'

'Most women are, darling, and always have been. But somehow, I don't think they always will be. The war has changed so many things. I don't imagine men will ever be able to put women back where they want them again. Not that my dear little Harold was ever able to do that!'

That was better. I got a laugh out of her with that.

'Now – what we both need is a good slug of Harold's precious brandy. Then I'll telephone Philip and put it all right.'

'No! You mustn't!'

'Don't be silly, Helen. You need him. You can't face Michael tomorrow alone.'

'You mustn't. I don't want Philip here. You mustn't.'

She was serious. I thought, at first, she was just allowing herself a little stubborn pride that would easily be overcome by commonsense. Then I looked more closely at her and saw that she was perfectly serious. More than that – she was afraid.

'Look, darling,' I said cautiously. 'Be sensible. Michael's been through a lot. He had a bad war. He's had that . . . little breakdown. He may not be – how shall I put it – he may not be as responsible for his actions as one would hope. You ought not to see him without someone with you. Not that I'm saying he'd . . . no, of course not, but . . . well, to be on the safe side.'

'He said that if I brought anyone with me, he'd not let me see Hermione. I'm to come completely alone.'

'Is that really wise?'

'I must do exactly as he asks. Otherwise . . .'

'Oh, dear. I know, let's talk about it in the morning. You look half dead. Things won't seem nearly so bad over breakfast.'

Should I have kept faith with Helen? Or should I have telephoned Philip as soon as she was in bed? I tiptoed in after half an hour and she was sound asleep, practically unconscious, exhausted. If I'd rung Philip then, he could have caught the milk train and been with us by breakfast. Surely, then, he could have made her see sense.

I did nothing. I shall regret that decision all my life.

Helen looked much better in the morning. Just having a night away from Knapp Hill, a night away from tensions and explanations, seemed to have worked wonders. She seemed much less tense, more like herself. Yet she only trifled with breakfast.

'Will he let me see Hermione on my own, do you think?' she asked, crumbling a slice of toast on her plate. 'If I can only see her, talk to her, explain . . .'

'She's very young,' I warned. 'Not even five yet. Don't expect too much.'

'She'll understand. I know she will. If only I can talk to her . . .'

She looked so elegant, standing in the hall, smoothing gloves over her ringless fingers. Her three-quarter coat was charcoal pinstripe, very severe, over a straight skirt of the same colour. A blouse of fine ivory silk and those wonderfully trim calves and ankles, the sheerest pale grey silk stockings and impractical grey suede shoes completely dispelled any impression of masculinity. The great gilded mass of her hair was piled into one of those new face-framing hats and a cocquettish eye-veil enhanced the twilight of her eyes. Seeing her, one could never regret the frills and furbelows of pre-war years.

She smiled at me, such a wan little smile. 'Thank you for letting me come. Thank you for letting me talk to you.'

She knew. I'll swear she knew. Or is that just hind-sight?

'I might be out when you come back. Ronald wants me to go with him to some little atelier he's discovered in Swiss Cottage, of all places. Goodness knows what he expects to find there. Do make yourself comfortable until I come back – if you can find anywhere at all to sit in this awful mess.'

She kissed my cheek. I kissed hers. I let her go. Alone.

Thank God I was back when Helen came home. Ronald's outing to Swiss Cottage had been a total disaster. He took me to see some artist whom he swore would be the *succès fou* of the decade. It turned out that the artist was a very dear friend of Ronald's. He was also very drunk. The paintings were very bad.

'Ronald,' I said, 'you're being just a little bit naughty these days. I hope you don't think I'm only a silly old woman with too much money for her own good.'

He looked at me with his treacle toffee eyes and swore he'd been as disappointed with the paintings as I was.

I don't know – maybe Harold was right all along.

So I was at home when Helen came back. It was my maid's afternoon off (they're so spoiled these days – one is so afraid of losing them) so, when I heard the taxi, I ran to open the door myself. She looked exactly the same, exactly as she had when she had left. Then I looked more closely.

There was an abrasion on the point of her chin. At the right hand corner of her mouth was a tiny tear, no more than the merest fraction of an inch long. High on her left temple, shaded by the pert eye-level veil, was the beginning of a bruise.

'Helen?'

'She wasn't there, Aunt Eglantine, she wasn't there.'

She started up the stairs, trailing her little fox necklet behind her, all the spring, all the youth gone from her step.

'Helen?'

'I think I'll just lie down for a little while, if you don't mind. I'm very tired.'

I paced around the drawing room for a few minutes,

torn between fear for her and reluctance to intrude on her privacy. She was a grown woman, a wife (of sorts), a mother. I ought not to go running after her as though she were five years old again. In the end, I decided to go up and check that she was all right. As I reached the bottom of the stairs, I heard the cry.

It was a sound like nothing I'd ever heard – or ever will, please God. A high, keening note of utter hopelessness. It shivered through the empty rooms and down the uncarpeted stairs. A sound that splintered the silence and left it crazed over like a broken pane of glass, never to be repaired.

Just once and then nothing.

Doctors are fools. I swear they have Lysol, not blood, in their veins. They keep their humanity locked up in their Gladstone bags.

'It's not a matter for the police, Mrs Hayler,' Dr Prowting insisted. 'They make a point of never intervening in domestic disputes.'

'Domestic disputes?' I raged. 'This is rape.'

'There is no such thing as rape between husband and wife, as you may or may not know.'

Pompous ass.

'Well, there bloody well ought to be!' I saw him flinch at my language. He was lucky not to get worse. I hadn't been in the 'purity patrol' without learning a thing or two! 'You've examined her. You've seen what that man has done to her. It's criminal.'

'That's just my point, Mrs Hayler. It isn't.'

'That girl is hurt. She's bleeding. It's barbaric.'

'The natural result, if I may say so, of resistance. If I understand correctly, Mrs Frampton has – ' He fiddled with his spectacles for a moment. ' – has denied her husband his rights for a considerable length of time. On this occasion, his ardour led him into a more forceful

258

expression of his feelings than was advisable – but no more than that.'

'Exactly. He raped her. That's what I said.'

'Not in the eyes of the law.'

'Then let the law be the judge of that, not you.'

'I would be called upon to testify to your niece's condition.'

'Are you warning me, Dr Prowting?'

Just for a moment, a man looked out from behind the medical facade. 'Mrs Hayler, take my advice, I beg you. Even if you persisted and the police did press charges of common assault – and I doubt very much that they would – there would be a most unsavoury case. Mrs Frampton would be asked some very personal questions, not always sympathetically. Her marital situation is . . . er . . . rather unconventional. Can you imagine what a determined counsel might make of that? Do you want to see her pilloried, to see her private life dissected? Do you want to hear servants quizzed about the disposition of bedrooms, about noises in the night, about the state of the sheets in the morning?'

'Would it come to that?'

'It would, make no mistake.'

'That's shameful . . . degrading . . . monstrous . . .' I ran out of words to express my indignation.

'And, in the end, all for nothing. The result would not be in doubt. A husband *cannot* – however much you may disagree – rape his wife.' He put his spectacles on again and, with them, the man disappeared and the doctor returned. 'I've given Mrs Frampton a light sedative – just enough to make her drowsy. My advice is to let her rest and let nature do the work. She'll get over it in a day or two.'

I doubted whether Helen would ever get over it, but there seemed little point in saying so.

After Dr Prowting had gone, I tiptoed upstairs to

check whether his sedative was working and to suggest that Helen might like a warm drink to help it down. The bed was tidied again. All evidence of the intimate nature of the doctor's examination had been neatly disposed of. Helen was lying down. I noticed that she was so thin that the bedcovers seemed to be barely mounded above her.

'Can I bring you something, darling,' I whispered. 'A little warm milk? Could I whisk an egg into it?'

'Dear Aunt Eglantine – being a nurse doesn't suit you at all! If you tiptoe around with that lugubrious expression, I might start imagining I'm really ill!'

She laughed and the sound made me feel that perhaps I'd badly over-reacted. Then I looked into her eyes. It was like looking down a deep, deep well. At the bottom, pinpoint tiny and wavering, was only my own reflection.

Helen wasn't there at all.

Of course, she wouldn't hear of my ringing Philip.

'He ought to be with you,' I argued. 'He must wonder when you're going back to Wiltshire.'

'Just tell him I'm going to stay a few more days with you than I'd originally planned.'

'He won't be satisfied with that. No man would.'

'He'll have to be.'

'For goodness sake – you'd quarrelled before you left – he must be out of his mind with worry.'

'I doubt that. He might be a little concerned.'

'Doesn't he have a right to know what has happened?'

'No one . . .' Helen's voice was a little whisper of winter wind and it made me shiver. '. . . no one has a right over me or my body. No one ever again.'

We agreed that she'd stay with me until her injuries healed and I had to lie to Philip to keep him in the country. With a little ingenuity and smooth talking I persuaded him to stay in Wiltshire until Helen was fit to be seen by her lover again. If he'd been half the man I took him for, nothing would have kept him away. But London in November is very uninviting and he was hunting with the Tedworth three or four times a week.

We concocted a convincing cover story. We even decided on a show that we could tell him we had seen together. *Birds of Paradise* at the Lyric. I found out about the plot, so that we could sound convincing.

Lies, lies, lies.

I even lied to Harold. Or, at least, I concealed the truth. He popped in most days from his club – just checking when the place would be habitable again, he said – and always stayed for tea or cocktails or whatever. When he was around, I managed to smooth away the furrow of anxiety that threatened to sit permanently on my brow these days. I looked in the glass and thought, one day it won't go away at all.

In twenty-seven years of marriage I had never lied to my husband. Not serious, not *proper* lies, anyway. I didn't like being forced to start.

Helen's face was scarcely marked. Michael had been very careful about that – it proved that he had been far more calculating and less carried away by passion than I had imagined. In a couple of days, her complexion was as flawless as ever. The bruises on her body would take about a week to fade. But the bites . . . the scratches . . . I shudder to imagine the abuse she had suffered. How could he? A man who had sworn at the altar to love and cherish her?

'With my body I thee worship . . .'

He should have gone to prison for that, for a very long time. If I had been judge, he would have done. But then, women always seem to interpret the rules with more emotion than accuracy. That's why there will never be a woman judge, I suppose. It's inconceivable that men would ever allow it.

Helen spent just a couple of days in bed and then only because I insisted. She was up on the third and fidgeting to get out.

'Just a breath. I'll stifle if I stay in.'

'But there's a frightful pea-souper. You can't go out in that after two days in bed. You'll catch pneumonia.'

'I'm not ill and I'll go mad if I have to stay in any longer. Let me go. I promise I'll just walk around the square like a good girl and then come straight back, if it makes you any happier.'

'Then make sure you pull your scarf over your nose and mouth. Whatever you do, don't breathe it in.'

She did more than just walk round the square. She was gone so long that several times I hovered by the telephone, trying to persuade myself that I didn't need to call the police. Anything might have happened. One heard such tales. She might have lost her way, missed her footing by the river, fallen under a bus.

Or worse. But some deep knowledge of Helen's underlying strength kept me from really believing in the worst. She wouldn't do that. Michael might have been weak enough to try to end his life, but Helen never would.

When I was small, there was something so exciting about a November fog. It assaulted all five senses at once: depriving us of sight; muffling sound like an old blanket; corrupting taste and smell; laying down a greasy film filthy to the touch. Bus conductors, carrying flares which added to the reek, marched six paces in front of their vehicles. Street lamps at noon glowed like rotten fish. Detonators were fired off to clear, supposedly, the railway lines. The pigeons never even bothered to get up in the morning. There always seemed to be a frightened housemaid, muffled to the eyes, lost on her way back from the corner pillar box. If we *had* to go out – and it was firmly discouraged – on our return, Nanny would always blow our noses ferociously. Then she would roll the handkerchief fastidiously up around the black horror inside.

It's not so much fun now. Now it's just a dirty, smelly, clammy inconvenience.

I looked out of the window, but could barely see beyond the empty window boxes. Sulphur yellow, insidious as an alley cat, the vapour seeped through chinks in the new window frames and filmed the spanking white paint.

I never heard Helen's feet coming down the street. I never knew she was back until the door banged. And only then did I admit to myself the fear that I'd been pooh-poohing all afternoon.

'Like it?' she asked, pulling off her hat and giving a neat pirouette. 'Good heavens, Aunt Eglantine, you're never speechless, are you?'

The heavy, waving mass of silver hair was gone. Relieved of its weight, it had sprung into baby-fine curls all over her head, like bubbles of sea foam. The sleek line of her jaw, her neat ears, the sensuous curve of her neck, were naked. Despite the fact that I had cut my own hair six years earlier, to see the same effect on Helen was somehow shocking. It was as though she had been caught in a state of partial nudity. Combined with her new, ethereal figure, the result was – frankly – erotic.

'Like it?' she demanded again.

'It's . . . it's stunning.'

And it was.

'Tomorrow I want to go shopping,' she said, sitting by the spitting electric fire and wolfing down quantities of tea cakes with bramble jelly. 'Nothing fits me any more. I feel like a scarecrow. All my clothes are hanging on me, I've lost so much weight. Will you come with me?'

'Yes, of course, it'll be such fun, just the two of us.'

I should have been glad that Helen seemed so much better. Surely it was a sign that she had not been scarred by what had happened. She seemed prepared to put it all behind her, with the enviable elasticity of youth. How very sensible. What cannot be cured must be endured.

Yet I was uneasy. She was *so* bright, *so* normal. Look at her now, licking bramble jelly off her fingers and laughing as though getting sticky was the funniest thing she had ever done. Then she was up, flicking through the evening paper, out into the hall to see if the late post had arrived.

Out of its cardboard sleeve she brought a new record and placed it on the turntable of my Aeolian. She wound the machine, checked the needle and lowered it onto the lead-in of the record. It was the Two Bobs, I seem to remember. Harold and I had seen them in *Bran Pie* at the Prince of Wales a few weeks earlier.

'I bought it this afternoon. Everyone's doing it.'

I watched her, slender and bright, dancing a shuffling one-step, alone in the glaring electric light and I worried.

Helen kept me to my promise the next day and we went shopping directly after breakfast. She dressed and undressed, was measured again and again as we progressed around the *salons*. A mannish walking costume from Creed; a couple of smart afternoon frocks, one in spotted foulard and one in rust crêpe marocain, from Redfern; a stunning dinner gown of black lace over a tube of slinky black silk-jersey from Lucille's. We looked into Fifirella and Reville's.

It was enough to swell any young head. Helen's figure was acclaimed wherever she went. She was the new woman. (How many times in history has there

been a new woman? I remember being one in the ninet-
ies!) Helen was *today*.

I started to get quite excited. Life had been so dull for
so long. Perhaps I had been just a teeny bit obsessive
about my plans for the house. It was marvellous to gad
about shops that weren't interior designers!

We were just coming out of The White House in
New Bond Street, where Helen had left an order for
wonderful underclothing in the loveliest colours, colours I would never have thought of – apricot, almond,
rose-beige – mouthwatering. I resolved to stop wearing
white. But if Harold ever noticed, would he even care?

There had been just one, tiny, embarrassing moment.
Helen had been tempted by an example of a silk nightgown with matching peignoir in palest amethyst. Long-
ingly, she had let the silk whisper through her fingers.
Then, 'No,' she said, 'it'd be wasted. There'd be no
point in wearing something like this with Philip
around. He prefers me *au naturel*.'

Her voice, so low, yet had a clarity that seemed able
to slice through the chatter around us. I saw several
heads turn in our direction.

When the maroons went off, I swear my heart stopped. For a moment – just for a moment – I thought it
was a Gotha raid! How silly! Yet it was incredible that,
in all the turmoil of events in the past week, Helen and I
had both forgotten what day it was. How could we?

His Majesty had asked for complete suspension of all
normal activities. All over the city, maroons exploded
and sirens were sounded. Flags were lowered on the
roofs of all public buildings. Trains came to a halt. I
read afterwards that aeroplanes, seeing the rockets go
up, throttled down engines and glided for two minutes.
Our country came to a standstill in memory of the Glorious Dead.

In front of us, a bus halted. The driver and conductor

stood motionless, hats off, beside it. The passengers stood in their seats, heads bowed. Motors halted and the occupants stood by them. In the stores behind us, assistants and customers stood in reverent silence. The stillness was uncanny. There was a lump in my throat like a golf ball and I just couldn't swallow it.

Tears were streaming down the cheeks of a woman standing near me, yet her tears were silent. I saw a man bury his face in his handkerchief. A child wailed once and his nurse popped a comforter into his mouth and shoogled the pram to silence him. An old man put his arm around the shoulders of a woman, who leaned against him, her shoulders shaking. He lowered his head to hers and they stood, armoured in grief. A pigeon took off with a clap of wings like applause.

When, after two minutes, the sirens and rockets sounded again, it was as though the city shook itself, gave a united sigh, and went back to work. Up and down Bond Street, drivers were turning starting handles and engines were being cranked into life again. Pedestrians blew their noses briskly and walked on. Bells on shop doors clanged and telephones rang once more. A woman snapped open her compact, squinted fiercely into the tiny mirror, powdered her nose, and tip-tapped off on high heels.

Life went on and Helen continued with her shopping.

If I didn't see much of Helen in the year or two that followed, I certainly heard about her. If half I heard was true, then no wonder she didn't have time to visit her aunt.

When I was young (oh, dear, I'm beginning to sound just like Harold!) young people had fun, of course, but we kept within our own milieu, so to speak, within our own class. Any indiscretions were easy to hush up. I couldn't understand this longing for low life that seemed to sweep over certain of our young just after the war.

Of course, the war had lowered many of the class divisions. For better or for worse, I'm not inclined to say. It is simply a fact that during the war, one often saw debutantes working alongside parlourmaids. Perfectly worthy men were promoted into the gaps left by the deaths of 'natural' officers. And, of course, there was a certain type that actually *profited* from the war.

Somehow, one always thought that the natural order might reassert itself once hostilities were over. One could understand that the aspirations of the working classes might have been raised. There's nothing wrong, I suppose, in that. What I could not and cannot understand is the reason why so many young people who ought to have known better became afflicted by a sort of *nostalgie de la boue*.

Take these treasure hunts, for instance. A perfectly harmless amusement, one might imagine. They started off as simple fun for a dull afternoon, a little like hare and hounds using taxis and buses. A few young people might while away the hours by following the route a chum was known to have taken and trying to catch up. A few years ago, I might have enjoyed that myself. But like all good things, the more people become involved, the more silly it all becomes.

The simple chase became more complex. Cryptic clues were dreamed up and followed by hordes of whooping young men and women in motor cars. More sober people began to complain about the noise and nuisance.

One morning, Harold passed his newspaper across the breakfast table to me without a word.

I looked at the photograph first. Amongst a milling mob of bright young people, I couldn't at first see what Harold was trying to point my attention towards. Then

I saw Helen. She was towards the back of the crowd, but her height and beauty were unmistakable. There was Philip, too, with one arm draped drunkenly around her shoulders and the other embracing a young man with a vacuous expression. The usual multiple headlines said:

NEW SOCIETY GAME
MIDNIGHT CHASE IN LONDON
50 MOTOR CARS
THE BRIGHT YOUNG PEOPLE

I didn't know quite what to say (an unusual circumstance for me). I looked again at the picture, at that blur of laughing faces. I unfolded my spectacles and put them on. Helen's face leaped into focus. She looked exhilarated, breathless with the excitement of the chase, more than a little tipsy – and deeply unhappy.

'I suppose,' said Harold hesitantly, 'it's all very clever, this treasure hunting – following the clues and all that.'

'Oh, yes. They say it's quite a skill really,' I soothed him. Then I went on to read the piece. It did nothing to quiet my anxiety.

A howling mob of young men and women, packed into fifty motor cars, had followed a trail of clues around London, sounding their hooters and trying to overtake each other. Some had hired taxi cabs to whisk them around the less well known back streets.

They had raced from Achilles' statue (a vulnerable point in Hyde Park) where a postcard of the *Death of Chatterton* had led them to the Tate Gallery. From the Pensioners' Garden in Chelsea (the warriors of Crimea have a garden), they had roared via Peter Pan's statue to Drury Lane (look out for Nell Gwyn). At one point, everyone had been crawling on the filthy pavement in

Seven Dials looking for an elusive clue. A huge breakfast and a string orchestra had greeted those who completed the course.

'I'm sure they don't mean any harm,' I reassured Harold, as I passed the newspaper back to him. 'It's just youthful high spirits. After all, haven't they just endured the worst four years in man's history? One must make excuses.'

From then on, Helen's picture appeared alongside most reports of silly goings-on. There was the night the Thames was set on fire with drums of petrol. There was the party that finished when the survivors commandeered the equipment of a road-mending gang just arriving for work and dug a huge hole on the wrong side of the street. A milkman's horse was kidnapped at the end of a circus party. Someone tried to lead him up the steps to the house, but the poor brute baulked and the milk float overturned.

I stood on the sidelines and worried, feeling like a silly old hen, flapping about her brood. It didn't matter how many excuses I tried to make for their behaviour. The antics of the bright young people made me feel very old.

They were so crass, so unfeeling. One treasure hunt involved collecting not objects, but people. Can you imagine? A car would screech to a halt in the small hours of the morning, disturbing resentful inhabitants who had to get up to work when the revellers were sleeping off their excesses, and a Billingsgate porter would be dragged off, or an Italian waiter, a flower-seller, a matchbox maker, a milliner, or a Wapping docker. Sometimes, two or three cars would arrive at once and a hapless 'clue' would be fought over.

I have no doubt that these poor people were well paid for their pains. That is not the point. What concerned me is that they were not seen as people, just as objects, as adjuncts to the game for the evening. What happened to them after it was over was no one's affair.

Helen and Philip rented a house in town, in Ellis Street. Several times I went to see her. If I arrived in the morning, her maid would say she was still in bed and couldn't be disturbed. If I arrived in the afternoon, she was out. I started to feel very resentful.

Of course, I was still going regularly to Buckholt to see Hermione. It was one of the great pleasures of my life to sit with that dear child on my lap and tell her a story. She was so loving. I would feel her solid little body pressed against me, I would feel the sticky pressure of her lips on mine and I would wish that I could steal her away and keep her for my own.

Once or twice, she looked as though she was bursting to tell me something. I would be convinced that she was about to speak – I knew she could if she wanted to – but no, it never happened. I used to feel bitterly disappointed. Her silence might have been easier to bear if she had not been so obviously intelligent. She had been silent by choice for so long. If she ever chose finally to speak, would she be capable of it? What a waste.

Helen's life style was driving a deeper wedge between her and her daughter. How could she not see that? If there ever had been a chance that Michael would relinquish control of the child, it had gone, once Helen's name became linked in public gossip with the notorious set she ran with. She would never get Hermione now. Never. She had given Michael every moral excuse, as well as every legal one, to hang onto his daughter.

And – almost as though she knew it – Helen's behaviour became wilder and even less predictable.

I went to see Price Malyon. He met me in his study. He had been working on a mound of papers, sitting behind a desk that was ostentatiously wide, of gleaming mahogany, with vicious claw and ball feet. I had the unworthy suspicion that the size of Price's desk was in direct proportion to his own opinion of himself. Still, he met me courteously enough and came out from behind his desk and drew up a pair of chairs by a small, out of season fire.

I begged him to put some limits on the behaviour of his son. But Price only laughed his throaty laugh and answered in a voice from which the rich Cornish accent had never been successfully eradicated.

'They're only having a bit of fun. Let them sow some wild oats while they're young – it doesn't last for ever.'

'I think they've sown more than enough,' I said and knew that I sounded uncharacteristically prim, but I was seriously worried. 'Have you *no* influence on them?'

'I could bring Philip to heel just like that.' He snapped his fingers in a vulgar fashion. 'Who do you think holds the purse strings round here? But why should I?'

'Because you're not doing him – or Helen – any good by indulging their every whim. Because you're actually encouraging Philip to be an idle layabout. When is he ever going to grow up and earn a living?'

'My son doesn't need to earn a living.'

'Of course he does. Or he ought to,' I snapped.

'Now you listen to me, Eglantine Hayler . . . when I was Philip's age, yes, and a damn sight younger, I worked eighteen, nineteen, twenty hours a day. I worked in the shop all day, went to night school half the night. I worked harder than any black.' His voice was rough with pride. 'And why? Because I was going somewhere. I wanted to *be* someone. And I am – just look around you. But I never had any fun on the way.'

I tried to placate him. 'Yes, you worked hard, Price, and you deserve everything you've worked for, but . . .'

'. . . so now my boys can enjoy everything I never

271

had. If Hector wants to breed skinny polo ponies and mooch around with straw sticking out of his ears, that's all right. And if Philip wants to be a drone and a play-boy, that's all right too. I can afford it.'

'You're a generous man, Price,' I said sadly. 'I thought you were a shrewd one, too, but it seems I was wrong.'

But of all the people whom I thought ought to be concerned about Helen, the one I least expected to come to me was Philip himself. So I couldn't have been more surprised when he turned up one morning.

'Helen's still in bed,' he said, with no preamble. 'She doesn't know I'm here.'

'And why are you here? Shouldn't you be sleeping off the effects of last night, too?'

'I didn't have to come, you know. I wanted to. If she finds out . . . Well, you might at least try to understand.'

'I'm sorry. I'm being very rude. Sit down, Philip, and tell me what's worrying you.'

He didn't accept my invitation to sit. He prowled around the room, looking more than ever like a nervous racehorse at the start. Looking back, I think Philip was the most handsome man I've ever seen. He was physically perfect. Nothing was out of place: not the well-manicured hands; not the thick, waving chestnut hair; not the aquiline nose. Any girl would have to be blind not to have a soft spot for a man like that. And if I sometimes thought that not a great deal went on behind that well-shaped forehead of his – well, that's probably just a cynical old woman talking. Yet I had never seen him exhibit an atom of imagination or emotion before this morning.

'I don't know what to do about Helen.'

I didn't answer. I didn't want to impose my own

personality on this meeting. I'd spent my life doing that, not always successfully. I was going to let Philip tell me how he saw the problem.

'She's . . . I don't know how to describe it . . . she's . . . If you read the newspaper at all, you'll know.'

I just nodded.

'I'm losing her. I can't cope with all the late nights and the drink and the drugs. I'm worn out. I want to get out of London – home – anywhere.'

'Why not go, then?'

'Helen'll never agree to come with me. I suggested closing up the house in Ellis Street yesterday and she told me that she wouldn't dream of rusticating in the middle of Salisbury Plain. She said if I want to go, I can go by myself. Then she went up to her room and wrote out invitations – over a hundred – for the party she's throwing next month.'

I tried to be forbidding – really I did – but Philip looked so pathetic. I know I've laboured the racehorse analogy a bit, but he really managed a good impression of a worn-out hack. I'll bet anything you like that Philip can sleep standing up! It would have been difficult not to laugh if I didn't guess he was in deadly earnest.

'My dear boy,' I said. 'Are you telling me that you just let Helen do whatever she likes?'

'More or less. What else can I do? I just want her to be happy, you see. She's had such a rotten time of it.'

'And you really think that letting her run amok is the right way to ensure her happiness?'

'I did, but now I'm not so sure. She's never satisfied, you see, always running after something more, something different. She's always *looking* for something and I don't know what it is. She's always bored. I'm afraid that one day she'll get bored with me.'

I looked at his beautiful, worried, not very clever face and felt terribly sorry for him.

Ought I to have told him? Did he have a right to know the reason for Helen's irrational behaviour? I seriously considered the idea of explaining about the rape, about the savage way marital trust had been abused, about how it seemed to have poisoned Helen's whole system. Philip was right in one way – Helen *was* running, but from something, not after something. I knew what she was running from. If I tried to explain it to Philip, would he understand Helen better?

I paused for a long time before making my decision. Philip just didn't have the emotional maturity to cope with information of such appalling brutality. Instead of helping Helen to rise above her betrayal, he was much more likely to do something daft – perhaps even something violent. Yes, that was more than possible. Philip was an adolescent with the body of a man. I couldn't take the responsibility of telling him. It was too much for me. I couldn't cope. I couldn't take the blame for what might happen next. Besides, was it even my secret to tell?

Instead, I asked pitilessly, 'Wouldn't that be all for the best – for her and for you?'

'And who would she go to from me? And who after that? And after that?'

'She might go back to her husband.'

'Never.' There was no ignoring the ferocity in that one word.

'Not even to get her daughter back?'

It wasn't the first time that thought had occurred to him. I could see that by the way his hands paused in the middle of lighting a cigarette. Then he flicked the match out and tossed it into the empty grate.

'That's what Cassandra said. She said that Helen's feeling guilty and she's trying to run away from it. But she can't run far enough or fast enough. Can't say I understood half of what she said, I'm afraid. Cass's too clever for me.'

'Freudian claptrap,' I snorted, 'but Helen does miss Hermione very much, you know.'

'Do you think . . .' Philip paused and blushed like a great schoolboy, '. . . it might make her feel better . . . do you think Helen would like another baby?'

'Good God – no!'

'I'm sorry,' he stuttered and coloured even more. 'I didn't mean to shock you. I just thought . . .'

'You haven't shocked me, you silly boy, but I've only just realized just how dim you really are!'

'But Cass said . . .'

'If you can't see why that is quite the worst possible solution, then there's very little I can do to help you,' I snapped, quite out of patience with him. 'Now why don't you run along before Helen finds out you're missing and you have to invent some great whopper to explain your absence.'

'Yes, yes, you're right, I must go.' He leaped up as though galvanized by the thought of Helen's anger.

I saw Philip out myself, handed him his trilby and opened the front door. He still lingered on the step, turning his hat round in his hands.

'I'm sorry to have made such an ass of myself,' he said, 'it's just that . . . well, I do rather love her, you see.'

Poor boy. How could I turn my back on him?

'Then my advice to you is to take Helen far away from London. Get her right away. Italy, Switzerland, anywhere. Just go.'

'But Helen won't . . .'

'Good heavens – you're a man, aren't you? *Make* her go!'

'And then, I'm a bit short of the ready. Pa's very generous, of course, but I can't keep going to him.'

'I think you'll find,' I said acidly, 'that your father'll be only too pleased to get you out of London.'

And I shut the door on him before he could come up with any more feeble excuses for doing nothing.

I lost my darling old Harold in October 1921. He went to bed before me that night, saying he felt rather tired. When I followed him an hour later, he seemed sound asleep, breathing very deeply. When I woke in the morning, he had gone.

He died as he lived – quietly, without making a fuss. He abhorred fuss, always had done. So when it was time for him to go, he just slipped away.

No one will ever believe how much I miss him. People used to look at us, I know, and wonder what we could possibly have in common. We were a comical pair: I have always been – well, volatile is the kindest description; Harold was steady, patient, tolerant. Some people may have thought him dull. I never did. He was always there, you see, loving and dependable, so patient with my little whims. He was the kindest man I ever met.

I miss him dreadfully.

Helen was in Menton when her Uncle Harold died. She didn't come to the funeral. Well, it was a sensible decision, really. By the time the news of Harold's death reached her and with the complete length of France to travel, she would scarcely have been in time. Instead, she and Philip sent an enormous wreath. It was very exotic – canna lilies and waxy stephanotis, a splash of bougainvillea, beaked strelitzia. The poor florist must have had a terrible time making it up; she must have raided every hothouse for miles.

Funeral flowers aren't really intended for the dead, of course. Are they? The dead don't wander around after the funeral, picking up cards and reading them, saying,

'I see X remembered me, then' or 'Nothing from the Y's, I see. You'd think they might have made a bit more effort' or 'Z has really pushed the boat out this time'! No, the flowers are really meant for the living left behind, to comfort, to show respect, to impress.

Still, I remember looking at that exotic wreath and imagining Harold's face if he could have seen it. He had such a naughty, wry little grin. It was part of his charm.

Everyone came. The Framptons: Anthony looking stouter and redder than ever; Clementine bang up to the minute in a cloche hat down to her eyebrows, trimmed with a sweep of egret feathers; Viola, still in crêpe and veils after all these years – ostentatious, I call it; Charley – surely that was a whiff of brandy I caught when he kissed my cheek. The Malyons were there too: Price and Harriet saying just the right thing; Adrienne with her little boy, Alexander – eighteen months old and she can't bear to be parted from him for a moment; Hector with a distant look as though he had seen so many young men die, what was one old man more; Cassandra, patting my hand and saying Harold would always be watching over me in spirit. So many people. All Harold's old business associates. Friends from his club that I scarcely knew. Everyone.

Michael was there too. I didn't want him near me, couldn't bear him to touch me – not after what he had done to Helen. I looked at him in his respectable dark suit and black tie, his hair completely grey now, his face drawn down in appropriate solemnity, and I couldn't believe what I was seeing. This sober, slightly dull, apparently sane man was a wild animal.

I wish Helen had come, but perhaps, after all, it was better that she didn't.

It's hard to pick up the threads again. I always thought I was the resilient kind. I couldn't see myself as the wan widow. I wasn't a Viola, making a lifetime's profession of grief. I have too much commonsense for that. But after twenty-nine years of seeing the same face across the breakfast table every morning, of hearing the same quiet breathing at night, it's very hard to adjust to being solitary. It's like suddenly being without a shadow. I would find myself thinking, 'Oh, I must tell Harold that' or 'I wonder what Harold will say'. Most unhealthy.

I would drift around my pure, stark, modern house, the one I had plagued Harold so unmercifully to let me have. There was no pleasure in the sleek lines of fitted cupboards. The chrome and leather chairs held no comfort. I couldn't warm myself at the blue and grey Cubist vision on the drawing room wall.

I felt nothing. There was no one to sharpen myself against and I was losing my edge. I could feel myself becoming bland and dull. I needed Harold's acerbic little comments, spoken with such deceiving mildness, to keep myself alert.

I needed an interest.

Hermione was adorable. She was growing so fast now, still more stocky than graceful, but her face was becoming the face of a girl and not a child, strong chinned and wilful. I indulged her disgracefully, once Harold had gone. I never visited without bringing some little present: a 5000 piece jigsaw of the 1911 Delhi Durbar; a little net to trawl for newts in the forest ponds; a paintbox too good for a child, but I fell in love with it because the colours had such marvellous names – Nymph's Thigh and Isabella (a murky white called after the unpleasant linen worn by the daughter of Philip II); a pogo stick (on which I practised surreptitiously myself). I even arranged a regular delivery of the *Children's Newspaper* for a little while, but it was so mind-numbingly pi that I cancelled it very quickly.

Yes, it was spoiling her, I know. But who else in her life spoiled her? And who else did I have in my life to spoil? Helen was back from her protracted Continental tour, but I saw as little of her as when she was abroad. Only the more lurid newspaper reports kept me in touch with my niece's activities. My advice to Philip had not been successful.

One evening, Hermione and I were dragging back after an afternoon spent on the mudflats of the foreshore, turning over stones to see what jumped out from below. It was well after nursery teatime and I knew I'd have to endure yet another roasting from Nanny, who never seemed to appreciate that children will get dirty when they are happy. As long as the mind is well-nourished, who cares about the state of the hands and knees? We were both chewing the last of our half pound of mixed aniseed candy, satin cushions, brandy balls and pear drops.

There was still one satin cushion stuck in the corner of the paper poke. I fished it out, peeled off the clinging shreds of the bag and popped it into Hermione's mouth. Obedient as a little bird, she opened her mouth and then, under my elbow, she caught sight of someone across the lawn and set off at a trot.

By the time I caught up with her, she was sitting on the knee of a tall, thin man in spectacles. If I say he had a 'nice' face, it isn't meant as a disparagement. It really is the word that described him perfectly. He had sharp, careworn features with gentle eyes. His clothes were what used to be described as 'good' tweeds, meaning shabby. There was something about him that seemed familiar, but I couldn't think what it was. Hermione certainly knew him. She looked quite at home on his knee and he seemed to enjoy it.

He struggled to rise as I arrived, but Hermione's weight was too much for him.

'Do forgive me for not getting up, Mrs Hayler,' he said. 'This white man's burden seems to get heavier and heavier.'

Hermione gave a grunt of protest, which was the nearest she ever got to communicating and she wouldn't do that much often.

'Of course, I remember who you are now. Captain Snape. How nice. The last time I saw you, you were in uniform.'

'Let me pour you some tea – it's still quite hot. Down you get, you minx, I can't reach.'

He set out a clean cup, but Hermione slapped his hand away and poured out the cup of tea herself, very carefully and only half-filling the saucer.

'She's very independent,' I laughed, trying to excuse her rudeness. 'We've all learned the hard way that Hermione likes to prove how grown-up she is. I hope that didn't hurt.'

'Not at all. I'll know better next time than to try to take over one of Hermione's jobs.'

'Thank you, darling, that's just what I need,' I said, taking the cup from her. 'It might be better if you cut along to Nanny now. We don't want her any crosser than she's going to be anyway, do we? Yes, I promise I'll come and see you before I go.'

'Would you like a story before you go to sleep?' asked Patrick Snape. 'You choose – anything you like – but I like adventures best. Pirates. Buried treasure. Or animal stories. Have you got *Dr Doolittle*? That's fun. Trot off, now, and I'll come up when you've had your bath.' He waited until Hermione was out of earshot. 'What a waste.'

'Oh, I don't think so,' I answered sharply. No one was going to criticize Hermione while I was around to defend her. 'She's a very intelligent child.'

'That's what I mean. She ought to be going to school,

mixing with other children, broadening her horizons –
there's nothing she couldn't do, if she wanted to.'

'She still can.'

'I don't think you realize, Mrs Hayler, just how disturbed Hermione actually is.'

'Aren't you being a bit alarmist? "Disturbed" is a
very strong word, isn't it?'

'And I mean it. Hermione isn't deaf – I've tested her
carefully. She's physically fit. She's intelligent. But
healthy children don't just refuse to talk. Her silence
must be a sign of some deep injury. Yet no one will tell
me why. It's a mystery. God knows what really goes on
in her mind.'

I was tempted to confide in him. I was really tempted
to tell him about the cruel event that had taken away
Hermione's mother and her voice at the same time. I
looked at his gentle eyes and worn features. There was
something so reassuring about Patrick Snape. He would
understand and, once he understood, he could begin to
do something about it. But it wasn't my secret to tell. I
didn't have the right to tell him about the dreadful night
when Michael Frampton had forbidden his daughter
ever to mention her mother again.

Instead, 'How knowledgeable you sound,' I said
lightly.

'I'm a teacher.'

'Of course, an expert. I should have remembered.
You even look like one!' I chuckled at his rueful
expression. 'Well, you're wrong about this. Hermione
is a perfectly normal child. She just doesn't have much
to say for herself.'

'I wish it were as simple as that.'

'She's not neglected. She does have lessons, you
know, privately.'

'I know. And from next week, I'll be giving them.
I'm taking over the local school now Mr Grafton has

281

retired and I've been asked to teach Hermione in my spare time.'

I sipped my tea reflectively. 'From what I've seen, Captain Snape, I think that will do very well.'

And now I thought a bit more about it, didn't Patrick Snape have a friend – a friend who'd made a promise to me he'd never kept.

'Tell me,' I said. 'What's happened to your friend – I can't quite remember his name – the flyer . . . you know?'

'Archie, you mean. He's . . . around. In fact, I'm waiting for him now. He and Charley Frampton went sailing this afternoon. There wasn't room for me. Anyway, I'm not awfully keen on bobbing about on the water.'

No, of course there wasn't room for three in Charley's dinghy. It was quite reasonable that Patrick should stay behind. Yet I could tell by the offhand way he spoke that he was unreasonably put out by the decision.

For some reason that I couldn't quite understand myself, I wanted to comfort him. He looked so utterly decent, so ill-equipped for dealing with the razzmatazz of modern life, so bleak.

'Lucky you to be left on dry land. So sensible. I always think that sailing is a greatly overrated pastime. I wouldn't dream of venturing on anything smaller than a luxury yacht – and certainly not in these chilly waters.'

But he wasn't listening. He was looking over my shoulder and the watchful expression on his face told me something I would never have guessed – not in a million years. Across the lawn came Charley looking, for once, suntanned and healthy. With him I recognized the stocky figure of Archie Byatt.

'You made a promise to me, young man,' I called when they were barely within earshot, 'and I'm going to make sure you keep it.'

★

Archie Byatt kept his promise. He began to teach me to fly that very same week. On Archie's advice I bought a reconditioned Avro 504K, an ex-RFC training machine. It looked a little the worse for wear, but was quite sound, chosen because he said that it was tame enough for a novice, but still fun to fly. I rented a field from a local farmer to use as a landing strip and we were ready to begin.

Until you've been in an aeroplane, you can never know what an exhilarating experience it is. The tension as pre-flight checks are gone through. The sickly smell of dope on the fabric, hot under the sun. The sick room odour of castor oil as the rotary engine is primed. The clattering roar as the engine fires in a reek of blue smoke. The dangerous feeling of curbed power as the revs rise. The fairground ride as we bounce over the rutted field, faster and faster. And then the earth just falls away.

Contrary to everyone's expectations, Archie was an excellent instructor. He let me get on with it with minimum interference. This might not have suited everyone, but it was ideal for my temperament. Charley Frampton was highly amused by my enthusiasm and invited me to stay at Buckholt for the duration of my lessons. Archie stayed there too. Patrick was by now living in the schoolmaster's house in the village. We made a jolly foursome – Archie, Charley, Patrick and me. We went everywhere together.

Hermione was doing very well under Patrick's tuition. He seemed to have a knack of communicating with her. To be honest, I was just the teeniest bit jealous. Until then, I had prided myself on being the only person able to get through to the child. Now Patrick's simple but direct methods seemed to be having some success. Nanny told me – and I could see it myself – that Hermione's temper tantrums, born of frustration, were

lessening. Unworthy jealousy apart, it was very satisfactory.

Viola's attitude, however, was less than satisfactory.
For some extraordinary reason, she seemed to have
formed an unlikely attachment to Archie Byatt. I
couldn't think of anything less suitable.

The poor child was probably lonely, heaven knows,
but after all these years of ostentatious mourning, I
couldn't imagine why Viola had chosen this moment to
return to the normal female preoccupation with the
other sex.

Archie did nothing to encourage her. In fact, if anything, I'd have said he did the opposite. Many a time he
brushed her off with a casualness that was almost brutal.
One might almost have said she enjoyed that sort of
treatment. Silly girl. Didn't she understand? No, I don't
suppose she did. How could she? I don't suppose she
knew much about the normal facts of life before she
married, let alone . . . well . . . *that*. And yet . . .

One afternoon I was wandering around the garden.
Hermione and I had been playing hide-and-seek and
Hermione had found a more than usually successful
hideaway. I remembered there was an abandoned
summer house, derelict and forgotten since the war,
overlooking the water at the very end of the garden. If
Hermione was hiding there, she'd never expect me to
find her.

It was a sad looking little place. Its thatched roof was
sagging and mossy. The ornamental stained glass
window panes were missing or cracked. As I came
nearer, I could hear movement. Yes, I'd got her.
Wouldn't she be surprised?

I was just about to call out, when I saw Viola come
out. She couldn't see me, but I was close enough to see
that her hair was tumbling out of its pins. She hurried
past me and still she didn't see me standing in the shrub-

bery. Her lips were reddened and puffy – the lips of a woman who had been thoroughly kissed. The skin of her chin and throat, always so white and sensitive, was abraded as though it had been in contact with a bristly surface.

I was still pondering this as Viola hurried out of sight. Then Archie came out of the summer house. He stood in the sunlight a moment, squinting up the garden. Then he straightened his tie, ran his fingers through his hair, put his hands in his pockets and wandered off down to the shore.

Well. Even at my age, I find there's still plenty I don't know about human nature. I don't know when I was so surprised.

What ought I to do? If I told Anthony, there'd be an almighty row that might well force Viola to do something silly, something she'd certainly regret later. If I whispered in Clemmie's ear that she ought to have a discreet word with her daughter, I couldn't trust that silly woman not to do something drastic.

In the end, I tackled Viola myself and made a mess of it. It's not like me to be embarrassed about a situation. Usually I'm quite capable of calling a spade a spade. But this was different. I was going to have to tell Viola some very unpalatable truths. When it came to the point, I looked at her innocent little face and muffed it. By the time I'd finished, Viola was more confused than ever. I don't think she had an inkling of what I was trying to warn her about.

Why should I try to shoulder the responsibility for other people's children?

Every night I studied the pocket manual written by Major Smith-Barry that Archie had tossed at me on the first day. In a very short time, I could recite its forty-two pages backwards – and frequently did! From the beginning, I was in charge of the Avro.

Archie sat in the instructor's seat, with the ability to communicate with me by speaking tube, but he allowed me to put into practice whatever manoeuvre we discussed before take off. As well as teaching me the conventional landing and take off, flying level and turning, Archie taught me to stall, to glide, to spin. He taught me the notorious Immelmann turn. He taught me to be at home in an environment naturally hostile to man.

From Archie I learned that the aeroplane is a nice-tempered, reasonable machine that obeys simple, honest rules at all times. He took away the mystique and replaced it with common sense. I loved it.

Archie was a great gossip too. He really enjoyed a spot of malicious meddling. It was difficult to understand why he should take an interest in some of the little nuggets of information he loved to pass on. It was from Archie I learned that Hector Malyon had been adopted as a Parliamentary candidate – for the *Labour* party.

'Good gracious,' I said, 'Hector is such a traditionalist. He's the last man I'd have envisaged waving the red flag.'

'Perhaps he's a secret Bolshevik. Perhaps he's been sent by the commissars in Moscow to undermine the English country gentlemen's way of life.'

'If you knew Hector,' I laughed, 'I don't think you'd say that!'

'It's a wonder we didn't have our own revolution before the war ended – the time was ripe, the people were ready for it. But the war ended too soon. Now we're all comfy and cosy again and it's all deadly boring.'

'You're a terrible boy, Archie, but you don't shock me one little bit. Just don't try that speech on Charley's father, I beg you. He'd have a stroke! I shouldn't think Hector stands an earthly, anyway.'

'Oh, I don't know. A brilliant war record. A pukka gentleman even though his Pa is in trade. By the way, have you heard the latest definition of *nouveau riche*? Someone who has to' buy his own antiques!' Archie kicked up his heels and laughed uproariously. Then he went on. 'Not a bit like his awful brother. He could rely on the disillusioned ex-soldier vote. After four years following orders given by chaps like him, obedience becomes a habit. All Malyon'll have to do is march up and tell them where to put their Xs – never mind what party he represents – and they'll all salute and do it.'

'You're very young to be so cynical, Archie.'

'Only the young can afford to be cynical. Only the young have the right. We haven't made our mistakes yet.'

'But you will.'

He just laughed and blew me a kiss.

One day after my lesson we had all gone out for lunch at a little pub on the Beaulieu River. To be honest, I wanted to show off my new acquisition. I'd got rid of the Vauxhall and bought a delicious little Bugatti Brescia – a most uncivilized vehicle – noisy, uncomfortable, with brakes whose performance left much to be desired, but, oh, the power! I actually held off a Bentley 3-litre on the Great West Road. Gorgeous!

Archie and Patrick travelled on Archie's flat-twin Douglas. Charley came with me in the Bugatti, because, with one arm, he couldn't hold on safely riding pillion. Viola had wanted to come too, but Anthony, showing unusually good sense I thought, had taken her with him on a little jaunt to Winchester, where he was seeing his solicitor and she could do some shopping.

We sprawled on the grass by the edge of the river. The tide was out and the shore smelled rich and rotting.

The channel in the centre of the river was a glittering trickle, a silken thread discarded on the mud. Oystercatchers probed with scarlet bills and tossed aside the seaweed with lost, piping wails. The sun bored through the thin piqué of my frock and loosened my ageing joints. I took off my hat and shook my grey curls, as coquettish as a girl. The taste of the beer was bitter on the soft part of my palate.

I felt very, very good.

'Solo tomorrow,' said Archie. Like us all, he lay flat on the grass. His head was lazily supported on Patrick's lap in a way that would have scandalized Harold. Somehow, that day, it seemed perfectly natural.

'Tomorrow,' I squawked. 'Am I ready?'

'Would I say so if you weren't?'

I grinned at them all in foolish delight.

'Good for you,' said Patrick. 'I thought I wanted to fly once, but one trip with Archie convinced me to keep my feet on the ground for good.'

'And then I'm off,' Archie finished.

As if his thighs lay under my own head instead of under Archie's, I felt Patrick stiffen. 'Where?' he asked quietly.

'Oh, I don't know. Somewhere. Life's no fun any more. There's no going back to Ireland since the settlement.'

'Thank God,' Patrick whispered.

'I didn't know you'd been in Ireland,' I queried innocently.

'Didn't you know?' Charley giggled. 'Archie and Patrick *were* the Black and Tans. Very exciting. Without them, the whole thing would have fizzled to a stalemate long before.'

'Don't talk such utter rot, Charley,' barked Patrick.

'You enjoyed it, didn't you, Archie? Go on, admit it. You loved every moment of it.'

'It was something to do, I suppose. After all, what have other men done since the war – started chicken farms, sold boot laces? Even tried for Parliament like Hector Malyon. That's not for me. As His Majesty's "trusty and well-beloved", I was taught to kill. Am I to blame if I developed a taste for it?'

I thought of all the stories I had heard about the Black and Tans. I thought about the night raids, the burning farms, the shots in the dark. I thought about the brutishness and the hatred and black, black secrets. I looked at Patrick sitting hunched in private misery.

'Find something you're good at and stick to it, my father always told me,' laughed Archie. 'So I did!'

I went solo the next day.

Early in the morning, before the mist had lifted, I was taxiing across the field. I had hardly slept all night, not with apprehension, but with excitement. Yet when the moment came, I was unnaturally calm. The rush of air through the open cockpit increased – I could tell as much by that as from the engine revs that I'd reached the critical speed. I gently plucked back the stick, remembering that the machine climbs much better in an almost level attitude than pointed wildly at the sky. Suddenly, I couldn't feel the wheels bumping off the turf any more. I hopped over the hedge at the end of the field and was flying.

I squealed excitedly into the speaking tube, but this time there was no one behind to hear me. I was alone.

For fifteen wonderful minutes, I threw the Avro around in every contortion that Archie had taught me. Far below, I could see them – Archie, Patrick and Charley – my three friends. They were puny figures, mere men, and I was immortal. I challenged the sun that morning and I outran the wind.

Overconfidence led to a dicey landing. I touched

down late and almost ran out of field, but managed to slew round at the last moment. The prop bit into the turf, trimmed the grass and freed itself. I was flung forward in the harness, then whiplashed back. When I killed the engine, I realized that my clothes were sticking to my skin with sweat. But I wasn't going to let anyone guess that I'd just scared the life out of myself. I swung out of the cockpit as Archie came running up.

'You bloody fool,' he yelled when he was still a dozen yards away. 'You could've killed yourself. You were magnificent!'

And he kissed me fiercely on the lips.

Their congratulations were very sweet. It was only later that I realized, with a jarring sense of anticlimax, that I had done what I set out to do. What next?

'I suppose you'll be going off soon, too?' I asked Archie next day.

'Not just yet. Michael Frampton has a little job he wants me to do for him. So I'll be here for a little while longer.'

'Oh?' Whatever Michael had in mind, I had a feeling that I ought to know about it.

'Yes, just a little something to keep me off the streets – and lucrative, too – poor, unemployed ex-officer that I am. A little research job.'

'Research? Something interesting?'

'I can tell by your face that you're absolutely bursting to find out. Well, I'm not going to tell you. It's private.'

'I'm not interested! Keep your silly old secrets!'

And I disguised beneath childish pique a very real worry about what Archie could possibly do for Michael that would be worth money to him. I tried to imagine Michael and Archie working together. It was a combination I didn't like – but I didn't quite know why.

'And besides – maybe I'm not in such a hurry to

move on, after all. I'm not at all sure I ought to leave old Patrick. Not yet.'

On the morning after Elsa Broke was killed, I decided that I was going to see Helen and nothing was going to stop me. For poor Celia's sake, something had to be done.

It was splashed all over the newspapers, of course. There had been a party near Hindhead – come as your secret self, or some such silly nonsense. As usual, a good deal too much champagne had been drunk and probably, although it was never disclosed, a good deal too much 'snow' had been sniffed. It seems that Elsa had quarrelled with the young man who escorted her to the party. She had driven off with someone else and the car had been found at dawn at the bottom of the Devil's Punch Bowl. The driver was unconscious and Elsa's neck was snapped.

The little maid who came to the door of the house in Ellis Street made her usual excuses, but I was in no mood to be stopped.

'If your mistress won't come down to see me, I'll go up to see her!' I brayed and swept upstairs, along the corridor and through the door at the far end. 'Helen, this has got to stop . . .' I began.

Perhaps I really ought to have waited downstairs. But, after all, I was, and am, her aunt – her only living relative.

In the gloom of the curtained room, the long sweep of Helen's back gleamed bone-white and sweating. Her head was thrown back and the tousled gilt curls were plastered to her scalp. Propped up on pillows, Philip had taken both her nipples in his blind, searching mouth. With calculated precision, Helen's hips rose and fell, just a few, measured inches at each stroke. Enfolding him. Nourishing him. Drawing him.

I should have turned my head aside. I should have closed my eyes. I couldn't. I looked and the scene had a terrible beauty that brought out the sort of flush I thought I had finished with all over my body.

All this I saw, with the clarity of a photographic flash, in the moments before Philip's mouth opened in a soundless cry, letting her breasts swing free. Helen shuddered and quickened her pace. She shuddered again, grinding herself hard downwards again and again. Then she fell forward, sobbing, onto Philip's chest.

The room was filled with the sound of their united breathing. Then Philip opened his eyes.

'I say, darling,' he drawled, 'here's your aunt come visiting. Isn't that decent of her?'

Helen rolled off and he sat up higher, grinning, camouflaging what he had to but not attempting to cover his chest decently. Helen propped herself up on her elbows, managing to drag the sheet up with her, so that only her shoulders were visibly naked. She reached across the night table, opened a gold cigarette case and took out two cigarettes. Holding them both in her mouth, she lit them, then popped one between Philip's waiting lips.

'Thanks, sweetie,' he mumbled, then he turned his devastating, boyish grin on me. 'Do you think you could be an absolute poppet, Aunt Eglantine, and toss me my robe? Thanks. Perhaps you might turn your back for a moment? OK – I'm decent now.'

Philip was up, his dressing robe wrapped tightly round his body. I couldn't help noticing that he was recovering only slowly from the inconvenience of my sudden arrival.

'I'll just toddle off, shall I, and leave you two girls to have a cosy natter.'

'Well,' said Helen after he'd gone. 'I must say – you

do pick your moments.' She picked a shred of tobacco off her tongue.

Now that I was actually here, I couldn't think what there was to say. I walked across the room and whisked open the curtains. Looking at the disorder of the room, I wished I'd left them closed.

They had obviously undressed each other slowly and lingeringly as they had crossed the room, sometime in the early hours of the morning. Spangled sandals, black patent dancing shoes, Philip's bow tie, a boiled shirt with gold studs and cufflinks still in place, a beaded slither of backless evening gown, black dress trousers looking uncannily as though they still concealed two legs. The trail led from the door. Closer to the bed, I averted my eyes from Philip's underwear. Hanging from the end of the bed was a whisper of apricot silk cami-knickers. One silk stocking was still tangled in the disordered blankets.

But it wasn't my Helen in the bed. It couldn't be. Not this woman with the evasive eyes and the sulky mouth. Her face was puffy with sleep, her movements slow and sated. She altered her position and the sheet slipped back. She was so thin that her breasts were indecent growths. When she reached over to stub out her cigarette, her shoulder blades were like budding wings.

'Helen, darling, can we talk?' I was annoyed to find myself pleading. That wasn't the mood I had arrived in.

'If we must. Look, why don't you go down to the morning room? Order some tea – whatever you'd like. I'll join you in a minute.'

She was a long time coming. By the time Helen joined me downstairs, I had regained some of the fizz that had led me to storm their bedroom. Her first words really put me on my mettle.

'I suppose you've come to tell me what a naughty girl I am,' she yawned.

'No, I haven't . . .'

'What a relief.'

'. . . because you're not a girl and you're not naughty. You're a woman and a bloody stupid one at that. Where's this all leading?'

'All what leading?'

'*Don't* be clever with me. I'm not in the mood. When are you going to come to your senses? These silly parties, the drink, the cocaine, the fast cars. Are you trying to kill yourself? I can think of less messy ways . . .'

To give Helen her due, she heard me out while I ranted on. At least, she didn't interrupt, but I don't think she was listening at all. She poured a cup of tea, tasted it, grimaced. She looked out of the window to check the weather. She rearranged a couple of stems in the flower arrangement in front of a pier glass. And all the time her feet and fingers were tap-tapping to a soundless dance tune.

'For God's sake, Helen, what's it all for? What do you want out of life?'

Her tapping fingers were still at last. When she looked at me, I knew that nothing I had said made any sense at all to her.

'I want Hermione,' she said.

HECTOR

The Soldier

The dream is always the same. I can feel myself sliding into it. I struggle against it, crying out that no, I don't want to dream that dream again. But I slither down the slope and it grabs me and I can't get away. I have to dream it.

I'm walking down a road, any road, anywhere. There's a man walking in front of me, any man, short, tall, fat, thin. I'm walking faster, so I come up behind him quite quickly. That's when I start to struggle to escape the dream, but it won't let me. I know what's going to happen next. I know the man's going to turn round.

When he does turn round, that ordinary man, any man, anywhere, he always has the same face. His face. He turns his face to me. He knows what I'm going to do. He knows and I know what will happen to him. For a split second, the knowledge is there, the disbelief, the shock, the horror. His mouth is open, a red hole. In a moment, he will begin to run, but I'm too quick for him.

And then . . . and then . . . I wake up. Not screaming any more, thank God, but sweating and shivering like a frightened horse, weak with the horror that lingers into consciousness, limp with relief that I'm awake. Adrienne does her best to comfort me.

'Was it that dream again?' she asks and gentles me with her steady little hands.

She strokes back my wet hair. She puts her warm,

strong arms around me and lets me hide my face between the pillows of her breasts, until her body works its magic again. I'm a man once more and in control.

But Adrienne doesn't know it all. She knows that I dream, but she doesn't know what is going to happen if I don't wake up in time. I can't tell her that.

In the daylight, I am in command. My mind does what it's told. But at night, I slip into unconsciousness and I dream.

What happens to the killers when the killing comes to an end? What happens when a whole generation of men has become accustomed to the daily sight of human bodies like so much discarded lumber?

I remember a trench near Plug Street. Some poor old sod had been buried in the parados by a shell blast, months before. His desiccated hand stuck out between the sandbags. It was winter and the hand was frozen. The company wag used it as a hook for his tin hat. 'D'you mind, chum?' he always asked politely before hanging it there.

I'm not the man I used to be. Who is? Who among the contemptible little band that sailed to France in August 1914 has come home still innocent? 'He that toucheth pitch shall be defiled therewith.' My hands will be dirty for ever.

But Adrienne showed me another verse, which said: 'There is a shame that bringeth sin and there is a shame which is glory and grace.' And if the shame of nations sweeps away the bad, old ways and replaces them with something wholesome and good, will it all have been worthwhile?

One good thing that the war has done is finish the old political system. Men who have been promised a country fit for heroes and been given less than nothing, will take what they want. Is it too much to ask? They want their jobs back; they want decent homes; they want food for their children; they want hope for the future. And by God, they deserve it. They have paid for it already – and much more besides. We owe it to them.

The war ruined the Liberal party and with it Lloyd George. Or was it the other way round? All those promises that were made with such hope in 1918 were impossible to keep. The people don't easily forgive broken promises. They'll stand firm when things are going badly. Promise them nothing but blood, sweat and tears and they'll rise up in cheers. Promise them the earth and fail to deliver and they'll never forgive.

The post-war boom was so short. We never realized that depression was so close behind. The whole balance of trade was altered. Countries that used to buy British manufactured products had been forced to find other, cheaper suppliers while we were occupied fighting the war to end all wars. They saw no reason to change once we began knocking on their doors again.

Lloyd George was a falling star and when the Conservatives, alarmed by his handling of the Irish question and by the implications of the Chanak incident, broke up the coalition, he was left with less than half a party to lead. As 1922 wore on, and by June the number of unemployed men reached two million, it became clear to me at last what I had to do with my life.

My father was delighted when I said I wanted to stand for Parliament.

'To think,' he said, 'a son of mine governing the country.'

And he was scandalized when I said I was standing for the Labour Party.

'A son of mine,' he thundered, 'on the same side as agitators and strikers and Bolsheviks? Over my dead body!'

'Don't be so melodramatic, Father. I'm not preaching red revolution. I'm talking about a legally recognized political party.'

'What's the difference, I'd like to know? This country was nearly brought to its knees by Bolsheviks in 1917 and 18. Look how the miners and shipbuilders let down you boys at the Front with their stoppages and their wrangling. The very police mutinied! Do you know that at one time the Fleet had only one week's coal supply left? Do you know that Churchill threatened to call up the Coventry aircraft engineers if they didn't go back to work? No, you don't. What do you know about anything at all? You weren't here.'

'No, I wasn't here,' I replied as calmly as I could, 'that's the whole point.'

'Aye, well,' Father muttered, 'now, don't get me wrong, Hector, I'm not trying to put you down. You're an honest, right-thinking man, I'll not deny, but you've no experience of real life. I just don't think you know what you're getting yourself into, that's all.'

'I owe a debt of honour, Father. Don't shame me by pretending it doesn't exist.'

What arrogance – to imagine that I could shoulder the debt of a nation. Every time I passed a man in the street with a placard round his neck: DISABLED EX-SER-VICEMAN NO PENSION BOOTLACES 3d or I Fought For YOU Now You Think Of ME Matches 1d, I would empty the contents of my pocket book into the man's tin collecting cup. And I didn't do it for the pleasure of seeing the man's face light up with joy and disbelief. That would have been selfish somehow – offering a sop to my conscience and going on my way rejoicing. I did it because I genuinely believed that every single person in the land had a duty to the men with the broken boots and the chestful of medals to see that their children were fed.

There was so little I could do. No one who shared with me the honour of wearing the 1914 Star, the proud badge of the British Expeditionary Force – and there were so few of us left – would want while I could prevent it.

I made sure that anyone I employed in the stables had a military record. I influenced my father to employ only ex-servicemen, once he was able to recruit groundsmen, gardeners and a chauffeur again. And of course, he'd already promised to keep open their old jobs for anyone who wanted them back on demobilization. I visited all our neighbours and tried to persuade them, not always successfully, to the same way of thinking. It became well-known in the area that no one was ever turned away from Knapp Hill without a square meal and a helping hand.

Charity! These men didn't want charity. They only wanted what was due to them. How could I, rusticating in Wiltshire, help more than a few? Then it became apparent that the government would not survive to the end of 1922 without calling an election.

Oh yes, I was arrogant all right. I thought that all I had to do was present myself at a party association meeting and say, 'Here I am. Use me.' And they'd all jump up and pat me on the back and say, 'Jolly good. We've been waiting for you'!

I didn't have an inkling of the sort of class suspicion my offer would arouse. They distrusted me. I couldn't understand why.

Looking back, it's surprising that the local Labour Party branch even agreed to see me. They could just have torn up my letter and tossed it in the nearest waste paper basket. I imagine that's what quite a few of them wanted to do. Instead, I was summoned to a meeting in a private house in a respectable part of Devizes.

I'd taken care not to overdress. I wore a pre-war

tweed suit that was too big for me because I'd lost weight, a soft shirt and the hat I usually wore when walking the dogs. I was prepared for men in heavy, shapeless suits, mufflers and awkward boots. I was surprised by the neatly-dressed, schoolmasterly type with immaculate stiff collar and cuffs, a gold pince-nez hanging on a chain around his neck, who sat at the head of a mahogany dining table. I certainly didn't expect the trim, youngish woman in a sober tailormade suit who looked like a bank clerk or a typist. I wasn't prepared for the disfavour that rose up from the five people in the room as I walked in. But I brazened it out and shook hands with each one of them before taking the upright chair they indicated.

They looked at me with some hostility before the schoolmaster said, 'Tell us about yourself, Mr Malyon.'

What was there to tell?

I could tell them I was Lieutenant Colonel Hector Price Malyon DSO and Bar, MC, once a regular soldier in Kitchener's contemptible little army and now adrift in a peacetime world I increasingly didn't understand.

I could tell them how much they needed someone like me, to give them credibility. I could tell them how important it was for them to be seen as a party of sane and much-needed reform, rather than as the bunch of raving red revolutionaries most people imagined them to be. If people like me were seen to support them, it might allay the fears of the property-owning classes.

Or I could tell them I was a coward.

Adrienne kept me sane. She understood, you see, as no one else at home understood, what it was all about. Vileness had laid hands on her, but it had passed on without touching her soul. She offered me her clean, sound body and her clean, sound mind. She smelled of soap and starch, of bread and butter, of woman. I wanted to bury myself in the smell and never come out again.

I can remember coming downstairs, that foul winter's night at Knapp Hill, and finding her alone in the hall. We had been expecting a Belgian refugee, of course, but it was so late and the weather so threatening that we'd given her up, imagining that she wouldn't arrive until the next day.

And there she was, a battered cardboard suitcase in her hand, her summerweight coat dragged over the mound of her belly to fasten with only one button, scrawny wrists and ankles protruding from the charity clothing. She ought to have looked pathetic. In the moment or two that I looked down on her, before she realized I was there, she looked magnificent.

There was a stubborn strength about the set of her shoulders as she looked around the strange place, taking stock of it. I watched her, in her pragmatic, un-English way, decide to make the best of things. Her spirit flickered like a flame in the darkened hall. I have been warming myself at it ever since. She had not been defeated. Nowhere near it.

Then she put down the suitcase and put both hands to the small of her back, letting out a little noise that was more sigh than groan. She looked up then and saw me. As I came downstairs, she looked up at me with those great, soft eyes. I had a little spaniel bitch once, who died in whelp, and just before she died she looked at me with eyes just like that, begging for the help I couldn't give her. I started to run and was just in time to catch Adrienne as she fell.

Most people nowadays, when they think of Flanders, if they think of it at all any more, think of a ravaged country, trampled into its own mud, torn apart by opposing armies. The very frontier between France and

303

Belgium is lost in most people's minds, blurred beneath the terrible title of the Western Front.

It wasn't always like that. People scarcely remember that 'poor little Belgium' even existed before August 1914. They forget it was once a fertile land with huge red cows grazing knee-high in buttercup-yellow meadows.

When the battalion berthed at a wharf right in the centre of Le Havre on 13 August 1914, we all crowded onto the deck of the troopship *Cawdor Castle* for a first glimpse of France. We looked down onto the Place de la Gare, fringed with a row of tamarisks, with offices and shops on one side and a rash of hoardings on the other, advertising outlandish brands of *tabac, bière, savon, parfum*. Above the railway station, in great red letters, was the poster we were soon to see everywhere:

> *Taisez-vous!*
> *Méfiez-vous!*
> *Les oreilles de l'ennemi vous écoutent!*

We stood on the deck and sniffed the exotic smells of bread, bitter coffee, strong tobacco, fish from the stalls set out in the square, and we chafed to set foot at last in France.

I don't think we landed with the spirit of exaltation now attributed to us. We weren't carried away by the emotion of the moment. I have read accounts of the early days of the war that make us sound like schoolboy Sir Galahads starting out on the quest for the Holy Grail. It didn't seem like that at the time to me.

For one thing, we were mostly older than the volunteers still at home clamouring to be allowed to save civilization from the boot of the Hun. We had memories of Ladysmith and Spion Kop, some of us, of the tawny hills of Hindu Kush and the boredom of garrisoning the Rock. We were professionals and left all that enthusiasm to the amateurs crowding into recruiting offices back over the Channel. We had been sent to do a job and, by God, we were going to do it as well as we could and then get off back home again.

I tried to dredge back through long forgotten school-boy history lessons. Was this the first time an English army had landed in France to fight anyone other than the French? I just couldn't remember, but I was pretty certain that the last time a British army had entered France, it had been on the way to defeat Napoleon. Or did they land in the Belgian ports and not in France at all? And was there such a country as Belgium then, in any case? I'd never paid all that much attention to any of my lessons.

Anyway, it didn't much matter. I'll bet they didn't get the extraordinary welcome that we did.

You know the sort of reception we were given. The newspapers were full of stories of cheering, weeping crowds, waving any item of red, white or blue they could lay their hands on: tablecloths, curtains, petti-coats. The extraordinary thing is that none of these stories is exaggerated.

Under a grilling sun, we marched five miles to the rest camp. The time hung very heavily there and it was difficult to keep our enthusiastic hosts out of the camp by courteous means. It was also hard to keep our men out of mischief, before orders came to move forward. By the time the lads had entrained for Landrecies in waggons stencilled *Hommes 40, Chevaux en long 8*, half of them had given away their cap badges and shoulder titles. The other half gave theirs away on the march towards Mons. The farther north we travelled, the more enthusiastic was the welcome.

At every station, crowds pressed fruit, chocolate, cigarettes, wine through our carriage windows, with

305

half-joking shouts of '*À bas les Boches!*', accompanied by vivid throat-cutting pantomime.

Once we had de-trained and were on the route, tables of food and drink were set out in the villages. Girls marched arm in arm with the Tommies, laughing and singing, doling out flowers and kisses in equal proportions. Even the dour CSM, Annetts, marched with a rose tucked into his chin strap and a silly grin on his face. When there were no more cap badges to give away, the lads handed out buttons and belts as souvenirs. The British Army marched hatless with their trousers held up by string.

Carrying 80lbs of equipment, in thick khaki uniforms, flannel shirts and woollen underwear, in temperatures of over ninety degrees, we trudged along the *pavé* the forty miles to Mons. Our hobnailed boots slid on the granite setts. Our ankles turned on the intersection between the cobbles. The newly-recalled Reserves had been issued with new boots. I saw one man whose socks had disintegrated and were mashed into the bloody pulp of his feet. Hatless men suffered terribly from the sun on their necks. At a nightstop in Maroilles, the lads hung up their soaking shirts and put on their worsted cardigans instead.

I remember passing Malplaquet. The obelisk that marked Marlborough's victory over the French excited quite a bit of interest amongst the men.

'That's where we whopped 'em last time out,' I heard a man say, but I didn't have the energy to put him right.

At midday on the Friday, we crossed the border into Belgium. In the pitiless sun, we halted in a meadow near a tiny village. The inhabitants carried out to us bread, butter and coffee in a brave attempt to feed three thousand men. A milkman and a fruitseller made their rounds of our ranks, both transporting their goods in the traditional dogcarts that looked so strange to English eyes, drawn by active, heavy-jowled, crop-eared dogs.

We reached the Borinage, one smoke-blackened, acrid-smelling pit village after another, running on into each other, so no one knew where one ended and the next began. Disfigured by pit-head machinery and slag heaps, seamed by a complex pattern of drainage channels and neatly cut in two by the sixteen-mile, ruler-straight, reeking, slimy Mons Canal, it didn't look like good fighting country.

And when we got to Mons, with its church belfry like a huge coffee pot surrounded by four little teapots, we turned round and marched back again.

Of course, there are all sorts of sound reasons why we had to retreat almost as soon as we had arrived. We numbered 70,000 or so men in all. The total German forces numbered 1,485,000 and we faced four corps and three cavalry divisions of von Kluck's First Army. The French, badly mauled – their casualties by this date about three times the total size of the BEF – had fallen back, leaving our flanks exposed. A ten mile gap had opened between us and the French, a gap quite wide enough for an entire enemy corps to drive through. We were in danger of being cut off and surrounded.

Relationships between the French General Lanrezac and our own commander were less than cordial and each blamed the other for the coming débâcle. Sir John French promised the French that we would hold our position on the canal for 24 hours. Some units, in fact, didn't arrive there until the 24 hours were nearly over.

In an early mist that promised another gruelling day, we dragged wagons, furniture, trees, anything that would make a barricade, across the streets among the terraced cottages. The Belgians came to help us with picks and shovels more substantial than the light entrenching tools we carried.

The bells were ringing for mass by the time we'd finished. Neat families, freshly washed and pressed, were making their way to church, picking their steps through the mess we had made of their streets. It was as though Mons had been divided into two separate worlds: a sane world where people went to bed and rose in the morning and breakfasted and worshipped; a mad one where we crouched in the streets behind the upended wardrobes and double beds we had commandeered from the sane people.

I walked up and down the line of prostrate men, stopping at each one for a quiet word. I knew their names; I knew their families; I knew them like my brothers. They were steady and calm, ready for the job they'd been sent to do.

'Take your time now, lads,' I said. 'Let them do all the running. Let them come to you, pick your target and fire at will.'

I got down, flat on my belly under a farm cart, squinting up the straight, bright street. The church door was open in the heat and the sound of singing was clear and sweet. We waited for the Germans to come.

This was the battlefield of Mons, not a carefully selected arena, just the place where we happened to be at the time, across the path of the advancing German First Army.

Down at company level, we didn't see it that way, of course. One never does. The big picture is for generals. The fighting soldier is only conscious of the man in the funny uniform who is trying to kill him. At most, we keep our eyes on the few yards of frontage that mean life and death to us.

We were in contact with the enemy. Yes, we were taking casualties – heavy casualties. But that's what war is all about, isn't it? You face that the moment you take the oath of allegiance to the sovereign. We were regular soldiers and this was the job we had been sent across the Channel to do.

The Germans came on in solid phalanxes of field grey. We just couldn't miss them. It was like picking off a row of tin cans on a wall. Our lads were at first astonished and then jubilant. This was something like soldiering! It was just like being back at Hythe, at the School of Musketry. Poor blighters. They were packed so tightly that each of our bullets found more than one target, frequently several. And still they came on, craftier now, sheltering behind the mounds of their dead.

We treated them to a 'mad minute' – 15 rounds rapid fire. I'm told the Germans thought we were equipped with machine guns – if only we had been! After we had finished, there was silence. And then out of the crumpled, stacked line of grey that filled the whole of our field of fire, came a long, long moan.

In answer to our fire, they brought up a couple of field guns. Then we were the sitting targets. So I gave the order to move back and regroup, beyond range.

We didn't know how heavy the casualties were all along the fighting front. We knew that we had lost badly, but never guessed that the pattern was repeated right along the line. Our new position was in an area of slag heaps. Those heaps were a problem. They were either overlooked by others or too hot to touch – or both. But we'd managed to make ourselves fairly comfortable.

The slag heaps were no protection against artillery. We couldn't dig in because of the heat in the core of the heaps. Anyway, the spoil just slipped and filled in the holes as fast as we dug. The air was filled with great puffs of black coal dust. Every breath made us cough and wheeze. We looked like bloodstained sweeps. It was impossible for stretcher bearers to reach the wounded because of the hail of fire that bounced off every square foot of open ground. We had to do the best we could with field dressings and iodine.

We held on as long as we could, but in the end, our only option was to abandon our position, falling back across the canal, destroying the bridge as we went.

I hope they were kind to the wounded. We had to leave them behind. It wasn't as callous as it sounds. Even Germans are human, after all, and it's rare for a professional soldier to neglect enemy wounded. Who knows when the tables might be turned? I don't say as much for conscripts, though. Sometimes they don't see things in quite the same way.

It was a good morning's work. We'd held them for a useful stretch of time. In our new positions, the afternoon more or less repeated the morning. But there were more than twice as many of them as of us. Under cover of darkness, we began the slow and painful business of falling back.

II Corps suffered 1600 casualties that broiling summer Sunday. Nothing, you might say, to the casualties in the battles yet to come. Thank God, we were not blessed then with the dubious gift of foresight. Those 1600 casualties represented more than 2 per cent of our total force, gone in one day. We couldn't afford continued losses at that rate.

Back along the same roads we went and they seemed twice as dusty and hard with our backs to the enemy. The cheering crowds were gone. Sometimes as we passed through a village, doors would open and frightened people, good people, would thrust water or bread or coffee into our hands. Then the doors would close again. I thought of them hiding in their indefensible little houses, waiting for the sound of German hooves clattering down the street or for the whoof of a bursting shell that would blast their frail shelter to pieces.

The roads were clogged, too, with refugees. Now

we were hampered by broken-axled ox carts, pitiful household goods strewn across the road, old men pushed in wheelbarrows, children in perambulators, terrified people who clutched at our sleeves and begged us not to abandon them. Behind them, they could see the billowing, black smoke of burning villages – perhaps their own villages.

They were running. We were withdrawing. The Germans harassed our withdrawal at every step. And it was bitter to yield a single yard of the route we had travelled so triumphantly so short a time ago.

I remember being constantly parched. Often, the water carts were impeded by refugees and couldn't keep up with the marchers. Sometimes, the horses in that heat needed to drink more water than they were actually transporting. Dirty, thirsty, exhausted from the heat, we rolled like drunks across the road. Men fell asleep where they stood when halts were called. The units became completely muddled, as men who had been unable to keep up rejoined the march after a rest at any handy point. We were withdrawing. But we were not retreating. There is a difference.

It's the smell I remember most: of bitter, greasy smoke and the tang of explosives; of blood and horse piss; of wounds beginning to suppurate in dirty bandages; of the fly-blown bodies of horses. Most of all I remember the smell of thousands of unwashed men. It hung around us as we marched, followed us as visible as a cloud. It was the smell of an army on the move. It was – so nearly – the smell of defeat.

Looking back, I see how close we were to disaster. If von Bülow to the east had kept his nerve, he could have smashed open the French centre that dreadful Sunday. Our rearguard fought constant, bloody, expensive skirmishes throughout the withdrawal, but the final, clinching assault was never launched. It was as though the

Germans never seemed quite certain of where we were and what we were doing. They just kept on stumbling over us as though by accident.

Perhaps they couldn't believe we were really turning back as soon as we had arrived. Perhaps they thought it was all part of some diabolical plan to lead them on and encircle them. If only they'd known!

We marched. We fought. We marched again. We slept where we fell. And when we woke up, we had to do it all again, under a sky white hot and melting at the edges.

They nearly got us at Le Cateau, where exhausted II Corps, sodden after a lashing summer storm, could not avoid making a stand. Yet somehow, due to poor intelligence or communications, von Kluck was unable to bring up his complete strength to finish us off as he should have done.

For eleven hours we held them off. For eleven hours we dug our heels in and would not be budged. But at what a cost.

The air was sultry, heavy with thunder. It seemed to press physically on us, like an ill-fitting hat. The noise of firing ebbed and flowed up and down the line, devil's music building up to an ear-splitting crescendo in one position, then faltering and dying away as another stubborn little huddle of men was overrun. Then it would break out somewhere else, as the Germans probed another supposed weak spot. But, though they came near it, they never broke through.

And we could still laugh. Corporal Maidment, neat and meticulous, was collecting his spent cartridge cases, wiping them clean and replacing them in his bandolier, for all the world as though he were on exercise on Salisbury Plain and would have to account for all he had expended.

'Missed some over there, Corporal,' the next man

said, pointing over our defences to where a pile of spent shell cases marked the spot recently vacated by an artillery battery.

A chuckle ran up and down the line as we waited for the next wave of attack.

When the order to disengage came, I looked around what was left of my company. Not a man was unhurt – except, amazingly, myself – and their fire, though still steady and disciplined, was less effective now. They were worn down, by heat, by thirst, by pain and loss of blood.

And they were all looking at me. They were all waiting to see what I would do to get them out of this mess. As though I were some sort of conjuror, they waited to see what little miracle I would pull out of my pocket. Didn't they know that magic is all an illusion?

Their expectancy was oppressive. I felt as though gravity had taken hold of me, grasping at my boots, tacking my tongue to the soft floor of my mouth. And still they waited for me to get them out. And I would, too. Every last man of them – no matter what.

'Right, sa'r'nt major,' I said. 'Time to draw stumps.'

'Righto, sir,' he answered and then a slimy, bloodstained bubble, just like the kind a child makes with soap and a twisted wire loop, oozed from his lips and burst.

People talk about the Angel of Mons stretching out his hand to silence the battlefield. They talk about St George holding back the might of the German empire. They talk about the ghostly bowmen of Agincourt turning back the German cavalry with shining arrows, as once they had routed the French cavalry on this same, sad, contentious patch of land.

Officially, it's all been discredited and laid at the door of some newspaper hack. Those with a scientific bent explain it all by talking about heat exhaustion, thirst and mirages, something called mass hysteria, whatever that might be.

Perhaps they're right.

I know what I saw. I don't talk to anyone about it. Why should I? Whether anyone else believes or not, makes no difference to what I saw. If I had come home prattling of white-hot, blinding light and a breathless silence over the battlefield, I should, quite rightly, have been shut away for the duration. Besides, it wasn't like that at all.

But I know what I saw. And I was not alone. All I will tell you is that the enemy could have annihilated us and, for some reason, they failed to. However you attempt to explain it, it was a miracle.

I'm sorry. I got diverted, didn't I? I didn't intend to bore you with my memories. We all have so many memories nowadays and we all think that our own are far more worthwhile than anyone else's.

What I was trying to explain was that it all started out as a proper war, a soldiers' war. In the beginning, it was a war of movement, just as it ought to be. Generals understood that. They could cope with it. They were at home with the concepts of cavalry screens and flanking movements and a race to the Channel ports that bogged down in the autumn rains of Flanders. Vlaanderen. The flooded land.

There were so many of them and so few of us. So we dug holes to shelter in. That wasn't good enough, so we dug deeper holes. Then we joined all the holes together in a long line. That's when it all started to go wrong. That's when it stopped being a proper war.

But by the time that happened, the British Expeditionary Force, the Regular Army, had virtually disappeared from existence. Oh, of course, there were quite a few of us left, here and there, but we were scattered, diluted by the flood of volunteers and later conscripts.

After First Ypres, only we didn't know it was *First* Ypres then (so ignorance really is bliss), I went on leave. When I came back, I was the only combatant officer left who had started the war with the battalion. I could look around and there was scarcely a face I knew. Eager faces. Steady faces. Bright faces. Let-me-get-at-'em faces.

Strangers.

Where was the orderly I had last seen in Nonne Boschen Wood heading up the line with a pail of tea in each hand, whistling tunelessly to himself?

'Where are you off to?' I shouted. 'It's pretty unhealthy out there.'

'I know, but if I don't go, the blokes won't get their tea, sir. Counting on me, they are. Care for a cup yourself, sir?'

He'd dipped me a tin mug of tea and said he'd pick it up on his return journey. I've still got the mug somewhere.

Where was the company commander who'd fished out his last remaining Oxo cubes and made hot drinks for the eleven men left in his company?

We were short of everything – ammunition, rifle oil, sandbags, barbed wire. We'd spent a perilous morning well in front of the line, defending a sapper working party putting up a single strand of barbed wire before the trenches.

'A giraffe could walk under that lot without bending!' exclaimed a middle-aged sergeant in disgust. 'It's enough to make a soldier weep tears of blood!'

Where was the corporal who'd dragged a tattered creature in baggy red trousers and a dark blue coat into the dugout early one morning?

'Beg pardon, sir, but we've found about sixty like him digging around in our woods. What'll we do with them?'

He was quite disgruntled when told that he was assaulting a Zouave, an ally, a comrade, with every right to be there. He'd hoped he had discovered a nest of spies.

'Well, they'd better not muck around with *our* trenches, that's all.'

It had cost us a lovingly-hoarded bottle of scotch to pacify the ruffled pride of the Frenchmen.

God, I had loved them, those dirty, awkward, stubborn, patient, wonderful men. Where had they gone?

I'm whole. Look at me. Strip off my clothes and look at me. Not a mark. Not so much as a scratch. Two arms. Two legs. The proper complement of two eyes, a nose and a mouth. My entrails neatly tucked away in the proper place. My cock rising to my demand. My lungs functioning and I don't even have to think about it – in, out, in, out – even when I'm asleep. I'm in perfect working order.

Why me? Why Hector and not Tom, Dick or Harry? Why should I be singled out to remain whole, when others deserved as much and yet they were soon just names on the daily casualty lists: officers, one name to a column; other ranks, a solid mass of type right across the page.

And when the war stopped being a soldiers' war and slid into a stinking morass that sucked men in at one end and spewed them out in pieces at the other, these men went on making the best of it. In spite of broken bodies, in the very face of death, they endured. I did not. I could not.

The simple fact of my survival has left me with a debt to repay. There are widows to be housed and children to be fed. There are men who will never walk or see or breathe easily again to be cared for. And there are politicians who must be made to promise – if necessary by force – that we will never, *never* go to war again.

No one was more surprised than I to be notified that I had been adopted as the official Labour Party candidate for the insignificant Wiltshire constituency of Upper Avon. I expect they hadn't been able to turn up another one.

I know I talked too much at the selection meeting. I'm not even completely sure what I said at the time. It's all a bit of a blank, I was in such a blue funk. High-minded piffle, no doubt. Philip says I always sound as though I'm preaching a sermon. (People like me need brothers like him, he says, to avoid becoming unutterably sanctimonious.) All I can remember is leaving the meeting in a muck sweat.

I didn't feel like going home straight away. There would be too many questions asked – particularly by my father – that I couldn't answer. So I took the car as far up the track to Roundway Down as it would go. Then I got out and walked along the ridge to Oliver's Castle. It was very late and there was hardly a light still on below in Devizes. Beyond that, there was nothing but windblown darkness and the bulky plateau of Salisbury Plain. Even without seeing it, I knew what I was looking at, knew and loved every rounded hill and chalky valley.

'Well,' I thought. 'I've done all I can. Either they want me or they don't.'

Adrienne seemed completely unsurprised by it all. 'But of course they want you,' she said, dropping a kiss on the back of my head as she read the letter over my shoulder, 'and if they did not, I would catch the very next train to Devizes and give them all what for! You will be a first class member.'

Philip gave a lewd snort.

'Is that not the right term? Have I made a mistake?' she asked with a little frown – she hated to make even the slightest error in the English language, even though I always told her her accent was charming. 'I thought one should talk about honourable members in your parliament.'

'A member,' Philip gurgled. 'A member is . . .' Then he caught sight of my expression across the breakfast table. '. . . I was only teasing, Adrienne. Sorry. You're absolutely right. Hector will make a splendid member!'

'Then what is all the laughing? Hector?' She turned her ferocious little frown on me. 'Have I said something foolish, please?'

'Don't pay any attention to Philip, darling. He has the sense of humour of a second former – if that.'

'Oh Lord! Just listen to the head prefect!' Philip rolled his eyes heavenward. 'I hope you're not going to turn into a middle-class prig, Hector, because if you are, then the sooner Helen and I hightail it back to the bright lights, the better.'

'You can't go soon enough for me,' I growled and turned my attention to the cooling kidneys on my plate.

I can't imagine that every newly-adopted candidate is invited to town by the soon-to-be Leader of the Opposition to meet him. So why me? I could only assume it was because I was something a bit out of the ordinary – a prospective Labour Member of Parliament coming from neither the working nor the intellectual classes.

Adrienne, of course, thought it no less than my due and was quite excited by a trip up to town. I could have done without being away from home precisely at that moment. I had three mares due to foal within a day of each other. Then, at the last minute, Alexander caught a feverish cold and Adrienne would not be persuaded to leave him. However, if I intended to take my new political career seriously, I could hardly begin it by ignoring a summons to meet my future leader.

My mood was sour, by the time I reached his chambers. On the way, I'd passed the Regent Theatre, where a matinee queue was forming for *The Immortal Hour*. Outside, shuffling in a wet, bedraggled line along the gutter, a busker band was amusing the queue. It was a scene I might have passed without noticing outside almost any London theatre. Broken boots, mufflers, well-brushed, shiny suits with rain-darkened shoulders and baggy knees. But these buskers wore their medals. I recognized the DCM, the MM, the 1914–15 Star. At least they still wore them and hadn't sold them for the half crown's worth of silver they contained. The people in the queue were wet and cold and not inclined to be generous. The rain dripped off the players' hat brims and slurred their wheezy instruments.

> *Though there's nothing in the larder,*
> *Don't we have fun!*
> *Times are hard and getting harder,*
> *Still we have fun . . .*

They all seemed to be coughing from cold and wet and malnourishment. But one had the filthy, gurgling cough of a man whose lungs have been shredded by gas.

I wanted to scoop them all up and take them along with me for sausages, poached eggs and tea at the Corner House. Instead, I emptied my pockets of all the money I could lay my hands on and tossed it into the open violin case on the pavement. One of the men gave me a half-hearted, incredulous salute of thanks.

A remarkable man, Ramsay MacDonald. He had the head of a Roman senator (Mother longed to sculpt it – she got her wish soon afterwards when he replaced J.

R. Clynes as leader of the party), a voice of naturally impressive melancholy and a surprisingly theatrical leaning in dress. I'm not saying I expected another Keir Hardie in flat cap and muffler, but the dapper man in morning coat and pinstriped trousers took me by surprise.

Why should I be surprised? Was that a sort of snobbery on my part? Yes, I suppose it was. I expected the illegitimate product of the Lossiemouth board school to show more evidence of his humble roots.

Of course, it was his brain that had got MacDonald where he was, his transparent honesty – even when it brought him the sort of unpopularity his anti-war stance had done in 1914 – and the tenacious staying power that is said to characterize the Scots.

His rooms in Lincoln's Inn were shabby, with a couple of worn leather armchairs before a mean gas fire and a writing table under a window adorned only with a dark green holland blind. The daylight that filtered through the screen of dripping laurel outside was tinged further by the blind, giving the room a curiously underwater feeling. Everywhere I looked, there were books, on shelves, teetering on the table, piled on the worn carpet. He offered me an unexpectedly decent sherry and we settled down to some mundane chat about this summer's weather compared with the extraordinarily dry weather of 1921.

'You know there will be an election before the year is out, Mr Malyon?' MacDonald said suddenly, looking up sharply from the decanter as he poured another glass.

'I know, sir, that's why I'm here.'

'So, tell me, what do you think you can do for the Labour Party in rural Wiltshire? Our stronghold is in the industrial north, on the Clyde, on the Tyne, among grime and the clatter of machinery and the exploitation of labour. In 1918 we put up only three candidates in five divisions in Wiltshire. Even in a railway town like Swindon, the best we could come was second. The others were nowhere.'

'I would rather ask – what can the Labour Party do for the men of Wiltshire? You will never form a government unless you can carry the shires as well as your traditional ground. Poverty is not just an urban problem. There are slums in country villages that can hold their own with the worst you can show me in Glasgow or Newcastle. Just as many people have no sanitation. There are just as many children bootless, stunted by rickets, with starved minds and bodies. These people have a vote too, but they're held back by tradition, by lifelong distrust of anything new – yes, and by fear that if they don't vote the right way, they'll find themselves without a roof. Yes – even today – in the 1920s!'

'You are a crusader, Mr Malyon.' And he gave the word 'crusader' a faintly mocking tone, as though the idea amused him. Or maybe it was only his prim Scots accent.

'I hadn't thought of it that way, but if you say so, then yes – I am. The people I'm talking about didn't hold back when they were called. They didn't hide behind the umbrella shelter of reserved occupations. They didn't have much to give – only their lives – so that's what they gave.

'And what are they given in return? Abolition of the Agricultural Wages Board. No minimum wage. An agricultural depression so deep that small farmers are forced off the land altogether and large landowners find it's more economical to go in for "slut farming" – letting the land run to seed for a spot of rough shooting – than it is to produce food for the nation. And whatever happens, the labourer is out of work. And don't forget that out of work means out of his tied cottage, too.

'That's what serving King and Country has done for

the countryman! Those are the people whose support you must win if you want to govern this land.'

Behind the facade of urbanity, I saw his eyes narrow. He *knew* what I meant when I talked about poverty. He *knew* what it meant to fight his way out of the trap of birth. Not everyone had his willpower or his luck.

'They will have a capable advocate in you, Mr Malyon, but the question is – will they have you?'

'Perhaps not. Perhaps their natural conservatism will reject your party this time, perhaps even the time after that. And I make no promises about staying with you.' The time for honesty had come. We had fenced around our major differences for long enough. 'At the moment, I see your party as the only hope for the forgotten rural poor. If that changes . . . if you let them down . . . I'm not committed to you in any way. I'm committed to the people of Upper Avon, no one else.'

'But first you have to win your seat, Mr Malyon.'

We'd done a lot more talking after that and it was late by the time I left Mr MacDonald. I could have caught a train home, but I was feeling surprisingly tired. Instead I decided to take up Philip's offer of a bed for the night. I could telephone Adrienne from there and check on how Alexander was feeling.

The rain had stopped. I paid off my cab in Sloane Square and decided to walk the rest of the way, up Sloane Street. By the time I neared Ellis Street, the evening was surprisingly fine, although the trees that edged the street still dripped water down my collar if I was careless enough to brush the leaves with my hat.

I could hear the noise in Cadogan Place long before I reached it. It sounded as though a whole maternity hospital's worth of babies had been left out in their perambulators to howl themselves to sleep. My guess was not that far out.

As a party, it was described in the press the next day as a howling success. I suppose that depends on whether you were trying to sleep anywhere nearby. The gardens were brightly lit and, at first sight, seemed to be full of children at a time when they ought all to have been tucked up safely for the night. That was at first sight. At second sight, I realized my mistake.

A six-foot man dressed in pale blue, smocked rompers, with a frilly bonnet on his head and a comforter sticking bizarrely from his moustache was dancing a smoochy number with a tiny young woman in knee socks and lacy petticoats reaching barely below her bottom.

Another girl in serge gymslip and black stockings, her panama hanging round her neck by its elastic, was being given a piggyback by a man in a little boy's sailor suit, his bare, hairy legs grotesque below short knickerbockers. The girl carried a hockey stick and was beating her mount, urging him on shrilly.

A Boy Scout and a Girl Guide were wrapped obscenely around each other beneath a tree. I hope for the girl's sake that the Boy Scout remembered the Scout motto.

Everywhere I looked, people bowled hoops, spun tops, dug in the flower beds with bucket and spade. A donkey race was being run down the central path. As the leader passed me, whooping and bouncing up and down on the poor brute, the animal stopped to stale. The rider slid forward onto its neck, helpless with giggles, as the other donkeys raced by.

I wandered completely unnoticed through the square. I might have been a shadow. It was as though I didn't exist. A crowd outside the railings was jeering, but the revellers paid no attention to that either. There were three or four gramophones, each playing a different record, yet people seemed to be dancing to something different again. They danced to a tune I couldn't hear, to a rhythm I didn't understand.

Then, through a gap in the crowd, I saw Helen. She was dressed as a nanny, in a severe costume quite unlike the baby frills of everyone else. Her head was hooded in a close, dark veil that was almost nun-like. I began to elbow my way towards her. One or two people complained if I trod on their toes, but most were not in a condition to feel my weight.

In a perambulator parked beside Helen was a baby, in long clothes and shawl, suckling from a bottle that looked by its colour as though it must have contained neat Scotch.

Someone squealed as I approached, 'Look out everyone, here comes Daddy to put us all to bed!'

The baby pulled the teat from his mouth. 'Bugger it!' he said. 'It's my brother!'

Once he had got over the shock of seeing me there, Philip was in one of his hospitable moods and insisted on escorting me to his house. He linked one arm through my own. With the other hand, he held up his long, lacy skirts.

'Will 'oo take 'ums home,' he cooed in a tiny voice. 'It's long past bedtime, but Nanny's having too much fun to look after 'ickle me.'

Somehow or other, I got him round the corner into Ellis Street. In the hall were two men dressed like Just William and playing with a train set. Philip lurched against me and I accidently knocked the engine off the line. One of the men went into a tantrum, lying on his back screaming and drumming his heels.

'Come and have a drink,' offered Philip.

'No, thank you. It's late. I think I'll just go on upstairs, if you don't mind.'

'No point, old man. They're all coming round for nursery tea when they get tired of playing. We're having egg custard and prunes and cinnamon toast and bikkies and . . .'

'And some hot milk before bedtime, to make sure you all sleep well, I suppose?'

'Oh yes,' he nodded, 'but perhaps just a little something more warming in it. Mustn't take these things too far y'know. So there's no point in your trying to go to bed. No chance of getting any sleep before the milkman comes.'

Philip sat me down in his study, opened a cupboard and poured out two stiff whiskies. As I downed mine, I looked across at my brother, six foot two inches of lace and broderie anglaise, and felt an extraordinary sense of unreality creeping over me.

I thought about the shuffling line of medal-wearing buskers, coughing in the rain. I thought about Ramsay MacDonald, that dapper dandy in his shabby chambers. I thought about Helen, icy as a nun, presiding over her nursery of romping grown-ups. I could feel myself, despite the noise in the hall, drifting away to sleep.

I longed to be home, with the sweet curve of Adrienne's bottom tucked into my belly and the softness of her hair stirring beneath my lips with every breath.

Adrienne and Alexander. They make my life worth living.

Can a woman rape a man? Probably not. In the end, the man must always be willing, or the deed will not take place. But on the night Alexander was conceived, Adrienne as good as raped me.

She flowed around me. Molten. Fluid. Ardent. Devouring. Her hands were magic butterflies. And what she did with her lips . . . oh God . . . She took the desert that was my heart and watered it and it blossomed. She opened like a velvet glove for me to enter, then closed like a snare behind me. She led me and drove me. I stayed with her to the very brink. When the moment came to withdraw, she made one final, tiny movement – just drew herself backwards down the shaft – and it was too late. She rippled around me, opening and closing. I was pumping, pumping . . .

I never meant to do it. It was wrong. It was beautiful.

Spent and still joined we lay, unable to part, until at last I slithered stickily out.

'I'm sorry,' I said, 'I'm sorry. I should never have done that.'

In the lamplight, Adrienne's eyes glittered and overflowed. The tears made bright tracks down her cheeks.

'Thank you,' she whispered.

I had never meant to be cruel.

Adrienne and Alexander. They make my life worth living.

I know I was nodding. I felt my head give a jerk forward and I snorted. And Philip, damn him, was laughing at me. He sat opposite, with his empty glass clutched in his hand, and laughed. The noise pierced through my drowsing. I opened my eyes wider and realized that he wasn't laughing at all.

I didn't know what to do. His breath came in great, heaving sobs. He lifted his face to me all blubbered, his mouth a square of misery, his nose running with snot.

'Oh God, Hector,' he moaned. 'I'm so unhappy.'

What do you do when your brother cries? When he was three or four, I would spit on my handkerchief and rub the grubby streaks off his cheeks. When he was ten or eleven, I'd tell him to buck up and stop blubbing. But now he was twenty-nine and what could I do?

'I don't know what to do,' he kept on. 'I don't know what to do.'

I walked over to the door to check the hall, because it

had grown suddenly quiet. I didn't want anyone to see or hear Philip in this state. But it had gone quiet because Just William and his friend had fallen asleep across the railway track. On the way back, Philip clutched my elbow.

'Get me a drink, old man,' he begged.

'You've had quite enough,' I protested, but it was only a token protest – a sort of big brother exerting his authority – because if anyone was in need of a stiffener, Philip was.

He gulped half of it down in one like a dog after a hard run. 'God, I needed that. Sorry, old chap, made a bit of an ass of myself, but the fact is . . . the fact is . . .' He put the glass down very carefully and then buried his head in his arms. '. . . I don't know what to do.'

'Suppose you try telling me what this is all about.'

'I'm losing Helen.'

'Another man? I'm sorry, but I'm not really surprised.'

Philip lifted his head then and the outrage on his swollen face was comical. 'Good heavens – no. Nothing like that. Anything but.'

'Then what?'

'I don't know – that's just it. She's changed. She's drifting away from me. I can't keep up with her any more. I'm running all the time, but I can't catch her. Parties. Dancing. Booze. I never see her alone any more. There's always someone around, laughing and making smart jokes.'

'You're just having a nasty bout of self-pity. If it's as bad as all that, why don't you shut up this place and come home?'

'She won't come.'

'Then go by yourself.'

'I can't leave her. I daren't. I don't know what she'd do next. All this . . .' He gestured wearily.

'I don't know how you can afford to live the way you do.'

'I can't, of course. But when I tell Helen, she just laughs and says she'll find someone else who can. She's changed . . . But she doesn't mean it. Not really. You know, Hector, I sometimes think Helen doesn't really like men. Not – you know – not like *that*.' And he winked.

I had a sudden horror that Philip might start inflicting the secrets of his intimate relationships on me. At that time of night and on an empty stomach, it would be more than I could bear.

'I don't think you ought to talk like that,' I said, sounding more like a governess than a brother. 'Some things are private.'

'You don't understand . . . I knew you wouldn't . . .'

'Try me.'

'You know, I envy you, old man.'

He held out his empty glass to me. I took it, but just put it down quietly out of sight.

'Most people would say that you haven't got much to envy anyone about, Philip.'

'Well, I envy you. You've got a lovely wife like Adrienne, a grand little boy, you know what you want to do with your life . . . you've got everything.'

'Now you really are getting maudlin. For heaven's sake, buck up. You've got what you chose. A London house. Smart friends. Another man's wife. What more do you want?'

'I knew you wouldn't understand . . .'

He got up then, in search of the bottle, and found it. His stained and crumpled draperies trailed behind him.

'For heaven's sake, take all that frippery off, can't you,' I snapped. 'I can't talk to you while you float around like the ghost of Hamlet's father.'

328

'I can't. They'll all be back soon. Got to keep in the spirit of things, don't you know. Can't let the side down.'

'Philip, I'm tired. I can't cope with all this emotion so late at night. Let's talk about this in the morning, eh? When you're sober?'

'I'm not as drunk as you think. Not too drunk to realize that I couldn't possibly talk about it when I'm sober. It's now or never.'

I wished we were back in the days when a grubby handkerchief could wipe away the tears. At least that was quick and didn't take half the night.

'Hector, would you do something for me? Please?'

I had an awful feeling that I was already deep in this thing and that Philip wasn't going to let me get out of it. 'Mmm? That depends,' I said noncommittally.

'Will you help me get Hermione back?'

Yes, I did hear him properly. And yes, he meant it. He was absolutely serious.

'Please. Help me get Hermione back for Helen.'

'If you're not drunk, then you must be stark, raving mad. No.'

'For my sake. Please.'

'No.'

Of course, I put that crazy conversation down to drink and completely ignored it. It had to end then, anyway. It had started to rain again and playing games in the gardens had palled – just as everything eventually palled – so all the bright young people had skipped back to Ellis Street for nursery tea.

They all tumbled in like end of term dismissal, shrieking and giggling and quarrelling, all, as far as I could see, in need of a good, hard smack on the bottom and sending straight to bed without any supper.

'Oh, goody goody gumdrops!' I heard one girl squeal. 'I just *love* spotted dick!'

And the guffaw that followed made me wonder whether she really had been referring to the sponge pudding.

I was trying to speak to Adrienne on the telephone at the time. The instrument was situated in a little lacquered box in the hall, just outside the dining room door. The noise coming through the door made it impossible to hold a conversation.

'Are you at a party?' asked Adrienne.

'There is a party, but I'm not at it,' I shouted.

'What?'

'I said there is . . . never mind . . . is Alexander all right?'

'He is a little better, but . . .'

'What? Oh, this is ridiculous. I can't talk to you like this. I'll be home on the first train tomorrow.'

When I went to bed, it was impossible to sleep. For the first few hours, I was kept awake by the noise of a gramophone at full blast. Once there was the crash of breaking glass, followed by hoots of laughter. By the time everyone had gone home – or fallen asleep where they were – I was too wide awake to sleep anyway.

I got up and pulled open the curtains, letting in the pale morning light. The gas lamps were still alight, looking in the dawn as sick and ghostly as by now most of the revellers must. I pulled up the sash. There is such a short time in the twenty-four hours when London smells like that, cool, green, unsullied, fit to breathe. I wanted to go home.

I would be very surprised if Philip could remember anything of our conversation by the time he got out of bed – whenever that might be. It must have been the drink talking. He couldn't have been serious. Could he?

★

Lloyd George and his coalition held on until late in the year. On 19 October, at a meeting in the Carlton Club, the Conservatives finally threw him to the lions and voted by 187 to 87 to end their support.

They appeared to have all sorts of good reasons. They resented Lloyd George's opportunist solution of the Irish problem by partition. They maintained that he had been criminally rash in threatening to draw the Empire into war with Turkey without prior consultation. They deplored the wholesale selling of honours – £15,000 for a knighthood, £25,000 for a baronetcy. (How much had his KBE cost my father, I wondered.)

Bonar Law became Prime Minister of a Conservative government and an election was called for Wednesday, 15th November.

Although not actively campaigning before the election was called, I had been getting around and making myself known in Upper Avon. I met with a surprising amount of suspicion. Country people are naturally conservative. In Upper Avon, they had voted for the same member for thirty-seven years and many people saw no reason why they should even dream of changing at this stage. The sitting member, Captain Cathcart, had never been opposed by a Labour candidate and had had no opposition at all in 1918, when even the Liberals failed to field a candidate against him. He had what looked like an unassailable majority.

But, as my father pointed out when he took me out for a walk and a pep talk man to man, I had three quite clear advantages.

'I have?'

'They're right under your nose – so make sure you don't waste them.'

'Well, you'd better point me in the right direction, then.'

'First of all –' He stopped to swing his stick at a

clump of nettles growing around the base of the wicket gate in the garden wall. 'What's that doing there? . . . first of all, you're a local man, not a stranger sent down from London to tell people what's good for them. They wouldn't like that. Everyone knows you. They remember you as a lad on that fat old pony of yours . . .'

'Poor old Consort,' I smiled nostalgically.

'They remember cutting you slices of bread hot from the oven – you were always hungry, no wonder you've grown into such a great beanstalk. They remember you falling out of the trees scrumping apples . . .'

'Remember when I sprang all Cathcart's keeper's snares? He marched me home himself and I don't think you've ever given me such a leathering as you did that day.'

'There you are then. That sort of memory won't do you any harm now. And then there's Adrienne . . .'

'Oh no, I'm not having my wife dragged into this. Electioneering can be a dirty business. I don't want her involved in any way.'

'Don't be daft. She's an absolute trump. A real bobby-dazzler. Remember the women's vote. That's well worth cultivating. Cathcart won't – too stuck in his ways. Probably hasn't realized they've even got a vote yet! Let Adrienne talk to the women – about their children and schools and what it costs to feed their families and how much rent they pay and . . . whatever women talk about. She'll have them eating out of her hand in no time.'

'I still don't like it.'

'You don't have to like it. Just do it!'

I looked down at my father's dumpy little figure. He was positively fizzing with electricity. Running his grocery empire seemed to have become all too easy lately. He grabbed this new challenge with both hands.

He's been a wonderful father to me. No man could have asked for better.

'I thought you weren't too keen on the idea of my standing for the Labour Party?' I laughed. 'And now listen to you! You've turned into my self-appointed agent.'

'Someone has to! No, I wasn't keen,' Father answered shortly, 'and I'm still not. But if you're set on it, then you'd better make a good job of it, that's all. No point in going off at half-cock. Now then – what else? Oh, yes. Your war record.' He tracked the flight of a pheasant, whirring over our heads, with his stick. 'Pow! Gottim!'

'No.'

'What do you mean – no?'

'Just no. I'm not going to make capital on something like that. It's too distasteful.'

'You're a stubborn donkey, Hector. Always have been. You don't get it from me, that's certain. I've always been able to recognize a good thing when I saw one – like your mother, eh?' he chuckled. 'I tell you, if you don't use your war record, it'll be like going over the top with one hand tied behind your back. The war's worth thousands at the ballot box to a man like you.'

'And have people accuse me of medal waving?'

'And who has the right to, if you don't? You can't just pretend it never happened.'

He was right about that. Everywhere I went, people wanted to talk to me about their war. It meant swapping yarns about Polygon Wood over a pint in the Antelope. It meant understanding when a woman showed me a stiff studio portrait that was all she had left to remember her husband or son. It meant feeling physically sick when the rector preached a sermon about divine retribution falling on a guilty Germany. Didn't he understand?

What was the point of exacting vengeance on individual German men and women? Hadn't they just answered their country's call? Now punishing the makers of war, that was different, but how do you punish a government without harming its citizens?

The punitive terms of the Treaty of Versailles reduced Germany and her people to beggary. The country was being stripped to pay retribution (and hadn't they done the same to the French in the 1870s? Yes, but that didn't make it right). One day they will find a messiah to save them from all this. One day a new demagogue will rise up and inspire belief in a new Fatherland. And then we'll have the same job to do all over again.

Captain Cathcart, for all his military title, had been just the wrong age for any fighting, even in any of the many messy little colonial bushfires of the last century. I went to hear him speak at an electoral meeting in the school at Collingbourne Kingston. I didn't intend to challenge him that night, just assess him. You could call it an intelligence patrol, rather than a trench raid.

I tucked myself in at the back, with a good view of the sparse audience and the platform. Captain Cathcart was a thin, spry little man with a brisk manner, quite able to dispose of the few tentative questions.

Tranquillity – the election slogan of the Conservative Party, defined by Bonar Law in a speech in Manchester as 'freedom from adventures and commitments at home and abroad'. It had undoubted appeal. No more living on the edge of a precipice, worrying whether we would share the fate of Belgium. No more Bolshevik spectre waiting just around the corner. No more being held to ransom by a workforce pampered by the full employment of wartime and grown too big for its boots.

Bonar Law offered tranquillity to a nation whose heavy industries were folding under the competition from newer, cheaper markets, whose workers had been forced to accept wage cuts.

'Tranquillity,' finished Captain Cathcart. 'I would like to end by quoting to you the definition of that word, on the authority of the Oxford English Dictionary no less: "freedom from disturbance or agitation; serenity; calmness". The party that offers that golden vision to the people of this land is the party to vote for. And now – ' He smiled and looked around. ' – I am ready to take questions from the floor.'

There weren't any. No one really knew what to ask him. He had represented Upper Avon for thirty-seven years. Everyone knew what he thought and felt about every subject under the sun and his views were straight down the party line. They didn't need repeating. So when he'd finished, everyone just drifted politely off home again. I quietly followed them. I had achieved my aim.

No one had challenged him about 'the Geddes axe' which had cut £64 million from the government budget. No one had asked him about the cuts in house building, in education, health or defence. No one had even wondered about the rumour that war pensions were going to be slashed.

I'd done my reconnaissance and now I was ready to go into action. Adrienne was an absolute brick. I couldn't have done it without her. She put a human face on my facts and figures. At every public meeting I held, Adrienne was there beside me on the platform and sometimes Alexander, too, reminding people that, above all, I was talking about preserving family dignity by making sure that no family need fall apart because there wasn't enough money coming in to keep it together. Put like that, it sounds a bit corny, but I don't think people saw it that way.

Together we canvassed every house in the constituency, knocking on doors, talking to people and above all, listening, listening, listening. Adrienne trudged up long, muddy tracks with me when the ground was too wet to get the motor any closer. She held sickly babies in her arms, listened gravely to mothers' grievances, examined primitive sewage arrangements.

'It makes me so angry,' she exploded as we closed the door on a broken down railway carriage where a bright girl had been forced to leave school to look after a sick mother and four younger children. 'That girl will grow up just a copy of her mother – too many children, too little money. If she could stay at school, she might have a chance of escaping all this . . .'

She held out a helpless hand at the battered carriage, the mud, the scrawny chickens picking in the nettles, the bare-bottomed toddler throwing stones at a tattered cat.

'You'd do the job better than I will,' I said and I meant it.

'I would if I could and I'd be damned good at it, too – you know I would – but who'd vote for a foreigner?'

'That poor woman won't vote for anyone. Why should she try to drag herself down to the village when she can scarcely stagger to the privy and back?'

'Don't forget her, Hector. When you are elected, don't forget her, will you?' Adrienne urged.

I couldn't have done it without her.

When 25000 unemployed ex-servicemen marched past the Cenotaph on Armistice Day 1922, I was there.

On the banner they carried was written 'From the living victims to our dead comrades who died in vain'. That said everything.

I marched in the ranks with men whose faces were marked now, not by fear of instant annihilation, but by the day to day struggle of keeping a family on next to nothing. They were hungry. Their wives had been turned into nagging shrews with the effort of trying to make every sixpence do the work of a shilling. Their children wore broken boots on stockingless feet.

They had fought for their country and their country had turned its back on them.

They could have screamed their protest down Whitehall. They could have hurled stones through the windows of politicians who had just dropped them when they had finished with them, like broken toys. They could have burned effigies in Parliament Square.

Instead, they marched in silent dignity. They still remembered how it ought to be done. Their ranks were disciplined. They formed fours as briskly as ever on the command, even numbers taking a backwards step of thirty inches with the left foot and a rightward step of twenty-seven inches with the right. There was pride – a justifiable pride – and still a swagger in their stride. This was no raggle-taggle army. The sound of their boots drowned out the jangle of medals.

When they passed the Cenotaph, they saluted their lost friends with a stiff 'eyes right'. For a little while, they forgot the sleet that blew in their faces and worked its way through the weave of threadbare suits. I could have wept for them, but I was on parade.

They were an unwelcome phantom of the Victory Parade they had marched in only three years ago. No cheers this time. No flags were waved. Hardly anyone stayed to watch, except the policemen whose duty it was to ensure there was no trouble.

But there would never be trouble from these men. That was part of the problem.

And when it was over, when they had delivered their message to an uncaring street, they didn't know quite what to do next. They broke ranks and milled around a bit, unwilling to split away from pals, reluctant to go back into the world that no longer valued them. Then the men who had a bus to catch, or a wife waiting at home, wandered off in ones and twos. And the men who slept in cardboard boxes poked the old newspapers back down their coats and slipped quietly back to the Embankment.

'Sir? Colonel Malyon, sir?'

I turned at the sound of the voice.

There was a cartoon that showed two Tommies, side by side, looking out on a desolate landscape.

'Is this the little village by the stream where we stopped on the retreat,' one asks the other, 'or is it that big place with all the factories and the cathedral?'

You have to have been there to appreciate the humour.

The town of Corbie was much like that, a street lined with rubble, with a door left standing locked and guarding nothing, or a shattered gable end exposing a pretty girl's bedroom with fluttering rags of rose patterned wallpaper, or a once glittering black leaded stove whose chimney now led nowhere.

Furniture had once been dragged out into the street to make barricades and, later, pushed back to the sides to clear a passage for one or other army. Scarred, splintered, the remains lay beneath the tumbled walls of the houses from which they had come.

And there was a piano. It wasn't much to look at, but a soldier had pulled a three-legged stool up to it and was softly trying some chords. There were keys missing, some notes wouldn't play at all, some jangled in a way that made the man wince. With patience and skill, he began to coax a tune out of it, a recognizable tune that drew his pals out of the *estaminet* up the street and around the piano.

He played *Broken Doll* and *Hold your hand out, naughty boy* and *Let the great big world keep turning* and his mates roared out the choruses. Then he seemed just to drift away and I recognized, mutilated by the missing notes, the plaintive sound of a Chopin nocturne. The audience listened quietly, but he stopped abruptly before reaching the end.

'Bloody awful machine,' he laughed, with a little embarrassed catch in it.

'That's nice, that,' said one. 'Who wrote it?'

'Chap called Chopin,' answered the pianist. 'A Pole.'

'As long as he wasn't a German.'

'Germans wrote some pretty good music, too. Listen.'

He accompanied Bach's multi-layered melody in a clear tenor and the gaps in the keyboard didn't matter any more.

> *'Schafe können sicher weiden*
> *Wo ein guter Hirte wacht . . .'*

There was a quietness when he had finished. Then, 'It's Sunday, you know, Davey. Play something for Sunday, will you?'

He played *Jesu Lover of my Soul*. Those who knew the words sang them, in all sorts of keys, quietly.

> *'Hide me, O my Saviour, hide,*
> *'Til the storm of life is past;*
> *Safe into the haven guide,*
> *O receive my soul at last.'*

Even those who didn't know the words, knew the tune and hummed softly with it. Then he played *The Day Thou Gavest, Lord, is Ended*. One by one, the voices faltered and fell silent, until only the mutilated piano finished the hymn.

In some perverse way, the scene made me angry. Soldiers shouldn't be like that. They can't afford to be weakened by thoughts of home and firelight and Sunday evenings. They can't afford to have hearts. It's too painful.

But I didn't really believe that. Not really. It would be easier that way, though.

The pianist suddenly banged down the lid of the piano. It sagged down over the keys on one hinge.

'Sorry,' he said tightly. 'Too dark to see any more, chaps.'

The next day we moved back up to the front line and it was some time before I came across the pianist again.

'I enjoyed your music the other night, Gledhill,' I said, doing the rounds one night and finding him on sentry-go.

'Thank you, sir. Bit of a duff piano, though.'

'Where did you learn to play like that?' I asked. 'What did you do before you joined up?'

'I was organist in our local church and I played in a dance band in the evenings, sir. A good one, too. You've probably danced to our music at all the best London dances in the season.'

While he spoke, he never took his eyes off the observation hole, straining over the blackness beyond the rusty wire. The other side was so close at this point that I could smell tobacco smoke. There was a constant murmur of voices and, although I couldn't distinguish the words, the intonation was somehow foreign. Yet in a way, it sounded like the grumbling and chaffing that could be heard any night in our own trenches. Somewhere out there, someone coughed, a weary, miserable cough.

'I doubt that,' I laughed, 'I've never been a dancing man. And what did you do during the day?'

'I was a music teacher, sir. Piano. Lessons 3/6d per half hour. Visits to pupils' homes extra. All examinations offered. Satisfaction guaranteed or your money back.'

I laughed again. He would be a good teacher, I imagined, with an encouraging manner and a quiet, steady voice. He'd be able to get the best out of his pupils, even the ordinary, bread and butter ones.

'So you've got a niche waiting for you when all this is over.'

'Oh yes, sir, I can easily pick up the threads again. And they're keeping my place in the band. It'll be good to see people dancing and enjoying themselves again.'

He hummed a little tune that I remembered hearing everywhere last time I was home on leave. Then, further down the line, a flare went up, a merciless brightness that sharpened the high points and drenched in even deeper shadow the depths of the desolation in front of us. We both tensed, waiting for the flurry of fire that would signal the discovery of some luckless wire cutting party. Nothing happened.

'Someone's jumpy tonight,' observed Gledhill.

'Yes, I don't much care for being this close to the other side myself.'

'Close enough to pinch the sausage off Jerry's plate!'

'Close enough to light his meerschaum pipe for him!'

Out in the darkness the German with the cold sneezed.

'*Gesundheit!*' yelled Gledhill.

And then we both ducked. But all that came our way was an answering shout of '*Danke sehr!*'

'Well, I promise myself to come and listen to you play one day, Gledhill,' I said, moving on down the trench, 'though I won't necessarily promise to dance!'

'I'll be watching for you, sir.'

'Gledhill! Good to see you again. How are you?'

I held out my hand. He didn't take his gloves off to return my handshake. I thought his grip was surprisingly limp for a man of his character.

'So, so, sir,' he answered. 'Mustn't grumble.'

He was thinner and older – weren't we all? – and wore glasses that I didn't remember. He took them off, folded them awkwardly and put them in a pocket. They left pinch marks on either side of a nose purpled by the cold. He stooped into his clothes as though he were trying to hide inside them from the slicing wind that jabbed at us around the corner. I felt embarrassed by my heavy overcoat.

'Look,' I said, 'it's bloody awful out here and we can't possibly talk. I'm just off to look for some tea. Why don't you join me?'

'I really ought to be getting along. I just stopped to say hello.'

But his look was avid at the mention of tea.

'Nonsense. I'd take it as a kindness if you'd keep me company. Between you and me, I haven't quite settled down into being a civilian again. It'd do me good to have a natter with someone who knew what I was talking about.'

'Well . . .'

I usually go to my club for tea if I'm alone. They do a decent spread there with hot buttered toast and potted shrimps or anchovy paste, something you can get your teeth into, not the dainty little flim-flams one has to put up with elsewhere. Mother always goes to Brown's and Cassandra wouldn't dream of anywhere but the Ritz. This time I decided to go somewhere different. Not, I must add, because I didn't want to be seen around in Gledhill's company. Certainly not. But because he looked as though he needed something even more substantial. So we went in for an early high tea at a nearby ABC, somewhere popular with the Whitehall clerks and typists for its shilling luncheon.

'I'm going to have a really good tuck in,' I said. 'I had to catch a train from Wiltshire at an awkward time and missed lunch.'

Encouraged by me, he ordered sausages, two poached eggs, grilled tomatoes and tea. To keep him company, I ordered the same. I didn't really want all that at that time of the day, but to have done anything different would have embarrassed Gledhill.

I shan't forget the expression on his face when the food arrived. He let the steam rise up from the tea cup and curl round his chin. He looked down at the plate and then quickly away from it again. It was like watching something very private. I was intruding just by being there.

I picked up my knife and fork. My voice rang out with a false heartiness to cover my shame at sitting down to a meal with a full stomach.

'No need to stand on ceremony,' I said.

Then Gledhill took off his gloves.

He still had fingers. At least, there were five protruberances still on each hand, longer than stumps, shorter than fingers ought to be. Seared. Charred. Papery skin white as bone. Mummified, weeping cracks at each knobbly joint. Suppurating scabs where the nails had been.

I looked down at the succulent sausages on my plate, then quickly away. The smell of frying made my stomach heave.

'I'm sorry, sir.' Gledhill picked up his gloves and began to ease them gently on again. 'I shouldn't have done that. Not when you're eating.'

'No . . . I . . . it's I who ought to apologize. I didn't

mean . . . I didn't think . . . it was just the surprise.' I
forced myself to look squarely at him and that included
his hands. 'It was thoughtless of me. Please, don't allow
your meal to cool.'

But he finished putting on his gloves first, easing the
fingers carefully into place, stroking out the wrinkles.
Then he picked up his knife and fork and began to eat
with a sort of clumsy dexterity.

'How did you . . . ?' I cleared my throat of rising
bile. 'What . . . ?'

'It was liquid fire, sir. Did you ever see it?'

I shook my head.

'It's black and sticky, smells like Wright's Coal Tar
only more so, much more. Everywhere it touches, blis-
ters, then Jerry sends over star shells and the whole lot
goes up. Nothing you can do. You can jump back from
ordinary fire, beat it out, but this stuff sticks, you see,
and you burn . . .' He looked over my shoulder and a
long way beyond that. 'I was lucky – chap near me lost
his face . . .'

But Gledhill was hungry and memories were not
going to get in the way of the unexpected luck of a
square meal. I picked at my plate until he'd finished.
Now I understood why he hadn't been able to fit back
into that nice little niche in the dance band that had been
waiting for him.

He put his knife and fork neatly to attention. 'I don't
suppose there'd be another cup in the pot, would there,
sir?' And when I'd turned the handle round towards
him and watched him heft up the brown earthenware
pot with one hand on the handle and the other clasped
supporting his wrist, he said, quite casually, 'Do you
remember that old piano in Corbie?' I nodded. 'That
was the last time I ever touched a piano.'

'Things a bit tricky now?' I queried.

'Rather. Not much call for a piano teacher with no

hands. I can still teach, of course I can, but I can't dem-
onstrate the finer points and my hands frighten the
children. The only thing I'm good for now is pedalling
a pianola!'

If they had been *my* hands, if *I* had been trying to
explain to a perfectly sound man what it's like to live
with part of my body roasted crisp as pork crackling,
my voice would have been thick with bitterness. But
Gledhill just discussed his problems quietly and matter
of factly, as though he were trying to explain the difference between crotchets and quavers to a particularly
backward pupil.

'I make a bit now and then in the evening,' he told
me, 'dancing at Covent Garden. Sixpence a dance.
Lucky I'd kept my evening dress in mothballs. You sit
in a sort of pen and, if a lady fancies you, she pays her
sixpence and you trot her out onto the floor. That's all
she gets for her sixpence, mind – just a dance – no
nonsense. I wear white gloves then and nobody knows.
But it's not much of a living really. And the things
they say . . . right in front of you . . . as though they're
talking about animals in a stall . . .'

'I wondered,' I said, clearing my throat, 'if you might
consider a different type of work?'

Again that painful, avid look, the same one he had
given the loaded plate. 'I'd do anything . . . I can use
my hands, after a fashion. I'm quite handy, really. I can
still write too, but no one'll give me a try.'

'There will be some writing involved. I'm standing
for Parliament in the coming election and I need an
agent. My father's standing in at the moment, but,
frankly, he's a bit too enthusiastic for me! I need someone to organize my affairs, keep track of my appoint-
ments, make sure I'm in the right place at the right
time . . . you know the sort of thing. I'm inclined to get

345

my papers in a mess and I think you're just the man I'm looking for.'

He nodded. 'Oh, I could do that all right, sir, I've always been a methodical sort of chap. I used to look after all the bookings for the band, all the paperwork, anything the rest of them didn't want to do. There's just one thing . . .'

'Yes?'

'I'm married.' He said it as though he were confessing to a particularly anti-social disease. 'She was a VAD at the convalescent home I was at and . . .'

'That's no problem.' I was thinking quickly enough not to leave an awkward gap before I spoke. 'There's decent accommodation with the job. I just hadn't got around to saying.'

I'd get my father to do up the empty land agent's cottage. There'd been no one in it since the war and he'd been talking of selling it. It was a bit isolated, but, with a spot of work, could be a pretty decent place to bring up a family.

'And if you . . . I don't want to sound ungrateful, but it's got to be said . . . if you aren't elected?'

'We'll know the answer to that in four days time. If things don't work out, I'll be trying again. I have a feeling that, whoever's elected on the fifteenth, they won't last long. I'd bet we'll be seeing another election in a year – or less. And then there's estate management, my stud records to be kept, bills of sale, all the usual sort of thing. Not quite a secretary, more of a right hand man. Not very exciting though, I'm afraid. Not what you're used to.'

He looked down at the table, then away. I turned my eyes from his emotion. It was wrong, all wrong. A man who had done what he had done ought never to be in the position of grasping with tears at anything tossed in

346

his direction by someone more fortunate. He had *earned* more than I could ever give.

I'd tried not to make it sound as though I were offering him a job out of charity. I'd tried to make him think he'd be doing me a favour by accepting the task of sorting out my muddled papers. Both of us saved face that way.

But Gledhill wasn't fooled. His gratitude heaped coals of shame on my head.

I'm not quite sure when the whispers began. They were so insubstantial at first, cobwebs on the wind. But, like cobwebs, they stuck. Were people becoming less eager to talk to me even before the election? Was it true that a few, a very few, people looked away, or over my shoulder if they couldn't avoid me?

I'm not sure. Adrienne says no, it was all in my imagination. Yet in the last few days before 15th November, I was beginning to feel ill at ease for some reason. I put it down to pre-election nerves, quite natural. I was anxious and seeing shadows in the corners that didn't exist. So Adrienne said. But I'm not so sure.

When election day arrived, I could scarcely eat for apprehension. What had we left undone, that we ought to have done? What had we done that we ought not to have done?

My father, with his usual practical efficiency, organized a fleet of motors, decorated with streamers in party colours, to carry elderly voters from isolated cottages to the polling stations. Because it was November, he ordered urns of hot tea – with the maroon tins of tea marked Malyon's in gold prominently displayed – to be posted at every exit. Wearing large red rosettes, Adrienne and I both toured every station in the constituency, shaking hands, saying our thank yous to party workers, radiating bonhomie and confidence. There really wasn't anything practical for us to do at this late stage – we just had to be seen – but it was better than sitting at home biting my nails and everyone else's heads off.

A couple of men ignored my outstretched hand. Adrienne said they hadn't noticed me, but I'm sufficiently large to be difficult to miss. She knew and I knew that they had deliberately snubbed me. That's politics. To make things easier, we both pretended it hadn't happened.

I didn't know what was going on and I didn't like it.

Counting in a small constituency like Upper Avon didn't usually take long. At every other election he had stood in, Captain Cathcart was tucked up in bed after a celebratory whisky long before midnight. Last time, there hadn't been a count at all. This time the result was close enough to require a recount. We stood around in the draughty school hall making nervous conversation.

'It's a devil, this waiting, eh?' said Cathcart. 'Not that I've had to do much of it before!' He gave an awkward little laugh.

'Not long now, I suppose,' I said fatuously.

'You've given me a good run for my money, anyway, Malyon. Jolly good effort – you and your lovely lady.'

'I suppose you'll miss going up to the House,' said Adrienne sweetly. 'You've been there so long. Have you any tips that might be useful to my husband? He's bound to feel a bit like the new boy at school for a while.' She linked her arm through mine and gave me a proud glance. 'Although I'm sure he'll settle down quickly.'

'By jove, you're a staunch one,' Cathcart said, giving Adrienne a startled look.

She didn't allow his 'little woman' remark to rattle her composure. She really looked as though she were quite certain of the outcome.

When they counted the votes yet again, for two pins I could have chucked the whole thing in and gone home. What the hell was I doing there anyway, making a fool of myself, trying to force a reluctant electorate to see things my way? What was so special about my way? Supposing I were wrong? Supposing all people really wanted was a quiet time, a spot of Bonar Law's tranquillity after the war? Most people had had enough fireworks in the past few years to last a lifetime. In this historically traditional area, what did I think I was playing at, trying to rock the boat?

'Why don't we slip along to the Antelope,' suggested my father. 'They'll have a fire on there. If we've got to wait, we might as well do it in a bit of comfort, instead of hanging around in this dismal place.'

'You go,' I answered. 'You might as well. No need for us all to be uncomfortable, but I don't think I could settle anywhere else.'

'Oh well, suit yourself. Perhaps I'll mooch about a bit longer.'

He lit a cigar and tried to look nonchalant, but anyone could see that we were each as tightly strung as the other.

At this time of night and with such distances to travel, not many people had stayed to hear the result. To be honest, not that many were interested. There were one or two sober citizens, shopkeepers and farmers probably, sticking it out on narrow benches in order to be the first with the news. There was a jaded-looking reporter from the *Wiltshire Gazette* with a full ashtray on the floor in front of him. I imagine the only reason he had to be interested in such an out of the way spot was that Cathcart was facing his first serious opposition in a generation. And in one corner was the usual noisy rabble, just lads really, good-natured, out for an evening's entertainment and sadly disappointed in this one.

Finally the returning officer declared himself satisfied and ready to make his announcement. We stood on either side of him and the time he took to clear his throat seemed to be endless. I could feel Adrienne's strong little hand in mine. She took hold of the ball of my thumb and gave it an encouraging squeeze. Over to the right of the stage, I could hear my father clearing his throat as irritatingly as the returning officer.

'Cathcart, Robert Frederick – three thousand, seven hundred and twenty-nine. Malyon, Hector Price – three thousand, seven hundred and fifty-three. I declare that Hector Price Malyon is duly elected the member for Upper Avon.'

It was over. I was Wiltshire's first Labour Member of Parliament.

Adrienne swung into my arms and gave me a short, snapping kiss, tipping her hat sideways. Her eyes were full and glittering. 'I knew it,' she whispered, 'I knew it.'

Cathcart leaned over and shook my hand. In the circumstances, he took it better than I would have done. 'Well done,' he said briefly. 'I can see I'll have to take you more seriously next time.'

There was back-patting and shoulder-clasping from every direction and then all the handshakers had moved aside and left me alone in the centre of the stage, facing the few tired faces below.

'At this time of night,' I said, 'I won't inflict on you the speech I sat up all last night writing! I'd just like to say – thank you, thank you all. I promise I'll always do my best for you.'

There was sporadic clapping, led, I suspect, by my father and then, through it, quite clearly, came the sound of hissing. I didn't pay much attention. After all, if someone wins, then someone else loses and it had been a close thing – there had to be plenty of disappointed voters. I didn't know quite how to get off the centre of the stage, so I just said, 'Thank you and goodnight' and turned to go.

'What about Samaria Wood?'

It was a cultured voice. I turned round, averting my face from Adrienne's puzzlement, and faced my accuser. A man had moved forward from the happily drunken group in the corner – a young man, stocky and broad shouldered, seeming shorter still because I stood on the platform. He was entirely comfortable in his close-knit body, poised, easy. His clothes blended with his drinking companions', but the way he stood, the way he looked at me, labelled him as something different.

My skin prickled, the way it used to do sometimes in the trenches, before an unexpected strafe would come over, or just before the soft, unmistakable plop of a gas shell. 'Malyon's having one of his premonitions again,' they used to laugh. But I was seldom wrong.

I looked down into his queer, colourless eyes, like water running over pebbles. I could see right through them. There was a long stillness between us. I felt my father put his hand on my shoulder, to draw me away, but the stillness lengthened.

His quietness was like a very dangerous animal, resting and not hungry, but you know as you tiptoe past that, if it wants to, it can just put out a paw and tear you apart. For the moment, it is content to let you walk away, but the next time . . .

And I knew, without knowing why I knew, that the time would come when it would be me or him.

'Tell us about trench Q.4.d.2,' the young man said softly.

I knew – I had always known – that I couldn't hide for ever.

In my dream, I'm walking down a road – any road, anywhere. In front of me is a man, any man. I'm walking faster than he is, so I catch him up. This is when I start to struggle, because I know what's going to happen and I don't want to dream any more. I struggle out of the dream like a swimmer with bursting lungs, up, up, to the surface and consciousness.

But this time, I don't wake up. I kick up to the surface, but I'm tangled in the dream. It wraps itself around me. It holds me down and forces me on to the finish. It won't let me wake.

The man turns round and faces me. From behind, he could have been any man, but now that he faces me, I know who he is. I know what I'm going to do and he knows too, because he opens his mouth to yell. Is he going to order me to stop? Is he going to laugh at me? Is he going to plead?

I'm holding my Webley service revolver. I'm dreaming and I can feel the weight of it. The handle fits into my grasp. It's warm because I've been holding it ready for some time, waiting. It's heavy – so heavy that I can scarcely lift it – my arm moves up so slowly. I look along my arm and the revolver is an extension of my arm, just as we were taught once, long ago. It doesn't seem so dangerous when you think of it like that. It doesn't seem so much like a deadly weapon if it's part of your arm.

I look along my arm, along the gunmetal glint of the barrel, to the little sighting nock at the end. Beyond that is his face, still with the mouth open, knowing what I'm going to do but not stopping me.

I squeeze the trigger.

I didn't wake. The dream didn't let go of me until it had finished. It made me watch his head explode. It

352

made me watch the purply black hole in the front burst out like a volcano at the back. It forced me to watch the lava erupt in fragments of brain and shards of bone that fanned out, dangerous as bullets themselves.

If it had not been a dream, the debris would have been blasted away from me. He would have been blown backwards off his feet by the force of the shot and the contents of his skull would have gone that way too. But because it was a dream, he toppled over onto me, hands clawing, howling his outrage at what I had done. Dabs and gobbets and morsels of brain splattered out over me, sticking to me like the liquid fire that had burned Gledhill, marking me for ever, so that I would never be able to hide again.

When I did wake up, I was clawing at my face, scraping off the disgusting mess, kicking out with legs tangled in the sheets. The howling was coming from me and the hands that gripped my wrists were Adrienne's.

I had frightened her. I had frightened her nearly as much as myself.

'Sorry,' I croaked, 'sorry, sorry.'

She leaned over and switched on the light by the bed. Everything looked so ordinary. Her sweet, rounded body hung over me and I buried my face in her breasts.

'Is everything all right? Hector? Adrienne?' came my mother's voice from the other side of the door. God, I must have been making a noise to wake her up at the other side of the house.

'Yes, we're fine, Harriet,' answered Adrienne. 'Just a bit of a dream. Nothing to worry about.'

She padded over to the door and opened it. I heard her try to explain away the awful sounds I had heard myself make by telling my mother that the tension of election night had left me a bit restless. As though I were a child who'd made a pig of himself at a party!

She slipped off and when she came back she was carrying a little dish and some cotton wool.

'Just let me give those scratches a dab with iodine, darling. I'll try to be gentle but it'll sting a bit.'

The sting told me how badly I had mauled myself. Seeing it in the shaving mirror next morning was still a bit of a shock. I couldn't think how I was going to explain this away. Of course, Cassandra couldn't resist making a clever remark.

'My, Hector, you look as though you'd been shut up with a man-eating pussy!'

I folded the newspaper noisily and tried to concentrate on the details of the election results.

'What's the matter? Did the pussy get your tongue too?'

'We had a puncture on the way back from the election last night,' invented Adrienne. 'It was terribly dark and I'm afraid Hector caught his foot and fell into a bramble patch.'

'How terribly careless. You're not fit to be seen. You can't let any of your new constituents see you like that. It looks as though you'd been fending off a jealous woman. Hell hath no fury . . . But then, no one would really believe that. Would they? Not when you so obviously have the ideal marriage.'

'It was a perfectly simple accident,' my mother interrupted tersely. 'It might have happened to anyone.'

'What does it feel like to be able to add MP to all those other letters after your name, then, Hector?' asked my father, wiping his heavy moustache.

'I'm not sure yet,' I confessed. 'Ask me again a bit later.'

'You'll have to go round today and thank all your supporters – and show yourself off to everyone else.'

'I'm not sure . . .'

Not looking like this I couldn't. Cassandra was right about that. I was a fright.

'Oh, but you must. No point in hiding your light, you know. It'll be expected of you.'

'You'll have plenty of company when you take your seat, I see. You won't be the only new boy at school,' said Cass, squinting at the newspaper over my father's shoulder.

'All the results aren't in yet, of course, but it looks as though there'll be a strong Conservative majority,' observed Mother, 'just as everyone expected.'

'Probably – nothing else was really likely,' I answered. 'The difference is that there's a new major party of opposition. We've pushed the Liberals back into third place and I have a feeling that's where they're going to stay. The Liberals are finished. With 142 seats, Labour is a creditable party at last. I told you – things will never be the same again.'

'I only hope you know what you're doing, dear,' Mother said. 'Do you think I might have some marmalade, Cassandra, or do you intend to use the dish as an alternative ashtray?'

Cass pushed the dish across the table with the same hand she used for her cigarette. The wobbling pillar of ash fell into it anyway.

'I wish you would at least wait until breakfast is over,' Mother complained.

'*I've* finished. So you've finally set the people free, have you, Hector? How creditable. But do tell me – don't you feel a bit like Sinbad, or whoever it was? You know – he let the genie out of the bottle because he felt sorry for it, but when it got dangerous, he found he couldn't put it back again, no matter how hard he tried.'

The House reassembled after the election on 20th November. In common with the mass of new Labour MPs

355

crowding the lobbies, sixty of them with neither a trade union nor a working class background, I was bursting to make my maiden speech. I knew exactly what I was going to say and, by God, they'd sit up and listen. It was at around about that point that I discovered the value of patience in parliamentary life. By the time the House went down for Christmas, I still hadn't had my chance.

Whispers. Whispers. They were talking about me behind my back.

Samaria Wood? Wasn't that where..? Didn't he..? Surely not. How do you know? Oh well, in that case . . . Haven't you heard..? Do tell . . .

I could hear them. When my back was turned, I could hear them whispering about me. Before long, other people would hear the whispers, too.

Unless I silenced them. Unless I followed them to their source and shut them off.

I suppose this was the first time that Alexander actually realized what Christmas was all about. He was two and a half – a bit more – and disgracefully spoiled. No, not spoiled really, not in the proper sense, but he was indulged to the absolute limit. How could we avoid it, when he was such an enchanting blend of my own rather severe, dark looks and Adrienne's piquancy?

And there was only Alexander. Despite our attempts to increase the size of our family, he remained our only child. Twice we had had hopes, but the hopes were not fulfilled. Adrienne used to console herself by saying that other people have to keep on trying to get it right, while we had produced a perfect child first time round, so we didn't need to improve on what we'd got.

I'd broken in a pony, just right for Alexander, earlier in the autumn – a little brown Welsh Mountain with quick, sure feet and neat head. There was a smart little saddle hanging on a rack in the tack room and a bridle that jingled on a hook above it. I couldn't wait to see my son's face when I took him down to the stables on Christmas morning to show him his first pony.

'Are you completely out of your mind?' exclaimed Adrienne. 'A pony? He's only two years old, for heaven's sake!'

'Three in April. Just the right age. I'm sure I was riding by the time I was three.'

'Hardly,' said Mother, lifting her head from a tediously long Christmas card list. 'When you were three, your father had just opened his first shop. We were living in a sooty terrace in Clapham. Cassandra was a baby and the kitchen was permanently festooned with malodorous laundry. I remember it well!'

If I ever stopped to think about it – which wasn't often – it always amazed me that my mother had loved my father so much that she had abandoned a privileged country house life for an aggressive young grocery manager. He'd made it up to her since – more than – but she must have had enormous courage to go through so much that her upbringing had not prepared her for.

'Well, just because I was deprived of a pony in my early childhood,' I returned, dropping a kiss on Mother's bent head to tell her that I was only joking, 'all the more reason that my son should not be. And Cracker really lives up to his name. You wait, Alexander'll be out on a leading rein with me before Easter.'

Philip and Helen came down to spend Christmas with us all in Wiltshire. It wasn't an arrangement that appealed to me, but, after all, it was Christmas. They brought an out of place languor, an awful, lethargic boredom that might have been fashionable in London, but cut no ice in the country.

Alexander had squealed with delight as soon as he set eyes on Cracker. I'd taken him down to the stables early, when the ice was still set on the puddles and our breath floated on the air in white gusts. The stables were warm, sweet with the scent of hay and acrid with the animals' overnight staling.

Cracker could barely lift his head above the half door and Alexander was far too short to see in. He craned on tiptoe, breathing heavily with the effort of reaching the soft, whiskered brown nose and Cracker blew hot, sweet breath back at him.

I slipped the bolt on the door and we went into the loose box. Alexander's thin little body was all bone and quivering sinew as I lifted him onto the pony's back. He flopped forward and buried his face in Cracker's coarse black mane.

'Ride, Daddy, ride,' he begged.

'Not just yet. You have to have breakfast first and then there's church and special Christmas lunch. But after lunch,' I said hurriedly as his face began to crumple, 'we'll go out together. Where would you like to go?'

'Down to the river. Feed the ducks.'

'All right. We'll fill Cracker's saddlebag with bread and take him down to the river after lunch. I promise.'

The lights in the house were just coming on as I walked back across the frozen yard with my son's thin little hand in mine. I tried to remember what the house had been like without Alexander trotting through it and couldn't.

Helen looked as wrong in church on Christmas morning as a lily in a cornfield. She wore a straight coat in some fashionably nondescript colour – probably Adrienne knew what it was – with a one-button fastening low on her left hip. From a high silver fox collar, her face looked out as calm and enamelled as a graven image. The bubble of curls that had rioted around her head when first her hair was cut was gone, replaced by a shining, silver-gilt helmet of hair, austere as a soldier-saint.

What a troublemaker that woman is. She has taken my jolly, uncomplicated, not too bright brother and turned him into a bag of neuroses. He's a lapdog, lying on his back with his paws in the air, waiting for his belly to be tickled. And that after she has devastated her husband's life and deserted her child.

Only now that I am a father myself do I see the enormity of that desertion. How could any woman behave like that and still have the effrontery to call herself a woman? My Adrienne is worth an army of Helens.

It was while Philip and Helen were down for Christmas that we heard that her husband wanted to make one last effort at reconciliation. He wanted to visit Knapp Hill and talk to Helen herself, to try to persuade her to come back to him.

Philip immediately went into a total funk. 'Good God,' he said, tossing the written request into my lap. 'That man can't come here.'

'Why not?'

'Here? It's indecent. Why can't he send a solicitor's letter like any normal person?'

'I seem to remember that he has. Any number. You used most of them for lighting your cigarettes.'

'Well . . . that's all they're fit for. Load of pompous rubbish. Don't expect me to be here and listen to him, that's all. I've got better things to do than that.'

'Like fornicating with his wife, you mean.'

'Oh, now listen . . .'

'No, you listen to me for once, Philip. Running off with Helen was the easy part. If you want to keep her, you've got to work a bit – for the first time in your life. It'll take courage to face this man, but it's the only decent thing to do. Perhaps if you talk to him, you can convince him that you're not just involved in a messy little affair, but that Helen is worth fighting for. That is,' I added nastily, 'if you really think she is . . .'

Philip turned his whipped, lap dog eyes on me. 'I'd die for her,' he said.

'If you'd ever been anywhere near a dead man,' I spat, 'you wouldn't say such a fatuous thing.'

Michael Frampton arrived on an iron cold January afternoon when the clouds were so heavy with snow only the chimneys seemed to be stopping them from falling down altogether. Philip had asked me to stay during the interview to give him moral support, but I'd no intention of sitting in like a gooseberry on what was going to be a very embarrassing meeting. Besides, I was coming round more and more to the opinion that Helen was bad for Philip and that it would be to everyone's advantage if she were to go home to her husband.

I did see Frampton getting out of his car – a dry, grey, stick of a man, too old by a generation for Helen. He moved stiffly up the steps to the door, a defeated man before the meeting began. It was difficult to feel anything but pity for him.

His driver took his car around to the back of the house and I went on to the stables. The horses were clean, uncomplicated. I didn't have to wonder all the time about their motives or worry about guarding my back.

I briefly considered taking Blenheim out for a run on the Plain, but the snow was too close and the packed chalk tracks hard enough to damage a horse's legs at anything faster than a trot. So after mooching around for a while, I decided to call into the office and check if Gledhill had anything for me to read or sign.

A brisk fire was burning in the grate. Gledhill had the lamp on and a pot of fresh tea stood on the desk beside him. The fire was snapping and the gas hissing in a companionable sort of way. Gledhill had his glasses on and was riffling through a muddle of papers that I had probably jammed into a drawer months before and forgotten.

He started to rise as I came in but I grabbed a chair and sat down, beating him to it.

'Anything for me, Gledhill?'

'I've mapped out your engagements for the week, sir. You're due in Collingbourne Ducis school tomorrow afternoon at three to meet local people, going on to Easton Royal and finishing at Pewsey. The following day, you're speaking to the ex-servicemen's club in Tidworth. Then there's a day off and the House reassembles for the New Year on the day after that.'

'Settling in well, are you? House comfortable?'

'Very nice, thank you.'

'Mrs Gledhill well?'

'Very well, considering. Not long to wait now. She says if it's a day overdue, she'll slide down the banisters to hurry things along!'

I smiled, remembering Adrienne's impatience for Alexander to appear. 'To tell you the truth, Gledhill, I'm hiding in here, if you don't mind. My brother's been trying to drag me into something I don't want to get involved in, so I've escaped.'

'In that case, sir, why don't you pull the curtains and I'll fetch you a clean cup from the kitchen. There's plenty in the pot.'

A willing conspirator, Gledhill went off and I walked to the window. The snow was just beginning to fall – big, fat flakes that scarcely seemed able to move through the frozen air. It was only mid-afternoon, but the pool of light from the window made the yard seem darker than it really was. Someone was walking across the yard. He moved out of the gloom and into the yellow square thrown by the window.

Careless, that. He ought to have known better than walk into a patch of light. He probably never thought that anyone would see him. Underestimating the enemy. It's the way men used to get killed. Weeks and months of taking every precaution – never raising your head above the parapet, never lighting three cigarettes from one match, always letting down the blanket behind you at an observation hole – then one day something happens to distract you, a letter from home, the prospect of leave and . . . that's that. Underestimating the enemy.

He walked into the pool of light and I was watching him. I could have blown the head from his shoulders at that range. Then instinct took over and he lifted his head and saw me standing there, watching. He didn't try to duck back into the shadow. He stood there with the snow whitening his head and shoulders and looked back at me, challenging me to do something about it.

Again I had the feeling that I was watching a dangerous animal, unpredictable, deadly. He had come closer, too close. He was within my defences. He was making my territory his own. Then the stocky young man with the transparent eyes got into Michael Frampton's motor and drove it around to the front of the house.

I moved then, crashing into the returning Gledhill with his clean cup, cannoning along the passages to the hall, but I was too late. Frampton had gone and Philip was standing in the hall looking as though he'd just been taken apart and put back together the wrong way round.

'Who was that with him?' I demanded.

'I don't know – his driver – what does it matter? Hector, I'm in one hell of a fix. Frampton's going to sue for restoration of his marital rights.'

'What? Don't be ridiculous. No one does that.'

'He's going to. I need a drink.'

Philip lost that yellow look after a couple of whiskies. It was only just coming up to teatime, so I locked the decanter away and stuffed the key in my pocket.

'God, he's a cold-blooded bastard,' he moaned, plumping down by the fire and propping his feet up on the fender.

'I suppose you hardly expected he'd come for a sociable chat.'

'Still – there are limits. Thank God I'd sent Helen away for the day. I swear he'd have knocked her down and dragged her off by the hair. Do you know what he called her? He called her a whore. He said that "the whore" must come back where she belongs. I'd say he was crazy if he didn't sound so sane. He said that unless she returns to him by the end of the month, he's going to take the case to court and force her to return.'

'I'm not sure he can do that, in this day and age. You can't treat women like chattels, not any more.'

'Can't you?' The look of hope on his face was child-like, innocent, pathetic.

'Well, I don't *know*, of course I don't. But it doesn't sound very likely, does it?'

'You didn't hear him.' Philip was sweating. His face gleamed in the firelight. I hadn't noticed until then how much weight he'd put on recently. 'If he says he's going to do it, he'll do it. Oh Christ, can you imagine? Just think what the *News of the World* could do with this one. Salacious details, pictures, housemaids' gossip – the lot. Even if the case fails – it must – just think what it could do to us. We'd be finished. And it won't do you any good either. You'd be hounded out of the House.'

'I thought the people in your circle – ' And for the life of me I couldn't keep the emphasis off the word 'your'. ' – didn't worry too much about little matters like marital fidelity and honour and self respect.'

'Whose side are you on anyway?' Philip asked petulantly. 'It's not what you do, it's how you do it that counts. You can do anything you like as long as you can get away with it. You know – a bit of fun, a bit of style. But this will be plain sordid. How can he do that? To his own wife?'

'I imagine he must have wondered in the past how she could do to him what she has done.'

'Don't be ridiculous. That's got nothing to do with it.'

'If you say so. So what are you going to do – give her back?'

'To that madman? What d'you think?' Philip picked up his glass, found it empty and tipped back his head to drain the last, reluctant dregs. 'But I'll tell you something – he won't get her without a fight.'

The next day, a quick chat with Father's solicitor confirmed that Michael Frampton is not as mad as he sounds. Unbelievable as it may seem in 1923, a husband is entitled to the – what's the phrase he used? – companionship, affection and society of his wife and if he doesn't get it, he may have recourse to the law. Of course, the courts are unlikely to order a woman to return, but they may enforce payment of substantial compensation to the husband. Worse – a husband may seek damages against the man guilty of adultery with the wife.

What does look certain is that only a madman would even dream of washing so much soiled linen in public. Perhaps it was only a threat. Perhaps he was only trying to frighten Philip as a last resort. If he actually goes through with it, it could be one of the most unsavoury cases in living memory.

God, what a mess!

Helen came to see me a night or two later. She slipped

into the library where I was catching up on some last minute reading before going back to London for the new session of the House. Everyone had gone to bed, I thought, Adrienne with a whisper to me not to be too late. Helen slipped in, the sound of the door and the sound of her steps unnoticed by me as I concentrated on the long-winded papers.

Suddenly, she was just there. She was still in the sliver of black evening gown she had worn for dinner, backless, its sleeves only suggested by long ropes of pearls that joined shoulder and wrist. She was a fallen angel, chained to earth. She slipped into the leather arm-chair across from mine by the hearth. Her feet were bare and pinched with cold. She stretched them out to the fire.

'You'll get chilblains, if you do that,' I pointed out, sounding like a finicky old man.

Like ashy fingerprints, there were smudges of weariness beneath her eyes. My bright reading light was cruel. It showed up the fine lines that linked her nose with her down-turned mouth. The hollows beneath her cheekbones and at the base of her neck had gone beyond fashionable thinness and were emaciated.

I had never seen Helen as a woman before. To me, she'd always been a beautiful statue, too perfect, plaster touched up with flesh tones. It was beyond my comprehension that anyone could love her – her husband, my brother, both besotted by an image no more real than Pygmalion's creation. Now, those shadows and lines, tiny imperfections, brought her down from the clouds and into the real world of men and women.

She was very tired, weary of the struggle, weary of the weight of two men's devotion. If it is a tragedy never to be loved, it might be equally as burdensome to be loved too much. Without opening her eyes, she spoke and the effort of communicating with me was almost too much for her.

'I've come to make a bargain with you,' she said in that peculiar voice of hers that seemed to turn Philip into a quivering jellyfish whenever she chose.

I didn't answer.

'I'll give you what you want and in return you must give me what I want. That's fair, isn't it?'

'That depends.'

'You learn fast,' she mocked. 'Never commit yourself. Lesson number one in the parliamentary handbook.' Her eyes flicked open, dusty as twilight. 'Very well. I'll make you my offer and lay out my terms. You can take them or leave them. No trading. No half-measures.'

'Go on.'

'I will go away, right away, abroad and never come back. I'll never bother this family again. I will make no future demands and I'll never try to see or contact Philip again.'

And as she said it, I knew this was the only answer. The flood of relief that followed her offer was quickly overtaken by anxiety that her terms would be so extravagant we'd never be able to meet them. Yet I determined that we would, whatever the cost.

'And in return?' I asked.

'I'll need some money, of course, enough to be reasonably independent and . . .'

Of course, I thought, money. She sees that the game's up here and she's getting out with as much as she can get away with.

'How much?' I demanded.

'Enough,' she answered coolly. 'No more than that and . . .'

And her jewels, I thought, and furs and a house, a motor car, maybe. What else?

'. . . Hermione.'

The last thing I had expected.

'That's all?'

'That's all I've ever wanted.'

And I believed her. I looked across the hearth at her weary face and a chink of understanding opened in the defences I had built against her.

'Why come to me?' I queried. 'Why not Philip?'

'He couldn't do it. You know he couldn't. You're the only one, Hector, who can get my daughter for me.'

'And if I do – if, somehow, God knows how, I get her away from her father – how do I know you'll keep your word?'

I shouldn't have said that. She'd given me no cause. She turned her face at an angle, revealing her famous profile. Once I might have suspected she'd done that on purpose, but, after tonight, I'd never be so certain again.

'You might find this hard to believe, Hector, but I'm very fond of your brother. He's been good to me. He's the only person in so many years who's even bothered to be kind to me. I can't hurt him any more. Just being here makes me a burden. If I stay, I'll drag him down and down – my husband will make sure of that – until we're like all the other seedy couples wasting their lives in second-rate French seaside resorts. Perhaps we'd end up drinking too much, staying in bed all morning, cadging meals off people who try to avoid us, getting old, hating each other, but we'd never be able to part because then we'd have nobody. You do see. I can't do that to him.'

'And all you want is Hermione and you'll go?'

'Give me my daughter and you'll never see me again.'

Well, how would *you* kidnap a child? This is the twentieth century, after all. Not even Helen could expect me

367

to gallop down the highway with a mask over my face, shouting, 'Stand and deliver'. All sorts of crazy plans presented themselves, each one less practical than the last.

I could put a ladder against the nursery window and carry her off. But she was nearly eight years old. If she was like her mother she'd be long and if she was like her father she'd be broad. I'd end up killing us both if she struggled on the ladder.

I could find out when she was going somewhere – a party or something – follow the car and force it off the road. But again, someone could get hurt and I'd frighten the wits out of the poor child.

I wished I could talk to Adrienne about it, I badly needed her common sense, but this was one subject where we'd never see eye to eye. Much as she deplored the fact that Hermione had been abandoned in the first place, Adrienne could never condone possessing the child by violence.

Whatever I did had to be done in perfect secrecy. After an obvious kidnap, there'd be a frightful hue and cry, with police swarming all over the roads. Somehow, she had to be spirited away in such a manner that no one would realize she was missing for several hours. We needed time to get her to Helen and then out of reach of English law.

What did Helen think I was – a miracle worker?

Ask and it shall be given. Seek and ye shall find.

'You do see, though, Eglantine, that's it's the only way?'

'If anyone but you suggested something like this, Hector, I'd call a doctor and a padded van!'

'But you'll do it?'

'Not under any circumstances. You're all being completely selfish. Has anyone thought of how Hermione might feel about all this? No, you're all too busy congratulating yourselves that you've found a nice, neat answer to a nasty problem.'

'But it is the answer,' I urged. 'The only answer.'

Damn, damn, damn. If she wouldn't do it! I'd lain awake for a week trying to work out a solution that needed no violence and wouldn't frighten the child into fits. This was the only, the *only* way.

'Listen, it's so simple. All you have to do is dream up some treat to take Hermione out for a whole day. They'll let her go with you, won't they, to a zoo or a circus or whatever? Then drive straight to Southampton – it won't take more than an hour – and hand Hermione over to her mother – her *mother*, for heaven's sake. Where's the harm in that?'

'And Helen will get on a ship, sail to France and live happily ever after? With a daughter she hasn't seen for four years? A daughter who's been told her mother is every sort of horror rolled into one? Who's closed her mind by closing her mouth? Wake up, Hector! This is the real world we're living in!'

'If you don't do this, Helen's life will be in ruins.'

'Helen's life is ruined already. All I can do is try to salvage something for her daughter. This isn't the way.'

'If you don't do this, I'll do it myself,' I threatened. 'One way or another, I'll get Hermione, no matter who gets hurts in the process. I won't have this family dragged down any further by that madman who calls himself Helen's husband. Helen's going to go and leave my brother alone, if I have to drag Hermione screaming from her bed to do it.'

'The war's over, Hector,' she said sadly. 'Why can't you let it go? There's no place for ambushes and trench raids and taking prisoners any more.'

Poor Eglantine. I liked her too much to enjoy threatening her, but I did it, all the same. Whichever choice she made was going to be wrong.

It was just a tiny paragraph. Whoever had clipped it out of the paper and sent it to me was making sure I didn't miss it. It was a snippet from the *Hampshire Chronicle* stating simply that an enquiry was to be opened into the death in suspicious circumstances of Lieutenant Colonel H. V. D. Vosper, who had been reported killed in action in April 1918.

With the same post came papers for Philip from Frampton's solicitor, the first salvo in his attack.

He wasn't out just to get Helen back. He was out to destroy our family.

When I was a boy, I had a book of puzzles and illusions. You know the sort of thing: two lines that appear to bend but are straight when measured, or appear of unequal length but are actually the same; if you hold the page in a certain way and move it towards your eyes, the rabbit goes into the hole. You know.

One of them was a black and white design. If you looked at it one way, it seemed to be a picture of a white goblet. If you looked at it again, it was two black faces.

It all depends on how you look at things.

I had shot my Commanding Officer through the head and dragged his body out in the dark to no-man's-land where, facing the enemy, it was smashed by shells and rotted, I hope, beyond all possibility of attribution of crime. I had then assumed command of the battalion, as one would on the death of the CO in action.

Of course, things like that aren't done in secret. We practically lived on top of each other in the dugouts. I did it because I had to and because I knew that the lads would back me up. We all stuck together, told the same story and so we lived. Otherwise we would have died.

God, how callous that sounds. In the night, I face him, screaming accusation. In the daylight, I know I did what had to be done.

How valuable was Vosper's life? To his widow and three children, of infinite value. Then put his certain death in the balance against the possible deaths of – how many? A platoon? A company? All of us? If a whole battalion, pitifully below strength already, was to be slowly dismembered across four hundred uphill yards of thigh deep mud, crucified on wire that our own bombardment had only tossed up in the air and flung down again in an even more impenetrable thicket, shredded by well-placed machine guns that raked the stumbling line from end to end from the safety of concrete blockhouses – how much was Vosper's life worth then?

We had done it before. We were to do it again. But never, in four years, had I seen so clearly the utter futility of it all. I looked at the men and knew I could not send them out there again. Enough was enough.

So I shot my Commanding Officer. It was a crime. Supposing everyone who had the wind up about an attack had done the same? What would happen to the war then, eh?

I had pleaded with him, begged him, hauled him up to the firing step, oblivious of snipers, and explained it all in words of one syllable. The men were ranged along the trench behind us, sullen and apathetic, punished beyond their capacity to think or feel or talk, no more sentient than animals in a slaughterhouse. Above the charnel house smell of the trench, the odour of rum was strong. The rum ration was supposed to boost morale before an attack and was about as effective as the condemned man's hearty breakfast. The stunning crash of our own guns had moved on from the wire. It was still there. We could see it still ahead – ravelled, strangling, unbroken. The guns spent themselves now against the ten foot thick walls of the concrete blockhouses where we had broken ourselves at dawn.

We looked out across the parapet – beyond the filthy band of detritus that rimmed the trench line, beyond the slashing steel mesh of rain that limited our vision to a few, foul yards of mud. Long, breathless sobs of agony told us where the wounded of the morning's attack lay. And as we listened, the moans turned to screams. It was still raining and the water was rising. In the shell holes where they had crept for safety, waiting for the dark and stretcher parties, trusting in their pals to come and get them out, our men were drowning. Alone with the dead, our friends were dying in a soup of slime and decay. And there was nothing we could do to help them. Behind me, Sgt Morris was crying.

If the CO had just got on the field telephone and told them that all our guns had done was to churn up the mud until the going was impossible. If he had just had the sense to realize that he was standing on the brink, with only one way to go. All he said was that we had been ordered and we were going. So I shot him.

I told Brigade that he had – and this contravening the C-in-C's direct orders that company commanders and above were not to be risked in no-man's-land – gone out on a recce the night before and not come back. When they wanted to know why the battalion had not attacked as ordered, I simply said that communications were down and we had received no orders. They fumed and sent down a reprimand that sizzled the wires, but by then it was too late. The attack failed, but no one really blamed us. It would have failed anyway. Nothing we did nor did not do could have made any difference. Things moved on.

And the men, knowing that they were alive and might have been dead, kept silent.

But five years later, which side of the picture would people see?

I don't know how Frampton had found it all out. But then, I don't imagine he did it himself. I suppose I always knew that one day I would have to face Frampton's pale-eyed killer. He had snooped and ferreted, greased palms where he had to, dug up what was better left decently buried.

And now it was him or me. I had always known it.

Eglantine was late. Helen was very restrained. She didn't pace up and down the waiting room, wringing her hands. She sat on the slippery leather bench, dressed in nondescript clothes, with her hands lying still in her lap, but she was so pale, I wondered what we ought to do if she should faint.

We had avoided the imposing waiting hall where the great liners docked on the transatlantic run. Helen was to cross to Le Havre on the anonymity of the ordinary cross-Channel packet. Not that Helen could ever look anonymous. Widows were ten a penny, but in the plain clothes that a middle-class young widow might affect, her beauty shone, pale and lustrous. No matter how much we might try to look ordinary, the few people who shared the waiting room with us would remember her when questioned.

I had to admire her. She sat still, but I knew she wanted to pace and smoke and talk. I knew because I wanted to do the same myself. I rubbed a clear patch on one sooty window pane and peered out. Gledhill examined, with minute care and for at least the fourth time, the faded travel posters decorating tobacco darkened walls. Deauville. Carlsbad. Zermatt. No one who sat in this waiting room had much of a chance of seeing any of them.

The longer we waited, the more likely it was that

Eglantine had thought better of her reluctant promise to hand over Hermione to her mother. I couldn't blame her. It was a mad idea. How could we ever have imagined that mother and child could just blend quietly into a crowd and never be seen again? She could dye her hair, hide behind spectacles, break out in spots, walk with crutches – Helen would still be Helen. When the pursuit began – and it would – Michael Frampton's bloodhound would sniff them out if he had to cross the whole continent of Europe on his hands and knees to do it.

I think we had all just about given up hope when Eglantine arrived, holding by the hand a rather plain little girl who was looking about her with intelligent interest.

'Where have you been?' I hissed. 'You're hours late.'

'Hermione had earache last night. If Nanny had had her way, she wouldn't have been allowed out at all today. But I can be very persuasive when I want.'

I looked at the child in her red coat and matching buttoned gaiters. A woollen tam-o'-shanter was pulled well down over her head, but I could see that both her ears were stoppered with olive oil-soaked cotton wool. Not only could the poor mite not talk, but she probably couldn't hear a thing today either. Sensibly, they weren't carrying luggage, so Hermione's curiosity had not been too much aroused in advance, and they managed to blend into the now increasing number of travellers more successfully than I had hoped.

I had a bad moment, when I thought Helen was going to leap up and make a scene. The last thing we wanted was hugging and crying and kissing. But she managed to hold her ground, though if I'd thought she was pale before, I'd been wrong. Eglantine came and sat on the bench beside her and the whole thing looked perfectly normal.

I could have kissed Eglantine myself. What an absolute brick she was! She had just taken the child, walked out of the house with her and here they were. Simple. Perhaps it wasn't such a crazy plan, after all.

Of course, Hermione didn't yet know what was going on. She just accepted the strange woman her aunt was talking to. Doubtless she was used to the oddities of Eglantine and considered today's journey as just one more example of it.

I didn't want to be around when she found out what was going on. I didn't envy Eglantine her explanations. Besides, I had something else to attend to. So I left Eglantine to make sure the next stage of the plan went off without a hitch. If she had got as far as this, I knew I could trust her to finish the job.

'Gledhill,' I said as we left Southampton behind and headed along the road towards Lyndhurst and the New Forest, 'I've got something else to do and if you don't want to be involved, I won't hold it against you.'

He just turned to look at me in question. The wind plucked the words out of my mouth and tossed them about.

'Once they guess that Hermione has gone, we'll be followed, no doubt of that. If they think about it for a moment, they'll realize that Helen has to leave the country. She'd never get away with it in England,' I shouted. It wasn't the sort of conversation that ought to have been shouted. Murder should be discussed in whispers, in the dark, not at the top of one's voice, in an open-top tourer. 'My guess is that we've got until dark, perhaps a bit beyond, before they realize what's happened. Hermione and her mother will be well away by then. But we can't take any chances. We have to give them as much time as possible.'

'I understand.'

'Do you? I wonder. If you want to pull out, just say so.'

'I'd do anything for you, sir,' he said simply.

We had plenty of time, by my reckoning – too much. It was too easy to think. Him or me, I told myself, it's him or me. There isn't any choice. Gledhill and I had a long lunch at The Crown in Lyndhurst and then, as the afternoon darkened, set off along the road to Beaulieu.

There's a choice of routes from Buckholt to Southampton, but I'd put myself in Byatt's place and eliminated all but one. He couldn't be certain, no matter how accurate his guesswork, what Helen had in mind. She might be going to France by the quickest route; she might have gone back to Knapp Hill en route for Liverpool and America; she might be making a dash back to London. She might, in fact, be almost anywhere.

So a good bloodhound doesn't tear off in a straight line. He circles near home, sniffing out his prey. Byatt would cast around, in widening circles: Beaulieu Road Station first, probably, then Lyndhurst, then north or east according to the clues. Someone, somewhere, must have seen an eccentric, middle-aged woman driving a fast car or a tall, fair, beautiful woman with a child.

We chose our site with care. There's a long, straight, fast stretch of road that ends in a left hand curve and a sharp right hand bend at a place marked on the map as Matley Bog. A motorcycle rider coming from the south has to throttle back in time to negotiate the curves. The bend is camouflaged by bushes that grow thickly right to the edge of the road. No houses in sight or in earshot. It was the obvious spot, but just to make certain, we drove all the way to Beaulieu before returning to set up our ambush.

Nothing complicated. Things go wrong if you're over-ambitious. Gledhill was stationed further up the road to make sure we chose the right person and that there was no other traffic on the way. Only when I received his signal would I tighten the rope we'd strung across the road between two trees.

Anyone riding a motorcycle too fast might easily misjudge the corner and spin off the road.

It was dark and cold and wet. No one was on the road at all. Crouching in the dripping bushes, I was beginning to get stiff with cold. We'd chosen the wrong road. Frampton hadn't sent Archie Byatt after all, but had gone himself in a motor car. We'd missed him. He was in Southampton already. He was on the way to France, in pursuit of Helen. Then I heard the engine note of a flat twin Douglas. I didn't need Gledhill's signal to tell me that this was our man, heading fast for Lyndhurst.

I pulled up the rope, fastening it off at about four feet above the ground around the trunk of a tree. It was so simple and so gratifyingly effective.

The rope took him across the chest. There was a twang, the engine screamed as the wheels lost traction and left the ground, a crash of splintering glass, a squeal of tortured metal as the machine skidded on its side along the gravel and then silence.

I was still crouching behind the gorse bush when Gledhill came running up. He tore with his useless hands at the knots I had tied in the rope. I left him still struggling and walked over to the wreck. There had to be no room for doubt. We had to have done the job properly. If not . . .

There was a smell of hot fuel. The front wheel of the cycle was a few yards away. The rear wheel was still spinning slowly, buckled and off centre. The rider was pinned under the engine, huddled and still. I had seen enough dead men to know that we had done all we needed to do.

Yet I still had to be sure . . .

I crouched down and turned up to the sky the broken face of Patrick Snape.

Black or white? Faces or goblet? Which is illusion and which real? I have been looking at the wrong image. I have mistaken the shadow for the substance. I looked at life and it was clear to me what I was looking at. Now, suddenly I am looking from a different angle and everything is changed. Certainties are uncertain. Priorities are unimportant. The ground beneath my feet is shifting. Black is white and white is black.

I learned how to kill and have forgotten how to stop. I am a murderer.

Alexander is sleeping. Fronds of hair the colour of my own feather across the sheet. It's still damp from his bath and curls at the nape of his neck where the skin smells of powder and soap. He has tumbled into a nest of feathers and every muscle in his body is flaccid in sleep. His thumb has fallen from his mouth. It is ringed by a ridge of callus from the furious sucking it suffers. His head is flung back and his mouth is open. I can see the two prominent front teeth that distress Adrienne, but to me they seem quite ordinary. Deep in his throat, he makes a sucking sound as though he thinks his thumb is still in place. His fingers are tendrils that curl around my heart.

I tuck back in place the blankets he has kicked off. The nursery fire will die down in an hour or so and the night is cold.

I remember that I promised to take him out on Cracker up to look at the white chalk horse on the Downs in the morning.

I'm holding my Webley service revolver. I can feel the weight of it. The handle fits into my grasp. It's warm because I've been holding it ready for some time, waiting. It's heavy – so heavy that I can scarcely lift it – my arm moves so slowly up. It doesn't seem so much like a deadly weapon when you think of it as an extension of your arm.

I'm not afraid. No, that's not true. I'm afraid that Adrienne will not forgive me.

ANTHONY

The Clown

Damned uncomfortable sort of age, this. Everything's too fast, too clever, too slick. Everyone's in such a tearing hurry. It makes me feel like some old dinosaur, left over from a past era.

I suppose it's always been like that. I know my father raged about my generation, when we were young – girls on bicycles, smoking in public, soft shirts – you know the sort of thing. But he *was* old at my age, whiskered and short-sighted.

I don't feel old, not inside, but I just don't quite seem to be able to keep up with the pace of things, these days. There seems to be a new craze, a new dance, a new cocktail, every week. No one has a proper name any more. Where are the Henrys and the Franks now? Everyone seems to be called Bubbles or Binkie or Pug. Pug – good grief!

'Good old Ant,' they say. 'Never changes.' But I do. My waist gets an inch or two thicker and my face gets a shade or two redder, but I still manage to keep smiling. Good old Ant.

Clemmie has to run now, to keep up. I see her getting thinner and brighter, smoking more, dancing faster with younger and younger men, at an age when most women are glad to settle back and enjoy their grand-children. That's it, of course. That's the problem. Four children and not a hint of a grandchild between them.

Viola was married two years before poor Harry went to war. When unsuitable young women were dropping war babies all over the place why couldn't Viola have obliged with just one child born in wedlock? Is that too much to ask? She owed it to us. And now she seems to be getting over the widowhood that I feared would last as long as the late queen's and is making eyes at that most undesirable friend of Charley's. She won't get a child from him – not a chance – and if she persists, I shall tell her why! Perhaps not. I might leave it to Clemmie to explain what Viola is clearly too innocent to have guessed.

Clemmie has whispered in my ear that I'm being a bit too innocent myself where that relationship is concerned. She says – and I can't imagine where a respectable married woman has come by her information – that Archie Byatt may not be as disinterested in Viola as I hope. She says that some men are capable of – what's her disgusting phrase? – 'looking both ways'. Good Lord! If he lays so much as one finger on my daughter, I'll horsewhip him!

No hope of a grandchild from Charley. Today's hard, smart young women aren't going to look twice at a one-armed drunkard. They say there's a shortage of men. They say that women are competing with each other for the few that are left, whole or otherwise. All I can say is none of them seems to be desperate enough to take on my oldest son. I can't say I blame them.

There's always the twins . . . well, they're young yet. Time enough to take life seriously when they come down from Oxford. I hope they manage to get one half decent degree between them. The way things are going, they'll need some worthwhile qualifications behind them. No money in land any more – I had to sell several farms for a song just to finance the twins at Oxford. 'You can rely on land,' my father used to say. 'You've always got something behind you with land.' Not any more. No money in any of the solid, gentlemanly ways of living that I always believed in. The only people who seem to make any money at all are the ones who're at home in this nasty, shiny, ramshackle world we're forced to live in.

Thank God for Hermione.

It's a bit of a shock when your brother goes mad. I don't mean slightly dotty – every family has some harmless old eccentric hidden away in the attic, doesn't it? I mean absolutely stark raving, barking mad. I shan't forget in a hurry putting my shoulder against his bathroom door and bursting in to find Michael unconscious in a bathful of red water.

He hadn't done it properly, Dr Hawley said. Typical. He'd cut across the wrists and damaged the tendons, but not cut deeply enough. Pussy-footing about. Oh, he'd have died all right, but it would have taken some time. If he'd made a really decent job of it and cut vertically along the artery, he'd have been dead long before we'd got suspicious and burst in. That's some consolation, I suppose. The publicity was bad enough as it was. I had to lean pretty heavily in certain quarters to avoid charges being pressed and it cost me, I can tell you – but imagine if he'd succeeded . . . It doesn't bear thinking about.

Who'd have thought that boring, sensible, utterly predictable Michael could have fallen so deeply in love that he couldn't face life without her? I wonder. Perhaps the whole thing was some awful aberration. Perhaps he didn't go mad when Helen left him, but much earlier – perhaps he was well on the way by the time he first met her.

A man doesn't get to the age of thirty-eight happily still a bachelor, with a comfortable town house and his sex life efficiently organized – whatever Clemmie might say – then drop like a pheasant in October at the sight of a pretty girl more than twenty years younger than him. Not if he's sane, he doesn't. I don't think insanity runs in the family, not as far back as I can remember, but you never know. It has to start somewhere. I might take off all my clothes and run starkers down Lymington High Street tomorrow, for all anyone might guess in advance.

If Helen had been a shop girl, he could've set her up in St John's Wood and they'd have lived happily ever after. That's the sensible way to deal with a grand passion. But you can't do that when her uncle and aunt are friends of friends of friends. So the poor fool had to marry her.

Of course, in some ways, you can't blame him. Helen was a beauty at seventeen and now . . . I saw her in town the other day. My cab was caught up in traffic and when I looked nosily into the one going the other way, there she was. My word, what a cracker! Worth losing some sleep over, I'd say! But no woman is worth losing your mind over. Absolutely no woman is worth wallowing in a bathful of blood for.

Poor old so-and-so.

It's all such a mess. Sometimes if I can't sleep at night I try to work out where we all went wrong. Which is more to blame – Michael's marriage or the war? Clemmie puts my sleeplessness down to too much port and cheese. Perhaps she's right. She says it's having an effect in another area, too. But dammit, she can't expect me to carry on like a young man at my time of life. What's she got to complain about? I can still perform. Maybe I take a bit longer to recover nowadays. And when she looks at me with that scathing expression, no wonder I'm not the man I used to be – it's enough to make a snowman melt. Perhaps I'll cut down a bit on the whisky last thing at night though.

Is it just my imagination, or were we a normal, happy

family once? I can see it all so clearly. It was always summer. The sun was always shining. The river was always full of fish. The coverts were always full of birds. Charley was bright and keen, a fine seat on a horse, a splendid shot. Viola was shy and sweet and pretty, just like daughters ought to be, and every young man around was mad about her. The twins were naughty, full of fun, typical boys. Clemmie was the perfect wife, the perfect mother, the perfect mate. She made me feel like a man, like a king. I was so proud of them all. We were all so happy.

It's not so long ago really, but with the war standing between me and my memories, it feels like a lifetime.

Perhaps it was never like that at all.

It's all such a mess. Michael may have come out of the asylum – only we called it a private clinic, of course, very discreet – with a clean bill of health, but I have my doubts. He put up a good front at first, but when he came back from that abortive visit to the Malyons having seen Helen again, he was back in the grip of obsession once more.

Like a man with a hole in a tooth, he was forever prodding and poking at his pain, airing it for discussion when it ought to have been decently covered and forgotten. I *knew* he and Archie Byatt were up to something, I just didn't know what. Even when that dubious young man's friendship with Charley had cooled, he was always hanging around. Nor did he seem to have any way of supporting himself, yet someone must have been paying his bills, because he always said his people were as poor as church mice.

They were up to something. Whatever it was, it led somehow to Patrick Snape crashing Byatt's motorcycle on a long, straight, dark road. And don't try to tell me that that terrible business of Hector Malyon's suicide wasn't tied up with it all.

Now that was a shock, if you like. A decent chap Malyon. Too good for his family. What would make a man like that want to blow his head off? He had everything. War hero. Nice little foreign wife. A son to follow him. No money worries. A brilliant Parliamentary career ahead of him, everyone said so.

Of course, one heard whispers that his war wasn't all it was cracked up to be, but what politician doesn't have to put up with rumours? If Lloyd George had really been up to everything people said he was, he'd never have had the energy to run a government! Malyon wasn't the sort of fellow to be put off his stroke by a few malicious whispers.

Mind you, they say there's no smoke etc etc . . .

I liked Patrick Snape too, much against my better judgement. Clemmie says you have to feel sorry for these men, that it's a kind of sickness that needs treatment, not a perversion. Medical claptrap. That's typical of this day and age. Too broadminded by half. Right is right and wrong is wrong and a pansy is a pansy and that's that.

Still, I liked Snape. Wouldn't have had him for Hermione's tutor otherwise. He worked wonders with her. She had been turning into a little savage, but Snape tamed her with kindness. Not even he could get her to talk, but still . . .

I knew there'd be hell to pay when the news arrived that Patrick Snape had been found with his neck broken at Matley Bog. But what had he been *doing* there? That's what no one seemed to be able – or willing – to tell me.

All the pieces are there, right beneath my hand, but no matter how much I shuffle them, I can't make sense of them. They won't fit together. But I know the connection is there, somewhere, if I can just put everything back in the right order.

Hermione went out for the day with her great-aunt on some sort of jolly. The poor child had earache and I heard Nanny complaining bitterly to Clemmie about the very idea of taking her out in that biting wind. But Eglantine can be very determined when she sets her mind on something.

'Nonsense, the fresh air will do her good,' she said. 'She can't sit moping over the nursery fire all day.'

I'd have been quite happy to sit moping over the library fire all day with a plentiful supply of whisky, if I'd been given half a chance!

So they went off together and weren't back by teatime. It was dark and Nanny started making an awful fuss, saying no one ever listened to her and she wouldn't be held responsible etc etc . . . You know. Well, it did seem a bit much to stay out so long, when the poor girl wasn't well.

Michael got in a fearful bate about it. Now, that wasn't at all like him. Normally, you'd scarcely think he had a daughter, for all the attention he paid to her. If it hadn't been for Clemmie and me, I dread to think what might have happened to Hermione. He'd probably have locked her away in some special school for abnormal children, but that wouldn't have been fair. Hermione wasn't abnormal, she just didn't talk. Dear little thing, really, when she wasn't trying to bite the hand that fed her!

But this time, Michael really kicked up because Eglantine hadn't brought his daughter back. There was an awful lot of shouting and running around. Most odd. I kept my head well down. Nothing to do with me. Then I heard the sound of young Byatt's motorcycle starting off down the drive and, by the sound of the gravel spurting back from the wheels, he was in a hurry.

I always felt a sort of relief when I knew he was out of the house. He made me uncomfortable. Now, I'm not the sort of man who thinks that *that* sort are always waiting for you to turn your back – of course not – but all the same, I didn't like him around. Only when I finally decided the coast was clear and came out of the library, I discovered that Byatt was still around and that it was Patrick Snape who'd gone tearing off on the motorcycle. And no one would tell me where or why.

Well, in the end it was all a fuss about nothing, because Eglantine and Hermione came home not long after that. Apparently, Eglantine's precious Bugatti had broken down and it had taken some backwoods mechanic ages to find out what was wrong. She went on and on about gaskets and bearings and things but she might have been talking Urdu for all the sense I could make of it, so I'm afraid I stopped listening.

Hermione looked awful. Well, no wonder, after having been dragged half around Hampshire in an open car when she already had earache. That woman really has no common sense. Nanny had all my sympathy as she hustled Hermione up to bed. I expect she was all right after a hot bath and a bowl of bread and milk. I must confess, I did tiptoe up to the nursery to say goodnight, but Nanny was very fierce and wouldn't let me.

It was about nine o'clock and we were just finishing dinner when the police arrived. I was called out to the library and told the news, so it fell to me to go back and inform the rest of the family. Wherever Patrick Snape had been going in such a hurry, he'd got no further than Matley. His body had been found by a passing motorist and, because he'd lived alone and had been riding Archie Byatt's cycle and because I was a magistrate, the police had decided we were the proper people to inform.

Awful. Awful. What a thing to happen. We were all terribly affected by the news. What a way to go – and after such a good war, too. We couldn't finish our dinner. We all filed out, shocked and silent, and it was only when we were sitting down with our coffee that the buzz of speculation began.

I never imagined Eglantine would take it so badly. I know she and Snape were close – too close, I might have said, in other circumstances. Harold had left her a very wealthy woman and she was, as I've said, not famous for her common sense. Middle-aged women can get very silly, I'm told. However, things being as they were, there wasn't likely to be a scandal between those two. Still, they were very good friends.

Eglantine was stricken, absolutely stricken, there's no other word for it. Everyone was talking at once, everyone was expounding his or her own theory why Snape had been on that road at all and I suddenly realized that Eglantine hadn't said a word. She was standing just inside the drawing room door, rather like a department store dummy that has just been propped up somewhere temporarily. She looked as though she were about to vomit. No one else noticed.

'I say, old girl,' I said, slipping over to her. 'Are you all right? Why don't you sit down? You've had a bit of a shock.'

'Anthony,' she said, looking at me and through me at the same time, if you see what I mean. 'What have I done?'

'Now, now, you mustn't blame yourself. Just because you were a bit late back with Hermione – that's got nothing to do with this awful accident.'

'Oh but it has, it has,' she insisted. 'It's all my fault.'

'Come on now, come and sit by the fire. A brandy's

what you need – best thing for shock. You'll see things differently after that.'

She let me lead her over to the fire. As I took her elbow, I could feel the tremors run through her and into me. We'd only gone a few steps when I heard the first crash.

'Good God,' I burst out. 'What now?'

I never could stand Archie Byatt.

He was breaking up his room, very thoroughly and systematically. Right at the top of the house, in one of the unconverted cubicles left over from the war, Michael had installed Byatt, saying that he spent so much time at Buckholt, he needed a place to call his own. And now he was breaking it up.

By the time I arrived, panting from the four flights of stairs, splintered glass and china from the washstand littered the floor. The curtains and curtain rail had been hauled down and the plaster was cracked. The upright chair had been reduced to matchwood. With a chair leg, he was smashing the window panes, one by one. I stood in the doorway, shock and lack of breath preventing me from saying a word, and watched him finish the last of the windows. From a pocket, he brought out a wicked-looking clasp knife and began to slash the bedclothes into long, regular strips.

Mad. Quite, quite mad. There were flecks of blood on his face, where slivers of glass must have flown back at him. His right hand was bleeding quite badly. His mouth was open and his lips were joined by gummy ropes of saliva. My skin crawled in horror as his arm rose and fell, rose and fell. The knife blade glittered with every motion. I tried to shout and only a croak came out.

But he stopped and turned to look at us all, clustered in the doorway, trampling over each other in an attempt

392

to see everything that could be seen while shrinking from the agony of Byatt's eyes. He was suffering. I couldn't stand the man, but I pitied him then. He was suffering more than any man ought to. I looked into his eyes and down into the pit of hell.

'Daddy, Daddy, *do* something,' begged Viola. 'I can't bear it!'

Michael was breathing down my neck. I grabbed him and pushed him forward. 'You brought him here,' I hissed, 'you sort him out.'

But Michael dug his heels in. 'I can't. I can't. Why me? Why don't we just lock the door and leave him alone until he gets over it?'

'Let me talk to him.'

Eglantine pushed through the crowd of us, scrawny, pale, authoritative. We all fell back, relieved that *someone* felt responsible for this scene.

'Leave us alone,' she commanded.

I felt obliged to protest at that. 'Look here, he's dangerous. You can't be left alone with him. Anything might happen.'

'But it won't,' she answered and I believed her.

'Are you sure . . . ?'

'For heaven's sake, Ant,' Clemmie broke in. 'If she's crazy enough to go in there with that maniac, she deserves all she gets.'

Eglantine shut the door firmly. We could hear the sound of the key in the lock. Immediately following that, there came the biggest crash yet. My guess is that Byatt had overturned the dressing chest. I turned to go back, but Clemmie grabbed me by the arm and propelled me downstairs.

I needed a stiff one or two after that, I can tell you. Clemmie went straight off to bed, saying that all this emotion had absolutely worn her out. Michael hung around for a while, looking worried, as well he might.

Somehow or other, he was at the bottom of all this, I just couldn't work out how. After half an hour or so, he turned in too.

I thought someone ought to sit up in case poor old Eglantine needed help – although what use I might be, I couldn't quite be sure. However, it was a gesture. I took a decanter and glass into the library and stoked up the fire. It might be a long night.

There were no further crashes. For all I knew they might both have been dead. Somewhere around two o'clock I did creep upstairs to listen outside the door, but I couldn't hear a thing. That was either a very good sign or a very bad one. I stuck it out for another hour, then tottered off to bed. Well, the fire was dying and I was doing no one any good by sitting down there getting sozzled.

Wonderful woman, Eglantine. More courage in her little finger than the rest of us had put together. I don't know what she did in that closed room that night. She never told us. The next morning at breakfast, there she was, looking more gaunt than ever, a sad old woman, but quite definitely alive.

'Well,' I said, walking over to the window to sup my porridge looking out across the frosty garden. 'What a night, eh?'

No one answered. Not a lot anyone could say. We were a pretty glum lot that morning, I can tell you.

'Awful about poor old Snape,' I went on. 'Awful. Does anyone know who his people are? They ought to be told. Probably want to take the body home and all that.'

Clemmie gave an ostentatious shudder. She was looking quite worn out. The events of the night, quite naturally, upset her. Then, first thing in the morning, she'd had to face a furious Nanny telling her that Hermione's earache was much worse – that's what comes of gallivanting all over the countryside against medical advice – that she had a raging temperature, she needed a doctor and would be lucky if she didn't lose her hearing in one ear. Ghastly woman. Exaggerating, of course. Well, I hope so. Still, one can't be too careful with children. Whatever was Eglantine thinking of, dragging her away like that on some silly expedition? Whatever the reason, it can't have been *that* important.

'There'll be an inquest, of course,' Michael observed, looking up from his toast. 'It could be very unpleasant.'

'No reason why it should be – I mean, they're all pretty harrowing and so on, but this must be quite straightforward. Accidental death. What else could it be?'

Michael looked across at Eglantine and she looked back at him.

'Of course,' he said.

Now, they think I'm stupid. Dear old Ant, they think, such a sweetie, but never notices a thing that's not laid out on a plate right under his nose. But I do. There was something going on, I could smell it, but I'm damned if I could work it out.

Afterwards, I cornered Eglantine before she could slip away.

'Well,' I demanded. 'What happened?'

'All sorts of things have happened,' she answered in that irritatingly matter of fact way she has when she's trying to hide something. 'What did you have in mind?'

'You know what I mean. What happened in Byatt's room last night? Where is he?'

'Nothing happened. We talked and he's gone home. I ran him to the station to catch an early train. It seemed best.'

'Is that all?'

'What did you expect? That he'd cut my throat? Don't be silly.'

Actually, exactly that thought had been bothering me all night. I had had an awful dream, just before daybreak, that Eglantine had been cut to ribbons just like the bedclothes. I woke up in a muck sweat, but I had no intention of confessing that to her. I felt such a prize idiot.

'Anyway,' she went on, 'you weren't so worried that you made any effort to check on how things were going. I could quite easily have been cut to ribbons for all you knew or cared. But I was in no danger. Archie's my friend. We talked about Patrick and . . . things and then he went home.'

'Good riddance! Best thing he could have done. I take it he won't be back?'

'I couldn't say. I hope not. There's nothing for him here now. But I had the feeling he has some unfinished business, I'm afraid. I don't think we've seen the last of Archie Byatt.'

Damn! Damn! Damn!

Patrick Snape's mother and two surviving brothers came down to Hampshire for the inquest. I had them met at the station and taken to the school house. It would be empty until we could find another master. In the meantime, they could stay there for a few days and pack up Snape's belongings.

I didn't meet his family until the inquest, which was held in the school where Snape had taught. There was no need for me to attend. I went out of respect and – yes, I might as well admit it – out of curiosity. As I expected, it was a very brief proceeding. There were just a few witnesses to be questioned.

Michael testified that the deceased had been disturbed

by his war experiences and was prone to sudden moods of violent and irrational activity.

Good grief, hasn't he ever heard of perjury? Anyone less prone to overexcitement than Patrick Snape, I have yet to meet. He was the sanest man one could imagine. Yet Michael stood there, with a concerned expression, the Bible still warm from his hand, and swore black was white. Why?

The motorist who was unlucky enough to find the body merely stated the place and circumstances. The policeman who attended the scene told us about the estimated speed of the motorcycle, the bend in the road and the weather conditions. The doctor stated the precise cause of death, in his opinion. The deceased had suffered multiple injuries as a result of the crash – he went on to list them and I could feel my ears buzzing and my head beginning to spin – but death had been caused by the severing of the spinal cord due to fracture of the neck.

And that was that. One life neatly wrapped up and labelled Accidental Death. Patrick Snape deserved better than that.

Afterwards I made myself known to Mrs Snape. She was a very respectable, dignified woman in black, although perhaps not *quite* what I had expected. I lifted my hat and murmured my condolences.

'. . . and if there's anything at all I can do,' I finished, 'please let me know.'

'We need nothing from you.' Her eyes were level with mine – her son's clear hazel eyes that saw straight through humbug – and it wasn't a pleasant experience. 'My son could have come home to the people who loved him when the war ended. His family, his home, his old job were all waiting for him. He didn't want us. We weren't good enough for him, once he became an officer. Instead, he chose to come here and now he's dead. You've done more than enough for me and mine, Mr Frampton.'

And on the arms of her two remaining strong sons, Mrs Snape turned her back on me and walked away. I ask you, was that fair?

I was passing through the village that evening when I saw the hearse leaving the school house on its way to the station. Behind it, upright and dry-eyed, rode the family in a hired trap. Behind that again, was a waggon carrying the trunk and the few tea chests that were Snape's earthly possessions. I stopped my car and got out, lifting my hat in respect as the coffin passed, along with any of the villagers who were passing. Most of the school children had gathered to see their teacher go. Some of the smallest were crying, wiping their noses on pinafores and sleeves. I had had no idea that Patrick Snape had made himself so well-liked in such a short time.

I felt I ought to speak to them. As Snape's employer, it was my duty. It was wrong to allow them to creep away with their burden, as though none of us knew or cared that there had ever been a man called Patrick Snape. But the memory of his mother's scorn kept me silent, rooted beside my motor, my hat in hand.

And then I remembered that, because she was still unwell, no one had told Hermione.

What could I do? What could I say? That night I went up to the nursery. I took Hermione on my knee. She was warm and soft and smelled well-scrubbed. I sat and chatted to her for a while and she looked at me with those wise little eyes. Wise, lost, unchildlike eyes. I couldn't find the words to tell her and just said good night and went away again.

'What can I possibly say?' I asked Clemmie.

'You don't have to,' she answered. 'I've already told

her that Patrick Snape found another job and moved away.'

'You told her what?' I gasped. 'That he just packed up and left her – without even saying goodbye? How do you think she must feel about that? She loved the man, in her own way.'

'You surely don't expect me to tell her the truth, do you? She's only a child, after all.'

Blow after blow, they all crowded in and all I remember are scenes like the magic lantern slides of my boyhood. The trouble is, they're all jumbled up. Clemmie, of course, says it's the whisky. But where would we be without a drink – eh – in times like this?

The only reason Michael had the courage to lie so blatantly at the inquest was that Eglantine had gone. If she'd still been with us, she'd have denounced his black lies to the heavens.

'Patrick Snape unpredictable?' I can just hear her. 'What utter rot! He was no more unpredictable than I am!'

Well, perhaps that wouldn't have been the most sensible thing to say, not coming from Eglantine, but you know what I mean. She'd have defended his character against all comers. She would never have countenanced the cynical manipulation of the truth that took place that day. But if it wasn't an accident, what was it? And do I really want to know the answer?

Eglantine had left us suddenly because of the awful business of Hector Malyon. A telegram had come for her on the morning after Snape's death. She'd been gone within half an hour, roaring up the drive in her frightful little Bugatti. It made you wonder whether women ought to be allowed on the road at all. They're such a prey to their emotions.

Two deaths on one night and they try to tell me there's no connection. Of course, I suppose lots of people died that night, somewhere – old, sick, in childbirth – and no one is trying to make a connection there. But two healthy men, in families connected however tenuously, don't die in violent circumstances on the same night without something fishy going on.

I wish I were a cleverer sort of chap.

The most almighty furore blew up after Hector Malyon's death. Who'd have thought it? The skeletons came positively clattering out of their cupboards all over the place. Of course, you can only believe so much of what the more lurid newspapers would have us believe. Even if only a half – a quarter of it – were true, then there had been some pretty murky goings on.

Of course, all the old scandal of Helen and Philip Malyon was dragged out, dusted down again and hung out for inspection. I strongly objected to seeing our family name appear in circumstances like that. I telephoned Max Aitken in person to complain about certain nuances that had appeared in the *Daily Express*. Highly moral twaddle! He was very sympathetic, of course, but I didn't notice much of an improvement in the tone.

Helen had dragged the name of Frampton into the gutter. It would be very hard to forgive her that.

There was to be an inquest into Malyon's death, of course. I toyed with the idea of going along. It might have thrown some light on the things that were puzzling me. On second thoughts, I decided not to go. Well, it wouldn't have been entirely in the best taste, would it?

Michael went, however. Of course. It was too much to hope that he might show a morsel of good taste these days. I had given him up completely.

It all came out and what a lot there was. Can you imagine Hector Malyon as a murderer? Michael told me that the gasp that ran around the dingy room when that was revealed showed that no one else could believe it either. Michael came to see me in the library on his return from Wiltshire and described the events of the day.

'It was an absolute sensation – yes, thanks, I will have a small one – the hacks were scribbling away so fast their pencils were smoking!'

I handed him a glass and settled myself on the opposite side of the fire. 'Murdered his commanding officer? And got away with it for all this time? I find that very hard to believe.'

'So did we all. It seemed like very bad fiction. Not at all in character. But once you know about it, there's an awful kind of logic about what happened next. He arranged an "accident" to remove his blackmailer and then committed suicide.'

'What's the point of committing suicide if you've got rid of the person who's threatening you?'

'I don't know,' Michael shrugged. 'He must have been thoroughly deranged. Guilt? To protect his family? Who knows what was going through his mind on that last night.'

I sat silent for a while and tried to arrange the facts as Michael had related them into some sort of order. Hector Malyon had – for whatever reason – been guilty of the murder of his superior officer when on active service on the Western Front. Patrick Snape had uncovered this and was blackmailing Malyon. So Malyon had arranged the motorcycle "accident", then gone home and blown his own head off.

As Michael said, there was an awful kind of logic about it all. It was in the best traditions of the more lurid crime novels. If you didn't know the men involved personally, it made some sort of horrid sense.

At best, even if he hadn't *actually* committed murder

in France, Malyon's parliamentary career could have been ruined by the mere suggestion. He would never be able to prove he *hadn't* done it and the uncertainty would have made the ultra-respectable new Labour Party drop him like a hot chestnut. At worst, he would be hanged for murder. One can see why, faced by a slimy cad of a blackmailer, he might choose to rid the world and himself of an unworthy wretch. Then what? Overcome by remorse, he blows his own brains out?

It all made sense in a way, unless you actually *knew* the men involved. Hector Malyon committing murder? Patrick Snape a blackmailer? Nothing would convince me of that.

'It's not possible,' I said at last. 'It just doesn't make sense.'

'Of course it does,' Michael urged. 'Nothing could be clearer.'

'Are you really trying to tell me that Patrick Snape is — was — a greasy blackmailer? I'm sorry, I just can't buy that, as the Americans say. Good God, the man's been in and out of my house for years. I've seen him nearly every day since he took up the post of tutor. He's been so good with Hermione.'

'I'm not suggesting he wasn't. Just that none of us can possibly understand everything about the man sitting next to us. You just never know.'

I looked across at my brother and realized the simple truth of what he had just said. 'And how was all this mud actually raked up?' I demanded. 'Where did it all come from?'

'From Archie Byatt, actually,' Michael said coolly.

Well. So it must be true, after all.

'Archie had heard gossip from soldier friends,' Michael went on. 'You know what men are like — worse gossips than women, once they get going. So he did a little detective work and uncovered some very unpleasant facts about the death of Colonel Vosper . . .'

'How could he at this late date? All the evidence must be – ' I shivered ' – long gone.'

'It wasn't exactly a secret crime. Half a battalion witnessed it, but it was in all their interests to keep quiet. But after so long, one or two began to feel more secure. It took only a little greasing of their tongues by Archie to find out what happened. And Malyon's behaviour once he was threatened with discovery proves it must be true.'

There was a flaw in that statement, but I couldn't quite put my finger on it.

'And was there no one at all,' I asked, 'to speak up on his behalf? I find that very sad.'

'His family, of course – they wouldn't hear of it – so distressing. His agent was quite forthright – said he'd been in the battalion throughout the war and there'd never been a breath of suspicion about Colonel Vosper's death. But when he was actually questioned about dates, it turned out that he'd been on leave at the time in question. So that put paid to his evidence. At the end, there was a bit of a scene . . . very distasteful . . . I don't want to go into the details . . . one understands that Malyon's wife was under severe strain, but still . . . no, thank you, I won't have another. And if you take my advice, neither will you.'

Amazing woman, Eglantine. I've always thought you could push her under and hold her down and she'd still come up smiling. But this business broke her – absolutely broke her. Of course, she's getting on – nothing like as young and spry as she pretends to be. Now I come to think about it, we're about the same age, she and I. Well, perhaps she's just a few years older. I hope I'm wearing better than that.

She turned up – unexpectedly as always – a day or two later and asked me to accompany her to Hector Malyon's funeral.

'Good God, no,' I exploded. 'I'm not as completely insensitive as people seem to think I am!'

'Please, Anthony, please. There's no one else. I hate to ask you to do this, but I've got to the end of my strength. I've been to Patrick's funeral and it was awful. I don't know how I can bear another one. I *have* to go – you do see that – and I'm afraid I'm going to make a nuisance of myself. I shall take the wrong road, or my car will break down, or I shall run over someone's pet Peke. And if anyone talks to me, I shall crumble into dust.'

'But what do you expect me to do about it?'

'Just be there, please. Make sure I arrive on time at the right place. Don't let me embarrass anyone by wearing the wrong clothes. Hold me up so that I won't fall over the church porch step.'

'I'm sure you won't do any of those things.'

'I might. You never know what I'll do next. Or – you never know – I might scream "murder".'

I looked at her raddled, broken face and realized with a thrill of horror that, while she probably wouldn't do any of the other things she had suggested, she was quite capable of carrying out her last threat.

'And it really wouldn't do any good, would it, to anyone who is left if I were to do that?' she went on. 'Nothing can be put back the way it was. I could lay this whole thing open, like a frog on a dissecting table, but that won't bring back Patrick or Hector.'

'You might,' I began, hesitating to meddle, yet fascinated by the power of dawning knowledge, 'at least make sure that when they are buried, the facts are not buried with them.'

'They're dead. What difference can it make to them?'

I thought about Mrs Snape's face as she had turned

away in contempt from me. Now that she had read in every newspaper that her son's death was not an accident after all, but the natural result of his own despicable dealings, what good would it do her to dredge up yet more filth? I thought about Malyon's little Belgian widow. Would she miss her husband less if she knew who had driven him to murder and his own death?

Snape was a blackmailer and Malyon was a murderer. Knowing that my brother had stirred the whole violent brew in order to take his own perverted revenge didn't make those facts any less true. Eglantine was right. Nothing we could do or say now would make the dead any less dead.

So I accompanied Eglantine to the Malyon funeral. I didn't attend, of course. I put my foot down over that. I'm not that insensitive. I drove her to the Malyons' house and then went on alone to the bleak little churchyard swept by the winds coming off the chalk downs. I parked my car outside the gate, then went to sit in a far corner out of the wind and out of sight.

Clemmie had been furious with me when she found out where I was going. She said it was morbid and creepy. Actually, it was the first time for ages she had even noticed me. I had been feeling a bit of a nuisance, like a smelly old dog one is too fond of to have put down, for much too long. It was rather fun to have her screaming at me and throwing her hairbrush across the room again. Just like the old days!

Still, I went. I dropped Eglantine off well in time for her to brush up before the cortege left the house. She was looking breakable, as though she might shatter at the slightest touch. Two funerals in one week and she had cared so much for them both. It was more than anyone ought to endure.

'Don't worry,' were Eglantine's last words to me. 'I shan't disgrace myself, or anyone else. But thank you for being here.'

From my vantage point, I saw the little cortege arrive. Just family. All the people who might have been expected to follow the coffin – the business acquaintances of his father, the old army friends, the representatives of the Labour Party – had all stayed away, as though the company of the dead man could taint them in some mysterious way. He was a murderer after all, even if an unconvicted one. *Not* the funeral one might wish to be seen at.

Yet the church was full. The people who came were not the ones who would have taken a front pew. They were the local people, the ones who had known him as a boy, the ones who voted for him, the ones who trusted him to speak out for them when they couldn't do it themselves. It made no difference to them what Malyon was accused of. They didn't believe it. They came to pay their last respects.

From my bench beneath the churchyard wall, I watched the little family group follow the coffin from the lychgate to the church porch. There was an icy sleet in the air. It piled a crinkly blanket of dead leaves over the snowdrops that sheltered among the roots of a beech tree. It got under the opaque black veils of the women and tugged them indecorously about. It whipped petals off the flowers that decorated the coffin and blew them across the churchyard almost to my feet. I huddled into the astrakhan collar of my coat and thought bad thoughts about Eglantine.

Price Malyon looked like an old, old man. There was no trace left of the bold and brash opportunist who had won a lady's heart and made a fortune out of people's appetites for tea and Dundee marmalade. He didn't look strong enough to be out on such a raw day. He could only shuffle up the path, yet still offered his arm in support to his son's widow.

Such a little thing, fragile and tossed by the wind. From where I sat, she didn't seem to look where she was going. If she once looked down at the uneven path, or over at the man on whose arm she rested, I didn't see her. She was looking at the coffin. She was watching her husband borne along in front of her by six strong men. Even at that distance, I could feel the dry eyed, burning intensity of her gaze. It was as though she was able to look right through the oak and lead that encased her love. Had she been the one to find him, I wondered, slumped with his shattered head on his desk? Or had they kept her from the sight, had they held her back at the door, so that she would only remember him as he had been, strong and alive and whole?

A little boy was holding her other hand. He was frightened and puzzled. He kept looking from his mother to his grandfather and then to the box that was carried in front of them. Cruel, that, I thought. They ought not to have brought him. What were they thinking of to allow it? Yet his father had just vanished out of his life. What could they tell him in explanation, if he wasn't allowed to follow his father to his last resting place? How else was he to know where he had gone?

They followed two and two behind. Two tall women, Lady Malyon and her daughter, I suppose, identically swathed and unrecognizable. Philip and Helen, her bright hair unmistakable even through the veil. I wondered what she was feeling, walking there within the family she had destroyed. Eglantine, dry and brittle as a dead twig, followed with a prim little man in glasses.

The rector met the cortege and they vanished into the church. I brought out my hip flask and took a little nip. Yes, I know it wasn't the time or place, but it was damned cold. And, to tell the truth, it wasn't just because of the cold that I had the shivers.

I could hear the organ and the sound of singing, but the wind had risen so much that I couldn't hear what the hymns were. It was a very short service. I wondered what the rector found to say about a man who had taken life – his own as well as someone else's. In fact, the more I thought about it, the more surprised I was that he'd agreed to hold a service at all. When I was young, a man like that would have been slipped into an unmarked grave in the farthest, dankest corner of the churchyard. In my father's day, he'd have been bundled into a suicide's grave at the crossroads.

They blamed it on the war, I suppose. That seems to be the way people get round any sort of abnormal behaviour these days. When someone acts in a totally unsociable way, we all nod wisely and say, 'Of course, he/she had a very bad war. It's not surprising that he/she goes off the rails now and again. One must be understanding.' But what would happen if we all seized on that excuse when we wanted to behave badly? I ask you!

They were all out again in no time. It just felt ages because it was so bloody cold. This time everyone followed the coffin to the grave. I was amazed how many people had come. Despite what had happened, Malyon must have been very well-liked. Whatever anyone else believed, here on Salisbury Plain they had faith in the man they had voted for. Hector Malyon was to be laid to rest in the heart of his constituency, within sight of the bare and inhospitable land he had represented for such a short time.

They all followed the rector across the churchyard to the freshly dug grave. The mound of earth, already grey with chalk, was dusted, just like my coat, with little hard pinheads of sleet. I lost sight of what was happening then. Too many people were in the way.

And then I saw him. Like me, he'd been standing against the wall and had been nearly invisible in the sleet and fading light. I watched him walk across to the cluster of people. Somehow, the crowd just seemed to dissolve in front of him. Some people are like that. They have this power to make other people notice them. It doesn't matter how small they are, how seemingly physically insignificant, they give off a sort of force, an energy field – just like a wireless transmitter is said to do. I don't understand how. Everyone can feel it. With a look, they can part a crowd.

That's what happened. He just walked very quietly towards the crowd of mourners and it opened up in front of him. From being able to see nothing, suddenly I was able to look down a clear avenue to the graveside itself.

Archie Byatt stood at the foot of the grave and looked down on his enemy.

It makes me shudder even now to think of it. Everyone was very still. I was holding my breath and I don't think I was the only one. If I said that I was conscious of an atmosphere of pure evil, you could safely accuse me of exaggeration and say I'd had more than the one nip from my flask. Maybe. Looking back, I can't recapture the horror that I felt at the time. But I know I felt it. It was very real at the time.

Byatt bent down and picked up a handful of earth. Slowly, he straightened and stretched out his arm. Then, grain by grain, he crumbled the frozen earth over the coffin. It was so still, I swear I could hear the patter of its fall. Probably not.

There was an awful finality about his action. He was drawing the line after the sum total of Hector Malyon's life had been calculated. And when he had finished, he looked down and smiled.

'That's for Patrick,' I heard him say.

Everyone stood quite still where they were. I couldn't have moved if you'd paid me for it. He turned and began the long walk back down the avenue of faces. He'd gone about six paces, when there was a terrible scream. The voice was not Eglantine's, as I had half expected and feared. It belonged to Malyon's widow.

'Murderer!' she screamed in a voice that raised the hairs all over my body. 'Murderer!' God, I hope I never hear a sound like that again.

There was a flurry amongst the mourners. They closed ranks and I lost sight of Archie Byatt.

Eglantine drove home. She said I'd had too many little nips to make me safe to drive. What nonsense. I always drive better when I've had one or two. And after all, I'd never wanted to be there in the first place. I'd only come because she was afraid she'd be too distressed to get home without assistance. I'd had a frightful afternoon and she blamed me for trying to make myself a bit more comfortable. She never thought how I felt, not once.

It had been an awful occasion, made even worse by its ending. Archie Byatt's insolent gesture had so enraged old Price Malyon that he'd collapsed – right into the grave. He'd been rushed home and, when Eglantine telephoned later in the evening to find out how he was, she was told that he'd suffered a serious stroke. It was touch and go whether he'd survive. Personally, I'd rather die than remain alive in that condition. I hope if it ever happens to me, Clemmie'll have the decency to put me down. Perhaps I ought to leave written instructions, somewhere safe . . .

Yet when I thought about it, the little Belgian widow's scream of 'Murderer' had been before her father-in-law had collapsed. The flurry around the grave-side had definitely been after she'd shouted. Was she implying that her husband had been hounded to such an extent that he'd taken his own life? How much did she know about the way my brother and Archie Byatt were involved in her husband's death?

If it came to it – how much did I know? How much do I want to know? Was it all simply a nasty little case of blackmail and suicide, or was Michael more deeply implicated? Still, I can't for the life of me see how.

Now that I'm older and not so keen on being out in wintry weather, I've taken to reading a bit. Nothing heavy, you know, but I do enjoy Mrs Agatha Christie's detective novels, especially that funny little Belgian Poirot – what a card! And I've been wondering, what would he make of it all?

I have all the facts right here in front of me. I just don't seem to be able to put them all in their proper places. And the reason is that – like a jigsaw that seems to be going well, but can't be finished – one piece doesn't fit. One piece has been forced into a slot that seems to be right, but isn't, so the whole shape of the puzzle is altered.

Patrick Snape a blackmailer? That's the piece that doesn't fit. Take it away and what do I have in front of me? What *was* he doing at Matley Bog that night? Where was he going? When I have worked that out, I'll have the answer to it all. I'm not at all sure that I really want it.

I tried to say as much to Clemmie when we were going to bed.

She peered into her dressing table mirror, made a smiling grimace, eee-ooo, eee-ooo, eee-ooo, over and over again and patted the underside of her chin for a full half minute.

'Don't try to be clever, Ant,' she said, running a smoothing finger along the frown lines between her plucked brows, 'it doesn't suit you.' Then she turned round. 'Oh God, just look at you. Why can't you undress in your dressing room, like any normal man? What do you think it does to me, having to look at you in your socks and shirt tails? You're about as exciting as a boiled potato!'

So I slunk off and finished changing in my room. I thought about that poor little widow, only a girl, alone in her bed. What must she be feeling, when she puts out her hand and touches the icy sheets where the warm bulk of her husband ought to be? When she cries in the dark, no one will hear her.

My eyes felt hot and prickly when I thought about her. And they weren't just maudlin, whisky tears. How awful to be alone. How awful to have no one to put his arms around her and love her.

When I got back, Clemmie was in bed. I slipped in beside her and cuddled up close against her back. She was warm and alive. The curve of her body against mine was so familiar. Through the slippery stuff of her nightgown her breasts were wonderful, softer now, more like marshmallows than the firm fruits they had once been, but I wanted them so badly. I could feel the blood rushing downwards, surging, filling me, engorging my cock.

Clemmie took my hand and slapped it smartly back.

'*Nobody* sleeps in a double bed these days,' she stated. 'It's about time we got rid of this monstrosity and bought some nice, new twin beds.'

'You don't really mean that, darling, do you?' I nuzzled at the back of her neck.

'I most certainly do.'

Thoughtless of me. With everything that had happened, she had far too much on her mind for me to expect her to put up with my fumblings. I am a selfish beast, sometimes.

HELEN

The Wife

I am a destroyer. Everything I have touched has crumbled into dust. My hands leave dirty fingerprints, soiling, despoiling, wherever I go. I have destroyed my husband. I have ruined my lover and his family. I have sacrificed my child.

All I ever wanted was someone to be kind to me.

I sit in this chair and listen to the stertorous breathing of Price Malyon. His breath is rasping in and out, so slowly that my own breathing almost stops in anticipation as I wait for him to draw the next. Perhaps it would be better if there were no next breath. Perhaps it would be better if he just slipped away, quietly, now, before he wastes into a dribbling, helpless hulk. He would hate that.

I could help him on his way. Nurse is in the housekeeper's room, having her tea. Harriet is in the studio – she can still distract her mind by working, producing savage ugly images that mirror her thoughts. I don't know where the others are. It doesn't matter, as long as they don't come in here. I could just put a pillow over his face – very gently – and those painful breaths would stop.

Price was good to me. In return, I could be good to him. That would be the only kindness I have ever done this family. I want to do something for them, before I go. I slide a pillow from beneath his head. It is pulpy in

415

my fingers, warm from his body, smelling sour beneath the starch and carbolic.

I haven't the courage.

Philip was kind to me. His kindness was like manna to the Israelites. It fell on my starving soul and fed me. He was rain in my desert. All the dried up springs of my body were filled by him.

It's hard to credit how empty I was before I met him. No one was actually unkind to me, of course not. Yet I might even have preferred that. It would have been something positive to fight against, something real. I could have kicked and yelled, fought back. I couldn't fight indifference.

I'm older now. Now I could cope. I'd find my own way out. But I was *seventeen* when I married Michael Frampton. Before I was eighteen, I knew what a terrible mistake I'd made.

If I had been older . . . If my mother hadn't died . . . If Aunt Eglantine hadn't seen Michael as a knight on a white horse . . . If there had been no war . . . If Father had left any money at all . . . If Michael's ardent court-ship had left me a moment to look around and see that there was more in the world than marriage . . . If he had just let me draw a breath . . . If I had been plain and stodgy . . . If anyone had warned me what I was doing . . . If I had been older . . .

Hector would be alive.

Adrienne would not be a widow.

Papa Price would not be lying here while I sit with a pillow in my hand and wonder if I have the nerve to use it.

Some men shouldn't marry. This is no criticism of them. I suppose the same must apply to some women, too. I just don't know any. Some people, then, are not suited to marriage. They don't have the ability to give, to . . . to *share* themselves. They are private people, with private minds and bodies. There is nothing wrong with that. They are probably very good people. But they shouldn't marry.

Michael was one of those. He was a good man. He was upright and moral. He would never stoop to deceit. He respected women. He honoured God and the King. I never had to worry that he might be seeing other women, or drinking too much, or gambling away his last penny. He was a pattern of good behaviour. In the eyes of the world, he was a model husband.

Yet because he married me, he was driven to violence, to rape, to subterfuge, to conniving and corruption – whether he wanted to or not. He could no more avoid it than the leaves can choose to hang on the trees all winter. He should never have married. Some people shouldn't.

Or was it because he married *me*? With some gentle, loving, tolerant wife, might he have been happy enough? With some passionless, temperate woman, might his marriage have worked – in its own way? There must be plenty of marriages like that. They seem to work well, after a fashion.

I am not passionless. I am not temperate.
I am a destroyer.

I was seventeen and no one had ever spoken a kind word to me. Clementine gossiped and chattered, bustled about her wounded officers, organized, arranged and rearranged. I was of no more interest to her than the floor she walked on.

I would see her sometimes, coaxing Anthony upstairs. She would stand on the lowest step and hold out her hand. She was temptation. Her smile promised him anything he wanted – anything at all. And he – dear, sweet, blundering Ant – would drop whatever he was doing. His red face redder with anticipation, he would take her hand and follow.

I tried to shut out the images. I would go and take a walk along the river, or play a game of table tennis with one of the more able convalescents, or read or write a letter for one of those who could not. And all the time the images came crowding – of limbs entwined, of skin glistening, the muted cries, the scent and sounds of love. I would grit my teeth and shut my mind, but my thighs would grow heavy and I could not stem the rich ooze of moisture.

I envied them. From the time we came back to Buckholt after our few days in Penzance, Michael never touched me. Not once.

I had known what to expect. Aunt Eglantine had made sure of that. My mother was too ill to do more than get through the next day in the last few weeks before my marriage, so Eglantine took her place. She invited me for tea one afternoon, but, when I arrived, instead of having it served in the drawing room as usual, she had a tray carried up to her bedroom, so I knew something was going on.

'Right – it's time you knew what's what, so let's not beat about the bush. There's absolutely nothing to worry about,' she said briskly. 'There's far too much nonsense talked about a perfectly natural act. Now, you might find this hard to believe at the moment, but you'll probably enjoy every moment of it. I do.'

She went on to describe the physical facts in astounding detail. Then from a drawer she produced a remarkable array of sponges and syringes and told me plainly what had to be done with them, should I wish to avoid conception, which, of course, I didn't. A man of Michael's age would want a family as soon as possible. My mother had managed to tell me that much.

I couldn't believe what I was hearing! Aunt Eglantine laughed, a rich, throaty, cigarette ash laugh.

'If you could see your face, it's an absolute picture . . . Don't worry, that's just the mechanics. Nothing to it. Now, what I'm going to tell you next is much more important, so listen carefully. Women are just as capable of enjoying the act of union as men are. So pay no attention at all to those fade-away types who tell you they just lie down and put up with it. If they do, it's their own fault. There are men who are insensitive, of course, or ignorant about what their wives need, but it's up to the women to put them right. No false modesty. If you don't like what's happening, or you'd prefer something else, then say so.'

'I don't think I know enough about it to express any preferences.'

'Instinct, darling. You're doing what comes naturally. Whatever feels right – is right.'

'Oh.'

'You're lucky in one way. You're marrying a mature man. Michael must have had plenty of practice, so he won't rush at you like a runaway train! Young men get so excited. Believe me, it's very irritating, being left high and dry because one's man has . . . shot his bolt, as they say, too early. No wonder some women suffer from nerves – it's sheer frustration! At his age, Michael will have developed technique, finesse, stamina. Lucky you! He'll know how to give you pleasure and in doing so, of course, he knows he will increase his own. Simple. Share and share alike.'

She looked at me as though she expected some sort of response. 'Is that . . . is that *all*?' I asked.

'Good heavens, no. That's the joy of it – you never do know all there is to know. I'm still learning! Now, what else? Yes. You may be rather alarmed by the sight of the extended male organ. Don't be. Whatever it looks like, you'll be able to accommodate it quite comfortably, in time, if not at first. They're all different. The variety is endless. Size is neither here nor there. My dear old Harold is not what one might call an impressive specimen . . .'

I didn't feel I needed to know this.

'. . . but we've had enormous fun together for years. It's all a matter of adjustment, you see. You do see, don't you?'

'I suppose so.'

'Well, if you remember nothing else, remember this. It's fun. Enjoy it. When Michael approaches you for the first time, don't shrink under the bedclothes. Open yourself to him. Make him welcome. The quicker you do that, the better for both of you. Goodness, my darling, you're setting out on an adventure, the greatest adventure there is.'

I already had an inkling of what she was talking about. Michael's kisses had aroused strange, shameful, delicious sensations. The way he moulded my body against his, the way his arms mastered me and supported me at the same time, the warm, secret places of his mouth against mine, sweet and sour . . . And when he let me go, I always felt as though a treat had been snatched away from my greedy hands. I felt as though I were on the brink of a discovery. There was something wonderful, just out of reach, something I wanted and very soon, very soon now, I should find out what it was.

On our first night together, I remembered what Aunt Eglantine had said and was prepared to be startled but not disgusted by the naked male form. I never saw him. He slid out of his robe and between the sheets with all the sleight of hand of a conjurer.

He felt nice, though. I didn't think I was going to be disgusted. He felt firm and warm, rough with hair in places, but satin smooth in others. He was broad and square, with hard, flat planes where I had curves. Very pleasant to touch. Very pleasant to hold.

You didn't prepare me, Aunt Eglantine. You weren't honest with me.

I wasn't ready for a man who scrabbled and butted against the small resistance my body put up against him. I wasn't ready for a man whose weight pressed me into the mattress so fiercely I couldn't breathe. I didn't know he would hurt me.

'Stop it, stop it,' I gasped into the pillow that was stifling me, 'you're hurting me.'

The object, the *thing* that was tearing at me just wilted away. I wasn't prepared for a man who wept on my breast, then got up and spent the rest of the night in an armchair.

Aunt Eglantine said, 'Whatever feels right – *is* right.' This didn't feel right.

Perhaps it was my fault, I thought as I lay alone in the wide bed. I must have done something wrong. I must have misunderstood what I had been told and my ignorance had caused this fiasco. I had been nervous and too quick to complain. Never mind. Whatever it was, we could put it right together.

Aunt Eglantine said, 'If you don't like what's happening, or you'd prefer something else, then say so.' So I did.

Breakfast was served in our room. I waited until Michael had finished his second cup of coffee, then I said, 'Michael, you're very heavy. Do you think next time you could alter your position just a little, then I wouldn't be so squashed and it might be easier for you to . . .'

At the look of shock on his face, my voice faded

421

away. He looked as though he had lifted the cover off his breakfast plate and found some loathsome reptile. What had I said? It was only a suggestion. I only wanted to co-operate.

Technically speaking, the next night was an improvement. At least, penetration was achieved. I felt myself tear, as I had been warned I would, and then I felt Michael go rigid as the hot flood pulsed through him. He gave a terrible cry and rolled off me.

That must have been the night Hermione was conceived, because my husband never touched me again. At least, not for many years and I have tried to blot that event right out of my mind. I *choose* not to think about it, ever.

Now that I'm older, I know that sexual compatibility is like a lucky dip at a village fête. You rummage around in the bran tub and if you're very lucky, you get what you always wanted, first dip. Some children use all their pocket money dipping again and again and are never satisfied with what they get. Some – most – are disappointed but make the best of it anyway. They are the ones who never, never admit to their friends that they could have done better.

But I was seventeen. Only a few months earlier, I had been a pigtailed schoolgirl. What did I know? I thought it was the end of the world.

If someone had just been kind to me, I could have borne it.

Not that Michael wasn't polite. He was scrupulously so. He never abused me, or blamed me for the travesty of our married life and – I'm positive about this – he never sought consolation elsewhere. In his own way, I think he must have loved me. His way was not my way. And after two years, he left me. To volunteer for the Front, even as a noncombatant, was a grand patri-

otic gesture from a man of his age. He deserves credit
for that.

On the night before Michael went away, I lay awake
until the house was silent, then I slipped into his dressing room, where he always slept in a narrow little bed.
He was quiet and still, but I could tell by the quality of
the silence that he was awake too. The room was quite
dark. I felt my way across to him.

'Michael? Are you awake?'

'Yes.'

'Can I talk to you?'

'Yes.'

I sat down on the edge of the bed. The darkness, the
smallness of the room, the need to whisper, gave our
conversation an intimacy we hadn't shared for a long
time.

'Must you go tomorrow?'

'I rather think I must.'

'Why?'

'Well – you know – one must do one's bit.'

'You're not going because . . . well, just because of
us?'

'Not just because of that, I promise you.'

'I shall miss you.'

He put out his hand and groped for mine.

'You're trembling,' he said.

'I'm cold,' I lied.

'Come closer. Let me warm you.'

I lay down. Michael flipped the eiderdown over me
and put his arms around me. He hadn't done that for so
long. Perhaps the sense of next day's parting softened
him. We lay for a long time, quietly, thinking of how
things could have been between us, if only we'd got off
to a better start. I seemed to have put myself in the
wrong, right from the beginning, with the best of intentions, but you know what they say about intentions.

And the longer we were estranged, the more impossible it became to put right.

But did that really have to be true? Or was I just making excuses for the fact that we were both too stubborn and proud to take the first step towards reconciliation? Perhaps now was the moment. Perhaps now, in the silence and darkness, we could begin the process of healing. I knew I didn't have the right words, but sometimes words just get in the way.

I put out my hand and stroked his hair, tousled from his restless night, back from his forehead. He didn't repulse me. Braver, I let my fingers trail softly down his cheek. The arm that encircled my shoulders stiffened. Although the blankets separated us, I could feel the tremor that ran through his body. Then I put my lips against his and let them stay there, undemanding.

I nearly won. So nearly. I felt Michael's mouth soften beneath mine and begin an involuntary response. Then he went rigid and jerked back as though I soiled him. He pushed me away from him and turned his back.

I crept from the room. I heard Michael give a long, shuddering sigh.

The next day, my husband went to war. I didn't see him for two years.

I was left with Clemmie who distrusted and despised me, with Anthony who was too lazy to offer any comfort, with Charley, damaged almost beyond repair by his experiences and too drunk to realize that the cure was in his own hands, with Viola, pouring out her fears and grief into the only open ear she could find.

Self-pity is a very destructive emotion. Looking back, one sees so clearly how wrapped up in ourselves we all were, each one of us. Clemmie bitterly resented the fact that the war was claiming the last of her youth and caught at each day as it flew by. Anthony was more worried about preserving his shooting and fishing than the fact that his family was falling to pieces in front of him. Charley, drinking at first to dull his physical pain, carried on because there wasn't anything better to do. Viola always thought that black suited her better than any other colour.

There I go again. Bitter and self-absorbed.

I was busy playing the role of deserted wife and young mother for all I was worth. Michael had gone, but that pitiful encounter in Penzance had left me with something so precious, so very precious. But upper-class women don't rear their own babies. It's just not done. They hand them over to nannies who draw up rigid timetables and shoo 'Mummy' out of the nursery and complain about interference with their methods.

I remember taking Hermione out in the twilight to look at the bats. It was a warm, sticky night and the air was thick with insects down by the river. I stood quite still, with Hermione in my arms, as the bats swooped low, scooping up their supper. We could hear the flitter-flitter of their leathery little wings. Hermione stretched out her short, pudgy arms. I shall never forget the expression of enchantment on her face. Then one bat swooped nearer than the rest. Hermione flung her arms around me in a sticky embrace and giggled into my neck. She was firm and chunky and altogether delicious. I felt a surge of gratitude to Michael for giving me someone so wonderful before he left.

When I got back, of course, Nanny was on the war-path. Clemmie had promised to 'speak' to me and she did so, quite firmly, saying that I had no business wandering around in the dark with my own daughter and that it mustn't happen again.

'Nanny knows best,' she told me, 'and quite frankly, we're so lucky to have her – what with a war on and everything – we daren't upset her. Where would we be if she handed in her notice because you insist on meddling so much? It'd be easier to manage without you, darling,' she finished, with a little, tinkling laugh that was meant to show me that she was only joking, of course, 'than do without Nanny!'

Michael came back a sick man. By then, Hermione had been whisked kindly and efficiently out of the reach of her nuisance of a mother.

I fell like a ripe peach into the hands of the first man to shake the tree.

I'm not making excuses. What I did was wrong and no amount of justification can change that. Philip was kind to me and I mistook my gratitude for love. How was I to know? I'd never met the real thing.

Philip does love me. I know that. He didn't mean to. He just meant to have a fling with a pretty girl. Love crept up on him when he wasn't looking. That doesn't mean it isn't genuine.

I don't love him. I like him. I enjoy his body. I'll always be grateful to him. But I don't love him. He deserves better than that.

Papa Price's breathing is slower now. Each inflation of his chest is a rattle of effort that scarcely stirs the bedclothes. The dropped side of his poor face is dark red and his lips have a plummy tinge. He might manage better if he were propped a little higher, but I am holding his extra pillow and trying to screw up the courage to do him the last kindness I will ever do.

The Malyons were so good to me. They took in their young son's mistress and never said a word of reproach in my hearing. They accepted me and never made me feel that my presence was an embarrassment they could well have done without. As, of course, it was.

Philip and I could have conducted a messy little affair. Lots of people do, I'm told. It takes a lot of ingenuity and a good memory. They suddenly acquire aunts who need nursing on their death beds. 'But I'll only be away for a couple of nights, darling, surely you can do without me for a little while . . .' Or there are urgent business meetings that go on too late for it to be worth coming home. 'You do understand, don't you, sweetie? I'm sorry to miss your birthday. I'll make it up to you. Promise . . .' Or worst of all, there are understanding husbands and wives who never kick up a fuss because they are up to the same game. They know the form. Never rock the boat. 'Don't you worry about a thing. I'll be much too busy to pine and the time'll simply fly by. Miss you . . . kiss, kiss . . .'

We were not furtive. Those stolen afternoons in seedy little hotels were not for Philip and me. We never drove for hours, an eye always on the clock, along country lanes searching for an accommodating inn. No giggles and twanging bed springs. No half-dressed grappling on the back seat of a motor with rain drumming on the hood. No Friday to Monday house parties with conveniently adjoining rooms. There was never the urgency of passing time, the *panic*, souring our coupling. Never the unacknowledged fear that the knock on the door might not simply be the chambermaid.

We were in love – or so I thought. So we chose to be together. The clean thing, the honourable thing, was to make a break with the past and start a new life together. We flouted convention. We stood hand in hand in the bright, clear air. We didn't care. We didn't give a damn about what the world thought, as long as we could be together.

What we didn't realize was that in defying conventional morality we put ourselves beyond the pale. The world would never forgive us. As Philip once said, in an uncharacteristically penetrating moment, 'It's not what you do, it's how you do it that matters.'

Our adultery wasn't wrong – not as the world viewed it – but the fact that we were living together could not be tolerated. We could fornicate ourselves silly, as long as it was done behind the facade of marriage. Once I left my husband, I put myself in an untenable position. A woman without protection. Easy game. Any man's meat. Once Philip tired of me, I would slide down and down . . .

But he didn't tire of me. The poor, dear fool fell in love with me instead. And all I could do was make him miserable, because by then I didn't know what I wanted.

Yes, we had lots of friends. There were simply masses of people who came to our parties and drank our drinks. Such fun. Papa Price – Sir Price – was known to be generous to his younger son and no one ever turned down any of our invitations. And all the time they were waiting to see us fall.

We fell. Oh, how far we fell.

I made a bargain with Hector: Hermione for Philip. Simple. He would give me back my daughter and in return I would relinquish my hold on his brother. Hector saw it as a hold, I'm sure of that. He always acted as though he thought I'd cast some sort of spell on Philip, as though I were a malevolent fairy holding him against his will. If the spell could be broken, I could imagine Hector reasoning, then his brother would be free. That sounds simplistic, I know, but Hector was that sort of man. Chivalrous men with a strong moral streak often are. Things were black or they were white; they were good or they were bad. No in-betweens. And I knew that he put me very firmly in the bad category.

So I gave him a chance to act as the hero of the fairy tale. I set him an impossible task, as the bad fairies often do. Emptying a lake with a sieve was nothing to what I asked Hector to do. I knew that he would fulfil the task, because that's the way these tales always go. Against all odds, conquering ogres and wizards, he would return my daughter to me. We would both get what we wanted and the spell would be broken.

Folk tales are full of bargains that go wrong and of people who get what they ask for, only to find out too late that it isn't at all what they expected, after all.

I didn't question Hector about the details. I left him to get on with it. When he told me to be in the waiting room of the Channel ferry packet on a particular day, at a particular time, I did as I was told.

Hector kept his side of the bargain. He delivered Hermione.

We waited and waited. Hector's face grew steadily greyer with tension as the hours went by. I thought that if David Gledhill didn't stop drumming on the window sill with his poor, burned fingers, I should scream.

She wasn't coming. The plot, whatever it was, had failed. I should never see my daughter again. Did that matter so much? What was she to me after so long? Hadn't I deserted her and lived happily all these years without giving her so much as a passing thought?

Oh, no.

Hermione had been three and a half years old when I left her. Now she was nearly eight and I wanted to see her with a ferocity that frightened me. If anyone – anyone at all – should stand in my way now, I felt ready to tear them to pieces.

And then she was there. My daughter. Just when we had given up hope. My daughter.

I half started up from my seat and I had to beat down the longing to run across the room, to wrap my arms around her and nuzzle into her neck, to swing her off the ground and hold her close, close, close.

Of course, I didn't. That would have frightened her to death and, above all, would have torn away the cover of secrecy that Hector had insisted must be maintained, no matter how difficult. If I wanted to be able to keep Hermione, Hector warned, I must do nothing to draw attention to us.

So I sat with my fists clenched so hard that the nails cut into my palms. Aunt Eglantine and Hector were muttering together in a corner. They looked so like conspirators that I almost laughed – so much for Hector's pretence at normality. And, from the protection of the pulled down brim of my hat, I watched my daughter.

Such a solemn little thing, so silent and withdrawn. She stood alone in the centre of the waiting room. Her red coat and gaiters were a blaze of colour in that dreary place. She was looking around with wide, grey eyes. Dear God, she was so like her father. I remember Michael had just that way of standing, considering, assessing his surroundings, not willing to make a move in case it should be the wrong one.

That wasn't normal in a child. Why didn't she climb on the benches and look out the windows at the bustle of the docks? Why wasn't she pointing, asking questions? Why didn't she interrupt her aunt and ask what they were doing in this strange place? Why didn't she *do* something?

This is what I have done to her. I have turned my bright happy child into this hesitant, unchildlike little person. Because of my selfishness, she has been stunted. Like a shoot sprouting in the dark, she has grown twisted and unnatural. She has been shut into her own silence and can't find the way out. I'm suddenly afraid that it's too late to undo what has been done.

But I *will* make it up to her. I *will*.

If she were older, I could explain. She'd understand. I know she would. I could tell her that I had believed it was for her own good to stay with her father. I could have taken her with me, but to what? God knows I longed to take her, but her father would have moved heaven and earth to get her back. And he'd have won. No court in the land would have awarded custody to an erring wife. Hermione would have been torn between us, like a carcase between jackals, and the result would still have been the same. She'd have been returned to Buckholt, by force of law if necessary, in the end. Better, surely, to leave her there, where she had been born, where she was secure and stable. I only left her because I loved her too much to take her.

I could have told her all that, if she were only a few years older. But what would a not-quite-eight-year-old make of it?

Hector and Eglantine had finished their furtive conference. When he and Gledhill left, Aunt Eglantine came over to talk to me. I listened, but I was watching Hermione. She never took her eyes off her aunt. Like a small dog, she watched and waited for the signal that meant they were going off again together.

'Darling, this is your last chance,' Aunt Eglantine said. 'Please, please think again. I know you're making a terrible mistake. I could just slip off back to Buckholt with Hermione and no one need ever know.'

'No,' I hissed. 'No. This time I'm not giving her up. Hector has made a bargain with me. He's got to keep his side of it.'

'A bargain?'

'Never mind. It's between him and me. I'm not leaving without Hermione.'

'I never thought you could ever be so selfish. Helen –

431

think. Have you even considered *her* at all . . . how will she ever understand what's happening . . . ?'

'She will. She will.' My voice was rising and Eglantine put a restraining hand on my arm. 'I'll make it up to her. I swear. It's going to be all right.'

Hermione was too far away to hear what we were saying, and her poor ears were stoppered with cotton wool, but she must have been able to sense the tension. She was looking at us, from one to the other, now more frightened than puzzled.

'Then let me try to explain it to her,' begged Eglantine. 'I can't just walk away and leave her. I can't just disappear. Let me take her for a little walk and try to make some sense of all this for her.'

'You'll come back . . . ?'

'Of course I'll come back. What do you think I am – a kidnapper? Hermione darling, shall we go for a little walk and look at all the ships?'

She held out her hand and Hermione took it with the first smile I had seen on her face. She wore mittens with red and blue stripes that matched her tam-o'-shanter. Her hand curled in Eglantine's with such trust.

Of course, they came back. Eglantine wouldn't do that to me. They came back after a quarter of an hour that felt as though it had lasted for ever. Eglantine's mascara had smudged beneath her eyes and the tip of her nose was red. I told myself it must have been very cold walking along the waterside, but even I couldn't really believe that that was all.

Still hand in hand, they walked up to me. Then Eglantine passed over my daughter's hand to my care. It lay so small and still in mine.

'She understands now,' said Eglantine. 'She's a good sensible girl.' She crouched down and kissed Hermione's little puckered mouth. 'And when you've settled in your new house with Mummy, I'll come and have a holiday with you. We'll have such fun, the three of us, you'll see.'

She kissed her again, a short, snapping kiss, then stood up and walked briskly out of the room, without looking back. I listened to the sound of her feet clipping down the steps.

Hermione screamed.

'Aunt Egg!' she screamed.

And that was the end. I had failed.

Aunt Eglantine hurtled back into the waiting room, her coal-scuttle hat awry. 'She spoke,' she sobbed, 'she spoke!'

And she swept Hermione up in a huge hug that left me standing alone on the rim of the abyss. The little girl wrapped her arms and legs around and clung like a burr.

I just walked away. There wasn't anything else to do.

I went back to Knapp Hill because I couldn't think of anywhere else to go. Because I wasn't supposed to be making the return journey, I had to catch the train out of Southampton, then change at Salisbury.

I had made a bargain with Hector: Hermione for Philip. Hector had kept his side of the bargain. He gave my daughter back to me. It wasn't his fault I couldn't keep her.

I stood on the platform and thought about keeping my side of the bargain. Nerves had prevented me from eating since early the day before and I knew I was light-headed, but my thoughts seemed to have a perfect clarity, as though all the dross had been burned away in the last few hours, leaving my mind clean and pure.

I had promised to leave Philip for good if only I could have Hermione. I had been given her. Now I was bound to keep that promise.

The train pulled slowly into the station. The great wheels ground along the rails, almost hidden in shifting curls of steam. Passengers were already thrusting open doors to get down. There were porters pushing laden barrows, people shouting, a whistle was blown on the adjoining platform. There was a basket of burbling pigeons. A woman was hauled up the platform by three yapping wire-haired terriers. They all seemed strangely distant. I was removed from it all. No one was looking at me. No one would even notice.

I had made a bargain.

The train had almost reached me now. Its wheels ground slower still, but heavy, so heavy. A final hiss of steam and I was lost in a camouflaging cloud. It was wet, heavy, touchable. I could feel myself swaying, disorientated by the sudden loss of vision.

'Hold on, madam, hold on!' The hands that grabbed me by both shoulders were rough and urgent. 'It's all right. I've got you. It's all right.'

I was hauled back, back, from the brink.

'Come over all faint, did you? You didn't ought to stand so near the edge. It's dangerous.'

I looked up into the worn, worried face of the man who had either forced me to break my promise to Hector or had saved me from an appalling accident. Had I just suffered momentary giddiness? I still don't know the answer.

'Silly of me . . . I'm so sorry . . .'

'Supposing someone opened a door and hit you? It wouldn't be the first time.'

'I'm so sorry . . . I didn't think . . .'

'Here, you ought to sit down and have a cup of tea. You've had a nasty shock. Come into the tea room – or shall I fetch you one out here?'

'No, no, I must catch this train. So sorry to be a nuisance . . . you've been most kind . . .'

Before the journey was over, the lights were lit in the carriage. Reflected in the grimy window pane, I still saw Hermione clinging fiercely to the only person who had loved her enough to stay with her, the one stable point in her shifting world.

Late as it was when I got back, I seemed to have arrived before Hector. He would be astonished to see me back at Knapp Hill again. He'd probably be angry. Quite rightly so. I'd broken my promise, when he'd gone to such lengths to keep his side of it. It wasn't going to be easy to explain.

I couldn't be bothered to dress for dinner, so I said I had a headache and asked for a tray to be sent up to my room. Before he went downstairs, Philip pestered me about where I'd been. When he came back up after dinner, he started again. I made up a pointless shopping trip, but of course he didn't believe me. Poor thing, did he really imagine I might have been unfaithful to him? Didn't he know that the game wasn't worth the candle?

One day I might tell him, but not now . . . not now . . .

By the following morning, such terrible things had happened that I knew I could never tell him.

Philip and I had stayed awake late, discussing the implications of Michael's threat to sue for restoration of conjugal rights. Philip was scared to death of the law. We lay on our backs and stared at the ceiling. Philip's hand cupped my left breast, but his desire was only a desire for comfort.

It was obvious that this was going to be the messiest case for years and we just couldn't see a way to get out of it. Yes, we could just have slipped away to the Côte d'Azur or Tuscany and faded into decent obscurity, but, as I once tried to explain to Hector – I couldn't do that to Philip. It would be too selfish. I couldn't ask him to give up so much for me, even though he swore he was ready to.

Other than that, we couldn't think of anything we could do but face the music together. As it is, it seems we shall be spared that indignity.

So it was late before we put the light out. Philip, of course, fell asleep at once – his method of solving problems involves a great deal of whisky to 'clear his brain'. I couldn't sleep. Over and over, I could hear the terrible shriek, 'Aunt Egg!'

Every time I shut my eyes, I was jolted awake by the terror in my daughter's voice. It had been rusty with disuse, harsh as a peacock's cry, a desolate, far away sound.

What had I done to her?

I was still lying awake in the dark when I heard someone knocking at another door. Cassandra was whispering urgently to Adrienne when I looked out into the corridor.

'Quick, quick,' I heard her urge, 'we're still not too late.'

She and Adrienne ran off towards the stairs. They were only halfway down the top flight when we all heard the bang. I knew what it sounded like. But it couldn't be that, could it? Surely?

I shook Philip awake and ran out and downstairs. Cassandra and Adrienne were well ahead of me. As I ran, a terrible dread surged through me.

There was a light shining under the study door. Cassandra stood in front of it. She was grasping Adrienne by the wrists, holding her back.

'Don't, don't,' she pleaded.

Adrienne was beating her little balled fists against the taller woman and with each blow she gave a gasping grunt. I ran faster. Whatever we had to do to her to prevent it, Adrienne must not be allowed through that door. But I was too late. She lashed out again at Cassandra, fierce as a she-wolf, caught hold of her hair and yanked. Cassandra stumbled forward, tripped on the edge of the rug and Adrienne was through.

Oh merciful God, let me forget it.

There was blood. So much blood. On the wall that backed the desk. On the books and bookshelves, the pictures that decorated the wall, the lamp that lighted them. Not the clean, red sort of blood that we all see when we cut a finger. Dark. Clotted. Clinging. Mixed with spongy tatters of tissue and sharp shards of bone and strands of Hector's thick, black hair. That – and the smell.

And Adrienne. No tears. No screams. Just a desperate whimpering, a thin thread of sound made by an animal that will soon bite off the paw that traps it in the snare. With little, frantic hands, she tugged her husband up from the desk where he had fallen. Although he was heavy and she was small, she folded his body in her arms and laid his poor, shattered head on her breast. There was no top to his head and it lolled forward on a neck like a snapped stalk. Adrienne shifted herself carefully, pinioned under her burden, until he lay comfortably against her, his dangling weight supported by her body. The whimpering stopped. The only sound was of Philip retching out in the hall.

She bent her head and kissed her husband and when she lifted her face again, her lips were all dabbled with blood.

Nurse has finished her tea. She has bustled back into the sick room, all starch and hairpins. She has found me sitting with her patient, a pillow in my hands. She looks across at the bed and gives an exclamation of irritation. Only now am I conscious that the room is quite silent. There is no painful rasping coming from the bed. Papa Price is still.

She snatches the pillow from my hands and tucks it

437

back where it belongs. I didn't have to use it. I need not have agonized over the decision.

'I thought he looked uncomfortable,' I explain. 'I was going to adjust the pillows.'

'That sort of thing is much better left to those who know what they're doing. Surely you knew that he could breathe more easily propped up?'

She is not angry, just annoyed that her patient has slipped out of her grasp when her back was turned. He was going to go, anyway. She was going to lose this one, no doubt about that. But it's so untidy to go when she's not even in the room. How unsatisfactory. Having a cup of tea? How's she going to explain that one away?

This is what I have done to the family that was kind to me. This is how I have rewarded them. But there is still one, final kindness I can do for them in return. I shall not dishonour my bargain with Hector. Simply to go away is not enough. That's too easy. I must make a gesture that will cut me adrift from Philip, and he from me, for ever. I must pay the full price, without stinting, for what I have done to the Malyons and I must not grudge the payment.

In the morning, I shall go back to my husband.

The simplest way, the kindest way, would have been just to slip away, without explanation, without tearful goodbyes. Philip might have been hit hard by the abruptness of it all, but in the end, he would suffer less. In the end, he would get over it. Philip is like that.

There wasn't much packing to do. I didn't want to take any mementoes of my time with Philip. Better that way. I would take his motor though, just as far as the station and leave a message with the station master to let the family know where it could be picked up. By evening, I would be back at Buckholt and my penance would have begun.

I was standing in the bedroom, looking out of the window – I didn't seem to have the willpower to get any further than that – when I heard a tap at the door. Adrienne slipped in.

I hadn't seen her since the afternoon of Hector's funeral, when the doctor had given her a sedative to quieten her after that agonized cry of 'Murderer!' No one but Adrienne – and perhaps the strange young man who had faced her across Hector's open grave – had understood what she meant by that.

'That's for Patrick,' he had said and only Adrienne seemed to know what he was talking about. With my inner ear, I can still hear the rattle of the frozen earth as it fell from his hand, grain by grain, onto the coffin lid.

Adrienne was diminished. There seemed to be so little left of her. Black seemed to drown her. She was swamped by the hugeness of the colour and all it stood for. She looked over at the bed and the open suitcase lying on top of it.

'I thought you might be going,' she said.

I just nodded. I didn't know what to say. Her presence galvanized me into actually doing something, so I rolled up a pair of stockings, snagged the silk on a ring, and placed them into the empty case. Then I lifted the pillow and took from under it the nightgown I had worn. It was still warm. It smelled of Philip. I let it slither back through my clumsy fingers. It whispered off the bed and onto the floor, a shimmering puddle of violet.

'I wanted to tell you,' she went on in a small, relentless voice, 'that you're doing the right thing.'

'Oh, you can always rely on me to do the right thing,' I answered bitterly. 'If a little late.'

'Helen, listen – no, *listen* to me. You mustn't go

439

because of what you think we feel about you or because you need to punish yourself. We love you, all of us. This is your home now. You'll always be welcome here. The only reason you need to go is because it's the *right* thing to do. It always has been.'

'You're so sure . . . even now, after all this . . . you're so strong . . .'

'If only you knew . . .' she began and the fierce control that kept her upright and sane shimmered like a mirage. She folded her arms around her body, drawing herself back into her protective, black carapace.

She walked over to the window and stared out of it for a while. Looking for something to do, I picked up the fallen nightgown and stuffed it into the case.

'Hector was murdered,' Adrienne said softly, 'you know that, don't you?'

I was appalled by the matter of factness in her voice. She might have been discussing the weather.

'But I thought . . .' I blundered. 'Didn't he . . . ?'

'Oh yes, he killed himself, all right. It was his finger that pulled the trigger.' She turned and I looked into her eyes and down into depths of pain that I couldn't even begin to imagine. 'But he was murdered all the same. He was hounded and hunted until he took the only way out that they left him.'

'But everything that was said at the inquest . . . Hector couldn't have done that. He wasn't a murderer. It was crazy. No one who knew him could ever imagine that he'd shoot his own CO . . .'

And my voice trailed away. She knew, I thought, she knew all the time, but she's never going to admit to it, because that would be to admit the unthinkable.

'He couldn't have . . .' I finished.

'No, no, of course not. No one who knew him would ever believe that. But he was a sick man, Helen, and a proud one, very sick and ashamed of what he thought was weakness. I sometimes thought it might have been easier for him if he'd had honourable scars to show for the wounds the war inflicted on him. Whatever he may have done, he thought it was right at the time. The law could never punish him as severely as he punished himself since then.'

'And you know who was behind it all?'

'Oh, yes, I know,' she said. 'I know and I won't forget.'

'What will you do now?' I asked.

'Do?' Adrienne replied, as though I had asked the most stupid question she had ever heard. 'Why, live, of course. I have a fine son, a good mother-in-law, a comfortable home. I am better off than many women. Hector has gone . . .' Her voice husked and broke. '. . . but nothing can devalue the time we had together. I know what it's like to have had a husband who loved me. Some women are never ever lucky enough to have memories like mine. And there is still Hector's work to do.'

I looked at her blankly.

'There will be a by-election, you know,' she explained, 'quite soon, to fill the empty parliamentary seat. I intend to stand in Hector's place. He had such hopes, you see, such great plans. He never had time to carry them out. I can't sit back and let all he hoped for go to waste. Waste is a sin. I campaigned with him, canvassed with him. I saw all that needs to be done. I *know* what has to be done. So I must do it, if Hector can't. I owe it to his memory. But, oh Helen . . . oh, Helen . . . I ache . . .'

I put my arms around her, feeling the sharp, little bones and the tensile power of her will. I was supposed to be comforting her, but I could feel her strength flowing into me, like a hot, powerful tide. She was courageous in a way that had nothing to do with her physical strength.

Her grief didn't destroy her. It didn't undermine her. It shored her up in a way I knew that I could never emulate. She was reaching out, even from the pit of her grief, reaching out to touch me and hold me up. She was holding me and she would not let me fall into despair. She teetered on the brink, yet she held out her arms and pulled me back before I fell for ever. And in return, I owed her something. I owed them all something.

I *would* go back to my husband. I *would* be Hermione's mother again. I would patch and repair and make good. I would *make* it work. And when I faltered – and I would, often – I would think of this moment and begin the slow, careful task of repair again.

Adrienne bent her head and laid it against me, but she did not cry. We stood together like that for a long time.

EPILOGUE

The woman who came back was not my mother. But Aung Egg said she was and Aunt Egg never told me a lie about anything – not about how far away the moon was, or where babies really came from or where Patrick had gone – not anything. So why should she lie about this?

The woman who came back didn't sing. Her chest wasn't soft. It was bony. When she tried to cuddle me, she held me too tight, so that my breath was squeezed out and I wriggled to get free. Then she looked sad and turned away. Didn't she understand? If I squeeze my kitten, Minkie, too hard, she spits and fluffs up and I have to drop her before she scratches. But I love Minkie so much that I just want to scoop her up wherever I find her and wrap myself all around her and not let anyone else have her.

Does the woman feel like that about me?

I think she's a sad woman. Sometimes I spy on her. She doesn't know I'm watching. I lie behind the shrubs in the garden or peep through the crack when the door isn't closed. I can go anywhere I like and nobody knows I'm there. When she's on her own, she doesn't read a book like Aunt Egg or a magazine like Aunt Clemmie. She just sits and looks sad. Her hands lie still, thin and white. Her face is quiet and watching, as though she can see a story happening in front of her.

I don't like to see her cry.

She and Daddy sleep in rooms right next to each other and there is a little door between them, so they can go in and out without waking anyone up. I know what Daddies and Mummies do in the night together. Aunt Egg told me. It's silly, but it's the only way to make babies, she said. Are they making babies in there, all night? If they made a baby, she really would be its mother. Would she still want to be mine if she had a proper baby of her own?

I don't think she will have another baby, though. I tried the little door between the rooms and it was locked.

So I can still have her for my own mother.

If I want her.

She reads me stories when I'm ready for bed. She doesn't read them like Aunt Egg, walking round the room and making all the right voices, so that we both laugh. She reads them quietly, as though it's a secret between us both, something very special that no one else shares but us two.

I heard them talking once. They didn't know I was right above them, in the crook where the great branches of the cedar tree meet. Grown-ups never talk in front of me. They raise their eyebrows and nod their heads in my direction, but they never say anything interesting. That's why I have to hide. Otherwise I'd never know anything at all.

Aunt Egg said, 'Don't force things, Helen. A child's idea of time is quite different from yours. Stop rushing towards her and let her come to you when she's ready.'

Then *she* said, 'I don't know if I can bear it much longer. I'm not as strong as I thought I was.'

'You are, you are. You can't give up now. What do you think it would do to that child if you went away again?'

'She wouldn't care . . . she scarcely notices I exist . . . and how can I blame her for that?'

'You're wrong, you're wrong. Can't you see? You must keep trying. Be patient, darling, please. Stay a little while longer, I beg you.'

'I don't know . . .'

How long is a little while? Will she go away when it's over?

She doesn't squeeze me too hard any more. Sometimes she just lets her hand trail over my hair, so that it

446

hardly touches me. It makes me shiver all over. I don't squeeze Minkie any more either. My fingers scarcely ripple her fur, from her neat little ears to the tip of her stripy tail. Minkie shivers under my fingers and rolls over onto her back. It's nicer than being squeezed.

I showed her where the curlew nests were today. Lovely, pale brown eggs with chocolatey splodges lying in a scrape in the ground lined with a scrap of heather. In a little while, there will be fluffy chicks and then they'll fly away.

We walked home for tea. She tried to hold my hand, but I wriggled out of her fingers and ran off in front. It's not that I didn't want to hold her hand, but she was walking too slowly for me – I was a chick scratching for food in the heather.

She looked sad. She didn't understand. Another day it would be nice to hold her hand.

She heard me creeping up on her this evening. Her ears are getting sharper. It was Nanny's evening off and Rose had gone down for her supper. The sun and moon were in the sky at the same time. It was easy to creep out.

She was standing all alone in the garden, with her face turned up to the sky. I was as silent as I could possibly be. My nightgown hem was wet with dew and stuck to my ankles. The grass was cold and the air was warm.

'Look, Hermione,' she said softly. 'Look at the bats. If you're very, very quiet, you can hear their little wings flutter . . . do you remember . . . ?'

And I remembered . . .

Then Rose came running out into the garden, scolding me and saying she was sorry, she'd not turned her back five minutes, only to get a bite of supper . . .

But I remembered . . .

There are suitcases in the motor car. She's wearing her

smart London coat and hat. She kisses me on the head and on the lips. She doesn't squeeze me, but I can feel she wants to. Her hands are shaking and her voice has gone trembly. She lets me go very slowly, then turns her head away, like I do when I'd rather die than let anyone see I'm crying.

She gets into the motor, not looking at anyone, and Liddell starts the engine. The gravel crunches under the wheels.

I scream and scream.

'Mother!'

Tripping and stumbling, I run down the steps. The car stops and my mother gets out.